Dear Soldier,

I served in the militar

MW00936150

I send you this book, which I wrote over 10 years, as a token of my appreciation for your service. That it is my book, and not the book you were hoping for, is unfortunate and I apologize.

Until recently, I made all the copies of The Born and the Made by hand. The Born and the Made is the first handmade novel ever to achieve a finalist position in the 29-year history of the Minnesota Book Awards. I tell you this so that you know the novel has been vetted for literary quality and enjoyability by someone other than my wife, my mother and my mother-in-law.

It did not win. I blame THE MAN.

Via the independent publishing arm of a certain internet-bookstore of some repute, I've designed this special "MILITARY SERVICE MEMBER EDITION," which I then purchased myself, as the author, on the cheap, and now donate to you.

Please accept this meager tribute for your noble service.

Thank you.

Robert Emery Spande
3 A D/3-8 Cav
Gelnhausen, West Germany
1985-1988
bobspande@gmail.com   http://robertspande.com

To all the friends who were with me in the writing of this tale:
To Ignatius Riley and The Shrike, Mike Allred and The Intruder -
- To The Great Thirst, The Incal and The Milagro Beanfield War -
- To S.T. Joshi and to Ray Russell -- To Stephen King,Richard
Matheson, Caligula and Robert McCammon -- To Falconhurst,
ERB and Mad Love -- To Cornell Woolrich and The Divinity
Student -- To The Black Stallion -- To Star Trek II The Wrath of
Khan -- To Wolfen and The Hollow Men -- To Gormenghast,
Kurt Vonnegut and The Quartzite Trip -- To Cthulhu and The
Once and Future King -- To The Krone Experiment and The
Seven Mysteries of Life -- To Dan Curtis, Kolchak the Night
Stalker and Trilogy of Terror -- To the Murphy's Aero Space
Filler Pad -- To the Sullivan Ballou Letter, David Bohm and John
Willie's Bizarre -- To Greater Magic and Stanyon's Magic and
The History of Magic -- To Tom and David and Tony -- To
Peyton Place, A Pattern Language, The World's Greatest
Adventure Stories and R.F. Delderfield -- To Ghost Story and
Shadowland -- To Teilhard De Chardin, The Universal Horror
Cycle and Star Trek TOS -- To Sociobiology, The Hour of Our
Death, Philosophy in the Flesh and The Marriage of Cadmus
and Harmony -- To The Exorcist and Legion and Elsewhere -- To
the Weird Tale -- To H.G. Wells pursuing Jack the Ripper
through Time -- To Jessica, Logan and Francis -- To Frank
Einstein and Joe -- To Jane Yolen and The Night's Dawn Trilogy
-- To the Girl of the Sea of Cortez, Mike Oldfield, Slavoj Zizek
and to Dr. Rat -- To How to Build a Flying Saucer and It
Happened in Boston? -- To Noam Chomsky and Martha
Washington -- To the JLA, the JSA, The Avengers, The Metal
Men, The Doom Patrol, The Challengers of the Unknown, The
Seven Soldiers of Victory and to Sgt. Rock -- To My Pals with
the Long Hair -- To Stanley Kubrick, Werner Herzog, Steven
Spielberg, David Lynch and John Carpenter -- To the
Bloomsbury Pocket Movie Guides, The Library of America,
Studies in the Horror Film from Centipede Press, and Cemetery
Dance's Novella Series 1-6 -- To DC Archives and Marvel
Masterworks -- To Taschen and Signet Paperbacks, Fawcett
Crest and Viking -- To John dos Passos and Stand on Zanzibar --

To Dhalgren and The Three and Four Musketeers -- To Coraline
and Weird Fantasy and Lost Girls -- To Tristram Shandy, Samuel
Barber, Aaron Copeland, Eiji Yoshikawa and Weaveworld -- To
Jack London, Jean Toomer, ComicBookGirl19, Laura Ingalls
Wilder, Arthur Russell, Horace McCoy and Tess of the
D'urbervilles -- To The Manitou, The Fury, Blow-Out and Willy
Wonka -- To Peter O' Toole and William Shatner -- To John
Crompton and House of Leaves - To the eternal magnificence
of John Williams, Jerry Goldsmith, John Barry and Popul Vuh
But most of all,
To my Wife and Kids,
I love you

The Born and the Made
By
Robert Spande

"...nature is great and reason is small."
Giacomo Leopardi – Zibaldone

There is Copeland.

If there is a municipality immune to the folkways of the rest of the country, Copeland gets the prize.

Secluded in the Heart-Shaped Forest, which it endlessly devours, inward and inward, the town of Copeland has no need for the rest of America, except for nourishment. Copeland gets fed from afar. Food and stuffs are replenished by trucks returning through the barrier of the Heart-Shaped Forest from their distributions.

The outside world would have a hard time getting in, even if it cared to try. Sure, there are movies at the theater, books in the library, newspapers and commerce. But it is as if these transact across a barrier of time, and something more than time - a gulf of inertial resistance to the flow of the world itself.

This gulf opposes theories, prejudices, fashions and trends of all stripes. There is no Quantum, nor Relativity in Copeland. Vietnam is something to be listened to on the radio; no Copeland man signs up for the draft, and, somehow, no government agency seems to care. Equality of the races and the genders is fuel for the rest of the country to burn. Women work the wood with the men. A black man can do anything he is fit to do, though, admittedly, he may have a tougher row to hoe.

Things are not perfect - Copeland is no Utopia - not by a long shot - but the corrosive divisiveness coming to a head in the rest of the country is anathema here.

It makes one wonder.

The town of Copeland sleeps in the crook of the Heart-Shaped Forest's arm, smoking and glittering as if in envy of the clouds and stars above.

One aspect of Copeland knows no sleep, however.

Like an anatomical organ, ever trudging, the Copeland Lumber Mill churns eternal.

The sawmill renders the fresh-chopped trees that amble down the lane of the Meritimus River into angled shapes and rectangular pieces.   In testament to this, hundreds of crosshatched stacks of 2x4s -- an impossible, limitless plenitude -- march back from the river docks, awaiting distribution by truck and boat.

Atop one of these stacks, far back toward the rear of the mill, sits a raven.

The huge bird observes, with its gloss black eye, the body of a woman sprawled supine near the garbage bins, in a widening pattern of her own blood. If it were one of the folk of Copeland observing, instead of a raven, the blood might seem to assume the shape of wings, the shattered green glass surrounding her head, a halo.

The raven turns its placid gaze to a man standing above the fallen woman, just done sawing at the poor woman's neck with a fish-scaling knife.

The man looks north, toward the road, with a face of frustration. He studies his work a last time: the intimacy of betrayed flesh no one should ever see, before turning toward the south side of the building. He walks calmly out of the dark bird's sight.

The raven looks back to the woman.

The woman looks into the black eye of the raven until her own eye dims.

The woman slips reluctantly into death.

Inside the mill, the work continues, unmindful of the freshly murdered woman outside the east doors. The night shift workers joke and bicker, and work the wood.

Just north, on the main road leading from town, an old man shuffles mill-ward, muttering, wheezing. A pickup passed the old man going the opposite way, some five minutes prior. The dusty wake still hangs in the air, as if to purposely torment the old man's breathing. He is drunk on cheap wine, not tired enough to sleep in the cold, yet too tired to walk all the way home.

He knows of an inviting vent at the back of mill that blasts hot air all night long, and he intends to sleep under it.

East, through the forest, at the top of an earthen rise comprised primarily of two elements: dirt and bones (graveyard bones, Indian bones, bones preceding all record), two teen boys -- twins -- slip like eels from the window of their home, a tiny, decrepit dwelling.

When the twins are sufficiently far from their tarpaper shack of a house, they crouch in conspiratorial whispers before heading off through the trees, toward their mysterious ends.

They pop out of the forest onto the Mill Road, startling the drunken vent-seeker.

"You near gimme a infarction!" The town drunk barks.

Neither of the twins says a thing. Shoulders hunched, hands stuffed deep in their pockets, they hurry guiltily past the man, north, away from the mill.

Upon reaching a safe distance, one of the twins emits a loud fart, and they both crack up.

The old man blearily regards the diminishing twins for a moment, before turning back in the direction of the mill, with a disgusted shake of his head.

Inward a tortured mile of forest from the twins' shack sits a log cabin, under a bright green roof.

In the small bedroom, atop an old sleigh bed, an ancient woman jumps bolt-upright out of a nightmare. Sweat is like a second skin all over her, from her glistening forehead to the bottoms of her feet. The old woman sweeps apart the hand sewn curtains that block the light of the moon from her sleeping head (for privacy is of no concern at all).

The dame scans her clearing with intense blue eyes, as if in search of the nightmare's author.

The Old Cross Bridge waits nearby, spanning an endlessly burbling creek that empties into a nearby waterhole, a waterhole always inviting of the children who splash in its shallows, long into the autumn.

The road crossing over this bridge leads to another house, not a log cabin, but a real family home.

The teen boy fights at his covers, his dreaming, of unrequited passion and danger.

His younger sister, in the next room, lies peacefully on her back, in a fashion vaguely reminiscent of a corpse in a coffin.

Mom and Dad slumber in their bed, in an attitude of military formation, as if ready to combat anyone who might threaten to wake them.

Across a patch of forest is Builder's Cemetery, delimited by a cold iron fence. Is there some person crouched in the branches of a tree above one of the graves?

Upon closer inspection, there is not.

Some rows back, however, we are captivated by movement among the gravestones. It's a trio of older teens, two lads and a lass. She dances weaving among the stones, enticing one of the boys while, unbeknownst to her, grievously disturbing the other.

Beyond the cemetery is a small area of tiny houses, more roughhewn than the rest we meet. This part of Copeland seems to fend for itself, creating spaces in the forest and populating those spaces with buildings and systems without assistance, or interference, from the municipality.

Ad hoc phone and electricity lines string the trees above the houses. The roads are unpaved dirt. Herb and vegetable gardens comprise nearly every yard. Garments gesticulate from the laundry lines like gentlemen in congenial disagreement.

The residents here, few in number, are Negro and Native men, women and children.

Now we approach Copeland proper, and Main Street.

Before we travel down it, let us stop and consider this tidy house. Nestled in Copeland's only official neighborhood, the shrubs are trimmed with aesthetic purpose. The sleeping flowers in their boxes are as content as domesticated flowers might ever be. A bright green mat entices welcome at the base of the meticulously swept steps.

In the tiny parlor, snoring on the couch (having immediately succumbed to the warmth of the fire he has only just made), a strikingly handsome man in his mid-thirties dreams the last pleasant dreams he will ever dream.

Here is Main Street, along which resides the supermarket, the post office, the police station and the diner. Way at the end of Main Street is a small public library. Over from that, the liquor store, owned by a woman who now sleeps in the small residence at the back, muttering impatiently to her sister, who never lived at all.

The Pink Motel is at the edge of town.

The motel has no room 13. There is a room 14, however, and in that room, a married couple, just passing through, have lost their fitful struggle with sleep and are making love like they invented the practice.

Their mutual climax is wistfully noted by the single woman in 12, traveling cross country to disburse her father's will among herself and her hated younger siblings. That unpalatable event will transpire the next day, at 3:30 pm in Red Wing, and makes the woman fit to bursting with anxiety; she can't get a wink of sleep.

The sounds of passion are also heard by the man over in room 11, on his way from New York to Texas to deliver an important message to a man he has no idea is already dead by misadventure.

All of these rooms' residents are destined to pack up and leave the very next day, and, as intriguing as their circumstances may be, have nothing to do with the remainder of this tale.

Remember the handsome man sleeping in front of his just-made fire? The handsome man's father is of some concern here.

The handsome man's father lives in the wealthier, elevated part of Copeland, overlooking town. The lanky old man is the only legal resident of the mansion, and has been known to stalk its halls, deep in the night, or so his guards and chauffeurs, otherwise known as the Burlymen, have been so indiscreet as to describe, when in their cups.

But not tonight. Tonight, the lanky old man got to sleep early.

The lanky old man wakes with a start as one of his Burlymen knocks urgently at his bedroom door. He spits vituperative as he drags his lanky frame out of the bed.

The Burlyman hands the lanky old man a phone handset, which he takes and puts to his lanky old ear. On the other end of the line is the night boss of the sawmill, of which, the lanky old man is the despised owner.

The lanky old man knows that every one of his employees at the mill, from the highest boss, to the lowest sawyer, hate him to his marrow.

He eagerly approves.

The night boss on the other end of the line is no different.

The man seethes between anxiety and animosity as he reports that a dead body has just been discovered behind his sawmill by a bum looking for a place to sleep. The lanky old man better come quick. The lanky old man asks his manager if the police have already been called, to which the manager replies in the negative.

"Good," says the lanky old man, "Don't.

"I'll be right there."

So wakes the sleepy town of Copeland.

Part 1

The Dreadful Passing

"If I love you, what business is it of yours?"

-Goethe

ChApTeR 1

We played down near the Old Cross bridge in our bathing suits, like a couple of happy pigs. Cot was a dainty girl, but her demeanor cast a shadow, large and dangerous. I was of a normal size and disposition for my 15 years, I guess.

Cot roared her 11-year-old voice like the banshee. Above her sandy locks she swung a makeshift cudgel around and around.

"C'mon you!" she boomed. "I'll make you into cat food!"

Her invisible assailants swarmed. Cot dealt them death blows, one after the other. I finished my rolled cigarette and flung the remainder into the creek.

"Damn, but you're loud," I admonished her.

At that, Cot cut through the crowd of demons, or ogres, or zombie-army-soldiers, and jumped on me. I tried to get up, but too late. Cot caught me in the gut with her fighting club and knocked me back down against the old willow, catching my spine on a gnarl, forcing the wind from my lungs.

She then proceeded to scream in my ear with such vigor that my eyes watered and I forgot for a moment where I was.

Then she was gone, down the south trail, into the dark of the forest. Her pretty hair bouncing behind her was the last to disappear into the gloom of the growth.

I muttered, collecting myself. I had a swipe of barky gunk across my belly from Cot's attack. It refused to come off by way of civilized rubbing, nor did it succumb to scraping.

I jumped back into the waterhole. The water was chilling in the grace of heat on that early fall day. The creek blinded me, reflecting filigree brightness.

I could still hear Cot, crashing away in the brush. I called to her and the crashing stopped.

"What?" came her small reply.

"We have to be back home!" I yelled.

"Oh... crap," I heard her say, more to herself than to me.

I paid her no mind, but washed off my face and blew spray at the tops of the trees. When I got back up to shore, I was surprised to see Cot was already getting dressed.

Finally, we tramped on home.

Lucius, our both-older brother, spied us coming. He ran to receive us with his usual cuff to the temple. Cot was quick and evaded him while I just stood there for mine.

"There's more friggin' diggin' today Johnny!" he screamed, after the fashion of a drill sergeant, his face in my face.

"Cripes, I remember... That's why we came back when we did."

This was a comment sufficiently craven to earn a roll of Cot's eyes.

"Trying to evade your duties is what you're doing! ATTENTION!" He all but bellowed.

"I ain't doing no attention Luce," I sighed.

Luce immediately adopted a weird stance and unleashed a complex judo move on me. My brother aimed his attack primarily at my head, but was sure to take advantage of the nearly limitless pain possibilities of my solar plexus.

I was suddenly on the ground. Some blood trickled into my mouth from an unknown source. I heard Cot's girly voice whispering to our brother:

"Tonight when you're sleeping I'm gonna take some roach powder, mix it up with some Drano and pour it right in your ear - don't matter which one. Then you'll be sweet as pie. I've been reading up on it --"

Still blind, I heard an issuance of outrage from Lucius. To his credit, he acted as any person might, who cannot divine the sincerity of a given mortal threat. He stormed toward the well-hole, or should I say, away from the author of his chemical lobotomy, snatching up his shovel as he went.

I don't blame him for fleeing; Cot's threats were uncannily stomach-dropping in their delivery. I count myself lucky that I was rarely on the receiving end of one.

Cot helped me up as I wiped at my eyes. I gave her a smile to tell her that my jaw was not broken and my teeth were all there. She smiled back her sweet smile.

ChApTeR 2

We heard the evil news when Lucius got back from the store.

After digging for a couple hours, we broke off, Lucius to Bill's Supermarket for milk and beer, me to my room to read my comics. While I read, I could hear Cot humming to her passel of dolls, through the wall.

About an hour later the sound of the truck drumming up the rut-torn road echoed off the pines.

Luce fairly exploded up the wooden steps and through the screen door.

"Miss Holly's been killed!" he yelled to all occupants.

For a second, my mind did not register what he said, but my body got it. A song of adrenaline pierced my guts like I was zooming down the Matterhorn at the state fair.

Miss Holly was our teacher.

There was trampling in the hall and Cot at my door, staring at me wide-eyed. She was well aware of the depth of feeling I had for Miss Holly. Cot gave me crap about it all the time, with her sly inquisitions when she caught me in reverie, no matter where.

My stomach continued to drop, tears coming to my eyes as I strode past her to the front room.

My brother, also aware of my feelings, spoke with what I can only describe as reverent awe.

"Murder," he said.

ChApTeR 3

I wanted to look handsome at the funeral service in the event that Miss Holly's eyes might scan the attendees through the lid of the casket. Of course, I knew rationally that this would not happen. Yet, I could see it over and over in my mind, like a movie, and unreal though it was, the idea held sway over me three days later, on the day of Miss Holly's funeral.

I looked at the moth-eaten suit stretched over my frame. It was small but sufficiently black, and solemn.

Whether I was handsome was for Miss Holly to decide.

Cot and Luce flanked me on the long walk to church. Both Mom and Dad were gone to work at their respective jobs, and could not join us. This was just as well, I suppose, given what was soon to occur.

ChApTeR 4

Murder, my brother had said.

The word had hung in the air, around us and through us. My momma, whose name was Janice, dried off her hands and approached from her kitchen.

"Luce, what did you say?"

"Mom, Miss Holly was found dead. Somebody killed her."

Momma had looked over at Cot and me. I knew she was mulling over whether we should be hearing any more of this. I looked her dead in the eye and I gave a direct order, if only telepathically, for her to let us stay and hear.

She clearly received my message because her eyes got a little shiny. Mom turned back to Luce and said, "Go on, Luce."

Lucius took a deep breath as he looked at me and said, "She was found behind the mill."

There was a heavy silence. I said, "Luce, who done it?"

"You ain't gonna believe it," Luce answered.

ChApTeR 5

Now, as we trudged to the funeral service, shaking in our skin with the cold shivering back, I felt sadness like a shroud on me. I would never see Miss Holly smiling across her desk, ever again. I started breathing heavy, and maybe some tears escaped. Lucius turned his head so as not to notice.

Cot sidled up to me and nudged me so as to push off the bad feelings. It worked to a small extent and Luce was able to turn his face back to us.

We could see townfolk approaching from different directions, mostly on foot. The road became treacherous with tracks and ruts, so we started across the green expanse of the church lawn.

The entire landscape of our small town stirred inside the lobby of the church. The luminaries of our town were in attendance as well.

From top-down there was first the Mayor of Copeland, latest in a seemingly endless procession of patriarchs bearing the township's name. Everett Copeland had his wife in impatient tow. She stopped and started like an auto with a bad clutch as he made his rounds.

Then there was Chief Constable, Gregor Kamen, who went to kindergarten and all the grades thereafter with my Mom. It was in his company that Luce had seen the main suspects in Miss Holly's murder get dragged off to the halls of justice. Their heads were down low Luce had said.

Chief Constable Kamen was not really talking to anybody. He was scanning the faces of the attendees. Kamen's scrutiny was so intense, so searching, I was given to wonder as to whether the two in custody were the responsible parties.

ChApTeR 6

Their heads were down, Luce said, their hands manacled behind them. Police jackets were over their heads but Luce knew who they were.

"It was the Donnel twins," Luce said. The drill sergeant had evaporated, replaced by a respectful young man. "Ol' Bandana is the one who found Miss Holly's dead body. I talked to him. He says they, uh... he says they..."

Momma's hands came up in a short, halting gesture. Luce paused, and seemed grateful to do so.

Stillness pervaded.

Mom turned away and quickly walked back into the kitchen.

Luce looked uncomfortable. He too turned away and closed the door, walking out to the truck, pretending he had something to attend to.

Cot and I exchanged meaningful glances. Neither of us was sure what Luce was unwilling to say, our mother unwilling to hear. We could tell it belonged to the realm of the awful, and the adult.

Cot shuffled toward her room and slipped in, closing the door behind her. She sought solitude for some surplus pain, bothered in a way that remained inaccessible to my boy self.

I went to my own room and covered my head with my pillow.

ChApTeR 7

Cot saw the way Constable Kamen was scrutinizing the funeral attendees. She came to the same conclusion that I did, that perhaps the Donnel boys were not responsible for the death of Miss Holly, as Bandana had claimed to the police.

Kamen's eyes met those of another man across the way near the front door.

Reverend Saulk was greeting people as they arrived, shaking hands, nodding and patting. Saulk looked sad and tired through the paternal set of his face, as he returned the Constable's nod.

Then a horse drawn buggy pulled up and Miss Holly's old Momma came out. Her name was Sadie Holly. She stepped down the fragile steps of the conveyance on the arm of an even older black man, Copeland's postman, Thomas. They hobbled up the church stairs through the stilled crowd like a boat among reeds. Sadie Holly's hair, though white, retained an aura of the blonde tresses of her youth.

Cot looked particularly dismayed at the sight of Miss Holly's momma. As the ancient woman passed by us, her smell wafted of mothballs and medicine. Cot started crying quietly and Luce, to the surprise of us all, put his arm around her.

A gleaming black car pulled up. A powerfully built man in the striped shirt and red suspenders of the Burleymen stepped out and opened the back door of the car.

William Wickley the Third emerged squinting into the light of the day.

William Wickley The Third was an ancient creature, comprised primarily of severity and acuteness. He grimaced with distaste at the tableaux of attendees. A good portion, the millworkers resourceful enough to escape the mill and attend the funeral, grimaced back at him.

Wickley grunted in seeming approval of this transaction. He started toward the entrance, his Burlymen following, and trailing his son, Robert.

My animosity toward the man may be perceptible. William Wickley owned the sawmill where my parents were at that moment slaving away, and behind which, Miss Holly's body had been found.

Everybody in the town called the man Winky, which I always thought was a compression of the man's full name, but which ultimately turned out to be based in the nature of certain intimate occurrences that had come to light, events I was too young to be appraised of.

Winky's eye passed over the three of us. His disdain was in evidence. We were, after all, the unwholesome spawn of a couple of his own, degraded employees.

Trudging behind the pack was Winky's son, Robert. Robert was maybe 30-some years. His thick crop of hair was golden in the sun, relatively incandescent amongst all the black. Robert stood to the side, next to the Burlyman.

Robert looked very sad. He had good reason. Miss Holly had been his girlfriend.

Winky began talking animatedly to Saulk, pausing only to glare intensely at anyone who threatened to approach.

Winky went low toward the Reverend's ear and started whispering, the more percussive and wet moments causing the unfortunate man to flinch spasmodically. Winky's face reddened, the whiteness of his eyes enlarging, looming. His yellow teeth flashed like bone knives.

Robert took notice and put his hand on his father's gangly arm. Constable Kamen walked over and interjected himself into the exchange, which seemed to force Winky to calm down a bit. Then, Winky, after a bit of tie-smoothing, started in on the Constable. Kamen withstood it admirably. Winky stopped abruptly and walked into the church, his spindly legs carrying him in strides of parabolic importance.

The Reverend looked dismayed. He made excuses to an approaching parishioner and too left the scene, but in the opposite direction, toward the church offices. Kamen's eyes followed Saulk as he hurried away.

Kamen turned and looked directly at me.

I could feel my eyes visibly widen. I grabbed Luce's elbow and indicated my desire to go inside.

Luce walked us all into the church proper. We sat near the back.

My perverse desire was to sit right up in front, like in class, but the basis of that desire, that I could somehow catch Miss Holly's eye, her living eye, was powerfully weighed down with its own somber impossibility.

I submitted to Luce's quiet direction.

ChApTeR 8

Reverend Saulk had just finished a painful immersion into the life of Miss Holly, punctuated by the passing out of various items the Reverend had collected in the last three days, items of historical and metaphorical significance to her story.

Miss Holly's students were all in attendance. However, their shenanigans were not. All of us, to a kid, were brought low and fighting epic sadness. We passed Theda Holly's memorabilia among us, and when items finally got to me, they were dotted with other's tears.

After being passed a childhood drawing depicting three crayola-grey elephants of descending magnitude, chaotically signed Theda in the corner, and completely dampened by previous appraisers, I realized I could not bear much more. If Luce's weird breathing was any indication, he was in a similar predicament. Cot was silent between us. I considered slipping out the door behind me.

The Rev's voice was charged and clear.

"Paul shows us in 2 Corinthians 3:2-3: "You are our letter, written on our hearts, to be read by all; and you show that you are a letter of Christ, prepared by us, written not with ink but with the Spirit of the living God, not on tablets of stone but on tablets of human hearts.

"These writings stay with us," continued the Rev, "and when someone close to us dies those teachings, those writings, remain etched on our hearts.

"I know Theda wrote on my heart. Ever since she was a little thing, Theda and Eli were strong in the Church."

Eli? I looked around the church at the locations of import, but saw no one who looked like an Eli.

Saulk continued, smiling down at Miss Holly's momma, dabbing at his own eye.

"I grew up with you, Sadie, from pups, in a land without cars and TV sets..."

Here, the Reverend's friendly smile faltered. He regarded Miss Holly's momma with an expression approaching concern. He stuttered on:

"... and I knew well your husband, Theda's father Kenneth, before he left us, what was it--fifteen years now?"

The Reverend was lost by himself in this quandary, before returning.

"All, compassionate, moral people, loved by the Lord," said the Reverend rapidly, by way of summation.

Reverend Saulk brought himself together to continue.

"How can folk defend themselves from such evil as brings us all together on this fine autumn day? Evil that is contingent, unnecessary, and unraveling of our most precious designs?"

Such words were shocking to hear in this context, and I was not the only person to think so, given the shuffling and muttering that ensued among the congregants.

"The Lord has given us powerful remedy!" the Rev shouted, trying to reel us back in. "In His Love, we find the Shield and the Balm, and the Certainty..."

Saulk's right hand ascended, gesturing as he turned round to this point, possibly the central thesis of his sermon. Indeed, the hand seemed to dance next to him like a second individual entirely, commenting, and none too favorably, on his words.

The sermon seemed to have lost its mark in the wake of the weird moment the Rev had shared with Miss Holly's momma.

"...the Certainty... um... oh yes, the Certainty is that the slings and arrows of this life are but shadows of shadows. The best truly is to come!

"For it is with certitude that I tell you Sadie: your best days with your daughter, and your husband are still in front of you. No matter how dark the day, no matter how deep the pit, there is the Shield, and the Balm, and the Certainty..."

The Reverend glanced down at Sadie Holly over the top of his bifocals. Perhaps he was trying to gauge some quality in Miss Holly's momma, how she was responding to his message.

The Rev furrowed a bit more this time, closing his folder quietly. By doing so, the good Reverend seemed to have excised a sizable portion of what remained. He reached up and pulled off the glasses.

"To Sadie Holly, I say this," Saulk paused, seeming to build up energy for the words he was about to utter. Miss Holly's momma was still as glass in the front row.

"You have proved yourself through your hardships, your love of God and your incredible strength. You will walk with Theda again, Sadie. She has written on all our hearts. We love you, and are here for you, Sadie, together, strengthened by the Lord's gifts of the Shield, the Balm and the..."

Something about Miss Holly's momma seemed to derail the Reverend's closing arguments. He was peering down at Sadie Holly like she was an unexpected result in a scientific presentation. Saulk seemed just about start up again, but then he clamped shut. Everyone in the church followed his gaze.

Sadie Holly's head was moving. Swaying back and forth, left to right, increasingly violent.

She was shaking her head, no. No! No!

"The Lord won't never forgive," she whispered, her whipping head modulating her words. The acoustics of the church conveyed her soft speech to every ear in the place, resulting in a white-noise chorus of murmur, and breath intook.

Miss Holly's momma stood up sharply and her purse fell to the floor, clattering objects all over the place. She stepped forward, unmindful as she crushed a small mirror under her foot.

"Not you," she whispered, pointing up at Saulk with a claw-like hand.

"NOT ANY OF YOU!" Sadie Holly bellowed.

We - all of us - every damn person in that church, startled. Miss Holly's momma turned her claw round to the attendees, bolting them to their pews.

Her gesture rested on Winky, sitting with Robert, some rows back. Winky seemed to shrink from Sadie's pointing hand, as if it were emitting poison.

Then, the accusing digit drifted over to Winky's son, Robert.

Robert Wickley's head was hung.

Miss Holly's momma collapsed on the floor.

Thomas, who had been sitting next to Sadie Holly, tried to get to his feet, but was unable to. He fell back into the pew, his legs actually rising into the air for a moment.

There was a susurrus of alarmed whispers from the church goers. Then, Constable Kamen, who had inched closer to the front as Mrs. Holly was talking, and had rushed over a second too late as she fell, spoke quietly to Reverend Saulk who was leaning down from the pulpit,

"She ain't breathing Rev."

The whole church silenced. All we could hear now were the strange sounds of the recussitory attempts, poundings and wheezings and other such awful noises.

Luce pushed me and Cot out of the pew and fairly shuffled us out of the church.

"Just keep walking and don't say nothing," was all he told us. Cot looked wide-eyed at me, but did as she was told and remained silent. We mutely followed Luce all the way to our house, where I fell into my bed. I contemplated the ceiling's flow of shadows, until sleep overtook my racing mind and I was subjected to roiling dreams in dark landscapes.

ChApTeR 9

Let us wend past, to days when Miss Holly breathed and smiled at me from her dappled wooden desk.

Miss Holly was killed right at the start of the school year. So, the time I describe was a more distant memory, with a summer intervening. I feel it was this summer's break from seeing Miss Holly that so intensified my crush. As if her absence caused my heart to grow so fond, that just the thought of returning to school was an exciting one, if only to see her again.

Miss Holly had been, before she was pulled from me, my teacher for the whole day. Out there where we lived, we did not go from teacher to teacher to learn different subjects as students do in urban settings. We had the practices of combined grades and one teacher all the day long.

I could not help but steal furtive glimpses whenever the opportunity presented, appraising Miss Holly with an adoring eye, whether the woman was teaching or writing in her papers. Every so often, Miss Holly would catch me at it and flash a smile, as if to say:

"It's ok - I don't mind that you love me."

Once, my chronic distraction found me doodling in my notebook instead of reading the assignment. I looked up from my drawing to see Miss Holly staring dead at me. Her face was drawn into a mask of absolute impassivity. I got to look into her eyes right then. I don't think she even knew it. She was off somewhere in dense thought while we students were silently reading.

Finally, she turned her face away, to the sun from the window.

The initial reason I loved her so was primordial, so simple.

Miss Holly looked just like the woman on the cover of a book I often gazed at for minutes, hours, for the entire duration of my childhood. The book was *Savage Pelucidar*, by Edgar Rice Burroughs. The cover displayed a fur-bikini clad, raven haired beauty, flanked by two ravenous saber-toothed tigers. The image was used again, for another Edgar Rice Burroughs novel some years later, called *The Cave Girl*.

The Cave Girl was strong, full hipped, looking me boldly in the eye from the cover of that book. The fantasies I derived from the image remained with me a long time.

Miss Holly's eyes were as mischievous and powerful. Miss Holly seemed as if she could readily tame tigers, yet in my fantasies, she always submitted sweetly to me.

ChApTeR 10

When I woke, there were some neighbor ladies at the dining table, talking to Momma, just come back from the Mill. They kept their voices low when I was near but they couldn't help but get loud from time to time. The ladies still wore their funereal finest.

"Her undergarments were nowhere to be found!" gasped Mrs. Remedy, who hailed from the house south of us. Momma shushed her with a warning look in my direction. Mrs. Remedy was cowed with a shame that quickly evaporated, once Mrs. Cooridy, our northern neighbor, rejoined in a heated whisper, that I could not apprehend.

My memory of these two neighbor women is so awful and ungenerous, their names will hereafter be preceded by the definite article, 'The.' I do this in accord with the conventions of monster-naming, in alignment with such standouts as The Wolfman, The Mummy and The Thing.

Momma was pretty silent during all of this, shaking her head occasionally, no doubt at the callous talk flinging back and forth around her, but seeming like it was the enormity of the tragedy that caused her to do so.

Momma had been fond of Miss Holly. They were classmates when they were kids. They might even have been friends. I made a mental note to ask about this.

Daddy and Lucius came in from the garage. The men could not even attempt to hide their disgust at the nature of the conspiratorial commiserations transpiring at their food table. The neighbor ladies stopped talking, looking staidly and defiantly at the men as they passed to the basement stairs, but Momma was red with shame.

My momma was a good woman.

The Cooridy (whose son had been horribly mangled and blown up in a war she herself exhorted the poor boy to attend, the ripped remains of whom she nonetheless insisted upon viewing, which caused vital pieces of her mentality to float away, making her rude and forgetful and wacky), munched at a piece of toast as she recounted what she heard in line at the post office from the cousin of Tom Billingsly, the Killdeer County deputy assigned to watch the crime scene, until the police from Hunstable came to investigate.

"Denise said that Theda Holly was killed somewhere else. Somewhere inside, most likely in someone's garage or pole barn or basement. There were cobwebs in her hair, she said."

I tried to blend into the furniture so that no one would make me leave the room, so the women would forget I was even there.

The Cooridy continued.

"Denise also let loose with this, and I find this particularly revealing, considering what I've always said about the Holly woman, about... you know what I mean. Anywho, there was apparently some evidence left on her--evidence of a horribly scandalous nature--and this evidence was of an amount enough to suggest that more than one person killed her! Now we all know the twins were in custody and just released to their parents. This evidence suggests that there were even more than two suspects, and heaven knows that they never would have released the twins if they were guilty. So, I'm given to think this might be some sort of orgy situation gone bad, something like that."

The Remedy nodded her head solemnly, as if the likelihood of an orgy situation gone bad was all but foregone a conclusion.

The Cooridy's words hit home. The twins had been released! It must have happened right after the funeral.

"Well, she was just a little too pretty to be a teacher if you ask me," decided The Remedy.

Suddenly Cot appeared in the hall directly in front of me. I was able to stop her in her tracks with a fluctuation of my eyelids to the wider. Catching my warning, Cot dramatically backed up to the hallway wall, listening, her teddy unicorn thing in the crook of one small white arm. It was then I noticed the shadows of both Dad and Lucius in the stairway to the basement, as if the dark shapes themselves were interlopers to the women's talk.

"As y'all know, the Holly woman was seen more than once in the company of Winky's boy, Robert, and that they were of a habit to visiting some of the nicer venues out of town, like Harold's Steak and such. Word is, Winky's boy might just be mixed up in this mess, and that Winky is marshalling his forces to cover it all up, and did some framing-up of those poor twins, which is why they were hauled to jail in the first place," The Remedy added, wholly in a breath.

The neighbor ladies paused, eating of their toast and drinking of their coffee, both looking at Momma expectantly. This was her cue to offer up whatever gossip she had gleaned from the workplace, the whole reason our neighbors had pounced from their lairs, the moment Momma had returned from the mill.

Momma, being who she was, said nothing at this juncture.

I thought about what I had heard. The Remedy had mentioned Winky's son, Robert.

Robert Wickley was generally considered by the people of Copeland, people other than myself of course, as having evaded the nastier encumbrances of his genetic due, such as Winky's bald pate, his power madness and his lack of humanity. The attitude prevailed that Robert, son of Winky, boyfriend of Miss Holly, was a genuinely upright fellow, looked up to by most, especially those mill workers who prayed every night for Winky to be mangled in an industrial accident, so that Robert could inherit their sawmill.

At the time, I naturally considered Robert Wickley a villainous jerk, but that was only because Miss Holly liked him.

Robert and Miss Holly had been an item for about a year. It was well known to all of Copeland, hardly the stunning news that The Remedy's scandal rag reportage made it to be.

But gossip knows no goodness, and to the neighbor ladies, Robert was just as likely as anyone to be of the nature and discipline of a cold-blooded lust-orgy murderer.

The Remedy's eyes shifted from her cohort's to those down-turned of my momma's. It was clear that this visit was not going to be the information windfall these ladies had hoped for. They began to shift uncomfortably in their seats.

Momma didn't look up when she said "Thank you ladies for dropping by... that was real sweet."

Cot tiptoed back to her room. The shadows withdrew into the basement. I hightailed it quietly to Cot's room while Momma showed the neighbor ladies out the front door.

"Well what do you make of it?" Cot asked.

"I can't say I understood any of what they said, but it's pretty clear they didn't like Miss Holly one bit, the bitches."

"What did Cooridy mean about that evidence?"

I sighed. "I think she meant that, you know, a group of people murdered Miss Holly."

"Like a devil cult?"

I hadn't even thought of that wretched possibility. The image of Miss Holly in the clutches of a devil cult was a dispiriting one.

Through the closed door I could hear Dad berating Mom about the quality of her guests. How they were conniving harpies out to sharpen their claws on the misfortunes of others and whatnot. Momma remained silent. I wished that Dad would ease up on her.

It was not Mom's fault that The Cooridy and The Remedy were conniving harpies, any more than it was Dad's fault that their husbands were irritable drunks.

"You know what we gotta do, don't you?" said Cot to me in a whisper, right up close.

"Aw, hell no I don't!" I whispered back into her face. "I'm goin' fishing before Dad or Luce notice I'm gone. Then I'm going to bed and then tomorrow I'm gonna do it all over again, plus a shitload of well-digging, so I got no time for what we gotta do, Cot!"

"Johnny," said Cot, with all the authority of a field general, "you and me are gonna go see the twins."

ChApTeR 11

We made out of Cot's window like prison escapees evading the eye of the searchlight.

The Donnel twins, Reginald and Bobby, lived in a tar paper shack at the top of a rise (possibly a mass grave from Indian War times), in the dark interior of the forest adjoining our property. Cot and I knew that if we started due south and walked for some minutes till the floor of the forest dipped precipitously, then followed its steady rise toward a clearing in the trees, we would find their home.

The day was leaving. Fog was stirring at the base of the trees. The lurking whiteness lent the setting of our journey a sublime creepiness, evoking, more than anything else, death, itself.

Cot was never one to show agitation, or fear. She did not conceive of horrible figures in the gloom as I did, nor did she half-hear the noises in the night that had me twisting this way and that. She trudged purposefully ahead of me, looking back from time to time without affect. I did my level best to keep my fear from registering on my face, but I know I was not wholly successful, as her gaze lingered on me occasionally, as if to make sure I was ok.

Cot was ever the elder.

When we got to the Donnel place we made the traditional non-verbal noises to call them out, and after about five minutes Bobby Donnel appeared next to us, as if out of thin air. Reg was not in evidence.

"What you two want?" said Bobby Donnel to the ground at his feet.

"Just checking on you," said Cot. "We heard they had you up to the jail for a few days –we wanted to look at a real jail bird."

"They had the wrong guys. Everybody knows that."

We nodded. We knew the twins were innocent and our eyes said as much.

"Well?"

"Well what?" asked Bobby Donnel, irritated.

"Well, tell us about it dammit! Christ almighty you were in jail! You gotta tell us about it!" Cot yelled at the boy.

Bobby Donnel knew it was so.

"Well that dick-nose Kamen picked me and Reg right off the street as we was comin' home from playing pool with the Hoddy sisters. We didn't know what it was about. I thought he was gettin us for killing old what's his name's ewe, back in March."

"You did that?" I asked, dumfounded.

Bobby was taken aback by his own admission and blurted "Hell no! But I thought that was what he was trying to pin on us." Color rose from his neck.

He continued, "Anyway, he took us right into the morgue and there was a body on the metal. He pulled back the sheet and there was Miss Holly, deader than shit, eyes wide open and staring right at us. Her neck was all fuckin' ripped up - it looked to me like someone had been trying to saw her head off. No blood though; they'd cleaned that up. Reg just puked a mile right there, all over everything.

"Kamen told us we did it, and everybody knew it cuz we was seen, which was a big ol lie, and that we were gonna swing by our necks. It only made Reg puke again. But I think Kamen knew right away that we di'nt do it. Mostly cuz of Reg pukin all over like that. It was kind of funny."

"Tell us about Miss Holly," I said.

Bobby looked at me weird... sizing me up.

"Well she wasn't naked, tho I could almost see her boob in her smock if that's what you mean..."

"No, I want to know about her face."

"Her face?" exclaimed Bobby.

"Yeah, what was her expression?"

He paused for a span, looking from the bottom to the top of a long birch tree, then said,

"It was bad Johnny, she looked real sad."

My heart hurt when Bobby said that. I didn't say anything back. I just looked at Bobby in his face, hoping he would modify what he said, somehow take away the dark force his words carried in their evocation of Miss Holly's last moments.

But he was silent.

Cot said: "Did you hear anything? Any of the cops talking?"

That kind of jerked Bobby up from a sorrow he was in. His face brightened.

"Actually, I did hear a bit of something while we was in stir..." he looked back at his house, presumably making sure his old man wasn't about, then pulled us farther into the trees at the edge of the clearing.

"I didn't hear it from the cops, I heard it from Bandana himself."

"Bandana? The one who said you two were the killers?" I asked.

"The same," said Bobby. "That smelly bastard was in the cell next to us getting clear of a serious drunk he was on. He barfed and shitted the whole time and when he wasn't doin' that, he was looking at us, kinda like he had something to say.

"So Reg, who was in poor way hisself, yells at him, 'What you want, you drunk fuck?' and Bandana just keeps lookin' at us like he's all full of knowin' bout us and he just caint bring hisself to speak it. So that night, when we're all sleepin', I suddenly get woke up by this whistling sound, not like someone whistling a tune, but more like wind whistling thru a broke window. Only its Bandana, and he's crying and muttering to hisself, all blubbering like a baby. It was sick.

"So I yell at him to shut the hell up. Bandana turns his face from the moon in the window - he's glowing white on one side, his eyes all wide and shit, and he says to me, 'You'll be out of here soon boy. I know it weren't you that done that gal in.'

"I says back to him, 'Well thanks for the fuckin sweet thoughts you fuckin liar, now shut your crying so's I can sleep!'

"I went back to sleep, and when I woke up, Bandana was gone from the cell. I asked a guard 'bout it and he said that someone had posted up Bandana's bail and got him up outta there, and that it didn't matter cuz the sheriff didn't believe his bullshit story anyways, and that we'd be outta there that very afternoon, and we were."

With that, Bobby was clearly done with his story. He looked to us for critique.

We both admitted of the tale's significance, and of our admiration for his jailhouse experience, which Bobby found edifying. We all made general motions of positivity and separation. Bobby mosied back toward his house. Cot and I started into the misty dark toward ours.

I looked back as Bobby closed his front door. I saw a figure in the window on the north side of the house. It was Reg, white as bone and not looking at all happy. He was watching us depart. He was shaking his head.

No.

ChApTeR 12

The long walk home was made more so by the dark that descended, and the cold. But Cot and I kept busy, ruminating over what we had learned.

"Why do you think Bandana would lie to the cops like that, Johnny?" asked Cot.

"It's pretty obvious that he saw something but he's afraid to say the truth of it. He's worried if he talks, the real murderer will get him."

"So he fingers the Donnel twins? Doesn't that seem strange?"

"The guy's a flippin drunk! Who knows what makes him say what he says!" I yelped at her. Cot was taken aback.

The two of us parted, not physically, but we took our own routes home nonetheless, Cot worrying over her thoughts, and me, I fell to thinking about my viciously murdered teacher.

ChApTeR 13

Have you ever lost a love?

The most unexpected and painful aspect is the sudden obliteration of romantic direction and all romantic focus, of all romantic satisfaction. Your love still flows outward, but with no direction, no focus, no purpose, it evaporates uselessly into the air.

ChApTeR 14

I knew I loved Miss Holly because of the Warm that would hit me. It was a Warm I felt in my face and my torso, accompanied by the slightest adrenalized thrill in my stomach. I would often watch her at her teaching, at the board, or at her desk, while the Warm expanded in my torso, like ink in water.

My face would fill with the most extraordinary pleasure, like a mask.

Miss Holly remained oblivious of me. Yet the Warm of my love for her flowed outward, from my face and body sometimes making me delirious.

So strange, the aspects of love that stay with me after all these years. The body feelings, the thrills, the Warm, the feeling in my face. None of the lofty ephemera of love toward which humans aspire in the mode of poetry and sonnets. For me, it was the Warm, and the flow outward of this body feeling.

It goes far to show how poorly we mold ourselves, how much we are made by the others who come to us, and go.

We slept that night to a powerful dark wind that brushed tree limbs against the windows. My sleep was dreamless and in the morning I woke to such a refreshed, rejuvenated feeling that it was nearly disturbing to me in light of the events of previous days.

ChApTeR 15

For a couple of weeks, things were almost normal. My parents got along real well in this stretch, coming together as they sensed the bad feelings from our neighbors closing in on them.

The Cooridy dealt us glares like we were leprous outcasts as we passed on our way to school. After Momma's resistance to the neighbor ladies at our dining table, the cool wind of reproach blew over our house quick.

School was a trial of replacement teachers, some of whom did not even last the entire day. Our class became a gang of ill-mannered criminals.

The tacks in the chair, the mouse in the desk - every mean prank and dirty trick in the book was brought to bear on those foolish enough to try teaching us.

One sorry fellow's coffee cup mysteriously lost its bottom, delivering a torrent of hot liquid directly into his lap. He started to cry. The class erupted in laughter.

It was nightmarish, the stuff of horror films.

The irreparable loss of the object of my desire made me rueful and bitter. It is amazing how much I thought of my stricken Cave Girl.

Many nights, as sleep approached, Miss Holly's image, smiling broadly in her supportive, lovely way, would arise unbidden behind my eyes. I would jolt to wakefulness, my stomach zinging.

Sometimes, when I was lucky enough to reach deep sleep, my dreams would become elaborate dramas of Miss Holly's sudden reappearance in my life, never questioned, seemingly natural.

Miss Holly often lay beside me and the dream delivered what I never got in life -- the flowing back to me of her love.

On waking, this all flew away, leaving me hollow.

But the worst, without doubt, was the actual imagining of her last moments.

So curiously intense was the adrenaline in my guts as I followed Miss Holly to her end, that sleep on those nights was all but impossible. I curled in my bed and tried my level best not to think a single thought.

ChApTeR 16

One crisp September morning, we sat down to see a black man up at the front of the classroom. He wore narrow metal rimmed glasses and a gray three-piece woolen suit. He was the very caricature of a teacher, excepting in his race.

I had never seen a black teacher before.

When everyone was settled in their seats, the man walked up in front of his desk and leaned back against it.

"My name is Edwards, Rufus Edwards, Mr. Edwards to you," he said, his voice piercing the room. "I know you have never had a black teacher; it's been explained to me a thousand times. But you have one now. And I am here to stay."

Terry Scald, a perpetually dirty fifth grader who always bugged Cot to play with him, snickered dramatically. Emboldened by our string of victories over the intelligentsia, he puffed like a challenging parliamentarian.

Mr. Edwards ignored the lad's posturing. He brought himself to height and spoke: "I've heard all the horror stories about you people, that you are half 'Lord of the Flies' half 'Animal Farm.' Nothing you do will get me to quit this job."

Terry Scald burst out again, about half a guffaw's worth of mirth this time. Some of the bolder savages in the class broke up laughing, too.

Mr. Edwards paused, gathering, enlarging, it seemed.

"What's your name fella?" Mr. Edwards asked.

The question hung in the air, demanding an answer. Terry's brow furrowed a little. Finally, the boy puffed up even more, petulantly responding, "Terry Scald."

Mr. Edwards nodded. He turned around, dug into a leather satchel on his desk. He reached into the bag and pulled out the most beautiful book I'd ever seen. It was like a book from a movie, impossibly thick and richly appointed in leather binding, with an ornate buckle. The edges of the cover were studded with gold buds that flowed into gilded vines traced all along the edge. The edges of the pages were a deep matte crimson, looking more like velvet, than paper

46

He unbuckled the book and opened it to the page marked by the blood-red satin bookmark sewn into the spine. He started writing in it with a pen from his pocket. It was clear our new teacher was writing Terry's name in it.

I looked at Terry and Terry was concerned.

Mr. Edwards said to us: "This is a book you do not want your name in. I usually write a student's name in it the first day, as an example, but for the most part you have to be pretty bad to make it in here. If, by the end of the year you have not gotten me to cross your name out, by being particularly good, your name will still be inside it when I give the book back to its owner. You do not want that, Mr. Scald.

"No one would want that."

Terry seemed anxious, as if his underwear had suddenly assumed an uncomfortable configuration. It seemed like Terry was about to say something, but nothing came out. We all waited. Terry shrank back into his chair.

That was my first introduction to Mr. Rufus Edwards.

ChApTeR 17

In later days, it seemed that Cot was distant to me. She withdrew into her room and wouldn't come out for hours. She sang to herself in there. Sometimes I could hear her talking. She was deep in herself and I tried to stay back and let her be.

Sometimes, especially when perusing my sister's journal without my sister's permission or knowledge, I could tell Cot was worrying about stuff no little girl should be troubled with. Miss Holly's death seemed to grow Cot up all too quick. Her face looked more and more like Momma and Dad's did, when they listened to the body counts from the war on the radio.

Sometimes when Cot was like this, her breath would start coming out in a funny rhythm. Her eyes would alight on mine, looking back into hers, concerned. Finally, she would relax. Cot was safe in front of me because I loved her without judgment, and she knew it.

Momma and Dad were different too. Dad never did seem to take his eyes off of Momma these days. She would be engaged in domestic activity, and Dad would just be watching her, as if to make sure she didn't fly off into the air and away from him. Was it Miss Holly's murder that made him like that? Did he think to himself, Thank the Lord it wasn't you honey?

Momma looked at Dad hard too. Especially when he took that first bite of dinner. He would catch her at it and both their eyes would light up. It made me want to grow up and have a wife of my own.

Lucius, on the other hand, was becoming a little strange. He was drinking a lot more beer. A lot more. He would take the truck to destinations unknown for many hours at a time, sometimes all of the night.

Most disturbing was his expression. He used to look pissed-off all the time, with his forehead all wrinkled, his eyebrows arched.

Now he always looked surprised. His eyebrows were high on his forehead and his mouth didn't stay closed a lot of the time.

He wouldn't ever answer when you talked to him.

Momma would get enraged at his lack of response. After calling him a couple of times, she would charge right up to him and start smacking at the top of his head.

"I am talking to you Luce!" she would yell.

Cot inevitably decided to get to the bottom of Luce's situation.

"You worried?" she asked me. I was reading on my bed.

"Yeah I'm worried," I said.

"What should we do?"

"What can we do? Talk to him? That ain't gonna work. He forgot how to talk. To us, at least."

"Any idea what he does when he goes off like that for hours?" Cot was swinging a big long fake candy cane that Momma adorned our steps with every year, though Christmas was months away.

"Not a clue. But if I know you Cot, you want to follow him next time he goes."

"You know me then," she said.

We couldn't follow Luce on foot, as he would be in his truck. But we knew he always left the house around 9:00 pm so me and Cot snuck out around 8:30.

We walked opposite ways down Walker Lane. Cot waited at the next intersection, her way, and I did the same, my way. We could not follow him, but at the very least, we could figure our brother's general direction and winnow our search in later days.

About an hour later, our truck sped toward me and zoomed left on Mary's Place. I found this odd – I was sure he would have gone Cot's way. Luce turned right on Pleasant. Then he was gone.

I went and got Cot. She was throwing pine cones into a tree, trying to hit something.

"I see you're paying close attention to oncoming cars."

"I got ears," she said grumpily.

"Well you can just stop torturing that tree, cuz Luce came my way. I'm sure you musta heard it."

This stopped her. She turned to me. Her expression said: "And…?"

"He went north on Pleasant like he was late for a very important date," I said.

"North on Pleasant? What the hell is that way? A whole lot of nothing."

We looked at each other then. We both knew what was north on Pleasant.

ChApTeR 18

Builder Cemetery's long and storied past accrued legends every year, it seemed. Only last year, Tommy Whidlaw said he was out there drinking with some buddies and witnessed a creature described as tall and thin, like a man, "but kinda see-through."

Tommy said the see-through man's face was like cracked chalk. He wore a old fashioned, brown suit with an aquamarine stone set into a bolo tie, holding a bowler hat in his free hand. The see-through man was crouched in a tree above a particular grave, just looking down at it, almost into it, or so it seemed. Tommy said he and his friends watched the see-through man for about fifteen minutes. The man never moved, never even shivered, all crouched in the tree like a big monkey, knees up around his shoulders, one hand above on a branch above steadying himself.

"Thing was," said Tommy. "and may God split my ass if I'm lying, but when the moon was out from behind the clouds, I swear to you, I could see it right through the guy's chest." Tommy said it was like looking through gauze.

Then, suddenly, the see-through man was just... gone.

No one saw him go; he did not seem to disappear. Everyone just noticed simultaneously that he was no longer there.

Tommy said they drank at their Kentucky bourbon for a while, working up their courage. They set out as a group to check out the grave under the tree. It was an old grave, a perfect tablet, like half the Ten Commandments, sticking slightly pitched out of the earth.

The gravestone said, only:
Darling Kealan
Loved by Mom
Loved by Dad
Loved by God
1896-1901

Cot and I went looking for the grave ourselves after hearing the story, and sure enough, there it was.

ChApTeR 19

It took us about 25 minutes to get to the front gate of the cemetery. It was pitch dark now, no stars in the sky, just a haze of charcoal clouds above. We looked all over the graveyard from our vantage at the gate, but saw no one, just a lot of stones breaking the earth. There was the occasional bit of graveyard ostentation, the reaching angel, the obelisk, mostly displaying the name "Copeland."

No Luce, though.

"I don't think he's here," said Cot.

I brought myself up on the fence. "I don't see him."

"You want to go in there, Johnny?"

I shook my head in disbelief, gaping at my sister, "Are you crazy? Yeah, I want to go in the graveyard in the dark of night more than anything."

Cot looked from stone to stone, ignoring my sarcasm. Her face was becoming increasingly fraught with worry. She didn't even realize it. Her breath hitched a little and she looked startled. I waited, but she did not come out of her state. Her breath hitched again.

"Cot?" I whispered.

She snapped out of it and looked at me. She was the old Cot again. Calm, adult Cot.

"I never liked this place," said Cot.

Cot looked at me impassively. I jumped down off the fence.

A crypt loomed inside the gate, a brick block with an iron door. I imagined the wretched state of the moldering corpses it housed, the moldering corpses of one of the founding families of Copeland. The name above the door was Denizen. I had heard the name from my parent's lips, most likely during one of their mutual nightly debriefings at the dinner table.

As I read the name, there was a horrible screech of metal and the iron crypt door slivered open.

The iron door of the house of death cracked open, not ten feet from my horror-struck countenance!

ChApTeR 20

Cot grabbed my hand and pulled me behind the stone pillar of the gate. What happened then, right behind, occurred out of our sight, due to that pillar. I was breathing very heavily. Cot rubbed my arm to calm me down.

There was another scream of metal and we could hear the crypt door opened a few more inches.

My imaginings of the Denizen crew's privileged corpses transformed to images of shambling zombies with dusty blood pouring from their desiccated eye sockets, ravenously raking the air for juicy, living flesh. I covered my mouth with my hand, clamped it there to hold in the scream that was boiling in my stomach.

Then the door exploded open with an anguished iron snarl. We heard running. It diminished away from us, sounding like more than one person.

Cot chanced a view around the pillar. She gasped and pulled me to look. There was Lucius, running for all his might away from us to the gate at the opposite end of the cemetery. There was another boy with him, whom I did not recognize in all the dust and distance, and a girl -- it looked like Stacy Steebler -- who I knew worked at the laundry in town. They were full-bore running. When they hit the gate, they burst right through it; it wasn't chained like this one was.

The sound of two distinct engines starting, revving immediately to pitched whines, split the night. I had a flash of realization. I looked around – there was nowhere to hide. We could try to make the corner of the cemetery, but there was no time.

We had to go inside.

"C'mon Cot," I said. I pulled her toward the low part of the gate. She looked at me alarmed, but came right up to me. I picked her up and set her over. She scrambled down the other side and stood statue still, not taking her eyes from me. I pulled myself over.

I jumped down and we hightailed it to the back of the crypt.

We crouched down. The two vehicles caromed our direction on the road skirting the cemetery. Lucius' pickup was in front. A red mustang with the other two inside followed. Its front window was dark, but one chilling sight broke through.

The girl's weird smile bobbed and danced against the rest of the blackness, reminding me of the grin of the Cheshire Cat, strangely unsettling and similarly disembodied. The uncanny image of her floating smile gave me gooseflesh.

For a moment, it seemed as if there were a third individual in the cab with them, a person small enough to sit in the limited space at the rear of the Mustang's cab.

I could not discern any features of this third person, or even if they were truly there at all.

We inched around the crypt to keep our cover as they moved.

Then, the vehicles were gone in a night of dust.

Cot started back over the gate. While she climbed, I looked into the open iron door of the Denizen crypt. It was all blackness in there. My eyes adjusted and white forms began to resolve, wavering it seemed.

I turned to retreat over the gate.

But wait. What was Lucius doing in the crypt? I stopped. Cot was burning her eyes into mine.

"What, Johnny?" she whispered harshly.

"I need to check out what they were doing in there, Cot." I responded, already preparing myself for Cot's excellent reasons why I should not, why I should instead march right over the gate to see us to our warm beds.

"I'll be here," was what she said.

I turned toward the crypt, with an irritated huff. As the dark entry filled my vision, the white shapes inside resolved to dusty caskets on stone shelves, enshrouded with white fungus. I could see nothing else. The floor was dark, as were the far reaches of the room, and the corners.

I didn't think I could go in there, into that dark.

I walked to the edge of the doorway and reached my arm into the gloom. I felt out in front of me, then down near the ground. My hand touched a thing. It felt like a glass cup. I pulled it out. It was a small candle.

I lit the tiny candle with a match from my kit, shining it into the crypt. On the floor was a pack of cigarettes and some white spots that turned out to be cotton balls. There was a strange smell in the room. A spicy sweet smell. A species of smoke? Of perfume? I could not tell, it was so faint against the backdrop of dead dust.

"Just a candle, some cotton balls, and a pack a cigs," I announced. "Wait --"

There was something red in there, on the floor. Just beyond the cotton balls, but I was too far away. Reluctantly, I stepped into the room. The thing on the floor was a circle of red, a nearly perfect circle. There was an angle inscribed, also in red, within the circle.

"There's a symbol written on the floor." I rubbed the circle with my finger and smelled. "I think it's lipstick," I said.

"Johnny, I want to go!" implored Cot, and Cot rarely implored. I hurriedly exited the house of the dead and made over the fence without a backward glance.

We tore on home, with the ghosts of Copeland at our heels.

ChApTeR 21

The next day at school, Mr. Rufus Edwards handed out small notebooks to every kid in class, even the youngsters. They were 5x8 and black. Inside were precisely cut, lined pages. Sewn into the black binding was an elastic strap to hold the whole thing closed.

"These notebooks are for writing in. Writing. No dirty pictures. No to-do lists. I see anything like that and we will have words." Mr. Edwards returned to the front of the room. He had us all write our names and addresses in the books and the name of our school and our class. Cot seemed quite taken with her little black notebook. She looked at me and smiled wide.

"Other than previously described prohibitions, feel free to write whatever you'd like inside. If you think up a poem or song, write it down. If you see something you would like to have a hand at describing, write it down. If you want to keep a diary, you may do so, although be warned, I will be collecting the notebooks from time to time and giving them the once-over, in order to chart your progress.

"What I've learned in my years, with a variety of students, is that it's so not easy for them to connect the word-making machinery in their brains to the writing-down machinery in their hands. It takes practice. So, you will be writing something in this book every day. There are no size or subject requirements. Try to keep it above one muddled, disjointed line of misspellings. The only strict requirement is that you write every day. If you do not, we will have words." Here Mr. Edwards placed his hand significantly on his leather satchel, in which hid the ornate book.

Some of the smaller kids shrank in their desks. Some of the larger kids did their best not to shrink in their desks. Not all succeeded.

Cot just kept on smiling.

This little black notebook changed my life. I wrote in my notebook every day. I could not help it -- I wrote almost exclusively about Miss Holly.

Starting off with some loathsome poetry, I proceeded to equally wretched prose. I was so young then, so inexperienced with my emotions. I will give you examples of this glop, only if germane to the furtherance of this story (and, as the author of this story, I have unique insight into the fact that this will never occur).

Cot used her notebook too. But she used it different than I did, as a tool to organize her thought processes, to assist in organizing her decisions. I stole into her room early on and at regular intervals, and read it through.

She, like me, wrote largely about Miss Holly. But different. I think Miss Holly's murder opened a door in Cot's mind, a door she would have preferred stayed tightly shut.

Suddenly, the world was a place where a beautiful woman, a good woman who helped people and was always nice and happy, could end up horribly murdered. Suddenly, Cot found herself in a world where the good did die young and the bad got off scott-free.

These were the thoughts that ricocheted in Cot's pretty head, when her breathing would stick in her throat.

Now, knowing Cot as I did, I saw there was no way in hell she could abide such a shift in her paradigmatic sense of the world. She had to do something. If Cot could not erase Miss Holly's murder from history, from the past itself, then her only option was to try to balance the scales retroactively, and catch her murderer.

The official investigation had come up empty handed. In fact, so bereft of results was the investigation, it seemed as if some force had interceded upon it, and the gossip of The Cooridy and The Remedy at my momma's dinner table seemed borne out.

I know this may seem a ridiculous prospect for an eleven-year-old girl to undertake, to catch a murderer. If Cot's realization about life's unfairness had been all, perhaps she could have let it go, relegated her cognitive discomfort to bad dreams and weird symptomatic behaviors like the rest of us do. But it was not all.

There was another aspect comprising Cot's dogged determination to bring Miss Holly's murderer to justice.

She did it for me.

ChApTeR 22

FROM THE JOURNAL OF COT CLEARY

Poor Johnny. He was moping all day. He loved Miss Holly just like a real man loves a real woman. Like Pop loves Mom. He loved her too much.

But she was lucky I guess. If you're gonna go, it's better that you are loved than that no one cares or remembers.

A lot of people loved Miss Holly.

I don't know if I ever want to love a person. It's kinda sick.

Johnny loved Miss Holly like those dippy guys that wrote poetry in the old days. He didn't even know Miss Holly, really. Johnny was in love with her picture in his head. Maybe that's the most powerful kind of love.

I don't know much about it I guess, thank you Jesus!

But to have the one you love killed. It's just so mean.

Even if it was just a fever dream, it makes me sick and sad and mad all at the same time! Johnny ain't ever gonna be the same. Not ever!

He could turn into anything from this -- he could end up a hermit. He could even become an ax murderer.

The killer thinks he got away with something. He got himself into a big old stew of shit is what he got.

ChApTeR 23

When Mr. Edwards picked up our journals a couple of weeks hence, both Cot and myself were taken aback. We had forgotten about this part of it. We both heard him say it, but back then, I guess neither of us thought we would write so extensively about Miss Holly.

When we got back from recess later, we saw both our notebooks splayed open, side by side, on his desk.

Our alarm was manifest. Especially to Mr. Edwards, who was watching us hard. After everyone was in their seats, he was still looking at us, his brow furrowed, his frown deep.

So, when Mr. Edwards held us back during 2nd recess, we were not shocked at all.

"C'mon up here you two," he said.

We moped up to the front. Mr. Edwards gestured to the notebooks.

"Johnny, you fancy yourself a jilted lover and Cot, you fancy yourself a private detective."

We said nothing, but kept our eyes on our feet.

"You think you are honoring the memory of Miss Holly by writing such stuff?" he asked. "Johnny?"

I shuffled and made noises, then, "Mr. Edwards, I felt real strongly about Miss Holly. I guess her death hit me kinda hard. I'm just trying to work some things out in my head."

"What it looks like to me Johnny is that you are taking some license with a poor murdered woman's memory! Someone picking this notebook up out of the blue would think that the author was an adult with mental problems, having an erotic affair with a feral, wolf-raised vixen, who happens to moonlight as a school teacher!"

Cot made the slightest noise of mirth. That made me angry. I let it show on my face, but didn't say a word.

"And Cot, just what do you think you are up to? I see things in your notebook that suggest you have been following William Wickley around without his knowledge or consent?"

"Really Mr. Edwards?" said Cot innocently.

"Really, Cot! Or am I to believe that this entry, dated two days ago, which states…

'0715 w.w. at post office.'

…means something else? Is it a description of a dream?"

Cot said nothing, as if awaiting further options.

"And it goes on!" exclaimed Mr. Edwards, proceeding to read aloud.

"'0830-0930 Winky breakfast Charlie's'

'1020 Winky Robert parking lot of the millworks. r.w. got in the driver's seat of a big black car. They talked for 10 mins and started yelling at each other. w.w. walked off, yelling behind him. R.w gave w.w the finger through windshield (super funny) and drove away fast.'

"Perhaps it is some new kind of poetry?" Our teacher asked the question with exaggerated interest, as if it were a genuine, pedagogical inquiry

"Yes, Mr. Edwards," Cot responded.

"Yes, what, Cot?" asked Mr. Edwards, menacingly.

"Yes, it's a new kind of poetry. Modern poetry, Mr. Edwards. Sir!" Cot said, with incredible sincerity.

I looked agape at Cot. She had been following Winky? Was she mad?

Mr. Edwards closed his eyes. His lips set into thin ridges. His hand crept toward the leather satchel, but stopped.

He looked at us both and then the stern teacher persona melted away from Mr. Edwards all in a moment. He drew himself up in his chair, his knowledge and concern broadening over his face.

"You guys, I can't imagine what you went through. Johnny, if you had such strong feelings for her… well, I'm just real sorry son. Real sorry."

I suddenly realized that Mr. Edwards was an exceptional sort of person, the kind you are lucky to meet once in a life.

All the mean impulses I felt toward him evaporated.

How strange.

"And Cot, I see how much you want to help your brother get to the bottom of that woman's untimely death. That's real admirable, and I mean that sincerely. Johnny, you are a lucky boy to have such a determined, brave and smart little sister."

Cot nodded, once, in accordance.

"But you are just kids!" Mr. Edwards shouted as he slammed the desk with his open hand. We jumped a mile. "I feel like telling your parents. If my own daughter had such delusions, I would ground her for a year just to keep her safe!"

I didn't know Mr. Edwards had a daughter. Apparently, Cot was reading my mind because she said:

"I didn't know you had family here, Mr. Edwards."

"Yes, I have family Cot. Believe it or not, I wasn't spontaneously generated by the school board for the purpose of teaching you urchins. I have parents and a wife and kids, just like a real person. My family, all of them, will be joining me shortly. They were prudently waiting to see whether I was run out of town on a rail before pulling up roots and coming here."

"I think you're going to do just fine here Mr. Edwards," said Cot. "I think you are the best teacher we ever had."

I was aghast. Better than Miss Holly?

Cot just looked straight ahead.

Mr. Edwards eyebrows shot up when she said that. He even looked pleased. Then he came to his senses and became suspicious, his eyes narrowing.

"For the moment, Cot, I will give you the benefit of the doubt, and will presume that you are not trying to butter me up... or change the subject."

"I'm not, Mr. Edwards."

"Fine then. But we still have a problem. You two are not thinking nor acting as you should be. You are both getting way ahead of yourselves. Johnny, I know you loved Miss Holly, but you are thinking about her way too much. You will never get over her if you don't start thinking about other things. There is nothing in your notebook but Miss Holly, Miss Holly, Miss Holly!"

"I can't think of nothing else!" I said, louder than I wanted to. "I've tried Mr. Edwards. I just dream about her all the time. When I'm working I see her, when I'm eating or playing. She has totally taken over my mind. It's like her ghost won't let me be."

Mr. Edwards looked directly at me then. "Do you really feel like she is haunting you, Johnny?"

I thought about it. "No, I suppose not," I lied.

Actually, now that the possibility had been brought up, it did kind of feel like Miss Holly was haunting me.

Why hadn't I thought of that before?

Mr. Edwards turned to Cot, his face soft again. "Cot, honey, you have simply got to cease this detective work. You are going to get yourself in a heap of trouble. What if Mr. Wickley had seen you following him? Do you think he would have been okay with that?"

"I would never let Winky see me, Mr. Edwards, I am way too careful."

Mr. Edwards sighed.

"Ok. Here's the deal. No more writing about Miss Holly. At all. Not one word. If you are writing about Christmas, and think you are allowed to even write the word 'holly,' you are sadly mistaken." The stern teacher was back.

Cot said, "Yes sir," and then I said, "Yes sir."

He snatched up the two notebooks. Cot gasped. Mr. Edwards stopped and looked at her.

"Mr. Edwards, suddenly I don't feel so well," said Cot, and fell right to the floor. It is amazing, the grace with which a person genuinely fainting attains the floor. Cot, on the other hand, clunked to the ground and bounced.

"Good heavens!" shouted Mr. Edwards, stepping quickly around the desk.

I ran to Cot, my heart pounding not in the least. I knew she was faking, but there had to be a good reason for it. I said "Cot!" and shook her violently. She made little noises. On the side away from Mr. Edwards, Cot pinched me hard in the leg.

"Stop boy, you're gonna rattle her bones apart," said Mr. Edwards. His voice crept back to some childhood accent.

Cot's eyes rolled sleepily and she brought her hand to her forehead. "Do you think I could have some water, Mr. Edwards?" she asked, sweetly.

"Yes, water!" Mr. Edwards jumped up and dug into his satchel, pulled out his white coffee cup, and raced out the door to the bathroom. When he returned, Mr. Edwards cradled Cot's head in his hand, actually dribbling water into her mouth like she was a just-borne calf. It was sick-making.

Mr. Edwards helped Cot into a chair. After a couple of minutes of the worst acting since silent movies, Mr. Edwards told us to walk outside, for the fresh air to enliven my sister.

Cot and I proceeded out into the sun of the playground. Kids were beating up on each other, pushing each other into the mud and twisting the parts of each other, vigorously.

Cot and I meandered to the far corner, near the tetherball post. She handed me the two notebooks, stolen while Mr. Edwards was out of the room, getting Cot her water.

"There is no way we're getting away with this Cot."

"Doesn't matter," she said. "All that matters is we got 'em. You stay here, I'm gonna go hide 'em."

Cot returned about five minutes later.

"You stink at fainting," I told her.

ChApTeR 24

When recess was over, and we returned to the classroom, there were blank notebooks on each of our desks. Mr. Edwards never mentioned the ones we stole.

At that point I realized that Mr. Edwards was on to us the whole time.

ChApTeR 25

Dad was reading the note Mr. Edwards sent home with us. Mom was putting the last item on the table. Yams. Cot was across from Luce, who sat, unwilling as a cat in a girdle, on my left. He looked not at all well.

"You fainted Cot?" asked Dad.

"She fainted dead away," I piped in.

Cot delivered a silent kick to the sweetest spot of my shin. I coughed explosively.

"I was just too hot, Daddy," she said.

"Cot, it's September."

"I was hot," she repeated. "The radiators were on too high."

"So, why does Mr. Edwards say 'Please keep a very close eye on Cot for the next week, or so. Cot needs constant supervision to ensure no further accidents befall her?'" Dad fixed Cot with a calm eye, that threatened utter destruction should she lie.

Cot, as always, was up to the task.

"In case I faint again?"

Dad was skeptical. He was a walking lie detector. My dad could ferret out a fabrication, no matter how sublimely wrought.

"Janice, I kinda think Mr. Edwards is trying to tell us something."

Momma sat down. She threw a pile of napkins to Cot, for distribution. "If he wanted to tell us something, he would have just told us," she said cheerily. Momma's dinners were not the place for anything save peace, and accord.

We ate and talked. Dad said a big piece of wood shot across the floor at work that day. Dad said it flew out of a debarker badly in need of calibration. When it hit the far wall, it sailed right through, easy as you please. He acted the whole scene out, his rigid hand played the errant piece of wood.

Then, Dad sat down and looked straight at Lucius, and said,

"Luce are you on drugs?"

Luce was slowly poking at his food, not really eating. He froze like petrified wood when Dad said that.

He turned his face up, to Dad. Luce was clearly at the end of some rope, his eyes hollow, his hair dark with an oily sheen. Lucius turned his eye to Momma, her dinner irretrievably ruined, to Cot, to me. Then he turned his head down, and slowly started nodding.

Dad's face presented an unholy progression of alarm, concern and creeping anger. Run through it all, some pride surfaced. Luce, after all, was telling a painful truth, a truth that would cost him.

Dad opened his mouth, but nothing came out. He closed his mouth. He jerked his head to the stairs where he and Luce slowly repaired to the basement, there following, conspicuously, for about an hour, no loud voices, no sounds of torture, and no copious weeping.

Mom doled out food to us, looking very elsewhere in her thoughts. She smiled sweetly to us and we all started eating.

The next day Luce was off with Dad in the pickup. Dad took him up to live with Uncle Bennett, just back from The Vietnam. All our prospects of discovering what had transpired in the graveyard went with him.

It was sad watching Luce go. He waved lazily to us as Dad pulled the truck onto the track to the main road. Cot and I waved back to him, but he wasn't even watching.

I have always despaired of such situations. To this day, I study my departee in the moment of parting, to perceive whether they are as broken up as I am, and I am invariably disappointed.

ChApTeR 26

"You think he was just doing drugs in that nasty crypt?" Cot asked.

We were back by the Old Cross bridge. I was smoking, which I liked to do there. It brought to mind Huck Finn and the freedom of youth. Cot was digging a big "X" into the ground with a stick.

"Yep I do," I said, "But I don't know what that symbol meant."

"I think I do," she said and started scraping into the ground with a purpose.

She drew this:

An inverse pentacle.

"I know what that is, Cot... that's a symbol for the devil," I said.

"Remember, we were talking about a devil cult?" she asked.

Yes! The horror! A devil cult!

"You think a devil cult did in Miss Holly, Cot?"

"Well, I don't."

"You don't?"

Cot threw her drawing stick into the forest. "No cuz if there was a devil cult, we would have to think that Luce was in it. And I know Luce is a jerk, but he ain't no devil worshiper, and he sure ain't no murderer."

Oh yeah, Luce. No way was he a devil worshiper. I could concede that part.

"So why were they in a crypt drawing devil symbols? And did you see what I saw? I thought there mighta been a third person in that Mustang."

"I don't know about that. I just don't think Luce was worshipping Satan," she said, almost to herself.

"Cot," I said.

Her head shot up, eyes daring me.

"What in blue blazes were you doing following Winky around? That man ain't right. If there is a devil around here, he is it! He would have eaten you raw if he'd a found you out!"

Cot's brow furrowed and her lips set in a thin line.

"He's got something to do with it Johnny," was all she said.

"You gonna tell me why you think that?"

"The way Winky was acting at Miss Holly's funeral, for starters," said Cot. "The way he reacted to Miss Holly's Mom pointing at him, right before she died."

I did remember. Miss Holly's momma pointed right at Winky before she collapsed.

Cot continued.

"I saw something - Winky made a jerky move, as if he was just about to jump in front of his son, to protect him, but then thought better of it. As if Miss Holly's Mom was pointing a real gun at them and he was trying to keep his son from being shot." Cot's hand, crooked and pointing as the grieving mother's hand had been, transformed into a gun and she shot a distant target, then blew smoke off the barrel.

"You think they both might have something to do with it?"

"I guess I do think that."

"All I can say Cot is that you can't be following people around, at least not unless I'm with you." I said sternly.

"Then I'll be safe, if you're with me, huh?"

"Yeah, cuz then you'll be safe," I affirmed.

There was a noise on the bridge. In its shadow, we looked upward, expecting to see old Winky there, slavering with the knowledge of our conversation. The Old Cross was a single lane bridge under a bed of gravel, at right angles with the spring creek underneath, thus the 'cross.' Leafy boughs impinged onto it, some scraping the gravel.

There was a human shape up there, silhouetted against the spikes of sunlight spearing the leaves. I hoped we were hidden in shadow, that the person up there could not see us. But then the person spoke to us.

"What say ya, little fish?" croaked an ancient female voice.

After a second's silence, Cot nodded my way, assigning me ambassadorship of our little country of two. I thought for a minute, and then gave the standard reply.

"Nothin," I said.

The shape regarded us, then shuffled back, out of sight, toward the far side of the bridge. There was silence. Cot looked at me in alarm.

Cot said, "What in the damn Sam Hill --"

"Ya must think me a child of yesterday's grouse," the old woman spoke. She was down under the bridge now, not ten yards away, shuffling right up to us.

She was about five-foot-nothing in her blue-striped dress. A thick, red shawl of dirty wool adorned her shoulders and a blue handkerchief topped her head. She could have been white, or Native, her skin was dark and creased with age. But her eyes practically glowed with their blue energy of life. Her lips were drawn in a prim smile.

"I ken nothin, and that ent nothin'" the gnarled woman said, indicating the pentacle that Cot had carved in the dirt.

I sighed. This looked bad.

"It's from the TV," I said.

The old woman regarded me with her electric eyes. "Nope twarnt what ye said afore young trout. Ye said yer own brother Lucius Cleary drew that devil mark in a crypt, is what ye said. I got ears and a brain and neither of em frozen, young trout."

"I know I didn't say his name," I said defiantly.

"I ken his name!" she grinned. "Just like I ken your'ns Johnny and Cot Cleary. And I mind yer not up to at-all good here beneath this bridge. You, boy, spoke of the late Theda Holly, ago. No good can come of that, young trout."

I had never seen this bizarre woman before. "Who are you?" I asked. "I don't know you from town."

"Theda..." The old woman continued, oblivious to my question. She worried a small object in her right hand. "Theda was a sweet 'un t'me. I would catch her in my wanders, but allus up t'other side of our forest. She was allus up for conversatin', that 'un. Allus give t'me some little gift." She looked down into her hand, at the thing I could not see. She shook her head slowly and put it in her pocket.

"So, it's your vision, young trout, that Old Scratch was up to Theda Holly's murder, ay?" said the woman.

I had no idea what she meant. I just looked blankly back at her bluest eyes.

"The Devil!" She yiped, and feinted at me, splaying her hands out and retracting them in an instant. I was startled into a jerk.

The old woman chuckled. Cot had her hands on her hips now.

"Just who in hell are you, lady?" she asked flatly.

"Statuette!" The old lady reared back, mockingly. "You speak!" She giggled.

I couldn't help it. I giggled.

The old lady heard me, and winked. Cot gave me a withering look. I remained sheepish and smiling.

The old woman looked mirthfully back and forth between us.

"I am Molly White," she said. "The Unsinkable!" She found this incredibly funny and wiped her eye of the resultant tear. "I ha' see'd ye here many a time little fish, but ne'er approached, for reasons of my own," she said, cackling softly.

Cot sized her up. "Where do you live?"

Old Molly was taken aback, by Cot's adult sound, no doubt.

"I live close, Cot, close enough to hear yer splashin and shriekin many a time."

"I'm surprised we've never seen you around here – we've been coming here our whole lives."

"Don't I ken't Cot, dear. If you fancy me an imposter of a dame ye never met, or a ghost, or what may be, go and ask yer Mom about me. She and I go back."

Cot nodded, as if to say, I intend to do just that.

Molly drew up close to me. She looked deep into my eyes and I was stricken still. "I'd give much to know what happened to my dear Theda. You believe that dontcha trout-John?"

"I do, Molly," I said, and sincerely felt it.

That seemed to pacify her somewhat. Molly paced the space between Cot and I. The trout thing was beginning to bother me. Was there some characteristic I displayed that reminded this woman of a trout? I pored over my list of attributes, but nothing came to mind.

"Right nice to meetcha," said Molly White and snapped her mouth shut like a machine. Walking back into the murk under the bridge, she was gone.

Cot and I stared at each other in amazement at the weirdness of the woman, her speech, and her appearance and disappearance as if from the gloom of the forest itself.

"We are just gonna have to do more following of Winky and that son of his. We don't have a choice," Cot said, as she walked over to the inverted pentacle in the dirt, energetically effacing it with the toe of her shoe.

The First Tale of Isobel Whitehead-Patrick
Early September, 1939

A mysterious experience occurred when Isobel was about 10 years old, in 1924, as she played in the Heart-Shaped Forest where it transected the Whitehead-Patrick property. The world at that moment had been sunlight slicing through the canopy, the air glimmering with displaced dew.

And then it happened.

~

When the experience had ended, or ceased to be, Isobel at first thought herself delusional.

Isobel had long consigned the event to the under reaches of her subjective knowledge, where it nourished her from afar, guiding her gently, yet inexorably, ever eastward. First, to a curious fascination with the forest throughout her childhood; then, to a four-year degree in Forest Science from Colwaitha College in Oklahoma City; on to a Masters earned from the prestigious Herontown University, and, finally, east-most of all, to her PhD aspirations at Bridgeford University, Bridgeford, England.

Her memories of the Heart-Shaped Forest were runnels through which flowed the rest of her life's work. Those memories, memories both present and absent, subliminally shaped her dissertation, which, for the last year and a half, had demanded that she travel farther out into the wide world than she ever imagined she ever would.

She would never have the opportunity to finish her dissertation now, and perhaps that was for the best.

Isobel considered the charcoal waves of the Skagerrak Sea as it bore her back to England. The impenetrable opacity suggested a solidity attendant more to the non-metals, than to seawater.

Indeed, for a moment, on the wet wood of the ferry's foredeck - a long, uncanny moment - Isobel Whitehead-Patrick was overtaken by a chill that that had nothing to do with the North Sea's pervasive local winds. The grey water that broke before her ferry was a dark infinity evoking a dimension in which Isobel's own human life was reduced to its contextually salient characteristics of fragility, impermanence and mortality. The concept that that the freezing churn before her would erase her forever from history, simply by stepping down into it, coursed through Isobel Whitehead-Patrick right then, raising the fine hairs and gooseflesh on her arms, bringing tears of awe to her eyes.

The hollowness of this experience was curiously enjoyable and life-affirming to Isobel, who breathed in, through her pointed nose, a cold lungful of the Cosmos.

The ferry's mournful horn brought Isobel back to the moment.

The year was 1939, the month, September. Saturday the 3rd. Roughly 6 pm.

All sorts of noises were coming from the bar area just behind the steel wall, noises of celebration and discontent.

Britain had just declared war on Germany.

Isobel came outside to escape the truly strange behavior surrounding the announcement, which had been made by a boatswain in three languages. The shipful of citizens, just realizing they had been plunged into a war, very like the previous war they had barely survived, and dawning upon what this implied for their nephews and sons, was more bizarre a surrounding than an exorcism, to Isobel's way of thinking.

Isobel became aware that she was nearly soaked through with spray. Her Amelia Earhart-designed extra-long flight jacket and her skirt, both leather, bought for a song, after the line was discontinued (but before the poor woman disappeared into thin air, causing the price of her clothes to skyrocket), pressed Isobel into her seat.

The tail of the horn's sound trailed away, and with it, her reverie. Isobel grabbed her satchel and wrenched herself up from a gaily colored deck chair that was, she whispered to herself, ridiculously out of place in this grey clime.

She was only now riding the North Sea from the Faroe Islands, where she had conducted over a dozen interviews, teasing from the islanders' accounts the neopagan symbologies nesting in their most pervasive ghost tales. Everything had proceeded splendidly, giving her the means to flesh out an anemic part of her dissertation, by using the relative forestlessness of the Faroes to her discursive advantage.

But then, even though there was no Faroe forest in sight, that strange message came to her, yet again, loud and clear, the message that had nothing to do with her dissertation at all. It came to her louder and clearer than ever before.

The message arrived only this morning, from the withered lips of an old man who appeared in a boat, as Isobel surveyed the swells of the sea, munching her sandwich on a Faroe rock on that Faroe beach. The smudge in the fog sharpened into a boat occupied by two ancient people, a woman aft and a man in the fore.

When they scraped a point beyond which the boat could no further go, the old woman planted a long stick through a hole in the keel into the shallows, fixing the boat to that spot. The old man laboriously clambered over the side of the boat to all fours in the water, soaking his sleeves and the heavy skirts he was, inexplicably, clothed in.

Isobel, who had stopped chewing at first sight of the small boat, and whose mouth relaxed into a stunned gape at the old man's watery shenanigans, put down the rest of her sandwich, spit out her mouthful and splashed up to the old man before he was carried away by the fabled undertows of those parts. Together they struggled to shore, impeded wholly by the old man's epic skirtage, until they slumped into the cold sand.

After the bellows of their four lungs were fully satisfied, the old man brought himself to knee and indicated toward Isobel, while looking questioningly back to the old woman in the boat. The old woman nodded her head and unleashed a guttural stream of abuse in an utterly foreign tongue, at which point the old man turned to Isobel and clumsily spoke the message, in English, a language with which this old man was obviously not familiar.

The old man spoke the message Isobel had repeatedly discerned herself; in a dream at the base of a gnarled oak in Wales, in a fevered vision, under the effects of ether, in a Wiesbaden dentist's chair, and from her own reading of other strange, coincidental occurrences throughout the whole of her sabbatical abroad.

Yet it had never been spoken by a human tongue to her, until now.

"Go home," said the beskirted old man.

~

Even as the old man spoke the words, there was an unpleasant feeling in Isobel's head. There was a spot, a location in her head that demanded Isobel stop looking at this old man and turn her reckoning inward. The old man watched Isobel's face evict all animation as the young lady before him searched and searched, inward and inward.

And then Isobel remembered. The mysterious event when she was 10 years old, playing in the lucky light of the Heart-Shaped Forest, was finally shaken and dislodged to the fore.

And that was that. Isobel said, "Okay," to the old man, and, leaving her sandwich for the birds, made back fast for England, within a few hours.

The words the old man imparted to her had not only concerned home, but had, Isobel was sure, somehow come from there. The old man had simply relayed the message that had come by way of some unfathomable network from the Heart-Shaped Forest itself.

The hailings in Isobel's dreamy states, had come to her as if on a beam, a distress signal.

Not Go Home, but, Come Home.

With respect to the mysterious event of her youth, the message made perfect sense, even as the message itself lent some semblance of sense to the mysterious event.

It did occur to Isobel that these turns might merely constitute an elaborate drama concocted by her fretting unconscious, in the service of simply giving up, throwing away the noisome monograph she was writing before it caused her real embarrassment.

These rude thoughts proved squashable, so she squashed them.

The hailing felt too real, too important.

Besides, Isobel had learned from the world what she had set out to learn.

~

A week and a day to break the news to the professor, pack up her things, say her goodbyes and disembark.

Isobel's travel choices on such short notice were dismal. She was forced to accept passage from Liverpool to New York on a steamer crammed to the gills with Jews fleeing the ill-tempered Adolf Hitler. In steerage, no less.

Her berth was barely 5 and 1/2 feet long. Her pillow was a paper bag filled with straw, which she ended up giving to a little girl who seemed all too grateful for it. Instead, Isobel rested her head on her canvas satchel, which she kept close. The rest of her belongings had already been sent home, to Copeland.

Every possible free space of the hold was carpeted with families, their luggage or their sleeping areas. The smells were exotic and human. As the 17-day trip progressed, the odors tended more toward the human.

The muttering, humming, intoning, the wails of outrage and pain, all mixed into the undertones of laughter and gossip, creating an atonal chorus to echo off the white-painted steel of the hold, quieting at nighttime only a little, and ceasing, never.

Isobel, who had travelled extensively, at a variety of comfort levels, found this journey opened up a world before her barely comprehending eyes that she had somehow managed to remain blind to, even as she had visited its most volatile areas.

For all her globetrotting, Isobel knew little about the suffering of great swaths of humanity, or the dark politics of bullying and thuggery unfolding across Europe. It whispered to Isobel that, for all her education, she wasn't nearly as world-wise as the little girl to whom she had given her pillow of straw.

Her travels in Germany were cast in a new light. Whether the blinders she wore during her visit (scarcely one year prior) were her own, or externally imposed, she had returned to Bridgeford from Germany blissfully unaware of this ship-full of troubles brewing just down the roads and just over the hills from her hotels.

Some things made sense now. The brown shirted men painting over grafitti'd bricks. The dire forbiddance of certain localities.

~

Isobel made friends with the little girl to whom she had given her straw pillow, by virtue of the fact that their faces, when they slept, were only about 18 inches apart. During the days of the voyage the girl would talk to Isobel endlessly, in perfectly acceptable English, smattered with Yiddish.

"All the windows of all the shops, my uncles Ephram's and Moshe's both, smashed to pieces! Those dirty Nazis took all the nicest dolls. My poppa's other brother, his little brother, Uncle El --"

The man sitting hunched on the lower bunk, just above the little girl, set his hand lightly on her shoulder, which made the girl's lips snap shut. Isobel had the impression that the man stopped his daughter's words, not to forestall her disclosure of unpleasant events, but simply to stop her from saying aloud his brother's name, as if her so doing might derail something hard won.

The man smiled sheepishly at Isobel, nodding his head once, in a quick prayer to the dead, a prayer compacted to a nod through God only knew what wretched circumstances. Isobel felt a shiver.

The man's little daughter looked up at him and understood this all in a moment.

The girl looked up at Isobel, who looked back at her. Isobel was speechless due to the ache in her throat and from trying to suppress quiverings of her face-parts. The girl seemed to believe herself muted, so Isobel wiped discreetly at her eye, saying, "Do you know any stories? I am a collector of stories you know, stories about trees especially."

The little girl, brightened. She got to her feet, allowing all the items to fall from her lap to the grey steel floor. Isobel tried to imagine the little girl in Isobel's own favorite childhood dress. She could not do it.

The girl's mud colored clothes, worn uninterrupted the entire voyage, seemed as affixed to her as her difficult circumstances.

The little girl whispered into her father's ear, then offered her ear for him. She nodded enthusiastically at his suggestion and, after one further whisper, diligently hidden behind her tiny hand, she sat back down and smiled up at Isobel.

"She wants me to tell it," said the father, to the eager nodding of his daughter.

The father thought for a moment and said, "A traveler was doing what he did best, travelling."

The girl giggled. Her father began to speak the story he had clearly told many times before.

"The traveler happened upon a man planting a carob tree (or sometimes it is a fig tree) along the side of the road. It was obviously difficult work and it made the traveler wonder. The traveler asked the man, 'How long will it take for this carob tree to bear fruit?' The man wiped his sweat from his forehead and replied, '70 years.' This surprised the traveler, for it was clear that this man would never taste the fruit of the tree he was planting. 'Do you plan on still being around in 70 years to eat that fruit?' The man looked at the traveler incredulously and shook his head. 'Heavens no! You see, when I was a child, I so enjoyed the fruit of trees planted decades prior, by men who never lived to sample their yield. I am doing the same for the children now, and their children,' said the man."

At which point the story was, apparently, over. The little girl looked to Isobel for her opinion.

To Isobel, steeped in the tradition of western story arcs, the fable was lovely in the telling, but did not pack the punch of, say, The Tale of Johnny Appleseed.

"You are less than impressed," said the father, a smile lifting his impeccably trimmed mustache.

"You speak English very well. What do you do?" asked Isobel, which made the man laugh in a charming way.

It did not charm Isobel however, or not overmuch. She could not tell if she was being laughed at.

The father, noticing Isobel's perturbation, immediately stopped laughing and in a rather humble way said,

"Forgive me. I was only amused at how quickly you changed the subject. I was a surgeon, a junior thoracic surgeon at the University Hospital of Surgery in Hiedlberg, and then for the last year or so, I have had to work for the Deputy Consulate of the British Embassy in Berlin."

"How fascinating," exclaimed Isobel, thankful that the subject had indeed changed. "What did you do for him?"

"I was his butler."

Isobel was again plunged into discomfiture.

The father, quick to notice Isobel's change of mood, said, "That is why our English…" but, he seemed to have embarked upon a sentence construction that was too much for him and he fell silent.

The little girl said, "He was a rude man. He was always very mean to Poppa," presumably in reference to the Deputy Consulate of the British Embassy.

Her father tensed.

"No, Sarah," he said. "That was his way of looking out for us. If he had been kind to us, it might have drawn scrutiny, made the bad people notice us. He made many a grave apology to me when it was just us two alone. Many times. He was a good man, and we owe him much more than I can ever repay," he said, as much to Isobel as to Sarah.

"Do you have a wife?" asked Isobel, immediately regretting having done so, for fear of the answer, given the trend of the conversation up to that point.

"She and my two sons tried to make the voyage in May. However, they were stopped in Cuba and sent back. We were fortunate to have been able to waylay them from where they… where they were headed after that," said the father. "They will be joining us soon, we hope."

The father considered Isobel.

"That story about the tree. It's important," said the father.

"Due to the centrality of future generations in its message?" asked Isobel, donning her Bridgefordian Cap of Hermeneutical Inquiry.

"In a way," responded Sarah's father. "More important is what the story implies."

"Which is?" asked Isobel, her Cap dissolving.

"An enduring faith in the Maker of all things."

"God."

"We do not speak the name of the Creator aloud," replied the father of Sarah, a finger to his lips.

Sarah shook her head solemnly.

"To plant the tree, as the man does in the story, implies a great faith in the Creator to steward the tree successfully to fruit, many years in the future. It implies that the Creator is invested in the process of life itself, not just human life. He is interested. He cares."

He looked for Isobel's response. She kept carefully averted while considering his words. Isobel was bothered, as the story enflamed her intellect in a mode no longer required, given her abandonment of her thesis.

Isobel's retreat into her own thoughts caused Sarah's father to make a movement of breath, to re-ensnare her attention.

Isobel looked up.

"Why so interested in trees?" he asked.

The question brightened and darkened her simultaneously. Isobel answered slow and uncertain.

"I was a student. I was writing my Thesis when I had to... I just had to leave. It concerned, which is to say, my doctoral thesis at Bridgeford concerned, the relationship between trees and a certain phenomenon that I am suddenly embarrassed to relate to you!"

"A doctorate at Bridgeford. Impressive. Do you fear I will not understand?"

"Oh, heavens no," and she stumbled, not knowing Sarah's father's name.

"I am Isobel Whitehead-Patrick," she said, proffering her hand. He took it. "Jake," he returned.

Sarah wedged in and took Isobel's hand from her father.

"Sarah," she said, matter of factly.

"Isobel Whitehead-Patrick," Isobel repeated down to her, with immense gravity.

"I am more concerned you will think me deluded and foolish. My thesis was on the relationship between deforestation and the rise in spirit related phenomenon throughout the world. There, I said it! You are the first people I have told who I was not required to. And telling you now, I guess I do hear the silliness in it."

"It's not silly," said Sarah.

"How marvelous, you saying that Sarah, for you are the first," said Isobel.

Jake brought Sarah into his lap. "This relationship you discovered, what does it mean?"

"Well," started Isobel staidly, as if preparing to engage in glorious battle to protect the ramparts of her theory, as if all she had ever met when describing it was resistance and ridicule, which was in fact true. She set her jaw firm and poured it all out in a torrent:

"It suggests that the relationship between trees and humans continues beyond the grave in some way. Indeed, there are certain theories of the chemistry and biology of plants that tell us that plants and trees are more intimately necessary to human existence than previously surmised. Some even speculate that plants breathe out what we breathe in and vice-versa. Thus, we humans live in a mutually beneficial, mutually essential relationship with the trees and plants of this world, a relationship far more complex than that we devour them and exploit them to our needs. I believe this intimate dance, if you will, continues post mortally. It continues after human death."

Isobel paused. She summoned her bravery and started to describe the rest of her findings, findings that historically proved the most difficult for others to swallow:

"This data I have amassed suggest further that there is, on this planet, a tree, or a thing that looks like a tree, that appears in, and then disappears from, certain forests, forests of local and global legend, such as Araymandr Forest in Sweden, where the trolls were said by legend to commune, or the Katrinaholze, where the legend of that name actually transpired. This tree-like entity comes and goes, is seen and then is seen to be gone from where it was seen. I suspect that this tree is vital to all life on earth.

"The Industrial Revolution and The Great War have wrought havoc with this arrangement. The deforestation that this epoch's tumultuous excess demands, has caused grievous injury, somehow, to our continuum of existence through death, and the result is, indeed, more ghosts.

"Ghosts apoppin and ghosts aplenty," said Isobel with a creepy little laugh that left Sarah in a pall.

"This tree you speak of, is it the Tree of Life?"

"It is," said Isobel defensively.

"From the story of the Garden of Eden?"

"Finally, someone who remembers the Tree of Life! Any westerner I ever talked to only remembers an attractive naked person named Eve eating an apple she should not have. I must always remind that there were two trees, The Tree of the Knowledge of Good and Evil, from which Eve and then Adam ate, and the second tree, the Tree of Life, the denial of which demanded Adam and Eve's expulsion from the Garden. For, if they were ever to have eaten of the fruit of the Tree of Life-"

"They would have lived forever," said Jake, with a tiny smile, chock full of knowledge.

Isobel was charmed, finally.

~

Some days later, Sarah crawled into Isobel's cot, deep in the night.

"I am scared of America," she said.

For Sarah to be scared was no small thing. However, Isobel did nothing to actively dissuade Sarah from this notion. Instead she told Sarah a story. It was the story of the recently remembered mysterious event in the Heart-Shaped Forest, when she was 10 years old.

"When I was a young girl, older than you, but young just the same, I was playin' a game of mumbly peg, do you know mumbly peg, Sarah?"

Sarah shook the dark silhouette of her head.

"It is a very stupid game, whereby a person, the stupid one, throws a knife between one's own feet while trying desperately to avoid skewering them. The feet. With the knife. Over and over. It is very stupid and I was enamored of mumbly peg overmuch, mostly due to its boyish nature and I was going through a phase."

Sarah snored lightly.

Isobel heard, yet continued.

"I walked into the forest that reached into our property. It was the Heart-Shaped Forest, a magic forest, I assure you, and I am perhaps the world's greatest authority on such things. I have a strong suspicion it is the only magic forest on United States' soil, which may sound strange to you."

Sarah only snored some more.

"Yes, I thought it might. The only magic forest in all of America. But it's true. Anyway, there I was, throwing a knife at my own feet drawing inward of the forest with each throw. The air was filled with light, I remember, and it dazzled me. I took at attempting to throw the knife at an actual target, other than the space between my feet, throw it so that the blade buried deep in some imagined enemy, with the handle vibrating from the force of it.

"I threw that knife, like I had seen done in the movies, holding the blade between my fingers and flinging it end over end at my target, and would you believe it, that knife thunked right into a fallen, rotted log, as if thrown by old Dan'l Boone himself. I was overjoyed, so I tried it again. I did it again. I was a true hero.

"However, on my third throw, I did not see the stone glimpsing up through that rotted log, and my little knife bounced away and I could not find it.

"I felt a curious sensation and looked down to see my pretty dress pinned to the inside of my right thigh by that knife. I saw it there, but I could hardly believe it, a knife poked in through the fabric, to the hilt, high up in my thigh.

"I reached down and pulled the knife out, and lifted my skirt to see my life just flowing out. The blood glooped out all warm over my hand, completely covering it in a red glove that I stared at, unbelieving, as my body shrieked alarm bells.

"For I had, by the sheerest of happenstance, struck myself a mortal blow. I had completely severed my femoral artery and had but moments to live.

"Moments, only!

"I sat back against the moss-covered stone, feeling the cold wet of reality for the last time.

"I heard a sound. I turned toward it to see an old woman, kindly seeming, smiling at me in all of the brightness shimmering in the forest. She spoke words I could not hear for there was an inchoate onrush of encroaching sound, filling my ears.

"Then from everywhere, from in my head, from out of my head and everywhere else, I could hear a moaning sorrow, like a choir of lament. I looked beyond the old woman and there was a small tree, and it was from this tree, this Tree of Life, that the sound came, I knew that for a certainty.

"I looked down at myself and the blood was gone from my hand and my skirt. I pulled up my skirt and the wound, so grievous and red, was all but gone. And then it was. Completely gone.

"The old woman smiled at me, and I smiled back at her. I tried to look beyond her to the tree, so that I could thank it, but it was no longer there. I could hear her now, the old woman, and she spoke in a strange way to me, in an unfamiliar, yet comforting, brogue:

'Place ye, me garland, that some many years hence, when ye be floaten the world over, and a sprightly old man approacheth, from out of the sea he come, and –' (here the old woman stopped and thought a bit, as if trying to come up with something particularly memorable) 'and that man - he'll be wearin a dress!'

"She cackled into her hand just then, as if this future prospect of requiring a man to wear a dress tickled her beyond all reckoning, but then the old woman stopped, fixing me with a look that brooked no distraction.

'When he does bid you return, then you do that thing and return to me, for saving your life this day, you do that thing!'

"'I will,' I said, and I asked her her name.

"'You call me Mabel,' she said, 'Mabel Leone Lighty.'"

Robert Spande
The Born and the Made

ChApTeR 27

The next day was an important one for me. It was the day the new comic books for the month went on the racks at Bill's Super Market.

There were a couple of comics I always asked Bill's son, Clint, to save for me behind the counter (Bill was cooped up in the nursing home and couldn't speak anymore).

In particular, I always looked forward to the new month's "Classics Illustrated."

Nothing could bar me from my comic book day ritual. I needed something to distract me from the death of Miss Holly, from Cot's weirdly determined investigations, and from the memory of the strange Molly White.

"Hey Johnny," said Clint, as I walked through the jangle of the door. Clint, just turned 23, was in all respects the owner of the supermarket, now that his Dad's stroke had taken him off to the land of the near-dead.

Here was a boy who had grown all the way up, in a month. It showed in the strain underlying his every light-hearted witticism and his every nonchalance.

Clint whipped a flat brown parcel at me. I missed it entirely, actually popping it into the air in my attempt to catch it. It landed in a frozen food bin filled with meat and frozen vegetables.

"Hey there, Clint," I mumbled back as I grabbed the package up out of the cold. A glance inside told me that the new "Classics Illustrated" was right on top. I could see the words "Joan of Arc" in white block letters on the cover. I had no idea what that was, but it mattered not a bit.

This was why I loved "Classics Illustrated." Every month, the Gilburton Company of 826 Broadway, New York, NY shared their comic book interpretation of some rare classic I had never heard of. Obscurities like "The Cloister and the Hearth" "Lorna Doone" and "The Midshipman Easy" stand out for me as titles so weird, I had no concept of the meanings of their constituent words. Occasionally, there was the familiar classic, like "Moby Dick" or "The Call of the Wild," and I ate those up with similar vigor.

I closed the bag, relishing the thrill at the prospect of my near-future engagement with the lines and the economies of the 4-color process. I could barely wait to pore over the clunky, out-of-place and all-too modern typeset, to apprehend the classic story, distilled from its hundreds of pages of text into a 53-page comic book. This was heaven to me.

I paid Clint, foregoing any more small talk. He understood.

On the walk home, I submitted like a dog to my impatience, taking out Joan of Arc and studying the cover.

Next to the words, "Classics Illustrated," read the declaration, "Featuring Stories by the World's Greatest Authors."

The issue number, number 78, was printed on the tiny image of a splayed-open book. Below that, a circle said, "15¢," and below that, a box said "United States and Foreign," presumably in reference to the price. At the bottom of the cover image was an ornate yellow box, trimmed in red and white that proclaimed:

ALSO-

A Pioneer of Science Story

A Heroic Dog Story

A Famous Opera

The words "Joan of Arc" rode over the top of the cover image in bold, white letters, strangely modern and out of context with the picture below.

On the cover, a maiden shepherd, no more than thirteen years old, her flock milling about her, kneeled in front of an androgynous, iron-armored angel. The angel regarded the girl with dispassion.

The angel's armor was entrancing to me, rendered in vivid red and yellow highlights, and green shadows. Colossal white wings emerged from the angel's armored back, dominating the cover's entire right side. In the distance behind the two, a bright cloud unfurled, dramatically enshrouding the figures in its glowing nimbus.

The angel handed a longsword to the kneeling girl, pointing dramatically off left of cover, as if to say, "Go! Take this sword and..." And what? Why the hell would an angel be handing a sword to a young girl?

I could not wait to find out!

I looked at the girl. Was she Joan of Arc? I figured she must be. The girl was clad in a red tunic with impeccably rendered shadows, the chiaroscuro playing all over her, like a maze. A white cloth wrapped her head. A long mane of auburn hair descending from it, down her back. The girl's hands were clasped in front of her in a prayer of supplication. Her eyes were locked devoutly on those of the angel's.

She was beautiful, yet serious and resolved.

At home I read the comic straight through and learned the tale of Jean d'Arc, Maid of Orleans. It was a story I did not know, portrayed as history, yet utterly fantastic. How was it that this story was not taught in school, nor in church?

Joan was a normal girl, circa 1400's. She lived in the French town of Domremy, and played with the other kids, just like a normal little girl. But she was not a normal girl. She talked to angels.

When Joan was a young teen, the archangel, Michael, let the girl in on a little secret. God wanted her to become a military general, fight the British, and reseat the French King Charles on the throne (he had gotten booted off). This struck Joan as a mite silly for a little girl to attempt, but her sufficient devotion saw her to it.

Joan travelled to see Charles himself, who was basically willing to try anything to become king. Charles ultimately gave her the job.

Joan used her new army to kick big ass in a bunch of battles with the British. She became a celebrity whose fame outranked even Charles' himself, a fact that stuck in the royal craw, even after Joan got him back on the throne. He was a real asshole.

Charles betrayed Joan, after all she did for him. The creep sold her to the British.

The dirty, rotten British put her through a series of bullshit trials, but Joan was so strong, steadfast and true, she sailed right through them, even when they tortured her.

So, get this. The jerks who had her locked up, unable to effectively convict her, proceeded to set her up. They stole her prison clothes and left men's clothes in their place.

Modest-to-a-fault-Joan foolishly wore the men's clothes, to keep from being stark naked, for God's sakes, and when she did that, the British charged her with wearing men's clothes!

Apparently wearing the other gender's clothing was about the biggest crime ever.

Because those flabby-faced, gap-toothed bastards burned her alive for it.

And that's the infuriating story of Joan of Arc.

The comic left me generally disappointed in humanity, and in the politics of 15th century France, in particular.

The story hit me hard. Mostly because Joan reminded me so much of Cot. They shared many of the same qualities, such as determination and steadfast duty. Like Joan, Cot seemed to follow a higher calling, and was similarly unstoppable. Cot also clung to her version of the truth like a sloth to a tree.

Hell, Cot had almost all the qualities of the Classics Illustrated Joan of Arc, save her pious belief, and perhaps a certain madness.

From that day to this, Joan of Arc has appeared amongst the group of people that live in my head. The people in my head I am embarrassed in front of, when I am bad, proud in front of, when I am good. People like Cot, and Miss Holly, and Captain Kirk, and many others. A whole gaggle of them nowadays.

ChApTeR 28

FROM THE JOURNAL OF COT CLEARY

I spent some time in town looking for Bandana. No one's seen hide nor hair of him since the murder. I looked and looked at all his haunts but there was nothing, not even a candy wrapper or an empty bottle of muscatel. So I just came back home. Johnny was in his room reading his comics so I hung out in the kitchen while Momma worked on lunch.

I talked to Momma about that Molly White. Ever since Momma was a kid she knew her! Momma said Molly White is a crazy forest lady, just like we thought, and has been ever since Momma was tiny. Momma told a story about how when Molly White was a teenager, way back in World War II, she fell deep in love with her neighbor boy. But then he had to go to war. And he never came back. But not because he was dead. It was because he married a French gal. Momma said Molly totally snapped after that one. That's how she became a crazy forest lady.

But then Momma went on to talk more about Molly. I kinda think Momma mighta known Molly White pretty good at one time. She talked real familiar about her.

She asked me if Molly White had shown us any acorns and made me choose one. I said what acorns? What do you mean acorns?

She said Nuthin, just acorns. I said No.

I told Mom we'd talked about Miss Holly.

Mom turned and looked out the window at the bird feeders we have out front. There were all kinds of tiny birds around the feeders, but they couldn't get any food cuz there was a gang of blue jays hogging it all. Dad calls blue jays bullies. Mom kept looking at them and looking at them.

What, Mom? I asked. She came out of it and looked at me.

I was friends with Theda Holly when we were kids, she said. My Mom and hers were good friends so I knew her since we were knee high to knee highs. We were best friends in high school too. Best friends.

I didn't know that, Mom, I said.

We had a falling out, she said, Theda was better than me at something and I couldn't forgive her for it.

Mom looked out the window some more.

I didn't say anything.

After a while Mom said, Molly White is harmless. I used to bring her bread from my Mom. Every week. It was like my Mom was paying her for something. It was one of my duties. She would have me in and I would help her with stuff. She took a liking to me. She did me favors.

What kind of favors? I asked.

She would tell me stuff about myself. Even stuff that hadn't happened yet. She told me I would marry your Dad.

My mouth dropped right open then.

She told me when I was your age, Cot. Told me his name and everything. Your Dad didn't even live in town then.

But I forgot all about it, strange as that seems, like Molly gifted me the forgetting with the telling. I only remembered right before our wedding kiss.

Reverend Saulk had just said Kiss The Bride. I was moving to your Dad to kiss him, when suddenly -- I remembered! I jerked in my breath and my eyes got wide. Your Dad stopped and looked at me. Everyone in the church was looking at me. I was embarrassed. I didn't know what to do, so I grabbed both sides of your Dad's face and kissed him a big one for all to see. I never told him about it--and you're not going to either Cot, ok?

Ok, Mom, I said. I love you Mom, I said.

I love you too Cot, she said, and went on looking out the window.

ChApTeR 29

On the day we were set to do more following of Winky, we went to school like normal. Mr. Edwards came in looking very pleased. We all imagined the worst. He clunked his satchel down on the desk and placed his white coffee cup into its stain-worn place of honor.

"Today is a big day for me folks," he said with his resounding voice.

"I want to introduce you to my daughter, Adria."

We all looked over to the doorway. There was a black girl standing there, looking about my age, maybe a tad older. She wore a lime green dress with white lace at the collar and sleeves. She held the school primer in front of her, almost like a shield. The girl looked a little frightened.

Mr. Edwards said, "I know you all will make her feel at home."

Mr. Edwards bored his eyes into those of Terry Scald, who suddenly noticed his own hands and set to studying them with singular interest.

Adria's eyes scanned us, from row to row. I imagined she was comparing us to the students she had known, the bad ones and the good. Was this going to be the best class she had ever attended, an unlivable hell, or somewhere in between? I saw her troubled and difficult history in that perusal. I decided then that I would try to be a friend to her.

She was also extremely pretty, and I hesitate to mention this in case my friendliness be seen as less than noble. I had never thought of a black girl as pretty. I had never really thought of a black girl at all. I didn't know any black girls, and to be honest, at that time there simply were not that many black people living in our vicinity.

I appraised her as discreetly, yet as thoroughly as I could. On closer examination, she appeared to have some strain running through that slightly orientalized her epicanthic folds, broadening her cheekbones. She was getting more and more beautiful, the more I took her in.

I looked at Mr. Edwards to see that he was looking right at me, and apparently had been while I was appraising his only daughter, ruminating over her attractiveness. I felt like my thoughts were broadcasting in a spectrum only available to jealous fathers and that Mr. Edwards was even now plotting my demise.

"Adria why don't you grab that chair next to Johnny Cleary. Sam, you move back one."

Sam Phillips, a lonely, put-upon lad with sallow features and flaxen hair, seemingly unfettered by such modern extravagances as nutrition and general care, sighed at this latest indignity and slid his stuff from the desk next to me to the desk behind. Adria walked quickly across to the desk and slipped silently into it. She sat with her eyes down, her hands in her lap.

I was shocked that Mr. Edwards put his daughter right next to me. Perhaps my face betrayed information of which I was not aware, some potential of an easier path for his daughter, a friendly protector. At least that's where my thoughts went with it. I decided I would try to follow.

I looked over at Adria and she returned the slightest oblique glance. I nodded and let a slight smile escape. I believe I saw her nod faintly back, but wasn't sure.

Then Mr. Edwards' onslaught began and he kept us working hard till recess.

On the playground, Cot and I gravitated toward one another. When Adria emerged from the school with Mr. Edwards's arm protectively covering her shoulder, we walked up to them. Mr. Edwards saw us approaching and whispered something in his daughter's ear. He looked back at us, at me, and I felt a bolt of his protectiveness strike me. He nodded at me and I nodded at him and he walked back into the school.

"Hi Adria," said Cot, "love your name."

"Hi," said Adria, "thank you."

"I'm Cot, and this here is my brother Johnny. He's retarded and can't understand words but if you wave at him he will understand. Just don't do it too quickly. He's excitable."

Adria looked alarmed for a second, but recovered quickly and started to wave at me with exaggerated slowness.

"She's just telling tales. I'm Johnny Cleary. Pleased to meet you," I said, in what Cot was able to discern as a spot-on imitation of my dad's way of greeting. This annoyed my sister immensely.

Adria stopped waving and accepted my hand. She looked right up into my eyes. I felt a distinct thrill go through me. Her eyes were big, chocolate brown and deep with knowledge. I felt like she could see right into me.

"Hi Johnny," Adria said, "glad to hear you're not retarded."

"Yeah, me too. How long you been in town?"

"Just a couple days. We've been setting up the house."

"Oh," said Cot, interested, "where's it at? Your house?"

"Over by the cemetery, the far side."

"I didn't know there were any houses over there," I said.

"There's a few. They're small. Ours is all filled up. I got an older brother and my Mom and her Mom and her Mom.

Our surprise must have been apparent.

"My great grandma is 101 years old and full blooded Ojibwe from Red Lake. But she's feisty. That's what my Dad calls her."

"Must be crazy -- the teacher bein' your Dad," Cot said.

"Oh yeah. I'm used to it. Has he written anyone's name in the Devil's Book yet?" Adria asked.

"Yes!" I exclaimed. "He wrote Terry's name in it his first day!"

"It's just an old book. The Unabridged Outline of History by H.G. Wells. He scratched off the name and painted some gold on it. Put on a belt buckle. He uses it on all his classes."

I actually breathed a sigh of relief. Adria giggled into her hand.

"Just don't tell anyone or I will be in big trouble, but you two seem nice and it's all I got to offer you," she said.

Cot locked her lips with an invisible key and I did the same. We threw our keys over our shoulders and I motioned toward the action area of the playground.

"You wanna play some tetherball or something?"

"Sure..." Adria said, sounding not at all sure.

As we walked, I could tell that Cot's mind was working. Her eyebrows were stitched all crazy across her forehead. She was looking hard into the distance as she walked. I'd seen this look before. It invariably proved worrisome.

Finally, Cot said, "We're solving a murder. Would you help us Adria?"

We all stopped hard in our tracks. I felt like bopping Cot on the head and asking her just how crazy she was, exactly, to expose our intentions to the daughter of the man who had prohibited us from this very ambition. Adria just looked from Cot to me expectantly, her hands in the pockets of her worn grey jacket.

"You mean the old teacher?" asked Adria.

"Yep," said Cot. "We are fixing to follow the villain who mighta done it, later on. We think he did it, he killed her and he's trying to cover it up. Johnny here was in love with Miss Holly and so we're gonna catch – "

"Cot!" I exclaimed, "Will you shut up! I was not in love with Miss Holly! I just thought very highly of her," I protested.

"Oh, you were in love with her, like a puppy to a chew," Cot returned.

I just sighed with exasperation, wishing we were alone so I could forcibly muzzle her. But if we were alone, of course, I would not need to.

"Dad told us a couple of boys killed her. He said they were caught and everything," Adria said.

Cot looked at me, expecting me to address this. I closed my eyes and imagined a peaceful scene. Counted back from 10. All the tricks. When I was ready, I said, "No those boys were innocent. They're not in jail anymore."

"We interviewed one of the suspects and he told us the whole story. It was a frame-up." Cot was acting like a hardboiled gumshoe. I shook my head in disbelief.

"Cot this is nuts." I turned to Adria. "Adria, we have just been talking about it some, wondering who done it. To ourselves. We're not trying to solve any crime," I explained.

"Yes we are," said Cot.

She continued. "In fact, this very afternoon, like I said, we are going to be doing surveillance on the prime suspect. And we need your help. The way I'm thinking of doing it, you could really help us out. So I'm real glad you came along. What do you say?"

"When?" was all Adria replied.

"Right after school. I think it'll take an hour maybe an hour and a half."

Adria looked at us real hard. "And you're not just pranking me, right?" She turned to me.

I opened my mouth but couldn't speak. Finally, I choked out, "We're not pranking you, but Cot is exaggerating like crazy—"

It wasn't working. I couldn't lie to Adria and make Cot into a liar all with the same lie. It was easily the type of sin that would come back to haunt me, probably within minutes. Both girls fixed me with their eyes.

"We're not pranking you," I said, defeated.

"Then I guess... I'm interested," Adria said, smiling. "I think it's exciting and so sweet of you Johnny. It must have been tough on you."

My cheeks burned. I was in Hell, conveyed there by an 11-year-old girl. I remained mute and let the mastermind resume.

"Here's what I have planned..." Cot began.

After telling Adria a little of the history of the "case" and about Winky, Robert, and even Molly White, Cot laid out her big plan. As I listened, my skepticism expanded into utter incredulity, seasoned with a liberal dollop of apprehension and even some admiration at her boldness. It was actually a pretty good plan. As long as we were not caught and chopped into bits by Winky.

ChApTeR 30

After school let out, and Adria had made excuses to Mr. Edwards, we all met up by the Alhambra theater.

Who's Afraid of Virginia Woolf? was on the marquee. The Alhambra never showed first run movies and this was no exception. It had been showing for weeks and looked like a duller-than-dull domestic drama with lots of adult problems and was in black and white, no less. I cursed the management whenever I passed for not showing monster movies and serials and cartoons like a proper movie theater.

However, I have recently seen *Who's Afraid of Virginia Woolf?* on BluRay, and I have to say, it's an excellent film, filled with domestic drama, adult problems, and in glorious black and white, no less.

Our first task was to go to the saw-mill under the pretext of visiting Mom and introducing her to Adria.

Mom worked in the administrative office. She was secretary to the financial officer of the company. She spent her days in a dull green room, her desk surrounded by steel file cabinets, two black, clunky plastic phones, a dented green garbage can, and a rickety fan that sent its invisible plumes back and forth feebly across the space.

She only had about an hour more of work, so we had to get hopping. Cot had laid out plans of attack for three different scenarios: 1) if Winky was in his office 2) if Winky was in his office but left while we were there, and 3) if Winky was not there at all.

Winky's office was kitty corner across the hall from Mom's and could be seen from her desk. Whenever his own secretary was absent, which was often, as she was older than a Sequoia, Winky would expect Mom to be constantly ready for his needs. He would often simply look up from his papers at her, boring his mean eyes into her from his office until she noticed and got up and came in to see what he wanted.

The mill itself comprised a huge area, with many tin sleeved buildings, dominated by the massive, corrugated tin saw-mill in the center. The mill yard was delimited on one end by the river, with huge docks and conveyors for lumber, and on the other end by the railroad tracks, where a line of lumber cars sat, waiting to be loaded or unloaded. A shiny new water tower loomed above it all, with the words "Copeland Lumber" written boldly across its silver head.

Mom's office was in the main building, tucked into the ledge of offices that overlooked the saw-mill floor. We worked our way past floor workers we had known our whole lives. I looked around for Dad, but couldn't see him, before climbing the stairs to where Mom worked. She was talking away to someone on one of the clunky black phones and in harried gestures motioned us to the corner.

"Well, my calendar is dated ten oh six, is there a later one?" chirped my Mom into the phone. She didn't sound at all like herself. She was yodeling, it seemed, as if she were trying to keep something in her voice from breaking out and ruining her conversation.

"Ten thirteen? I see. Well, I will certainly have a talk with someone about that. In the meantime, I will have Sally from the warehouse give you a call and setup a meet, ok Mr. Styme?"

There were abusive sounds from the phone, and a click. Mom set the phone down with a plastic thud, and jotted something on her blotter.

"Kids, this is not a good time for me. Wink—" she stopped abruptly. "Mr. Wickley is not in his usual good mood today. Not at all," said Mom as she wrote.

"This is Adria, Mom. She's Mr. Edwards's daughter. We just wanted you to meet her, is all." I said.

Mom changed her face to smiles, and said, "Oh?" She stood up from behind the desk and we all met up in middle. Adria and Mom shook hands and smiled at each other. I could see something extra in Momma's appraisal of Adria, most likely mulling over the future complexities of our new friend being a black girl in our whiter-than-white town of Copeland.

"Mrs. Cleary!" a voice boomed from the door. "Why are there children in your office?"

We turned to see William Wickley the Third, the palest, most cadaverous man since Solomon Grundy, stooped in the doorway. In his spindly hand he held a sheaf of papers that he absentmindedly began to worry and wrinkle.

Mom quickly stepped in between him and our little group. She indicated the papers that Winky was brutalizing.

"Is that the Marketing Plan, Mr. Wickley?" She eased it out of his grasp. "The kids just needed to see me about something. They were just leaving Mr. Wickley." She turned to us.

"Say hello to Mr. Wickley, kids."

Adria immediately said "Hello, Mr. Wickley," clearly thinking we would all say it together, at the same time. But her voice rang out alone in the dreary office. Cot and myself stood stone still. My breathing got weird and my body surged with chemical energy. I felt the urge to pounce on Winky and sink my teeth deeply into his throat, cutting off his breath, ripping into the chords and pipes, and just hanging on lion-jawed, till he expired, like an antelope on the savannah.

Cot stood there calmly, looking the man directly in the eye. Winky was clearly affronted. He snorted and came into the room. He walked right to Cot and bent down till his face was just above hers. She looked bravely up. He scrutinized her in a simmering way, as if she were a stock animal to be bought and cooked in his pot.

He said, "You look so familiar to me. Haven't I seen you lurking about town?"

Cot's expression didn't change. "We saw each other at Miss Holly's funeral. At least I saw you," said Cot, flatly.

Winky blanched and undisguised disapproval overtook his face.

"What an atrocious thing to say," he declared. "Mrs. Cleary, I suggest you teach your children to show more respect to those who provide the means by which they are fed, clothed and sheltered. By which you, yourself, are sustained, Mrs. Cleary, I might add."

Mom's face fell and she said she was sorry to Winky and promised to get us out of there post-haste. She said she intended to put etiquette higher on the list of our social priorities. She started to continue, but Winky held up his hand, long as a boat, and silenced her.

"I don't like children, Mrs. Cleary. Just get them out of here. And I don't like marketing plans! The worst tripe I ever read. It seemed like a list of lies. Tell whoever wrote that to go back to janitorial work, to which they are better suited!"

Winky turned, and in turning, cast his dark glance on all of us, but on Cot he lingered, as if challenging her. As if she made so much as a move, he would unleash his powers without limit, reducing her to so much ash.

He stormed out of the office muttering under his breath about the respective shortcomings of marketing plans and children. Mom put her face in her hands and rubbed. She apparently rubbed well, because when she unveiled her face it sported a sort of wild animal look.

"I wrote it, but thats ok." Mom said to the far wall, forcing a smile. She re-noticed us. "I'd say it's a good time for you kids to head out, don't you? It was a pleasure meeting you Adria, and I hope you and your family like it here in Copeland."

"Thank you Mrs. Clearly, really nice to meet you too. I like your office."

Mom seemed particularly appreciative of that comment, as if the mutual outlandishness of their exchanged pleasantries was in some way touching to her. She gave Adria a hug.

While this was going on, Cot tugged on my sleeve. I followed her eyes to Winky's office, where he was animatedly throwing his coat over his arm. He wrenched his briefcase up off his desk and stormed out, banging the light switch off on his way. As he passed Mom's office he glared in. From this perspective, he reminded me of nothing so much as an enormous dead baby bird wearing an expensive suit and wingtips. A giant baby bird zombie shambling home from the office. The concept made me smirk and Winky caught it just before his face crossed the terminator of the door.

My bravado vanished and fear tickled my guts.

I whispered to Cot, "I think we better just go home."

"Are you nuts? This is perfect!" she whispered back. "He just left!"

I rolled my eyes and felt Mom's guiding hand on my back pushing me toward the door.

"I'll see you guys at home. If Adria would like to stay for dinner, that would be wonderful."

Mom pushed us out the door and was turning back to the trials of her job all in a movement, before we could say a thing. Adria, Cot and I stood there for a second in the hallway. We looked around to see if anyone else was about. No one was. Mom's office was the only lighted one.

"That was him, huh?" whispered Adria.

"Yep, that's Winky." I said.

"He's scary," she returned.

"You don't need to stay, Adria," said Cot. "We could end up getting in some big trouble here. There's no sense you taking a chance. You helped us a lot, just giving us an excuse to be here. Mom would have been suspicious if we woulda just showed up with some lame story."

Adria seemed gratified that she did not comprise a "lame story."

"Okay," she said, "but I want to know if you find anything. I get the scoop from now on."

Cot and I nodded and Adria started down the hall away from the work floor toward a back door. Cot and I followed toward Winky's office. It was not Cot's plan to go in now, but to wait in the office directly opposite from Winky's and right next to my Mom's, till Mom left her own office and went home.

ChApTeR 31

And such we did, as the shadows lengthened across the small office. We simply sat on the floor, with our backs against the wall, under the window facing the hall. No one out in the hall would be able to see us unless they pressed themselves against this window, an event we were sure would not occur.

All we had to worry about was that Mom would come into this office for some reason. We could hear her voice through the wall. She was talking animatedly; it did not sound like work talk -- she was using her home voice. Then came the muffled sound of the handset being set into its cradle, and a long time of silence. We heard footfalls and our Dad's voice came through the walls, vibrating down the window glass. Mom and Dad talked for a while, then we could hear the sounds of Mom gathering her things.

They left the office and we heard the click of the light being turned off and the chunky sound of the door being closed. Mom said something to Dad as their footsteps diminished and then... stopped. Suddenly Mom's footsteps, much louder and faster, started approaching. Cot's wide eyes flashed to mine.

The steps echoed right up to our door and suddenly the light in our little office turned on, blinding us. Mom walked in, right past me, so close, her perfume wafted through my hair. She walked up to the desk across from the door, with her back to us. Mom swept through the clutter of papers until her fingers lighted on a particular blue paper that drew a happy sound from her.

She brought the paper up and read it intently, turning and walking to the door at the same time. She passed right by me and I looked at her the whole time. But Mom was intent on her reading and walked straight out of the room, flicking off the light and swinging the door closed, never once noticing her two loving children crouching like loiterers against a drugstore wall.

Our parent's footsteps receded and so did the more immediate of our fears. Cot smiled at me like she had just won a gold medal at the Olympics.

"That was amazing," she said.

"That was close," I responded, "We woulda been made into sauce if she'da seen us, Dad right here and all."

"Someone must be watching out for us!" said Cot, her smile still wrapped around her face. I was brought to mind of Joan of Arc, and wondered how many times she asserted the very same thing.

Cot inched the door open and made her way out in the hall with the bearing of an international spy in an enemy embassy. I was right behind her as she slowly opened Winky's door and we whisked ourselves inside, closing it, wincing at the click. Cot had the wherewithal to close the office blinds to the hall. Where did she get this stuff? It was like she had been reading spy manuals her whole life.

"What are we looking for, Cot?" I asked her.

She was already scouting around the office. I was stunned to see that she was actually sniffing the air as she searched. She had that look on her face, the "Cot look" of deep thought and concern. She did not respond to me but instead looked behind a picture on the wall. It showed a young but no less malignant Winky shaking hands with a young politician sporting a big nose and a shiny receding hairline.

Finally, Cot turned toward Winky's desk. She opened the top drawer and drew out a stack of papers. After rifling through them, she put them gently on the floor and felt through the drawer with her hands, careful not to upset the arrangement of things.

She put everything back and repeated this procedure with the other drawers. I stayed by the door, listening for footsteps and/or sirens. The adrenaline in my stomach was raging. I don't think I had ever been quite so nervous. I looked at Cot. She was utterly preoccupied and seemed unconcerned with the felonious nature of our activities.

She was rooting through the lower right drawer, when suddenly she whispered, "Johnny, look at this!"

I reluctantly approached the desk. Cot was on her knees with the contents of the drawer orbiting around her on the floor. In her hand, she held a framed picture.

"It's Robert and Miss Holly," she said.

And sure enough, it was. Miss Holly, beautiful Miss Holly, stood smiling against a rough wooden fence, such as one might find penning in livestock. She wore a light green dress with a torrent of cloth buttons down the front. In her hand was a bundle of wildflowers, bright and colored against the wood fence. My heart sprang near out of my chest it was beating so hard, with both fear and a resurgence of the feelings that had been recently waning. Her eyes were happy, happy in a way that I had not seen before. They spoke of her feelings of the moment, of the comfort she received from the arm around her shoulder.

The arm belonged to Robert Wickley, whom I have as yet not described to you in any detail. I could not help but hate the fellow, even though it was known that he was a good guy, especially to Miss Holly. When I thought of them together, I was confronted by feelings that made me want to throttle the man, or at the very least, push him into a burning pit.

I felt all these forces impinge as I looked at the picture of Miss Holly and Robert Wickley. And yet, for all my resentment, the picture was so honest and good natured, I could not help but feel their sweetness for one another shining from the photo.

I thought to myself, This man did not kill Miss Holly.

Then I saw the knife.

"What is that?" I asked aloud, pointing. Cot zeroed in and started scrutinizing purposefully. I was indicating the shape on Robert's hip, dark and long.

"It's a hunting knife," said Cot.

ChApTeR 32

We walked and we talked. The lumber mill was behind us. The afternoon was just behind the trees, the late day sun pouring up the road. Our breath preceded us and the chill of September settled around, penetrating our clothes. It had gotten cold fast after our long summer.

The picture of Miss Holly and Robert Wickley was safe, faced down in its drawer. The rest of Winky's office was back in its original order. We had slipped quietly away, down the mill's rear stairwell. The strange lawlessness of what we had done stayed with us, as penetrating as the late-September cold.

What ate at me the most was the thought of Miss Holly's face, smiling so brightly in the darkness of the drawer's cold metal, hidden with the hope that we would all forget her.

It all seemed perfectly obvious. Robert had killed her, and Winky was doing just what The Cooridy had said: "marshalling his forces to cover it up."

That's why the police weren't doing anything. It wasn't that they had no leads. It was that Winky had ordered them to stop looking. He had done with her murder what he had done with Miss Holly's picture. Turned it face down in the dark.

I silently promised Miss Holly that I would never let anyone forget her, ever. I would keep her name alive in this town, somehow. The picture in the drawer would see the light of day, even if Miss Holly in her coffin would stay in dark eternal.

Before the visit to Winky's office, I was having thoughts of abandoning the entire endeavor and leaving the mystery of Miss Holly's murder to the police. But now I felt the importance of discovering the truth inside of me, smoldering. If fourteen-year-old Joan of Arc could make herself a full-blown military general, and lead armies to victory in medieval France, then I could sure as hell do my duty and find Miss Holly's killer.

I came out of my reverie to find Cot considering me while we walked.

"You're sure thinking about something," she said, "I don't think your brain is used to hard labor."

"I'm thinking about how cold the creek is and if I could throw you in it all the way from here."

To my surprise, Cot did not succumb to my baiting, but returned to a quiet seeming solicitude, the target of which was unknown to me. She regarded nothing so much as the dirt she was kicking up, yet I could sense a strong emotional force welling in her.

I drew up and said, "What did we find out from that picture?"

"Miss Holly and Robert Wickley were in love," said Cot, without a beat, watching me close, knowing her words would wound me.

They did, but I didn't let on.

She could see right through, but said nothing.

"I saw it too, but that knife…"

Cot jumped a little when I said the word knife.

"It's just a knife, Johnny! Everybody has a knife. You have at least four of them!" she said, in too abrupt a way, as if she was suddenly irritated with me.

"I guess… but remember what Bobby Donnel said about Miss Holly's neck? How it was all ripped up? That knife coulda done that. If it's the kind I'm thinking it is, then it has a serrated edge on one side - good for ripping…" I said, suddenly aware of how callously I was discussing Miss Holly's end. Cot regarded me with a touch of sisterly loathing.

"God, how awful," she whispered, her eyes back on the road. I could see the worry encroaching on her as thoughts ricocheted in her head.

Cot suddenly turned quite distracted and wandered into the road, so I came up alongside her. There was a sheen of sweat over her forehead and upper lip that glistened in the afternoon sun. This was out of place with the cool of the waning day.

Together, by virtue of no more than the gravity of kinship we made back for the edge of the gravel, where browning yarrow still swayed. I spoke quickly to distract her.

"There's no doubt in my mind they were sweet on each other. I admit I don't understand how he could seem so happy with her and then just kill her like that."

"I'm thinking the same, Johnny," she whispered.

Why was Cot whispering? There was a look of apprehension on Cot's face that wasn't going away. If anything, it was getting worse. Her eyes were funny, non-smooth in their movements, jerky, almost vibratory. I remembered back to the time outside the cemetery, when her face had shown the same signs. Indeed, her breath started churning. What a jerk I was, continuing to talk about Miss Holly's death! I needed to change the subject.

But Cot was not even listening to me any longer. She stopped and put her hands on her knees. Her breathing became more labored and then I heard the patter of her tears on the dirt of the road.

"Johnny, I'm having a hard time breathing," she whispered, even softer than before.

That jolted me. My heart accelerated like a skipping stone.

I didn't know what to do. I approached her and started rubbing on her back, real gentle, and crouched so I could see up into her face. She was a mess of tears and snot that she wiped at with her hand, leaving a dark swath of grime. She was crying real hard now.

"How could someone do it, Johnny? How?" she croaked, as she tried to drag in what air she could. I drew her upright and started to talk, to soothe her. It did no good.

It occurred to me then, and is confirmed by me now, that here was the reason that Cot continually played the precocious pragmatist. The implacably impassive investigatrix.

These personae kept the emotions at bay that threatened Cot's very breathing. She had abandoned them that day, or perhaps just lost her grip on them, to her profoundest detriment.

Cot's breath hitched in her throat with short, ugly sounds. Panic flooded her face and she reached out and grabbed the sleeves of my jacket.

"Johnny," Cot mouthed, silently. Then her eyes got real wide. As I watched, her pupils began to expand, covering entirely the blue of her irises. Her face assumed a cast of what I can only describe as horror. Cot's lips parted and I could see her pink tongue, totally immobile. I knew she was unconscious, even though her eyes were open.

"Cot, baby!" I yelled into her unseeing face. I grabbed her and brought her close, absently kissing her clammy forehead. I knew there was something I should do, something I had seen somewhere, and recently. I slapped ineffectually at her cheek. I shook her by the shoulders and her head lolled to the side. I realized that I would have to get help and could either put Cot down at the edge of the road and run, or carry her in my arms to do so.

There was no way I could leave her. I cradled her up in a motion. She was as light as air.

It took me a few moments to get used to running and carrying her, but my will was as great as any hero's for those few moments.

The creek's burbling sound mocked me like the chuckling of small children.

Cot bounced in my arms, and I drew her close to settle her. I brought her cheek to mine and I felt the deathlike chill of her skin. I brought Cot in even tighter, my left arm under her, and snaked my right hand up to her face, settling her legs in the crook of that arm, running at top speed all the while.

Grabbing Cot's face, pinching it roughly between my thumb and fingers, I tried to look in her eyes, to see her pupils. Cot's face danced in front of me, one eye shut tight, the other slightly open, unseeing. When I let go of her face, her mouth jawed opened and closed through no will of her own.

"No Cot, no!" I cried.

The prospect that Cot had died invaded my skull and drove down into my body. It was like being hit by lighting. The realization ground me to a halt and my ankle gave in to some chaotic cause. I stumbled to my knees.

Cot flew out of my arms to the ground, rolling to her back, where she lay utterly, impossibly still. I crawled over beside her and put my hand on her shoulder, shaking her, sobbing. I had no idea what to do. Her face was all grimy and I wiped at her forehead with my palm, as if polishing her would bring Cot back from the dead.

I felt chilled and nauseous. And alone.

"Get up, boy," Molly White said, behind me.

I turned and she stood above me, blocking the setting sun, a dark silhouette with a glowing corona of unkempt hair. Molly White seemed a haloed angel. But not the type of angel one sees atop their Christmas tree. No, a dark and terrible one. Gone was the blue handkerchief. Molly White wore a shapeless garment that looked like an antiquated night shirt, as if she had just popped out of bed.

I stood and Molly moved past me to kneel by Cot. She put her hand on Cot's head, and then moved her fingers to Cot's throat, feeling for a pulse.

Molly White looked up at me with her razor blue eyes, intense in their settings. I felt like running from her so she would not tell me that my sister was dead.

"Turn around Trout-John," Molly White said.

I thought I had misheard her. I opened my mouth to speak –

"Face ye away, boy!" she commanded.

I did it. I turned and faced into the sun which, in the slurry of my tears, blurred into a wavering ribbon of light. Behind me, I heard the rustling of Molly White's shift as she turned back to Cot.

I heard her speaking quietly. I needed to see what was going on.

"Keep faced away, Trout-John," barked Molly White, as if she could read my intentions.

Then Molly White said, to someone else entirely, "She needs your help."

ChApTeR 33

That's what she said, I have no doubt in my mind. "She needs your help." She did not say it to Cot. She did not say it to me.

When she said those words, it was like some stage manager backstage of all of reality threw a switch, causing the scene to change. Some lights came up, others went down. The music darkened and the audience hushed in anticipation.

A sound emerged from behind me. It was a muffled singsong vocalization that raised the hair on my neck. If not for the setting, I would have ascribed it to the sorrowful humming of a small child.

I wanted to turn around, but I felt in my bones that if I were to do so at that moment, I would somehow ruin everything and Cot would die there on the road.

There was a pressure behind me, and the skittering of pebbles on the ground.

A potential of some kind began to increase, a tension in the universe, strained to snapping. The hair of my whole body was electrified and standing. Shivers of gooseflesh slid down my arms.

Something was near, something terrible, something behind me.

I could feel this presence approach Cot, and indeed, it was the author of the muffled humming, which suddenly broke out crystal clear, as if out of a just-opened window. The sound sharpened. It was unlike any voice I had ever heard.

Before I knew what I was doing, I turned my upper body slightly and my head slightly more, and looked behind me, feeling all too much like Lot's wife.

The sight that greeted my eyes was wholly impossible. Cot lay on the ground, on her back, her limbs splayed out. Molly White crouched near her, not touching her at all. Molly's head was down and her lips moved silently.

Up through Cot's chest, through the bright red dress that peeked through her opened coat, there grew a small, flowering tree. The tree itself was roughly the height of a man, with a bare trunk only a few inches in circumference. Some four feet up, the tree opened into a mass of spade-like leaves, with small purple flowers interspersed. The leaves and flowers thrummed with the wordless song.

I gaped in astonishment, the sight before my eyes so unexpected, so incredible, the image seemed to snap in half and brightness engulfed me, threatening to send me into a cerebral accident. I turned back and covered my eyes with both hands, moaning like a machine about to break...

Cot coughed and drew in a gasp that seemed to last ten entire seconds.

I turned again to see Molly White kneeling next to Cot, helping her into a sitting, and then kneeling, position. Cot coughed and gagged and puked a torrent into the gravel before she finally started to breathing again.

There was no tree. I rushed up and checked the ground where Cot had been laying. There was no hole in the road where a tree might have sprouted.

Cot looked around, seeming to discover where she was. She looked up at me and did a double take. She opened her mouth in amazement, her head shaking slowly side to side. She spoke.

"I saw her Johnny," Cot said.

"You mean Molly White?" I answered softly. "She's right here, hon."

Cot fixed my eyes with her serious way.

She said, "No Johnny. I saw Miss Holly. I just spoke with Miss Holly!"

ChApTeR 34

On the way to Molly White's house, Cot said nothing. She was lost in her thoughts as we walked. I neared Molly White and whispered, so that Cot would not hear:

"How did you bring Cot back? Tell me."

"Why, Trout-John I dunt ken yer meaning, lad. I breathed into her mouth, boy. Ent that what yer meant ta do when a soul cant breathe of its own?"

That was the thing that I had not been able to remember: mouth to mouth resuscitation. I had seen Kamen giving it to Miss Holly's momma at the funeral. I made a silent promise to Cot that I would learn all I could about the technique.

I said no more. I was already concluding that I had suffered some kind of hallucination, brought on by the stress and terror of Cot's brush with death. Therefore, I said nothing about the small tree I had seen growing out of my dead sister's chest.

ChApTeR 35

Molly White lived in a log cabin not far from the Old Cross bridge, just like she'd said. The timbers were dark with age and creosote, existing in a bubble of space provided by the thick trees all around, as if Molly had made some sort of bargain with the forest to hide her away.

There was a screened-in deck attached to the front of the cabin, filled with junk up to the ceiling. A narrow path led to the front room where we now sat. The Ben Franklin stove, next to which Cot was warming, breathed its heat onto us as we talked.

I now know, with the benefit of years and subsequent episodes, that Cot had suffered a full-blown panic attack there on the road. The attack had closed her throat like a drawstring bag. The concept of death, when it worked its way too deeply into Cot, was the culprit.

I have read a veritable library's worth of information on this subject since that day and it all says that Cot very likely underwent what is called a near-death-experience, or NDE.

You see, as she choked, Cot's deoxygenated brain started firing randomly in its protestations, activating disparate nerve centers with showers of neuronal activity. Loosely associated concepts and events were thrust together in those waning, darkening moments.

Memories, emotions, ideas, image and sound impressions, churned together in a boiling conceptual gumbo, a last meal, so to speak. NDE theory explains that, in her retroactive search for meaning, Cot's mind fashioned the meeting with Miss Holly she described to us in the warmth from the Ben Franklin stove.

But there are elements that exceed this comfortable explanation, as you will see.

What Cot told us in that cabin has never been spoken since, until now.

Cot drew herself together in her blanket, and spoke.

ChApTeR 36

FROM THE JOURNAL OF COT CLEARY

Sittin next to that fire felt so good after where I had been. I'd been to a place cold and dark. After that, I was whisked away to a place I could never even imagine. All the people whizzing past and the buildings so tall and vibrating near into invisibility. They were like the tuning forks that Jim Milsap smacks on his knee when he tunes our piano.

I told Johnny and Molly White almost everything. I kept some back. But I'll tell you.

Here's what happened.

I was with Johnny on the road from the Mill, coughing, hiccoughing and breathing backwards, and I didn't know why. My thoughts were racing around and smashing into each other like bumper cars. I couldn't catch my breath or my thoughts.

Then a curtain started falling, kinda slow, over the world. I wanted to stay on watching, but the curtain kept falling, Johnny's caring face was leaving me, and I kept on not breathing at all.

I was thinking coughing coffin coughing coffin, and the curtain fell all the way over me. And I died.

I wanted to shoot straight up. The feeling was overpowering, but I could not. I was not allowed. And then I was in that first bad place. It was a cold, dark place of silence and stillness. There was no air, and I did not breathe, or even need to. That was scary at first. I wasn't coughing anymore, and I knew I was dead.

At this point while I was telling the story, Molly White said that I probably wasn't ever even dead at all. I just looked at her.

I was dead all right.

There was nothing. I said it was dark, but that's not right. There was no color. But I could see myself. I could see my hands in front of me, I could see my legs below me. I had color. But where I was had none.

And I said it was cold, but that ain't right, neither. It was like the color. There was no sense of temperature or the solidity of the world anywhere around me. My body just stayed in whatever position I put it.

Then I felt something. It thrilled me, but only for a second. Because in that second, just to feel something, like I did when I was alive, made me bust out laughing.

Until I realized what it was. Then I stopped laughing. Cuz it wasn't a real feeling, like feeling the sun on your face, or a cool wind on your sweaty neck.

It was the feeling of someone watching me.

I felt a hitch. A bump.

Suddenly I was heading some new way, tumbling now. I felt I'd been... what's the word... diverted.

There was speed, I felt. I was heading somewhere, toward a destination that had been decided for me, but when I looked around me, it was all the same nothing in all directions.

Then I pushed through the nothing and I was sitting in a chair, pulled up to a small dining table.

I was in a food shop of some kind. I could smell bread and coffee. There was a table setting in front of me with a napkin and silverware and a water glass, and one across from me too. At first I couldn't see any people around me, but after a second I could see a stream of blurs whipping about. I don't know how I knew it, but somehow I knew these blurs were people, moving so fast they blended into rivers that shot around the tables and ran their course on the sidewalks and crosswalks of the big city outside the window.

I looked out there. Cars were zooming in blurs of motion just like the people. Tall buildings lined the street reaching up into the sky so high it made me almost sick to my stomach. The tallest buildings, the ones that poked into the clouds, seemed like they were blurred up near the top, shaking so fast they became ghosts.

There was sound, but it was all the same sound. It was a whooshing, windy sound that came from all places at once.

Then I heard a bell. A little tinkling bell and I looked up to see the door to the shop opening up.

In walked Miss Holly. She wore a long blue coat with fur on the collar, with a deep red scarf tucked around her throat. There was a big elephant brooch on her blue coat that looked like it was made out of solid diamonds, rubies and emeralds. She had an amazing wide-brimmed hat cocked on her head. She looked like a millionaire's wife.

She let the door close and looked right at me, smiling her big smile. She was yards away, but when she said "Hi Cot," I heard it like she was talking right into my ear. She walked toward me, passing right through the ribbon of blurs and pulled out the chair and sat down.

This is where I kept silent about some things when I was telling all this to Johnny and Molly White.

I hadn't said nothing so far to Miss Holly, my jaw was just hangin open useless. When she sat down across from me, I noticed that I didn't have to look up into her face. It was almost like I was taller or something. So I looked at myself.

First I looked at my hands. They were not my hands, but the hands of an old woman. I moved them around and they were definitely mine, but with long fingers, bigger knuckles and little wrinkles all over the back. There was a ring with a big old diamond on my left ring finger. I turned to the window, to see myself in its reflection, but it was too bright outside and I could see nothing.

I looked down at the table. There were now steaming cups in front of us. Mine smelled of cocoa, Miss Holly's, some kind of spicy coffee. I took mine and sipped. It was fresh and hot. I was totally confused.

"I'm sure you are totally confused, Cot," said Miss Holly. She smiled her teacher smile at me and I felt safe again in this weird place. She continued, "You don't have anything to fear here."

"So I'm dead then?" I asked.

She looked at me kinda crossways. "Yes, Cot, you are dead. But not as a little girl. You will live a long life and die far in the future when the world looks like this." She gestured out the window at the towering buildings.

"You mean fast and blurry?"

She smiled. "No that's just the way the world looks to us dead people, Cot," she said. "I mean when the world looks like this, all filled with office towers and bustle."

I tried to soak in what she said, but it didn't do much to make sense of what I was seeing.

Miss Holly leaned across the table and took my hands in hers.

"I brought you here to tell you to stop. I know you Cot, you will continue to dig, and digging into this mess will only get our brothers hurt, or worse. I don't want that to happen. I want them both to grow old and happy."

"That's real sweet of you, Miss Holly." I said. But then I thought some about what she'd said. Brothers? Plural?

"Call me Theda."

"Ok... Theda."

"Cot, you have brushed the web, and the spider knows you are about."

Miss Holly took a sip of her coffee and looked out the window as she spoke. "Hunker down and be a kid, and you will be safe as a mouse in a mill."

"But Theda," I said, "Johnny ain't gonna stop. He loved you like a six-foot-rose. He can't think of nothing but you before or after you were dead."

"Ain't is not a word, Cot, and watch those double negatives," said Miss Holly.

"Sorry, Miss Holly... Theda, I mean."

"You will stop," said Theda Holly.

"It would help a lot if you'd just tell me who killed you," I said.

"I wish I knew, Cot. All I can see is darkness and things with teeth whipping around in the air, like fish in shallow water. Fortunately, when it was all over, I was able to flee across the land, and escape those things and their teeth. Would you believe it, I hid in a tree! Which is why I am able to talk to you now. As to the rest, it remains a mystery.

"But I can tell you one thing."

I just looked at her expectantly.

"You should have more of that cocoa. It won't be on the market for another 25 years. Chocolate is brain food you know."

I took another swallow. It was delicious and warm all the way down to my stomach. I opened my mouth to speak, but then, a real terrible look come over Miss Holly's face.

She was looking somewhere behind me. I don't think she knew it, but her hand went up to that big elephant brooch and covered it protective-like. I was afraid to follow her look, but it didn't matter.

There was a faraway sound of a child singing a strange tune. It sounded like it was coming from the bottom of a deep well.

Miss Holly sprang to her feet, causing her chair to fall over. The window darkened, and I looked out to see the reason. I was shocked to see a small crowd of women, women that looked an awful lot like Miss Holly, standing just outside the shop. The ones in front had their hands pressed against the glass and were shouting. They looked scared. They were aiming their yells right at Miss Holly and were all yelling the same word.

Run!

In the next second, I was pulled outta my chair and I was back on the dusty road looking up at Molly White and gasping in breath like a newborn babe.

ChApTeR 37

Cot finished her story and turned back to the fire. Molly White looked at me with some significance and got up from the table. She pulled out some dishes from the cupboard and started to washing them in the discolored tub sink.

Molly White saw my confusion, her cleaning dishes that were already clean.

"Helps me think, Trout-John," she said.

We talked no more about any of it. It was dark now, and Molly White walked us out to the road, after a bit. She said nothing the whole time except "Goodbye, little fish," as we parted.

ChApTeR 38

The next day was Saturday. Cot told our folks she was sick, which was indeed true, sick unto death. She was just a shape under the covers all the times I looked in on her. I tried to talk to her, but she would have none of it. She was in her own world.

I thought long and hard of all that Cot had told us the day previous. I didn't know what to make of it. I believed her, I always believed Cot. But I could not wrap my mind around the possibility that she had really talked to Miss Holly on the other side of the grave. It just did not mesh easily with my own, long-derived beliefs concerning death and life.

Yet how could I explain what I had experienced? What had I experienced? I had been faced into the sun. My memories of that presence behind me, the tree growing dead center of my sister's chest. They could have easily been the spawn of some sunbaked, retinal after-image, as of anything else.

Except for the words Molly White had spoken, of those I was certain.

She needs your help.

Nothing made sense!

I gave up all of the thinking and concentrated on breakfast.

Dad had to work that day. Momma had the day off. I was eating cereal at the table, heaping sugar on the pile, when Dad came up to join me.

"You're coming to work with me today Johnny," he said.

I was shocked. "I am?" I exclaimed. Normally, I would have been pretty excited about going to work with Dad, but after the events of the day before, and our scurrilous activities at the Mill itself, I was more than a little nervous at the prospect.

"Cot will be able to rest and you can get a feel for what your old dad does all day while you are goofing off at school."

"I know what you do Dad," I protested.

Dad, now sitting next to me preparing his own bowl of cereal, paused and looked at me. He looked surprised and, way deep behind his eyes, a little hurt. "You don't want to come?"

The terrible son. The ungrateful, terrible son.

"No! I want to come." I paused, trying to think up a sympathetic reason for my obvious reluctance. "I'm just worried about Cot, is all."

"Me too," said Dad. But then he regarded me for a moment too long and it was clear that this time, as it was all the other times I lied, he was keenly aware of it. My guilt increased tenfold and I turned my face down and started shoveling in cereal to hide the flush in my cheeks.

We both chomped for a few moments without speaking. Then Dad put his spoon down with a clink. "You ever think about Lucius? How he's doing and whatnot up there with Uncle Ben?"

"I think about him all the time. Miss him."

"Me and your Mom too. We miss him real bad. But you understand why he had to go up there, right?"

"He was on drugs."

My Dad studied my answer as if it hung in the air before him. "Yeah, that's part of the reason," he said. "A big part, but only part. The real reason he's up there is that he forgot how to enjoy his life."

This was confusing to me. I did not respond.

Dad continued. "Sometimes people lose track of the fun of life. They end up concentrating on things they think are fun. But things aren't fun, Johnny. People are fun. Life is fun. Dogs are fun. Things are just things. They sit there. You have to concentrate on the fun stuff, not the things. That's why Lucious was messing with drugs in the first place. Your Uncle Bennett knows just what I am talking about. That's why I sent your brother up there."

"What drugs was Lucius doin, Dad?"

"Your brother got involved with some shady people, Johnny. People who were living in the darkness. Sidling up to evil." Dad liked to say stuff like "sidling up to evil." He fancied himself a bit of a philosopher-poet.

"What kind of drugs was Luce doing?" I asked again.

My Dad asked of me: "Why do you want to know, son?"

"I don't know. I just do," I said, but this too was a lie. If drugs had something to do with Miss Holly's death, I was determined to ferret out what information I could.

Dad appraised me and it seemed again that I came up short. He shook his head and breathed loudly out his mouth and then said, "Your brother was shooting heroin into his veins. Uncle Benjy also has some experience with people who shoot heroin, which was the rage in Vietnam. They'll just be up there doing their thing, and we'll see if we can't get them back down here come Christmas."

"Dad, was he doing heroin just by himself?" I asked.

Again the look. "No... he fell under the influence of a guy, Ricky Denizen. Rich kid from up the hills. You know him, Johnny? You ever heard of that fellow?"

Denizen! That was the name on the crypt Lucius and those other two were doing their drugs in. I couldn't wait to tell Cot. Even though we had both agreed that Lucius could never have been involved in Miss Holly's murder, this Denizen guy could certainly have something to do with it.

But today I needed to concentrate on Dad and let Cot get her rest. "No I never met the guy or even heard of him."

Dad and I finished up our breakfast and I went to get dressed. I passed Cot's room and listened at the door. Did I hear soft singing from inside? I continued on to my room and got ready.

Dad was waiting out front in the truck. When he saw me on the stairs he revved the engine with a big smile on his face. This was a long-held tradition with us, from the days of my childhood when it would fill me with a terrible joy.

I jumped up in the cab. The cracked window behind us suffused us with the sun. The familiar smell of metal and machine oil hit me and I was immediately comforted as I sank into the springs.

The ride to the mill traversed the exact spot where Cot had collapsed the evening before.

As we drove over it I felt a hollow chill. When the Mill loomed before us, this feeling intensified. At least, as it was Saturday, Winky would not be onsite. Work was different for Dad on Saturdays. It involved a lot of preparation for the following week's work. Not as much mill work as cleaning and maintenance and logistical preparation, depending on the wood that would be coming in or the shipments that needed to be sent out.

The truck bounced past some walkers, three hefty Italian-looking men, carrying lunch buckets and thermoses. They made happily rude gestures in Dad's direction, then scattered when he made as if to run them down in good fun.

We passed through the gate. I turned to Dad and asked, "Dad, could you take me over to where they found Miss Holly?"

Dad slowed the truck. He looked concerned. But he said nothing and put the truck in gear and made a wide turn in the dust. We drove past piles of cut lumber waiting for transport to the railcars or the boats. Dusty, tired men at the end of their shifts moved out of the way of our truck without looking.

Dad drove to the rear of the main building, past garbage bins right up to the door where Cot and I had only the afternoon before slipped out of one adventure and into another, darker one.

"See that door?" said Dad. I nodded. "She was found between there and the garbage bin." With that, Dad slammed the truck into reverse and backed away from the spot. The place where Miss Holly's body had lain receded from me. I could almost see her body folded there, laying in a stain of red. Cot and I had walked directly over the spot when we had left the Mill the night previous. The thought was staggering.

Dad said no more about it.

Which is not to say that he remained silent.

"Are you familiar with the history of Copeland, Johnny? Do they teach you that stuff in school or is it all just naps and snack time?"

"Funny, Dad."

"I'll take that as a 'no," Dad said. We walked through the cafeteria and toward the Mill floor. Dad paused to punch his time card with a loud Ka Thunk.

"This mill is the whole reason for our town," he continued. "Well, not this mill, this mill was built after the first one burned up."

I nodded, not really understanding or caring.

"I have worked here a long time, Johnny. I've worked with a lot of old codgers who did nothing but talk and talk while they cut, and I've learned a lot of stuff about this town. Stuff I want you to know. I was hoping to tell you about it and frankly, if you acted interested, it would make your old dad pretty happy. And, knowing about where you live can be very useful."

I said: "I'd like to hear about Copeland."

"Well, let's see. You come over here and have a seat while I finish up what I've been working on. This old thing is having problems - slowed us down plenty this week."

Dad sat himself down on a stool next to a treadmill track that terminated in a machine, which I will admit to you, haunted my dreams. It was the Debarker. Getting caught in between the heavy iron-studded wheels that ground off the bark, having my body trundled through and by the very whirring teeth that hammered and chewed me to a raw tube of meat, was precisely the scenario that popped into my mind the first time I saw the Debarker, and every single time thereafter, including this one.

Dad said, "So?"

I said, "So?"

Dad said, "Well you gotta ask me questions Johnny."

"I do?"

"Yes, Johnny."

Dad was prone to this, scenarios wherein we were forced to engage him, as opposed to feigning interest, understanding, or both. There was no way out of this.

"Ok," I said. I was going to let him have it. "What year was Copeland born?"

"What? The town? Towns aren't born Johnny, they are incorporated. Copeland was incorporated in 1882."

"I don't want to know when it was incorporated Dad, I want to know when it was born." That got him. He appraised me, looking kind of pleased.

"Well spoken, young yeoman," he said.

"All right… Copeland was born…" He appeared to mull this over for a bit, and then started right in.

"The whole reason for this town is the wood. You know we are surrounded by the Heart-Shaped Forest. 45,000 acres, bought up around 1840 by Jeremy Denizen. Yes, Denizen, just like we were talking about at breakfast, same family. He come over from Europe with his baby bride and his family fortune.

"The Heart-Shaped Forest was right in the way of a proposed railway line and Denizen timed the completion of the mill right when that line was finished. It was a small mill. No gang saws. No kilns, not much finishing."

Dad was totally ignoring the work he was supposed to be doing on the Debarker. I looked around. No one seemed to mind.

"Denizen worked like a madman to make this mill a winner. It started out at only about 5,000 feet a day. Soon it was the biggest producer in the state, and within three years they were cranking out three million feet a year, my lad. Three million! In those days that was a huge amount."

I marveled at my Dad's enthusiasm. He engaged you as if by force of will, independent of the topic of discussion.

"And things proceeded nicely. He built a big house with some of that wood, and sprang up a brood right quick. His wife started organizing the folk that lived in the crappy little enclave that had grown up around the mill. She made sure Jeremy hired a lot of carpenters and the architecturally minded to work the saws and the loaders, to man the carts, to cut the very trees themselves. So that's when Copeland started building itself. That was right before the war. 1861 or so."

"The war?" I asked.

"The Dakota Wars, boy! Heard of that one? It happened right here less than a hundred years ago for Christ's sake!"

"Sorry! Yes, I heard of the Dakota War!" I bleated, by way of defense.

"I sure hope so Johnny." He looked at the splayed-out pieces of the Debarker's innards on the square of oil cloth at his feet. It almost looked for a second like he was going to start working.

"The Civil War (I'm sure you must have heard of it) took a lot of the workers, but the U.S. Army needed the mill to keep producing, so allowances were made, but then yellow fever hit the mill hard, and the blockades upriver, and then the mill burned to the ground in 1865. Some say it's a little more complicated than that, but I'm not given to idle speculation."

"What do you mean?"

He came up close to me and whispered conspiratorially, "I mean that some folks say that the group Winky's granddad William Wickley Prime himself led, were a band of warrior Santee, and that he rewarded them well for their dark works, burning that first mill.

"Cuz then Winky-One came in and saved the day. Bought out the mill, bullied a partnership with Denizen on ownership of the Heart-Shaped Forest. Rebuilt the whole shebang with gang saws and steam kilns and high powered finishers and the whole nine yards."

"So that's when Copeland was born? When Winky's granddad built the new mill?"

"Well I guess it was being born the whole time, from the time of the buying of the Heart-Shaped Forest to the burning of the mill, through the creation of the new mill. The whole time Copeland was ebbing and flowing around this center. Maybe that's why they incorporate towns, to put a hard and fast date on things."

"So why is our mayor named after the town?"

"Well it's more that the town is named after him, or after his grandfather, Morris Copeland."

"Where did he come from?"

"Would you believe Morris Copeland was Winky-One's butler?"

"No way."

"Yes way. The butler became the Mayor of a town named after him."

"That's crazy. Why didn't Winky's granddad just become mayor himself and name the town Wickley?"

"Crazy like a fox, Johnny. Winky-One still had all the power. Morris Copeland was his butler for godsakes! His lifelong crony from a child! It's flippin' genius, if you ask me."

I mulled a bit, incorporating his words. "What became of Denizen?" I asked, picturing the dusty crypt and its mold enshrouded caskets.

"Denizen kept his part of the forest. Kept control of the transport end of things. The Wickley and Denizen families have been at each other's throats ever since. They tried to patch things up recently here, by uniting the families in the old way, but that went all to Hell."

"What way is that?" I asked.

"By marriage of course," said Dad. "Your old teacher, poor Miss Holly…" Dad looked at me with significance.

"Theda Holly was a Denizen."

ChApTeR 39

While Dad and I hashed out the history of Copeland astride the fearsome Debarker, a towering tall man was checking himself into the Pink Motel, so named for the lurid pink its owner one day decided to don the poor motel in, from the flamingo-colored baseboards, to the Bazooka-colored shingles.

The huge man picked up his keys from shabby Billy Horner at the front desk, who tried to make inquisitive small talk with the large man, to no avail. The giant then drove his dusty, boat-like Cadillac around to room 14. There was no room 13, as the hotel's owner, Denny Freemantle, was a man never at ease of his many superstitions.

The unknown man strode around to his trunk, opening it to reveal all that he possessed in the world. From this trove he plucked a red Samsonite travel bag and a red Samsonite suitcase. Being a large fellow, he did not avail himself of the wheels, but held both cases in one arm as he negotiated the flimsy door lock. He slipped inside room 14, closed the door and locked it. The huge man did not emerge until the next day, when our paths crossed, and stayed crossed, well beyond the end of this tale.

ChApTeR 40

What follows, I pulled together from stuff I heard, stuff I read. Some is what I, my own self, in further adventures, witnessed.

I am going to tell about Miss Holly's last moments.

At the time it was known that Miss Holly had met her lover, Robert, at the sawmill parking lot after school.

I cast a glance behind me as I walked out of the classroom at day's end, only the second day of school, to see her bent over her work. She did not look up at me. I imagine after the last of us left through the door, she breathed a sigh of relief, pushed her papers into her desk, and, when the coast was clear, headed off to make her date.

School ended at 3:45 pm. By 4:30 Miss Holly was waiting at the sawmill. No doubt, she sat on the hood of her car, dappled by sun and shadow.

That's what I see.

Robert picked her up. According to witnesses he pulled up next to her and she rather jauntily hopped up into his dark green ford pickup. They kissed. Robert turned the truck into a lazy arc and left the parking lot.

They were seen about 45 minutes later at The Rusty Nail, a local pub. They imbibed, Robert, a whiskey water, served in the too-tall glass for which the Nail was notorious, Miss Holly, a coca cola. They both were energized, happy, and speculation was, since the Nail was only a 2 ½ minute drive from the sawmill, the lovers had stopped at some remote spot and caused each other to be energized and happy.

But this mood did not stick around.

Robert was later overheard complaining vociferously about Winky, his Dad. Miss Holly calmed him by caressing his proffered hand. They both ordered a second drink with their food. In surprisingly short order, Robert ordered a third drink. The bartender, Lucy said that, following this, Robert was quiet, and his eyes were brimmed with tears.

The timely gossip surrounding this development speculated that Miss Holly had just, then and there, broken up with Robert. That's why he was crying, and that's why he killed her. Others suggested his father had brought him somehow to this low state, crying like a girl, in a bar, for God's sakes. Whatever the case, Miss Holly kissed him sweetly on the lips.

In this somber attitude they paid their bill (Robert handed Miss Holly the money and she took care of it) and exited the bar, hands clasped tightly together. This was the last any of the townsfolk saw of Miss Holly alive, and the overriding reason for the cloud of suspicion that dogged Robert during the ensuing months. The patrons saw them leave together, at approximately 09:30 pm, and then she was dead.

According to Robert, he urged Miss Holly to come home with him. He said she consented, but was insistent they go pick up her car. She was after all a teacher of children. It would be unseemly for her car to be seen in the sawmill lot overnight.

Robert drove to her back to her car. A few minutes later, Miss Holly stepped down into the dust and waved at him briefly, silently.

Robert said later that seeing her pretty face through the windshield, looking so brightly up at him through the blue dark, made him so happy, he started smiling like a fool. So, he turned his face away and drove the same arc he had before, off toward home, passing Bandana trudging purposefully toward the mill.

When Robert got home, he made a fire and waited. Miss Holly never showed up.

Miss Holly watched Robert speed off down the dusty road. She turned to her car but suddenly heard something that gave her pause. It sounded like the voice of a child. The strange high pitched mewling was coming from the rear of the central building where the garbage cans were stored. Was the child crying? No, it was laughing. She couldn't tell. She called out, "Hello? Are you ok?" Miss Holly started off in that direction, her steps tentative.

I imagine there was a chill of adrenaline in her stomach.

As she neared the corner of the building, the sound stopped. Miss Holly at this point was so spooked, she was sorely tempted to just turn and leave. But the possibility now existed that there was a child in trouble, or in pain, there in the dark. She envisioned a child in one of the large garbage bins. She imagined her own potential-future child crying in a dark, smelly garbage can. That did it. That spurred her on.

I see myself in her car for some reason, watching through the dirty window as Miss Holly steps farther and farther away into the darkness, until she crosses behind the building and is gone forever.

Of course I can't know what Miss Holly was thinking. It didn't happen like this. I pulled the preceding scene from a horror movie I recently saw. It was such a dumb movie. The scene played out just like I described. But, for all its silliness, it horrified me. I discovered myself clutching my knees with an aching grip.

This happens a lot.

My whole life I have been plagued with the questions, what if it was like this? What if Miss Holly had this look of terror, or this look of defiance or this look of resignation? Did she lose her composure and beg to live? Did she bargain with her murderer? Did she stay silent and refuse to speak?

Today's entertainment offers an ocean of different stories, yet so many revolve around murder.

There is a secret pool of viewers out there, a diffuse group of souls who have lost someone close to them by way of an obscure misadventure that dogs their entire lives, awake or asleep. They all play the game that I, still, to this day, play.

It's called I Never Thought of That Before.

ChApTeR 41

Miss Holly was found by Bandana at approximately 10:30 pm that night.

Inside the mill, the sawing and grinding of machine against wood filled the whole air.

Slowly, one by one, the dog shift mill workers perceived a keening wail that warbled in a different, perhaps moral, register.

They emerged to find Bandana standing over Miss Holly's corpse, howling like a wolf at the forest moon.

Rich Bowler, a strapping night boss and one-time self-proclaimed football hero, thinking that Bandana had himself perpetrated this outrage, jumped the banister of the iron staircase and landed feet first onto Bandana's neck and upper back.

Bandana silenced and crumpled, at which point Rich was restrained by some of the more evenly keeled of the group and made to go back inside and call the police.

However, Rick, a sometimes "Burlyman" of William Wickley's, which is to say, one of the toughs at the mill whom Winky utilized as drivers (and for protection when wandering through the clouds of seething hatred emitted by his own workers), instead called Winky, himself, who then came to the Mill looking unkempt and deranged.

After viewing the remains and consulting with advisors, including his groggy lawyers, William Wickley The Third called the authorities himself, from behind the closed shutters and door of his own office.

A finisher, Don Deets, a 56-year-old veteran of the mill, saw it all. This is from his statement:

From the Statement of Don Deets –

There was green glass in her forehead. It was all over, so I couldn't kneel down. I could tell right away someone smashed her in the head with a bottle of some kind, looked like a Dell Point Lager bottle to me. No! Wait… yeah, Dell Point Lager.

Could you tell how she had been killed?

Oh yeah. Big slice under the chin. I could see way back.

Way back?

Way back into the wound. In her throat. I could see neck bones.

I see. Is it your impression that the local indigent Vladimir Rickoltz, known as Bandana, is responsible for the crime?

Vladimir!! Haw! Vladimir… that is too funny. Wait til I tell the guys… Nope Bandana couldnta done that to a person. Vladimir… too funny. (pause) Poor fella…

Tell me about Robert Wickley.

I always kinda liked the kid. He hung around the mill a lot when he was little. Wasn't no Little Lord Fauntleroy, just a regular kid. Real interested in the business. Kindof a shame, we were all waiting for him to take over for his dad, edge that sour fucker out and none too soon. Oh shit -- Winky's not gonna see this, is he?

No, Mr. Deets. Can you tell me about the relationship between Robert Wickley and the deceased?

They were gah gah bout each other. It was kinda revolting. That was strange cuz they were like, you know, arranged? You know what I'm saying?

I believe you're saying that their relationship was designed and enacted by their respective families.

No Brilliantine, I mean their families set them up. As a couple. (Snort of derisive laughter).

I see. Go on.

They'd been goin' out for about a year, as I recall. They was set up on a blind date by my own cousin's wife who's a distant Wickley. She, every once in a while, you know, handles the dirty work for the more elite of the clan, if you catch my meaning.

They both didn't want to meet each other, it was funny. She met him at a family restaurant called The Red Shed, and me and my wife and all of Copeland seemed like was already there eating, even though everyone knows the Red Shed has shit for food. We all knew about their date and wanted to watch the festivities.

They were totally surrounded. They could tell something was weird. But they started warming up to each other right quick. The entire rest of the restaurant, including the staff, was eavesdropping, hoping those two would have a terrible time. Maybe that's what drove 'em together so fast. (Mr. Deets stops abruptly and looks upward, contemplating his own words).

Go on Mr. Deets.

Robert Wickley started taking her out regular. They took ballroom dancing lessons (my sister in law is an instructor), and then would go dancing regular at the Medina Ballroom every Friday night. They ate at that steak place a lot (youngest busses tables). Whole town would see em walking around, holding hands. Like I said, kinda sickening. They had their dirty fun too.

What do mean, Mr. Deets?

I mean they was seen making out and she would spend the night at his place and him at hers. They was for sure, you know, fuckin.

Could you elaborate on that?

Huh?

Could you tell us more about their sexual life together? Did you ever hear any stories? Or ever see them together in this way?

Did I ever see them fucking? NO!

Hear anything about it?

Just one of the boys saw 'em making out over by the creek, in his truck, and a couple times, I heard her car was in front of his house overnight. The rest is just 2 plus 2. Know what I mean?

I think so. We may return to this issue..

No prob.

So Mr. Deets, if Bandana did not kill Theda Holly, in your estimation, who did?

Well that's pretty obvious ain't it?

It was a hit, like in the Mafia...

ChApTeR 42

FROM THE JOURNAL OF COT CLEARY

Snuck out while Johnny and Dad were at the mill. Looked all over for that damned Bandana. Nowhere to be seen!

ChApTeR 43

The next day, Cot and I escaped the house early, evading Mom in her weekly church recruitment. The sun was hot on our skin even as the cool of the air chilled our shadows.

Soon, we could hear Dad's pickup start, and ramble away down our dirt road. Dad was driving, but he was not destined for a church seat. He was acting as chauffeur. I could see Mom bouncing in the passenger seat, incongruous in her bright flowery dress, her lips pressed in irritation at her absent, hell bound children.

Cot and I shared a joy as soon as the truck was gone. We exchanged smiles of triumph and headed back toward the house.

Cot was back to her usual self. When I asked her how she felt, all she said was, "I had some good dreams."

We returned inside.

She said: "How bout we walk into town and eat at Charlie's? You got any money? I got some," Cot veered off into her room. I heard raspy paper sounds and the clink of change. Cot was somehow always able to produce as much as ten dollars as if from thin air. She did some babysitting, but otherwise, was just a money magnet. Once it was in her sphere of influence, money did not escape from her.

"I ain't buying no food, Cot," I said.

"Then I'll buy it. I want to go into town and have some stuffed french toast."

"All right then. I could stand a chicken skillet," I dared her.

She narrowed her eyes at my expensive choice and went back in her room, presumably to secure more money.

An hour later found us at Charlie's Diner.

Donnie Hemple, the proprietor of Charlie's, looked at us askance. He asked, right off the bat,

"Waiting for your parents, are you?"

Cot looked at me.

I said, "No we're gonna have some breakfast Mr. Hemple, thank you."

My manners mollified Donnie Hemple, for the moment. I had no doubt he would relate our visit to Mom or Dad the next time he saw them. Donnie pulled a couple menus from under his arm, but Cot put up her hand, and said, "I'm gonna have the stuffed french toast, and he'll have the chicken skillet breakfast." Donnie Hemple's eyebrows ascended, but he said nothing as he wrote this down, except: "Juice?"

It was a little uncanny the way Cot put her hand up like that, just like Winky had done in Mom's office.

I started to answer, but Cot quickly said, "No, water's fine."

When Donnie left, Cot started in grilling me about my day with Dad.

She about jerked her neck off when I told her that Miss Holly was of the Denizen clan, and the news about who Luce had been shooting up heroin with.

I could see that gray crypt reflected in Cot's eyes at the mention of the name Denizen.

I told her the whole history as relayed by Dad.

The Heart-Shaped Forest. The first mill. The burning. The first William Wickley and his butler, Copeland.

"That sure makes things a lot more interesting," she said.

"Yeah...that's true." I agreed.

Our food came and we made it to disappear with astonishing speed.

"So maybe one of those Denizens, then?" I asked.

"But they're the ones who stood to gain the most from her staying alive," replied Cot. "I guess I don't know too much about that stuff. We should probably ask Molly White."

The mention of Molly White caused a shudder. I started to say something. Cot knew what was coming and shot her head around, looking for Donnie and the bill, irritation across her brow.

I shut up.

When Cot turned back to me, she did not meet my eyes. Instead she looked over my shoulder.

"Who's that guy?" she asked.

I turned.

At the window booth, a man was eating a hamburger for breakfast. Upon a closer look, I saw there was a plate of eggs, bacon and hash browns waiting for him at the edge of the table.

The man was mammoth in proportion, his huge hands dwarfing the burger as he wolfed it in three successive bites, unimpeded by pause.

The huge man grabbed a napkin from the large stack he must have extorted from Donnie Hemple, who was covetous of his napkins, and wiped his mouth.

Then, in a movement, this ursine creature cast his eyes directly upon us. We froze. The man pointed at us with forked fingers, and turned his hand, beckoning us to him. He motioned to the fat padded bench across the table from him. His meaning was obvious, he wanted us to come and sit with him.

I turned back to Cot, widening my eyes in reproach as I saw her get up to do just that.

"No way, Cot!" I whispered. "I never saw that guy before. He is not from here... he could be the goddamned killer!"

"Oh hush, Johnny," was all Cot said as she gathered up the remainder of her food and brought it over to this man who could have crumpled her like a wrapper in his front pocket. My thoughts turned to all the warnings from Mom and Dad about interacting with strangers. I churned over the awful scenarios that waited should we not heed them.

I quickly gathered my stuff and hurried after Cot.

By the time I arrived at the table Cot had already given the man our names.

"Nice to meet you Johnny," rumbled the man as he proffered the huge wedge of flesh that was his hand. "My name is Elijah Holly.

ChApTeR 44

He was her brother.

"I got a fire burning in me Johnny. I can't put it out, not ever again. It won't let me sleep nor work."

These were Elijah Holly's first words to me, as I shuffled into the booth next to Cot.

"I had to quit my job when I heard. I couldn't work another day. I haven't had more than an hour of sleep at a time since, and I don't know if I ever will again."

Even as the torment of the words hit, I found myself studying Elijah Holly's face, which I immediately liked.

He had a species of shaggy beard, gray in a patch at his chin. His eyes, which were comfortably fixed on mine were deep brown under thick, leonine lashes. I felt right away like this man could read the truth of me. This impression was magnified by the tiny glasses resting on his nose. They were too small for his face, too small for his whole self. But in that precise respect they soon became perfect. I wear a pair indistinguishable from them now, as I write. And I am a huge, fat man.

I was still swimming in the weirdness of his soul-baring words. His confederacy shone on me like light at church. I felt like his kin.

"I'm sorry to hear that," was all I could think to say.

"How come we didn't see you at the funeral?" Cot asked him.

Elijah looked at the table. A fierceness washed over his face and was gone. "I found out about Theda's death only this week. A few days ago, in fact. But I knew something was wrong. For years there's been this crawly feeling at the back of my head. Up until a few years ago, whenever I felt like that I would call her. Everything would be fine. We were close. Like twins." He regarded us, especially lingering on Cot. "Like you two."

He continued, "Unfortunately, in recent years, I have fallen out of touch with my family, for reasons of my own."

"How did you find out, Mr. Holly?" I asked.

"Call me Eli, Johnny."

"Eli," I repeated.

"It was this dream." He reached over and grabbed the breakfast plate and laid it right on the conquered remains of his hamburger plate. He mangled the eggs, meat and hash browns with his fork and knife. Then he shook the whole thing over with hot sauce. He forked a mound of this into his mouth and immediately continued.

"In the dream, Theda was with me in the old sun room of the house we lived in when we were kids, the house she was living in right up to the end." He paused, tamping something down inside. "We had wicker chairs, white and old and frayed," he finally said, "Those chairs would jab you a good one from time to time.

"The sun was on her so bright I could barely look at Theda's face. Then she reached over and tied a leather string around my wrist. Just like this one."

He displayed his right wrist. Around it was tied a black leather string. It was tied to his wrist with a simple thru-knot, leaving two ends poking out.

"She held my hand after she tied it, but instead of calming me or making me happy, her grasp filled me with a big rush of fear. Like there was some menace right outside the field of my vision, closing in, breathing down my neck. I tried to pull away but her grip tightened like a vice and I froze. I looked at her so I wouldn't have to look behind me.

"Her eyes were pleading with me, through all that brightness, begging me to understand some unknown thing, all the while the creepy presence at my back kept growing, like the Werewolf's saliva dripping on your neck, right before he pounces on you. I knew right then I was looking at a dead woman."

Cot was mesmerized, nodding unconsciously.

Elijah continued while he shoveled in more food.

"Somehow, I found myself awake. I thought about the dream, and it occurred to me that I had seen some leather somewhere just like the string Theda had tied around my wrist. I searched around my room, until I came upon a shirt I had just bought. It was clearance and cheap, but had once been dear. I bought it only that day. The designer's tag was attached to the shirt with a leather string. I took it off the shirt and tied the string around my wrist, hoping that it would reveal the secret of Theda's message. It did not.

"So, I called home here to the police station and Deputy Peede confirmed what I already knew, that Theda was dead by murder, and that the police had no leads on the murderer. My Mom was dead, collapsed at the funeral and did I think I could finally get my ass on home and deal with the resultant storm of sh--" Eli stopped himself.

"I still did not understand the significance of the dream, the leather string, nor the meaning of my sister's pleading silence."

Cot and I were a pair of mutes.

"The meaning of the leather string though..." Elijah Holly's voice trailed off. "It's finally clear to me now, what that meant."

He put forward his right wrist again and displayed the leather string. He pointed to the longer of the two free ends sticking out of the knot.

"Johnny, this is you." Then he pointed to the other end, shorter by a third, in the manner of a knot hastily tied. "And Cot, this is you. And the rest of it around my wrist is my promise to my sister to come back here and make sure you two are all right."

"How did you figure that out? How did you figure any of this out?" Cot asked, somewhat rudely. Eli almost said something but clearly thought better of it and clamped his mouth shut. He considered the air above our heads a moment.

"I just know. I knew it the second I saw you two eating there. What's confusing is, why? What have you been up to that has my dear, dead sister calling me up in the middle of the night?"

ChApTeR 45

Thus, Elijah Holly became the next in the line of folks to whom we repeated the story, each time further progressed and more strange, more awful.

We even told him about Cot's attack and presumptive death. Elijah started nodding without realizing it when Cot relayed her meeting with his sister. I could see a bond between Cot and Elijah, forged of their both recent visits by the late Miss Holly.

At the mention of Molly White, Elijah perked up, but he said nothing.

"All I know," said Eli, "is that I feel the first small patch of peace since I first knew about Theda's death, just finding you two. The nagging feeling that's been nipping at me has finally flown away! I feel pretty ok right now, my dear sister notwithstanding." He smiled at us broadly. "I think I am gonna have some hot chocolate. Can I get you two any? It's brain food you know."

Cot smiled and nodded her head like a sentry who has just heard the correct password. We drank hot chocolate with Elijah Holly, while he reminisced about better days with his sister.

"Like I said, we were close. And come to think of it, when we were young we had a small gang of kids we hung out with and your Mom was a member of that group."

"Mom? What do you remember of her?" Cot asked.

"She was just about angelic. She was the distant, preoccupied type. You mentioned Molly White before. Your Mom and my sister were over at Molly's White's house, a lot, which put them on the outs with the kids round here. Molly has always made this town of two minds. Some think she's the bee's knees, others think she is a witch, akin to the child gobbler in Hansel and Gretal.

"But your Mom was real sweet. Never talked bad about people, which, to my mind is the harbinger of assholery, if you don't mind me cussing like that."

We didn't, though were confused by the word harbinger.

"Your Mom would bring Theda with her over to Molly's cabin. I was never allowed in. That always pissed me off. I never really knew why, especially since..."

"Since what?" demanded Cot.

Eli Holly passed his gaze over us, clearly weighing what to say.

"Since--nothing, little one," he said. "Nothing at all."

Eli paid for his meal, and ours, and together we all left the diner. Cot was beaming that she didn't have to spend her hard-earned babysitting money. Using the calculus of youth, I determined that she owed me another skillet breakfast, but I figured I would break it to her another time.

"I can't imagine that you two are free today, but I think we need to do more talking and there are one or two things I could use your help with," Eli said, squinting in the Sunday sun.

"We ain't doing nothing today, Eli," responded Cot.

I shook my head in agreement.

"Nope, you youngsters go on home to your family. Love 'em up, too. Give your Mom a secret kiss for me but whatever you do, don't tell her that I am back. The time is not propitious."

We stood confused.

"The time ain't right," he amended. "Now go!"

His voice had such a force that we turned right there and ran off down Main toward home, smiling ear to ear, both of us. As we ran, Elijah's booming voice caught us:

"I'll be in touch!"

ChApTeR 46

Adria looked at me with her big brown eyes as she munched a sandwich. I sat across from her on the lawn of the school. It was warm for the season and the sun was baking through the cold. Kids were playing and eating their lunches all over the place. Cot was somewhere else entirely, playing harmlessly I hoped.

As if reading my mind, Adria said, "Your sister has a weird name – Cot. I never heard of that before."

"There's a lot about Cot no one's ever heard of before."

"What does Cot mean? I know what a cot is... the thing you sleep on... we've got one in the back room for when Mom and dad fight and she kicks him out of the bedroom."

It was disturbing to hear this intimate tidbit of domesticity about my teacher. I didn't pursue it, instead finding refuge in the Cot Naming Story. It usually irritated me to have to tell it, mostly because the story seemed to shine a garish light on my own, boring, ubiquitous name. But, sitting with Adria, I wanted her to think I was above such pettiness.

I wasn't, but I wanted to show otherwise.

"Cot was born in Dad's pickup truck," I explained.

"Mom and Dad agree that it was a horrible, messed up event. They say it scarred them both for all time." I had heard my Dad tell this story many times. I wanted to capture Adria with this story, as I had seen Dad reel in his many victims.

"I was four years old, going on five, but old for my age. I knew Mom was pregnant, what that meant, and even how she got that way."

If Adria was scandalized, she did not let on.

"It was five in the afternoon, and when Mom's water broke, I was in my room playing with my Lincoln Logs. I was building a really cool fort and when Mom came in and scooped me up, my foot hit the fort and demolished it. I was so mad at her!"

Adria laughed, covering her mouth with her hand. A small, triumphal feeling welled in me.

"The weather was warm, so Mom threw me into the bed of the truck. Her and Dad got in the front. That was the last they thought of me after that. The drive was crazy. I was bumping and banging around back there and they were yelling at each other up front, like there was a ghost in there with them, instead of a baby coming."

"Then Mom made a weird, loud noise, like a whoop, and the truck pulled over real fast. I tried to look inside the back window, but it was steaming up something terrible from the inside."

Adria's eyes were wide now. I could not help but ramp it up a bit.

"Then the screaming started. Both of 'em. Yelling like they both just fell into the Grand Canyon. Mom started hitting the window I was trying to look into, and it cracked, like a shot. Dad never repaired it. That crack is still there to this day, some eleven years later. I still catch him looking at it when he gets in the truck."

"That's sweet!" Adria said, in a high whisper.

"As quick as it started, it was over." I brought my voice low and closed in toward Adria. She closed in toward me. I could smell her clean skin smell. I wanted to touch her black skin right then, caress her arm or something. Would it feel any different than my skin? I had to find out. I reached out and put my open hand on her upper arm.

She felt just like anyone else. But, better than anyone else, too. Adria looked down at my hand on her arm, then back up at me. She didn't say anything.

"Just as I was about to jump out of the truck and bang on the door, there was a baby crying in there, little Cot screaming, all pissed off. I was getting to my feet to go see when Daddy started the truck up and pulled it in a big circle that sent me flying out of the bed entirely. I landed right in the grass. I sat up and watched the truck zoom away from me."

I was caricaturing and gesturing all of this and had to take my hand off of Adria's arm to do so, which was unfortunate, but necessary.

Adria was enrapt. I continued.

"I walked on home, crying the whole way. We hadn't gotten two miles. I walked down our road and I could see the truck there. Maybe 20 minutes had passed. I walked into the house and Dad was right there. He kneeled down and hugged me. I said, 'I fell out of the truck Daddy.' He took my hand and turned toward the bedroom hall. He said 'I know honey, we saw.'"

Adria jerked up and started to say something. I put up my hand, as if to say, "Let's not go there," which is what my Dad always did at this point in the telling.

"We went into their bedroom and there was Mom in bed, holding this baby. I walked up to her and she smiled at me. She looked real tired, but real happy. The baby was lying in her arms, feeding. I pointed up and said, 'Is that the baby's name?'"

"Mom didn't know what I was talking about. So I showed her there was a word on the baby's head, on the back. Mom looked into the mirror on the opposite wall and said, 'Cot.' cuz thats what the word said, in the mirror. When Cot was being born in the truck her head came to rest on this flyer for the Annual Copeland Cotillion that Dad had lying on the seat."

"Cotillion?" asked Adria.

"It's like a big formal ball. Like a dance. Dad had brought the flyer home from his work with the intent of asking Mom to go with him, even though she was super pregnant, which Mom always says was very romantic, when she tells the story. The letters C-O-T transferred right from the paper onto Cot's wet bald head, you know but backwards, and then they read the right way in the mirror. Well, from that moment on, there was no argument. Cot's name was Cot."

"It's like God named her himself," said Adria.

The posturing storyteller flowed out of me. I looked at the event of Cot's birth, which I have told countless times since, in a whole new light. I always add Adria's words when I finish the story, ever since.

"It's like God named her."

Adria and I looked at each other, right in the eyes, and quiet.

A deep thrill began to boil up inside of me, just looking into those lovely, dark eyes. I admired her mouth, its beauty, and saw the ends curl up slightly into a knowing smile. I met her eyes again, and could see she knew right then and there.

You like me, don't you? her eyes asked.

Cot came running up, out of nowhere, and tackled me from sitting to sprawling flat in the snow-dappled grass. She kept on running. Adria laughed and followed after.

"I know how you got your name!" Adria yelled after Cot.

"No!" wailed Cot. "Johnny you are a dead'un!" But she just kept on running.

I remained on my back, looking into the ultra-blue and white of the sky above me.

ChApTeR 47

The three of us made a detour on the way home.

After long negotiations of the night previous, we had come to agreement on who next to "pump for information," to use Cot's newfound phrase.

Cot had wanted to talk right to Robert Wickley. I had quashed that idea firmly and resolutely.

I was still not convinced that he was involved. Other than the knife in the picture, there was nothing, to my mind, that could overcome that picture's sweetness, and the clarity of their affection represented there.

There was someone else whose name gnawed at me. Stacy Steebler, the girl we had seen run from the Denizen crypt with Ricky Denizen and Lucius.

Stacy Steebler was a wayward girl who found solace in the polar attentions of both peace keepers and law breakers. That we had seen her with Ricky Denizen did not reflect well on her canoodling relationship with the newest of Copeland's Finest, Jr. Deputy Wilson Peede.

I had known her tangentially, but for practically my whole life. She was possessed of a predatory beauty, which is probably why I knew of her at all, the type of girl one sees and remembers. Stacy generally sported a grim demeanor and a monotonous voice, which somehow enhanced her small-town-stunner status.

Stacy was the primary evening shift employee of Sol's Laundry. Sol's did chemical dry cleaning and regular laundering, providing a few banks of machines for those so inclined to come in and do their own.

Stacy saw Adria and Cot and me coming and smelled trouble right quick.

"What you little shits want? I don't see any clothes in your hands. Just turn around and head out cuz I ain't buying any of what your selling."

"Hello Stacy," said Cot. "You know us?"

"I know you two. Her, I don't know and I don't care to. Doesn't mean I want to waste my time talking to you, or give money to your church or your school, so just turn around like I said. I'm busy!"

Cot, unfazed, said, "Then you know our brother, Lucius, right?"

Stacy snapped quiet. Her face pokered up, even as a blush crept up from her neck. I looked over at Adria and noted that her jaw was set. Adria was staring intently at Stacy, in a highly inadvisable way.

"What the hell are you looking at, girl?" Stacy demanded.

Adria said nothing in response.

An electricity was building in the room. Stacy looked from one to the other of us. She walked up to the counter and lifted the little door that was hidden there. Menace flowed before her.

Cot, as if to stop Stacy's forward movement, spoke, low and soft, so I had to turn my ear to her.

"We want to know what you were doing with my brother in the Denizen crypt in Builder's cemetery. We followed him. We saw you run outta there. We know you were shooting heroin. We saw the devil symbol. And now our brother is gone!"

"You SHIT!" screamed Stacy.

She lunged for Cot. I moved to block her.

Before I even got a step, Adria was in front of me, swinging her bag filled with books. It caught Stacy full in the chest with a hollow thump.

Stacy tumbled back into the hard edge of a dryer, smacking her head with a clang. She started wailing.

"You bitch I will KILL you!" Stacy Steebler sobbed.

But Adria was above her in a second, bringing up her book bag again, as she said,

"I recognize you from Saturday. My grandma was coming out of Bill's and you and your scuzzy boyfriend called her a bad name."

Stacy's face suffused recognition and surprise as Adria's bookbag came down full to meet it. The meeting of face with books made a sound that repulsed me, even as it gave me great delight.

"I don't like that word," was all Adria had to say, as she left Stacy and went to the door. She held it open and looked back at us expectantly. Cot and I looked at each other amazed, but neither of us had the will to resist. We walked out past the warrior girl.

ChApTeR 48

Adria locked into step beside us as we walked down Main, toward the road out of town.

After sufficient time had passed, as if to clear the intensity of the preceding scene from our palates, Cot said, "Doesn't pay to cross you Adria, does it?"

To which Adria replied, "Don't call my grandma a bad name."

We walked in silence, each of our minds turning a different grist. I couldn't help but to give Adria furtive sidelong glances, while we walked. I performed such glances scientifically, as I had once done with Miss Holly, as if to confirm the curious effect of previous glances.

The growl of a familiar motor sprang into our ears. It grew louder until it buzzed in the trees all around us.

We turned to see Ricky Denizen's Mustang zooming down the hill of the road. He was a dark shape behind the wheel.

In the passenger seat hunched Stacy Steebler. The three of us watched in a daze of unbelief as the black car zipped down the hill and then up toward us. Denizen was going to run us down!

I bleated incomprehensibly, pushing into both girls, like an impatient lemming. Terror informed my muscles and the girls toppled into a roadside ditch, as if thrown by a circus strongman.

It was a deep ditch. If Ricky went into that ditch at his present speed, he would be just as dead as his victims. The girls landed in a heap and hugged each other close.

I didn't want to jump in after them, just in case Ricky plunged in after, too frenzied to preserve the lives of himself and his creepy girlfriend in the passenger seat.

I say creepy, because of the dull slackness of Stacy's face, glimpsed in the moment before I made for the opposite side of the road. The car matched my movement like a cat cornering a mouse. I ran to keep my life, as Stacy's weird, slack-jawed murder-face crawled up my spine.

So I jumped.

Some part of the car grabbed the zipper of my jacket, as I reached the zenith of my jump. It ripped the whole thing from me, causing me to spin in the air like a dust devil. I landed hard and kept spinning into a rolling, tumbling mess in the gravel.

I did not wait a moment to assess the damage, but jumped to my feet and ran across the road, even as Ricky was skidding around for another run.

I jumped the ditch to the girls who were already up, mouths agape from what they had just seen. Together we ran into the forest, and out of the reach of Ricky Denizen's hungry Mustang.

We ran for all our might as Ricky pulled to a halt behind us.

"Run you little pigs! Run! Run! Run! Run or I will eat you little pigs! Run! Run! Run!"

Then Stacy Steebler's screeching rent the air, adopting none of the fairy story metaphor of her gleefully evil boyfriend.

"DEATH to you! ALL of you!" she screamed. The last part was lost in a growl of unhinged enjoyment. I looked back and could just see her doubled over with the effort of her screams through the trees. We continued to run like mad and didn't stop until we could run no further.

ChApTeR 49

"Good damn thing we talked to Stacy Steebler instead of Robert Wickley," said Cot, as we walked, shaking, through the forest. "That worked out just great."

"Shut up Cot," I replied, "Wasn't my idea to make her crazy like that. You're just lucky Adria BookWielder was there to save you."

"No kidding. Adria you are my hero."

Adria kept looking down, but a small smile crept onto her lips. "I feel pretty good about it," she said.

We all chuckled self-satisfiedly at that.

"'Course, now there is a price on our heads," said Cot.

I nodded my endangered head in agreement. I stole a glance at Adria and was pleased to catch her in the act of stealing a glance at me.

She smiled at me and I smiled at her.

ChApTeR 50

FROM THE JOURNAL OF COT CLEARY
I followed Winky again. I couldn't help myself.

Truth is, no matter how evil he might be, there's stuff about him I think is kinda neat. I would never tell Johnny.

I followed him three times now, but this is the first time I looked at him like he was a real person instead of the bad guy in a TV show.

Mostly cuz he looked real lost at one point. He was walking across the street. He stopped in the middle of the street and looked behind him. Looked in front of him. His mouth was moving. His eyebrows were all crunched together. A car stopped just short of plowing him over, but he didn't even notice.

I couldn't help it. I thought, poor guy, and almost left my hiding spot to go help him out.

But I didn't.

Then Winky caught his thoughts. He walked across the street, stopping in front of a shop window. He fixed his tie and straightened out his jacket in the reflection. An old lady came by and he looked at her reflection like she was a hobo in a 5 star restaurant. She saw him and walked right to the other side of the street.

Even that made me sad for him. I could see he was mad for getting confused and was just trying to distract himself with his tie and by scowling at that old lady. Anyway, after all that, he seemed like he was back to his usual jackass self.

Right off, he started crabbing at a paper delivery boy who was slinking by, for throwing the newspapers instead of quietly placing them on the door mats. I could hear him all away from across the street. The paperboy had already done my side and there was a paper on a doorstep not five feet from me.

It was all I could do not to pitch it at Winky's head right then and there.

He kept walking on after scolding the paper boy, the old, terrible Winky. When someone passed him by who he was willing to talk to, he seemed to try to be nice, but came off more as if he were suspicious or angry with them. They always looked like they were embarrassed or afraid of him.

A couple of times millworkers passed him by and everybody pretended not to notice each other.

Finally Winky stepped into Charlie's. He took a spot way far in the corner, with his back to the wall. He sat and read the news paper, especially that part that is just rows and rows of numbers. After a few minutes - not long at all - Donnie Hemple brought him over a plate of food. They said nothing to each other.

Winky barely ate, but that man drank 3 whole cups of coffee! Suddenly Winky checked his watch and he was up and out of the door. He didn't leave any money and no tip. I half expected Donnie Hemple to come chasing after him, but I could see Donnie still inside, just cleaning off Winky's mess and looking glum.

Winky walked from Charlie's fast. He kept his head down the whole time. He practically ran over to Billings Avenue. I had a hard time keeping up.

That's ok. I knew where he was going.

Robert Wickley's house isn't very big. I bet it only has one bedroom. But it's super pretty. He keeps up the yard and there are flowers in pots on the step and in the windows. There was a newspaper on the walk going up to the house, and Winky picked it up and I could tell he was cursing that poor paper boy.

Winky knocked on the front door, high above his head. He looked around as he waited, and I think he saw me! He looked hard right in my direction and I felt sure-horror in my guts. He scowled and looked harder. I was in some bushes, but my skirt was my white one, and I feared he could see it through the leaves.

I was getting set to run off when the door opened and Robert came out. He smashed right into Winky, who was looking my way, and Winky puffed up and turned and looked real mean at his son. Robert looked right back at his father in a daring sort of way and it almost seemed like they were going to have a fistfight. A yellow thing floated to the concrete step between them from the stack of papers in Robert's hand. Neither of them seemed to notice.

Winky shook his head and turned on his heel to the front gate, with Robert close on his tail. Robert was also shaking his head in a disgusted way. They stood together at the end of the walk. They didn't talk at all. They didn't even look at each other. In fact, they kept looking in totally opposite directions while they stood there.

They stayed like that for a long while, until suddenly an old taxi pulled up. Robert got into the back and Winky talked to the driver and handed him some money from his wallet. He kept repeating to the driver: "You wait for him!" until Robert yelled from the back seat, "All right Dad! Christ!"

That shut Winky up tight. He stood up stiff as a board and turned and walked back in the direction of Charlie's.

The cab driver looked upset and leaned over to the passenger door that Winky had left open and pulled it closed from inside. After fiddling with the fare meter, the driver pulled the old cab in a big u turn and a quick left, and was gone.

I waited a few minutes. Then I crossed the street and hurried up the walk to the yellow piece of paper I could see was still where Robert had dropped it. It was a little card with some printing and some blank spaces where someone had written today's date and a time.

The card said:

Brewster Psychiatric Services

Robert, your appointment with Dr. Patter is scheduled for (today's date) at 0945 am.

If you are unable to make your appointment, please cancel no later than 24 hours beforehand, or you may be charged the hourly rate.

Psychiatric Services! In Brewster! That's where the drive-in was we went to on summer nights when Daddy was itchin to see some movie, like Psycho or that one cowboy movie with the weird music. I couldn't wait to tell Johnny about this. I turned and ran like a bat out of hell to the front gate.

Which was where Winky grabbed me with a snarl by my arm. He shook me like a doll and said "I knew I'd seen you around, you little whelp. Why are you spying on my son?"

ChApTeR 51

During this event I was still in bed. I had begged off school by way of a fraudulent tummy ache and a fever.

I was, at this time and for some years after, the type who felt slighted if I used up a sick excuse for an actual illness. I cherished those times home alone, ruler of the entire house, snooper into drawers and cabinets normally off limits.

Momma stuck her head in the door. "Don't let me find out you were out playing, Johnny," she said sternly to me. But I could see the concern encroaching on her eyes. I had given a worthy performance of pain and illness. I turned over to face her like it hurt my very skin and bones to do so, and said, "I won't Momma," in a shaky, fevered voice.

She made a sound of fretting and came over and tucked me in tightly, so as to ward off the demons of sickness and escape. She generously swept my forehead with her loving palm. I was in fear of her noticing how truly non-feverish I was. But mother-love was all my momma was made of at that moment, and she said, "You poor thing, you are clammy as all get out."

She kissed me sweetly where she had rubbed. I felt as lovingly cared for as I had ever felt, genuinely sick. My eyes wet. This just added to the appearance of my deathly illness. Momma kissed me again right on my presumably infectious lips and turned about and walked out, her chunky heels clacking all the way.

It was only a few minutes after she had climbed into the pickup with Dad and was gone away up the road, that the phone rang. I just let it ring. Soon, it stopped. The silence that filled the air of my house was total.

Then the phone started ringing again. This time it seemed to ring on and on like it would never stop. I slowly got out of bed, mentally daring the insistence to end, and when it did not, I started hurrying, hoping to catch whoever it was before they hung up. By the time I neared the black phone on its stand, I was fairly running.

The voice on the other end was a familiar one, excited and loud.

It was Elijah Holly. After I answered, he said, "Johnny I've got your sister here and she's pretty shook up. Can you meet us up by the post office?"

"Well yeah I can but I'm kinda sick," I said.

Elijah said nothing, but the voice of my sister in the background pierced my ear with a shrill admonition.

"You get your faking ass over here right now Johnny Cleary, or I swear to God I will burn every comic you have!"

ChApTeR 52

Winky shook Cot like a doll.

"What do you have to say!" Winky yelled into Cot's face.

Cot had the presence of mind to squirrel away the yellow appointment slip into the pocket of her dress, and remained as mute as a stone.

"Well I do believe that truants are best dealt with by the authorities. I think I can persuade old Kamen to sit you in a cell until we get to the bottom of this!"

With that, Winky jerked Cot by her tiny arm, nearly pulling it from its moorings. Winky dragged her along with him back toward town. Cot had to doublestep to keep up with Winky's long strides. Where most children her age would be pleading, crying for release, Cot said not a word and shed not a tear.

The route they now took brought them right by the cleaners. Cot looked in the window as they passed. Stacy Steebler was inside, pouring a container of quarters into a dirty bank bag. When she saw Cot, she ran up to the window, all smiles at Cot's obvious predicament. Cot gave her a silent "fuck you," as she slipped beyond sight, but not before seeing Stacy's grin abate into her more familiar mask of spite.

They had just passed Charlie's, and were about to cross the street to the police station, Winky's fingers still deep in the flesh of Cot's forearm, when a voice behind them made the old man jerk to a halt. The little girl ran full into the back of him.

The voice said, "What's goin on here?" It belonged to Elijah Holly, just emerged from the front door of Charlie's, a breakfast cheeseburger still nested in his huge right hand.

Winky summoned up every vestige of his importance and spoke.

"And who might you be?" he demanded.

"I just might be the last fella you ever speak to unless you let go of that little girl's arm," menaced Elijah.

Winky snorted, aghast. His mouth and his eyes popped. Perhaps just a little bit of fear colored the answer that rushed out in a defiant torrent.

"I will have you know that I found this... this... child snooping around my son's house like a burglar! She was right at his front step looking under the mat for a key, I have no doubt, and if not for my timely intercession, would likely have broken and entered his house in search of ill-gotten booty!"

"I wasn't gonna take no booty Eli," said Cot.

"Of course you weren't Cot. You were just going to tell Robert his old pal Elijah was back in town, just like I asked you to. Right?"

Cot missed nary a beat with her affirmation of this spontaneous lie.

Winky shook with affected, dramatic laughter.

"Oh ho ho! Very good! It's all very clear now! This little grommet is your partner in crime! She was going to burgle my poor boy's house on your command, whoever you are. Perhaps we should all take a walk over to the police station and see what they have to say about a child burglar-vagrant team prowling our town unabashedly in the middle of the day!"

"Perhaps you should let go the girl's arm," said Eli.

Eli's words had a bit of blood-soaked growl in them. Cot felt Winky shake from head to toe, the way a soul might, at the spectre of a wolf, just come out of the forest. He slowly released her arm.

"She should be in school with the other kids," said Winky, trying to camouflage his unease. "I think I'll just walk right over to the station and have the constable come over and join this little discussion."

"You do that Winky, but before you do, know that I will be making Kamen aware of the clear marks of abuse on this girl's arm." They all looked down and sure enough, the imprints of Winky's fingers were still deeply ingrained in Cot's upper arm. Then Eli continued.

"And you be sure to tell him my name."

"Which is?" asked Winky with a resurgence of self-glory.

"Elijah. Elijah Holly."

At this, Winky backed off with a start. He had just been about to say something, and it came out anyway, all whispery, "How dare you call me Winky," but with all the context and meaning flown right from his speech, as some desperate awareness settled on the thin old man.

Winky little more than muttered it to the wind, as he shivered in his place and then quickly crossed the street, not to the police station, but the other direction, across Maple, toward the Mill.

ChApTeR 53

We stood round the post office pay phone and Cot vividly recounted these events.

She looked at me expectantly and I said, "Cot, why ain't you in school?"

"I was gonna go to school after following Winky, but he grabbed me from it! Why ain't you in school Johnny? Oh yeah, you're super sick with chills and everything."

Cot was referring to my performance of earlier that morning, during which she had pantomimed a jerking death over Momma's shoulder.

"Playing sick, eh Johnny?" said Eli. "Don't make a habit of that, I hope."

"Well, not a habit..." I replied, noting my debate-wise inferiority to Cot. Suddenly, everyone was looking at me. I was the one in need of remonstrance, not the angelic blond girl who had just let herself get scooped up by the very probable killer we were trying to expose.

Cot deigned to be magnanimous.

"Johnny doesn't do it overmuch, Eli."

"Well that's good to hear," he said.

Eli's presence was the only thing saving Cot from death-by-brother, and she knew it too. But then, I think Eli may have had his own knowledge, as he was suddenly rather mirthful watching us. He made a clap to draw our attentions.

"Actually, kids, I do have business in the police station. I need to go over there straight away and since you are here, I would like to talk to you a bit afterwards. Could you wait here until I return?"

"Sure, Eli," I said.

Eli smiled down at us and ran back across the street to Charlie's. He came back out a while later with his jacket on and a manila folder in one giant paw. His cheeks were filled with food and he was chewing furiously. He ambled right back up to us and handed me the folder.

"Don't look at this," was his message, after I had translated out all the food.

"I won't, Eli," I said.

Eli nodded and made some really epic chews followed by a gulp, like in a cartoon.

He said, much more intelligibly, "Thanks Johnny, just hold onto that and I will be right back." He gave Cot's hair a ruffle as he passed her and she pretended not to enjoy it.

He walked along to the Copeland police station, marshaling reserves of authority, it seemed, as he stepped. Cot watched over my shoulder until Eli was inside and then gave me the ok signal. I splayed open the manila folder and together we set about studying the contents.

Inside were a bunch of papers roughly organized with clips. Also, a white, rigid envelope.

Upon closer examination, the folder revealed a trove of data about Miss Holly's demise. There were statements from witnesses, bearing the imprimatur of Hunstable County, the agencies of which conducted the more complex aspects of the investigation. It was this very folder that produced the witness testimony of Don Deets, which you have already read.

There were the police reports of all the responding officers of Copeland, as well as those of the responding Hunstable detectives. A couple of clips in, were collected the forensic data and the autopsy report itself. Finally, the folder gave forth the statements of numerous of the townfolk of Copeland, including that of Reginald and Bobby Donnel, the first, ultimately the only, suspects detained during the course of the investigation of the murder of Theda Holly.

Cot speed-read as much as she could of the file. I cannot say the same, drawn, as I inexorably was, to the white envelope at the back of the folder. When we got to it, Cot looked at me in sort of a pleading manner, because she knew in some way, with some sense that could see right through the white opacity, what the envelope contained.

I drew it out and held it in front of me, while Cot distracted herself with the rest of the file's contents. I turned it over and quickly surveyed its closure, noting that if I were to open it and remove its contents, no one would be the wiser. It was only held closed with a length of red string, wound around an affixed paper disc on the body of the envelope. I flexed it in my hands to reassure myself of what I held. The conclusion was inescapable.

Photographs.

My impulse was to open it right there and then, and to look hard at what I presumed were the death photos of my loved teacher. I imagined there were photos of the murder scene, and most likely photos of the autopsy as well. So many questions that had burned my soul over the recent months stood to be answered by the simple opening of this envelope. But the most important question was the one I had posed to Bobby Donnel in the forest outside his shack.

"What was her face like?"

I don't know why I felt so strongly that seeing her last expression would enlighten me about the circumstances of her death, as if I would be able to see the face of her killer, reflecting from her eyes.

But even then, I knew that her killer's identity was not really what I sought. I wanted to look into Miss Holly's dead eyes and be admonished with the very horror of such a glance from this pursuit entangling Cot and I. I wanted Miss Holly to talk to me one more time, as she had perhaps talked to her brother in his dream, and my sister in her short death. I wanted her to tell me to stop.

Cot paused her reading to look back at me - and my choice was clear. I placed the unopened envelope back into the manila folder. I heard Cot's breathing calm and felt her rigidity loose.

And just in time too, for right then Eli walked out of the police station, carrying a plastic bag and accelerating like a speed walker. As he neared I could just make out what the bag contained, nestled in a cushion of brown sand.

Shards of broken green glass.

ChApTeR 54

"I don't feel comfortable asking you two inside. But we do need to speak about some things, so you got any better ideas?"

"We really don't mind coming in, Eli," I told him. Cot was looking way up into Eli's face.

"No. I just accused the most powerful guy in town of child abuse. The last thing I am gonna do is bring a couple of kids into my motel room. Just give me a sec and I'll be right back, I'm just gonna put this stuff up." Eli gestured to the bag of green glass and the folder. He crossed the lot and unlocked the pink door of room 14.

Eli opened the door and visibly stiffened.

He just continued to stand there, looking into the room.

When he stepped inside, the darkness of the room enshrouded him. Eli did not turn on any lights, and he did not close the door. Cot and I looked at each other, alarmed.

"Let's do it," said Cot. By some silent agreement as to the subject of her utterance, we started across the lot toward the open door of the Pink Motel, room 14. I was brought to mind of my foray into the gloom of the Denizen crypt, as that dark doorway loomed.

We could hear things emanating from within, scrapings and other sounds of indeterminate origin.

Cot reached out and grabbed my hand as we neared. Just as we got to the threshold, a huge shape overtook the blackness of the doorway, stopping us dead. Cot gasped and crunched down on my hand. But it was just Eli himself, his red suitcases tucked under his huge arm. He stepped outside, drawing the door closed. I pulled loose from Cot.

"Let's go kids," Eli said, already bee-lining for his big old Caddy. He opened his trunk and threw his luggage carelessly inside. He had a smaller satchel under his other arm, which contained the bag of glass and the folder we had perused. "Someone's been in my room," he said as he unlocked the passenger door. "Get on in."

"Where we goin'?" Cot asked.

"For now, we are just gonna get some air between us and this place. I don't know who would have gone into my room, and I don't know how they got in, but I do know that someone has taken an unhealthy interest. It could be Winky, I hope to hell it was Winky. At least that would make sense. But it's been hardly an hour and a half since he and I had words. Not much time to find out where I was staying and go and break in."

"It was him all right," I said. Cot stayed clammed up next to me. We were all in the front seat, Cot between us.

We passed the front office and turned onto Main. Cot said, "Don't you have to pay?"

Eli replied, "I paid a couple weeks in advance." and then said no more.

It occurred to me, during the twists and turns, how little we knew Elijah Holly.

I realized with a sudden and palpable shudder that we had no real proof that he was even who he said he was. This big guy just came into our lives only a few short days ago, claiming he was Miss Holly's brother, telling a sad tale. The fact that Eli told Winky the name was encouraging, but the way he had walked from the police station, holding what was clearly evidence from the crime scene itself, was not. He walked fast and nervous, like a shoplifter whose stolen merchandise is slipping from its hiding place. What if he was the killer?

ChApTeR 55

And now we were in his car, at his mercy.

Eli turned almost right away into the Copeland Library parking lot. Eli went to the far end of the lot, which was out of sight of the motel, turned his boat of a car in an easy arc and backed into a spot facing the street. He cut the ignition and a horrible smell filled the car.

"Sorry 'bout that kids. My car has gastro-intestinal problems."

We both laughed, myself, somewhat uneasily.

I was relieved that we were in the very public parking space of the library. There was an old man with a book waiting at the front door for the library to open. He watched us with unguarded suspicion the whole time.

Eli stopped me before I could talk, and said, "Are you alright, Johnny?"

"I dunno," I muttered.

Eli looked pained at this.

Could he hear fear in my voice? I felt that all my worry was broadcast to him.

"Let's get out of the car, kids," was all Eli said, as he opened his door and pulled his mass outside.

As Cot and I dragged ourselves out she gave me a look that asked, What is your problem?

We all met round front. I noticed Eli brought the satchel with him. He set it down on the car, made a big sigh that expanded his whole being, and said,

"None of this is turning out right. Johnny, I could tell you were getting a little worried back there. Thinking I might not be who I say I am, isn't that right?"

I was startled that he could size me up so precisely.

As he talked, Eli pulled out his wallet and thumbed through some pieces of ID, laying them out on the hood of the car.

"This is my driver's license," he said, and sure enough, it bore his name and his photo, looking kind of goofy. I noted it was from Delaware.

He picked up a serious looking card that had his photo right in the middle. "This is my work ID." Again, his name appeared in bold dark, and underneath that, a series of numbers. A light green watermark behind it all said "D.O.D"

"What is D-O-D?" I asked.

"Department of Defense. That's who I worked for before all this. Who knows, I will probably go back there after I'm done here. I hope I do."

"What did you do there?" asked Cot.

"I interrogated people. Asked them questions for the government."

"You mean like spies?"

"Like anybody. Anybody that didn't seem like they were telling the truth to the F.B.I or any other... entity. Not spies really, but more than a few lawyers and clerks and bank tellers and just regular people."

"Did you torture them?" I asked.

"Didn't need to. People always tell me the truth."

"No they don't. I've lied to you myself - a couple of times," said Cot, matter of factly.

This caused Eli to throw his head back and roar laughter. Cot looked terribly annoyed when he did that.

"That's not really what I mean, Cot. What I mean is that I can always get the truth of the information I am seeking from a person. It's kind of a talent of mine. And that's why the Department of Defense pays me my wage, cuz I can do it better than – well, better than anybody in the whole world, or so I have been told."

"Like in the car just now?" I asked.

"Yes, Johnny, exactly like in the car just now." said Eli.

"You knew I was getting worried about you. You could tell that I worried you were lying about who you said you were. But how? You didn't ask me anything about that," I protested.

"You were worried I was lying to you about who I was, and maybe even that I was carting you off to do you harm. You even worried that I might have killed my own dear sister."

"Johnny you are an absolute shitheel!" exclaimed Cot.

"Shut up Cot! I got to do the worrying for both of us since you are so trusting - and so crappy at following people! And how the hell do you know what I was thinking Eli? Goddamnit!" I barked, by way of addendum.

"It's my gift. It's what I do. It's why the government is so keen on keeping me at the G14 payscale."

We just stayed still, bullying the big man with our silence.

"I have this gift," said Eli, "an ability that I never heard of anyone else ever having. I am not too sure how I came to possess this ability, cuz it's not like a knack for remembering, or playing the piano, or multiplying large sums in your head. I do have some theories though, and while I am back here, I intend to pursue them. Honestly, I think it's got something to do with this place, where we all grew up," he said.

"What place?" asked Cot.

"The Heart-Shaped Forest," said Eli, sweeping his hand indicating the green all around us, rolling into the distance from every edge of town.

Eli continued, "When I want to know something, a question, some uncertainty, anything – I mentally pursue the answer to that question, or problem. When I do that, when I go into that questioning mode, something kind of strange happens. It's always happened ever since I was a little kid. I guess when I was young I didn't even know it was happening."

Cot and I leaned forward toward Eli in our anticipation of his next words.

"I hear movie music. Which is to say, music that I have heard in a movie at some time previous. This music plays in my head in a way that does not resemble remembered music, but is as if a small orchestra in my head is exactly rendering this music, informing me, through its expression, as to the truth I am pursuing."

Eli chuckled. "When I was a young child it was cartoon music, like those wonderful Carl Stalling tunes- so expressive and meaningful.

"Even when I have not followed the music's advice, I have discovered later that the music knew exactly what it was talking about. When the music guides me - I don't really know how to explain it - it's too subjective. But sometimes, for example, the music is from a scary movie and other times the tune chosen is light and uplifting, like from a musical comedy, like that one with Rock Hudson and Doris Day.

"It is, more than anything else, as if I am a character in a movie, a character unlike any other, who can hear the soundtrack. What an advantage such a character would possess, right? I mean, it would guide the character, tell them not to open that closet door, or go into that cellar, because something terrible is about to happen. Now the music wouldn't say, 'Hey, there's a big hairy purple monster in the closet.' Just something terrible. That's the way it is with me. It doesn't answer my questions outright. It's just that if I listen closely to it, listen in just the right way, the music leads me to the answer I seek. The music helped me find Theda's questions. It led me to you in Charlie's Diner."

Cot's face fell. "How in the hell are we supposed to believe that, Eli?"

"How are you to believe that you and I talked to Theda after she was dead, Cot?" Eli responded, his voice tender and low. "Or that you can be here right now, talking to me at all, when by all rights you should be in your grave?"

When Eli listed the strange things we had been through, all in a breath like that, it did seem like something out of a fairy story. And there was more, like Momma's story to Cot about how Molly White had told her Daddy's name when she was still a little girl.

But all things paled next to Cot's death and what I had seen on that dirt road. The tree that grew right up out of her chest...

Eli looked from Cot to me and back again, waiting for us to say something. It was all too clear that Cot was real put off by his answer, maybe since it reminded her of that which she seemed so intent on forgetting. But through Cot's well-practiced look of disapproving annoyance, I could tell she knew Eli was speaking some shade of the truth to us in that parking lot.

I watched her face, and while she made sure not to meet my eyes, I could see that Cot was scanning the distant forest, wondering about its secrets.

"It doesn't always come, the music. Especially since I found out about Theda. I am left in silence when I need the music the most, these days, it seems. This has caused me great distress, but, usually, I have been fortunate with it, especially at work, during interrogations."

We met this confession with silence.

"I'm not the only one around here with special talents, either," said Eli. "All my life I've heard of people from hereabouts who can do things no one else can do.

"There was Mr. Knohadley from over east. Kids used to say that he would call them to him in their dreams. I even heard him once, myself. I had a dream about a white dog. It spoke to me in old Knohadley's voice and told me that if I didn't quit walking on his lawn on the way to school, I would find my ass peppered with salt-shot. I never took that route ever again.

"Then there was that piano tuner's mom, Mrs. Milsap. She could play the piano without touching the keys. No lie. She would sit on the bench, close her eyes and start humming. Sounds would start coming from the cabinet, but it didn't sound like a piano. It sounded like a million worms and spiders slithering and dancing along the strings, without involving the keys or hammers at all.

"But the weirdest of them all was Jameson Corr. I went to school with that boy and he was fairly insane. Talked to himself, never-ending. Was always looking in the air around him, talking about things he could see that we could not. Things swimming in the air around us, watching us and listening. One day he went just plain nuts and got up on top of one of the desks at school screaming on about how the things were about to come through and get us.

"I stayed the hell away from that boy after that. He was one creepy bastard.

"He ended up disappearing one night soon after. His parents woke up and found his bed empty, but slept in. Weird thing is, the covers were not thrown back, the way they are when someone gets out of bed. They were still bundled around a boy who was just no longer there. That's what his sister said."

Cot and I were staring at him mesmerized, like he was telling ghost stories, his face aglow, not from a campfire below, but from memories past.

"I don't get it, Eli," said Cot, her voice reaching back toward her familiar incredulity, "We have lived in this town, in this forest, our whole lives and no one ever mentioned any spooky people with special powers."

Elijah Holly thought about it for a moment. Finally, he said, "Maybe someone close to you doesn't want you to know about this stuff."

ChApTeR 56

"What about the green glass, Eli?"

Eli looked uneasy when Cot asked that. He looked over at the red satchel still sitting on the hood of his car.

"Is it evidence?" I asked, already knowing the answer.

"It is, or was. Pretty much useless in that capacity, now that I have absconded with it," said Eli. "It's the bottle... "

Eli held open the mouth of the satchel. I noted that he did not take the bag of glass out for us to see, but only let us appraise it as it lay in the shadows of the bag.

I looked over at the library door, and sure enough, the old man was still peering steadily at us.

"Whoever killed Theda, smashed her over the head with this bottle," said Eli. "The Hunstable investigators weren't able to pull any fingerprints from any part of it. Smashed into too tiny fragments they say."

Eli looked deep into the satchel. "Bullshit, I say."

I looked back over at the old man by the library door. I realized that the old man was watching us with a measure of interest bordering on envy.

"I intend to check the bottle myself." Eli added.

"How?" asked Cot, "Its all smashed up."

"I have a few ideas," assured Eli.

"You gonna tell us how you got it?" I asked.

"Well, it wasn't as easy as I had hoped it would be. I generally tend to go into such situations with something approximating a plan, but not this time. It worked out ok, thank the stars."

ChApTeR 57

Here's how it worked out "ok:"

Eli had just left us violating his trust, perusing the manila envelope he had ordered me, however unintelligibly, to keep closed.

Eli was aware of the role the glass bottle played in his sister's death from reading the Hunstable reports. He knew that the investigators regarded it, evidence-wise, as a dead end. Eli thought different. He was of the opinion that the broken glass could bust the case wide open, to use one of Cot's newfound phrases. But he still had not worked out how he was going to achieve his goal of walking out of the Copeland police station with it.

He had appropriated the Hunstable report by calling in favors from D. O. D. friends with ties to law enforcement. However, in this instance, Eli realized that he would need to resort to out and out thievery of the broken Dell Point Lager bottle to get it in his hands.

How he was going to accomplish this, he had no idea. As it happened, his ultimate success, if such an act could be considered a success, depended heavily upon the music in his head, and not at all upon his professional associations.

Eli saw right off the bat that there was only one deputy inside, manning the desk. It was the aforementioned Junior Deputy, Wilson Peede, cop-half of Stacy Steebler's erotic triumvirate. The young cop looked fretful in the extreme as he spoke into the handset of his phone.

The music started rising from nowhere, seemingly just out of the limits of Eli's visual perception. The music was clunky and humorous, wrought by a detuned piano and most likely from a silent film he had seen, though the title eluded him. The music described a person who thought awful highly of himself, but who, in the cold light of reality, was something of an oaf. Eli figured the music was telling him something about the officer behind the desk.

Wilson Peede nodded to Eli and returned his focus to his phone call, at which point the music in Eli's head changed to a brass near-fanfare, punctuated with childish piano motifs that he initially thought referred to the police, until he realized it was a quote from Alex North's score of The Bad Seed.

The poor bastard is talking to his girlfriend, and she's a bad one, like the little kook from that film, thought Eli. Officer Peede did not seem to be having much fun doing so.

"Mind if I wait here?" Eli indicated the general vicinity directly in front of Peede.

Junior Deputy Peede nodded tersely.

Turning his mind to the problem of where the evidence room was, Eli followed strains of music that switched schizophrenically from Max Steiner's King Kong, when he was cold, to Alfred Newman's love theme from David and Bathsheba, when he was hot. The evidence room was a broom closet, administratively converted into an evidence room, by fiat, with the inclusion of a few extra shelves. It was in the foyer hallway, just behind him.

"Stacy, I haven't seen you in, like, four days. I'm gettin' a little antsy," said Junior Deputy Wilson into the unsympathetic handset. Peede continued in this vein, in a placating manner, all out of proportion, and inverse, to his station as a gun-wielding officer of the law.

"Don't be like that, baby," Peede pleaded.

Given the proximity of the evidence closet, Eli knew he had to get Junior Deputy Wilson Peede out of the room. To accomplish this, Eli decided he had to annoy the Junior Deputy into leaving of his own accord.

Eli whispered, "Sounds like you've got a firebrand on yer hands, huh?"

Peede shot him a look of confederacy (which Eli found unfortunate, considering his desire to discomfit the man) and said, while covering the mouth piece, "Pal you got no idea."

"Yah, I had me a gal like that once," Eli said, all in a melancholy, "She was about as sweet and juicy as a fresh clementine. That is, until I found out she was screwing my worst enemy in the entire universe. Broke my heart clean in two." Eli looked wistfully into his contrived past.

A dark cloud crossed the junior deputy's pimpled face and he shifted uncomfortably in his seat, as though it were warming up on him.

Peede removed his snap-on tie. He unbuttoned his top button, and said into the phone, "Be quiet for a second Stacy. Yer talkin' a mile a minute. Tell me, where did you say you were last night? I waited around the Iron Nail for about over a whole hour!" Peede infected his voice with deep hurt,

Stacy's response to this was epic, nay, mythic. Her voice screeched from the phone so loudly that it came to Eli's ears across the space of many feet.

"I don't have to answer to YOU Wilson Peede! Not to you or to your tiny prick!"

Eli made sure to wince dramatically.

Junior Deputy Wilson reacted as might any low-ranking peace officer whose manhood has just been slighted.

First, he coughed explosively, so as to cover up any emasculating abuse that might be forthcoming. Then, he turned red, from his scrawny neck on up to his waxy cheeks. Finally, he squeaked into the phone, "Just hold on one second, baby -- I'll be just a tetch."

With affectations of invulnerability, Junior Deputy Wilson Peede pushed a button, and, setting the handset into its cradle, got up from the desk. He swaggered into Kamen's office, picked up the phone there, closing the door with a bang, and twisting the blinds closed.

Seeing his opportunity, Eli made sure no one was approaching before sidling up to the "evidence room" door. He checked again around him and reached into his pocket for his keys. Singling one out, Eli rapidly unloosed it from the ring and returned the remainder to his pocket.

The key he chose was not a key in the normal sense at all. It was an ingeniously contrived lock pick which broke into two pieces, a pick and a torque wrench. He carefully inserted the torque wrench into the lock and gave it a bit of practiced tension. With his other hand, he slipped in the pick and let it slide over the springed posts inside the body of the lock. It had been some years since Eli had negotiated the picking of a lock of any sort.

After a few gentle probings, all the while listening to the tensions and resolutions of the music in his head, there was a satisfying click and the torque wrench spun clockwise and the lock gave way.

ChApTeR 58

Which was how Eli came to possess the bag of broken green glass. How was he going to make use of it?

"I learned some tricks along my way," Eli replied when I spoke this question to him. "If you still feel safe with me, c'mon back into my smelly car and we will start with the relevant detective work straight away."

"I feel safe with you, Eli," said Cot, looking up at him like he was a firefighter just finished conveying her from a burning window.

"How 'bout you, Johnny?" Eli asked, turning to me.

"I don't like that you can know my thoughts without me even telling you, Eli."

"Well it's not really like that, but - tell you what, Johnny," he said, gathering up the contents of his wallet, "I promise you, that unless the situation is very grave, like someone's life is at stake, I will never use my music to- know more about you than you are willing to give up your own self, ever again. How's that sound?"

"Like a promise you won't be able to keep," I responded, but still I put up my hand and spit into it. After a moment of confusion, Eli realized what I was about, and spit into his wide-open palm, and we shook, my own hand disappearing into his.

As we left the lot of the library, the old man at the door followed our movement wistfully, as if we were friends leaving on a long journey. I was happy to see the door open behind him. Mrs. Tunket, the town librarian, grumpily motioned the old man inside. He barely acknowledged the gray lady, and just kept watching our car, as I kept watching him.

Our destination, Kimberly's Liquors, was, by quick estimation, just about to open for business. The proprietor of the ancient establishment was Kim Lewis, but she was not the titular Kimberly. The store was named for her predecessor in the womb, also named Kimberly, but stillborn, all those many years ago.

In defiance of this fact, the living Kim, some 50 years old now, talked to the Kimberly who was never born, all through the day, her whole life long. She cared not a whit who might be in earshot. She had done so since she was a little girl. This was impressive, because no one in our town considered her to be all that crazy.

After Eli's description of our town's more exceptional residents, I was given to wonder if perhaps Kim was special too.

In any event, Kim Lewis was one of Copeland's priceless fixtures.

"Eli Holly I see you there and I can hardly believe my eyes," said Kim, the second we walked in. "Kids," she added by way of greeting to Cot and myself, but she did not so much as glance our way.

"Hey there, Kimberly. Been a long time. You ain't changed a lick," said Eli.

"You call me Kim," she said, with a glance to the side, as to somehow differentiate herself from her ghost sister, who was apparently standing right there.

"But you know that, Eli." Kim said. "Kimberly says hello."

"Good to see you Kimberly," acknowledged Eli, which caused Kim some mirth, given that Eli could see no one there.

Then Kim narrowed those eyes of hers and said to no one we could see: "I remember. I won't. 'Sides he's a grown man and seen his share of grief these last weeks." She returned her attentions to Eli and said, "I am so sorry for your loss. We loved Theda and your dear Momma as our own."

"Thank you, ladies," said Eli to the woman standing before him. "That does help, more than I can say."

Eli took Kim's outstretched hand and they stood gazing at each other in silence across the counter.

After a bit, Kim broke the spell and slipped her hand free, saying, "What can I do y'all for? I hope you aren't here to buy liquor for these children."

"Not as such, Kim," laughed Eli. "Nope, I am here on business, I guess you might say, but business that I can't have people knowing about."

"I never did much talking to people 'bout how money gets spent in my establishment. Now are you gonna tell me what you need, or am I gonna have to whup you like I did when I caught you and your little shoplifting friends. You remember."

"I remember well Kim. True as a Cherokee arrow you are. And a harsh disciplinarian."

Kim laughed quietly and indicated the whole of the store with a sweep of her hand.

Eli said, "I will have a case of Dell Point Lager in the bottle, Kim."

Kim stopped her laughing and set about looking quite grim. She started to speak, unknown if to Eli or to her ghostly sister, but then, with a concerned look at Cot and I, she clammed up and pointed to the far back corner of the store. "Doesn't come any other way Eli. But you probably know that too, don't ya?"

"I do Kimberly," he replied, equally as grim.

"Kim, goddamnit!"

I glanced back through the window as we walked out. Kim was having an animated discussion with Kimberly, raising her arms and pointing.

"Is she nuts or does she really have a ghost sister?" Cot asked Eli.

Eli glanced back to see Kim's antics in the window.

"I honestly have no idea," Eli replied.

After Kim's we made quick to the hardware store, where Eli charged us to purchase some Plaster of Paris. When we returned with it, we demanded Eli explain what he had up his sleeve.

"It's simple," he said. "I am going to take one of these bottles and empty it out. Then I am going to fill it with Plaster of Paris, and when that dries, I am going to break off the glass. Then I will have a Plaster of Paris mold of the interior of a Dell Point Lager bottle--"

"--And you're gonna take the pieces from the evidence bottle and build them around the Plaster of Paris!" shouted Cot.

"Exactly," said Eli, clapping Cot on the shoulder. "Just like a puzzle. Hopefully, when I am done, I will be able to pull some kind of finger or palm print from across the pieces. I won't be able to do much with it, except compare the print with folks you or me suspect. But that just might be enough."

"Where do you plan on doing this Eli?" I asked.

I guess I'll just go back to my own house," he said, "It's not like my presence here is a secret any longer."

Eli said this with a look of dread across his face like he was going to spend the night in a haunted house. As if he did not look forward to the prospect of the dark hours alone with the fresh-turned ghosts of his sister and his mother.

Robert Spande
The Born and the Made

Part 2

The Heart-Shaped Forest

"The mere presence of the idea was irresistible proof of the fact."

-Mary Wollstonecraft Shelley, *Frankenstein*

ChApTeR 1

The reconstruction of the smashed green bottle transpired in the basement of Eli's house.

Over the course of that month, the area devoted to the bottle's rebirth came to resemble, more than any other thing, a sort of shrine.

First, there was the curiously colored rug, deep red and oval, from some unknowable source, but seeming to have been snatched from the narthex of a cathedral. Atop this red richness rose an ancient secretary, dark of wood, ingenious in design. Eli showed us its many contrivant and hidden spots.

"This desk is from way back from the days when the Denizen family had control of the mill and the town. My momma made me promise it would go to no one other than my own offspring.

"But no offspring was forthcoming... "

Eli caressed the dark wood of the desk's outfolded top, pausing over a small depression marked by an inlaid rose. He pressed on the rose.

There was a click from underneath.

Eli reached under the desk. His hand emerged holding a sheaf of pictures, all grey and curled from a day long gone.

Eli shuffled through these pictures, pausing now and again, always careful to keep the images from our view.

Cot was awful impatient at this and kept trying to peek.

Eli was on to her and pulled them just out of her view, every time.

Finally, he came upon one picture and pulled it separate from the rest. This he placed faced down on the secretary. The rest went back underneath, a click signifying their swallowing by the ancient desk.

Eli handed the picture on the desk to Cot as if to reward her suffering impatience. She turned it around. Her eyes glowed at what she saw. She sucked in her breath. It stayed sucked in.

"What is it Cot?" I insisted.

"It's Momma and Miss Holly, and this boy... is this you Eli?" she asked.

Eli nodded his head.

I walked over, behind Cot, to see what she was looking at. The picture was in the lightest of grey tones, with a wide white border, jaggedly cut along the edges in the way of photographs of the 40's or 50's.

Three children played in the arc of spray from a garden hose, held by a hand belonging to some adult, the rest of whom was lost off-picture. The spray glinted white in the grey of the old photo. Eli was caught in mid-leap, jumping up through the spray, his child face contorted in agony or ecstasy, it was impossible to tell which.

"Did you have a crush on my mom, Eli?" Cot asked.

Eli practically blew snot out his nose in a chimera of gasping horror and snorting offense. He snatched the picture from Cot and handed it to me, silently fuming. He never did answer her.

Mom was caught in the background of the picture, just evading focus by a hair, which made her seem ghostlike amid the shiny grey. She looked up in an admiring way at the boy conquering the sprinkler, as if he were conquering something more imposing than the strands of weakly ascending water at low pressure. Theda Holly stood next her, in a bathing suit that looked pure black, her arms folded. She was almost stern as she looked directly into the camera, her eyes veiled in a dark shelf of shadow from her bangs. Why did I have to see that?

It threatened to turn my reluctant mind to her.

For it was during this stretch of time, thank the stars above, that my dreams finally began to change their shape, their content. No longer did I dream every night of my lost Miss Holly. She began to drift away and dissipate, such that, even when she visited me, I would sometimes not see her, even when looking right into her face. I wondered on waking if Miss Holly would approve, or would she be sad at this turn of events?

Then, one night, I had a dream of a place like my school, but not quite. The sky above was impossibly blue, the clouds so white, with shadows that painted a solidity and weight that clouds could never have in waking life. The school building (for I was, for some reason, sure that it was a school) was of a deep rusty brick that, like the clouds and sky, was of a color too deep to be believed.

When belief has no place to hide, like in a dream, it submits, and rolls over, like an old dog.

Adria and I kissed in a corner there, in a darker place where the brick walls met.

I, the dream viewer, watched myself kissing her from a short distance, but the feelings in me were those of a participant. My God, the contentment, like a force or a wave, bathing me from head to toe. And the Warm.

The dream may have only lasted a moment, a mere glimpse or a snapshot of our two wrapped, kissing figures, but the epic infusion into my soul of such romantic joy, prefigured every thrilling kiss I was ever yet to have.

I woke from the dream irretrievably in love with my teacher's daughter.

This dream was the final antidote for my fascination with Miss Holly, and her death. Following its visit, I found some rough peace with Theda Holly's passing, which transformed into just what it was: the untimely severing of a beautiful soul from this world.

I still loved and missed Miss Holly. I still mourned her. But, with the arrival of this dream of kissing Adria, I realized that, as callous as it sounds, I could live without her. I could continue to thrive and grow and love, even though the primordial generator of the very machinery of my love was no longer in the world.

But, of course, it was too late.

ChApTeR 2

Eli did just as he said. He poured out all the beer out of one of the bottles we'd bought from Kim and her ghostly sister. He poured in a mixture of plaster of Paris, all the way to the top. He set the green bottle atop the wooden, inlaid secretary, to fix the plaster in the dark of his basement.

The next morning, with a loving gentleness, Eli proceeded to tap spider web cracks into the green bottle with a tiny geological hammer. When the cracks webbed the glass to degree and order sufficient to his taste, he got a fluffy towel from the bathroom. He reverently wrapped the towel around the bottle, leaving only the green mouth exposed.

With a look of significance at both Cot and me, Eli took in a breath, raising the little hammer, and brought it down on the bit of green sticking up from the towel. The room filled with a tinkling, snowfall sound.

He then delicately unwrapped the towel from what now remained only as white, bottle-shaped column of plaster.

With that, Eli abruptly stood up from his stool and shooed us unceremoniously upstairs, out of his house. We had to leave the bottle alone for a little while, he said.

ChApTeR 3

That month, Cot came with me on Comic Book Day.

The sun was shining, with nary a cloud to disperse or dissuade a single ray. Snow had already been falling for a few weeks, and a recent storm left a good layer of the white stuff over everything. The world, as a result, was blinding.

I didn't know why Cot was so invested in joining me, but she wouldn't take no for an answer. Perhaps it was so she could ask me the following question.

"Why you gotta be in love all the time these days?" she asked, as we walked.

I did not like this question. It seemed expository of a fault in my character.

However, Cot's exasperation was sound, reluctant though I was to admit it. First, Miss Holly, and now my obvious beguilement by Adria. To Cot, it must have seemed like I was overcome by an exotic disease to which she, herself, remained immune.

"I don't know Cot, it's like I suddenly can't help myself," I said.

"You're like a whole different person these days," Cot observed.

"I bet it'll hit you even harder, " I warned her.

"No it will not!" she insisted. "Why would I want to get all goofy and dreamy? I got stuff to get done."

"I ain't reassured," I said.

"You're a zombie."

"You're a medusa."

"You're a artichoke."

"You are the fire hydrant outside the VFW that all the dogs and half the customers pee on."

"YOU ARE A...!" Cot bellowed, and suddenly she was wrapped around my knees and biting into my thigh, but lightly, and I was laughing, and falling like a bolo-ed ostrich.

"I am a what?" I laughed into the dust of the road.

"You are a... something," was Cot's muffled reply through her biting grimace.

With difficulty, I disentangled my legs from the complex of her grabby limbs and teeth.

This scene dispelled my discomfort at Cot's questions, somewhat. But it got me to thinking that Miss Holly had indeed opened a space in me, a space that was going to want to be filled from now on.

Cot's blue eyes raked mine and I thought for the hundredth, the millionth, time how lucky I was to have her still with me, and not dead from her attack on the road.

She snorted and shook her head in pity at me. She probably thought my goofy look had something to do with Adria, or Miss Holly, not realizing it was all for her.

Comic Book Day that bright December morning heralded yet another tale of Gods meddling in the affairs of mortals.

This one was Homer's The Iliad. I was gazing at the cover, making connections, wondering if the Gilburton company was trying to tell me something, when Cot asked if she could look at it, as if to see what all the trouble was about. I foolishly handed her the comic, and that was the last that I saw of it till long after we got home.

"This is really something," she said at one point.

"What? What is?" I asked, hoping for an inroad to recapturing The Iliad, but it was not to be.

Sensing my unalloyed subterfuge, Cot angled away from me, to the other side of the road, without a word.

You may wonder if Cot's play of hookey, the day she was caught by a rabid Winky on his son's doorstep, got her into any trouble from the school, or our parents.

The fact is, none at all.

I had been home sick, therefore under no presumption of school attendance. Cot, on the other hand, was expected to have gone to school, which she never actually accomplished that day.

Cot and I discussed the problem. We decided it was best if she just pretended she had gone to school. Since our parents were both at work, they were none the wiser.

Fact was, in those days, kids often had to stay home for one reason or another. They helped their parents in their labors, or looked after littler ones, or any of a bunch of reasons that the immediacy of Copeland life demanded.

When Cot and I finally got home on Comic Book Day, I made such motions, grumblings and shufflings as to convey my desire to have my comic book back. Cot was too engrossed to give it up.

We played grab-and-evade. Cot scrabbled backward over the couch to escape my reach and was in her room with the door closed in a blink. Since I never opened Cot's door without permission, a hard-won and inviolable proscription, she was safe, for the moment.

About an hour later, Cot pushed open my door, an act that gave her not even a moment's pause.

"Cot you gotta knock," I yelled at her, angry that she ignored the very courtesy that saved her sorry ass only an hour before.

"Why, were you masturbating?" she asked innocently.

"Cot! Where in hell did you hear that word?" I demanded.

"I heard it from you, Johnny. You were talking to the Baker kid about Barbarella from the magazines. I looked it up in the Funk and Wangle's."

"Stop eavesdropping on me and give me my damn comic."

"So, you were masturbating."

"No goddamnit, I was not masturbating. Now don't ever say that word to me ever again, and give me my comic book!"

"Did this really happen?" she asked as she put The Iliad into my hand. From what little I had seen of The Iliad's cover, displaying Zeus himself, directing the events of some ancient battle, I was pretty sure it had not.

"I don't know cuz I have not had a chance to read it, thank you!" I said, with great umbrage.

"Have fun masturbating," said Cot, as she left the room.

ChApTeR 4

The last day of school before Winter Break found Mr. Edwards in an uncharacteristically awful mood. He brooked no shenanigans on this presumably lax day before we were all set loose on the world for our two week furlough.

Too bad for Cot, who presumed otherwise and got herself in hot water for fighting with Danny Snitches on the playground.

"But Mr. Edwards it's the last day! You don't want to have to stay after school." she pleaded.

"On the contrary Cot, you have a huge number of school days before you. I would like nothing better than to assure myself that you will comport yourself in a more ladylike fashion through every single one of them," Mr. Edwards assured her.

"Besides you and Danny can help me close down the classroom."

So it was that Adria and I walked out of school that last day together, unencumbered by Cot's jealous curiosity at what was growing, unspoken, between us.

I still held tight to my dream of us kissing. Through many a classroom lesson, I fell into a disreputable state of fantasy, where, upon my ruled Big Chief notepad, whole adventures starring Adria and myself played out, unwritten, undrawn, as if the notepad were a window into another world, where my wishes were manifest and reachable.

Adria, like her father, was not herself. I tried to catch her eye throughout the day. The few times I succeeded, she was quick to look away from me, at anything else, it seemed.

"Adria," I asked. "What is going on? You haven't said a word to me, won't even look me in the eye. Did I do something to make you mad?"

Adria kept her eyes downcast on the road and didn't say anything for a long time.

"My family had a real tough day yesterday Johnny. We-" and there she stopped. To my surprise a sob welled up from inside her.

"Adria! What is it?"

We had stopped on the road. Adria, still not able to look at me, covered her face in her hands and wept loudly.

"I- we- lost-"

She could say no more. Her sobs soaked her mittens. I pulled Adria toward me. I hugged her as if she were a porcupine, which is to say halting and tentative, all the while trying to ignore the thrill it gave me to do so.

But Adria turned my uncomfortable, fumbling embrace around, falling into me in a way I cannot describe, her wet face buried in the folds of my winter coat.

I whispered, against my own intention, "It's ok, baby."

Adria suddenly stopped her crying and looked up at me. Her face was beautiful. Her eyes were wet all around and droplets glistened in her lush lashes. The lids were heavier, darker and thicker than before and the effect was, no doubt, what women the world over attempt with expensive eyeshadows.

Adria's face possessed a new vitality, especially her lips, which were smooth in their fullness. I wanted badly to kiss her, and in her vulnerable state, I believe she would have kissed me back, just to push whatever was troubling her far away. I looked from one tear dazzled brown eye to the other, waiting for her to talk.

But she didn't say a thing. Instead, she grabbed my hand in hers and pulled me running. We weren't carrying much for books, given the Christmas holiday, and soon we were running full bore, so fast our hands broke apart, and toward where, I had no idea.

We ran up Pleasant toward Builder's Cemetery, in the distance of which, lay the slowly growing clump of simple houses where Adria and her family lived.

Just past the cemetery, Adria moved sidelong in her running, into the forest that guarded the southern edge of the cemetery road. This unexpected change of direction resulted in my catching my boot on a root. I sprawled, an unwilling and inverted snow-angel. Adria waited patiently as I got right and brushed myself off. There was the hint of mirth in her tear-iced eyes as she started off again, but at a careful walk.

We slow-footed it through the snow covered forest. The crispness of the afternoon brought me all up to a moment. For the 10 seconds or so following, I made a memory, just walking through the pretty woods, with a pretty girl, and those 10 seconds are with me still.

When Adria stopped, not too far in, we were in a small clearing. The bright circle of visible sky above us gave shelter from the penetrating dark of the forest.

Adria pointed to a snow-blanketed mound in the middle of the clearing. After a few moments of staring at it, the mound resolved into the relief of a medium-sized, four legged animal. I guessed a dog.

"That is my dog, Buster. Daddy found him on the road yesterday, coming home from school." Adria was crying again, but kept on.

"He came and got me, on account of Buster was mine. Daddy said the ground was too hard for burying, so we brought him here, to this pretty place, and laid him down."

Adria crouched by her fallen friend, silently weeping all the while. I could tell she was mulling over whether to brush off Buster's face. She decided against it.

Instead she stood up and walked close to me.

"Thank you, Johnny," Adria whispered, and this time she hugged me. I didn't know what to say, so I just hugged her back, and, again, did my best not to enjoy it too much.

When Adria was done with her hugging, as I reluctantly loosened my grasp, she placed a light kiss where my jaw met my neck, just below my ear.

Maybe she was trying to give me a friendly kiss on the cheek and missed. Where she landed it, instead, was such a nexus of intimate pleasure, I felt my legs weaken, such that I threatened to topple us both over onto Buster.

I quickly turned around and started out of the forest, so she would not see whatever confessional portrait was playing across my face.

More than that, her kiss had sent a jolt straight down from my neck, to my loins, giving me the quickest, full erection I had, as yet, ever experienced. It was as if it had simply exploded into existence, straining visibly against the front of my corduroys.

I was mortified.

During the course of our exit from the forest, I made some adjustments and forced myself to calm down.

By the time we hit the road, things were better and I could turn to Adria. She was looking at me, kind of confused, as if she were wondering if her kiss had been a mistake. Then, it seemed she couldn't look at me at all. I felt terrible.

I was just trying to hide my hard-on!

"Well, thanks for letting me show you, Johnny," Adria said, switching her eyes between this horizon and that. "That's why I been sad today. My daddy too."

"Punishing Cot is probably making him feel much better right about now. I know it would me," I said.

She laughed and that made me laugh. I grabbed her hand and she let me. We walked like that down the cemetery road, both our moods elevating, every step.

Holding Adria's hand seemed to rejuvenate me, not just in spirit, but in body too, like she was vitamins and minerals and fruits and vegetables and all those things we were told to finish off our dinner plates to make our bodies strong.

The road turned a corner around the cemetery fence. We kept walking straight through a field of churned, frozen earth.

We parted there, but before we did, there was a communication between our four eyes, each one had a say. That look promised we would look after one another, tell each other our secrets, and that we were sweet on one another. There were no more hugs, certainly no kiss.

Just the sweet promise.

I turned away, exuberant, wild. I wanted to scream and run, just to dissipate the enormous energy Adria inhabited in me.

But I didn't want her to see. I just walked purposefully away from her, back toward the cemetery, with only a few furtive looks behind me at her dwindling figure. It started to snow again.

Perhaps, if I had not been fighting this massive internal battle, I might have seen the red Mustang lurking on the cemetery road, where it bent away around the fence.

ChApTeR 5

When I got home, there was bad news waiting. Both my parents were there, which was odd, because they usually got home hours after Cot and I did. My Mom had been crying. My dad was getting her a glass of ice water from the fridge.

When I came in, they both looked at me with something akin to resigned sadness, which caused my guts to drop. They tried to change their faces, but I knew what I saw.

"What's going on?" I demanded. "Is Cot ok?"

Then I heard a door from the hallway swing open. Cot came out to the dining room. She looked wretched and sad, even worse than my parents did.

"Mom and Dad got fired from the Mill today, Johnny," was what she said.

ChApTeR 6

FROM THE JOURNAL OF COT CLEARY

I never saw my momma brought so low as that. She was a kitchen zombie for many days after Winky fired her and Daddy. Just shuffled around in her robe all day long. She even did dishes she had already done, just like Molly White did, but I don't believe it was to help her think. She just never noticed the dishes were already clean.

Daddy was different though. He bloomed like no flower ever bloomed. He wore a big smile whenever Momma wasn't around, and when she was around he was constant trying to get her to look on some bright side he could see, but she could not.

She never even looked up when he did this, but he kept on.

One day, Daddy said something to her, I couldn't hear what it was, but he seemed to break through Mom's darkness. She kept looking down, but her mouth curled up at the ends, just a little. I could see she was fighting hard to keep on frowning, but she just couldn't do it.

"God-DAMN it's good to be away from that mill!" was what Daddy said, loud, and to us all, five times a day, if he said it once.

Him and Momma were good savers, and I was a good saver, because of trying to be like them. So, at first it never appeared to me that we were hurting for money. I had a lot of money saved up, and I just put it in the money jar and didn't tell a soul, not even Johnny, cuz I knew they'd never let me do it. Probably about 50-60 bucks I put in there. They never said nothing about it, so I don't know if they noticed it or didn't. Don't mind either way, it was fine with me.

Daddy's new haunt was his garage, and he spruced it up super nice, with all the tools one day hanging from hooks on a big home-made board that had holes drilled all over in even rows, just like at the hardware store.

Daddy took Johnny and me fishin' down by the Old Cross probably every other day. We ate a lot of fish after they lost their jobs.

Worse than anything was our sorry, screwed up Christmas. We couldn't afford presents so nobody got any. For some reason, Mom and Dad were giddy about this and kept saying it was "magical" and a "really real Christmas." Even Johnny told me he liked it, cuz Christmas didn't stress him out for the first time ever.

"I like that I don't have to pretend to like my gifts," he told me. What a maroon.

I thought it just plain stunk.

The only thing that saved Christmas was a little package left on our doorstep. Johnny ended up kicking it across the yard as he went out the front door. He snuck the package back in the house with the firewood he'd been sent out to fetch.

While Mom and Dad kept drinking wine and getting disgustingly googley with each other under the Christmas tree, we went to his room to open the package.

It was from Eli.

Inside the brown paper package, were two objects, both old, both beautiful.

A black lacquered fountain pen and a magnifying glass with an ebony handle.

Underneath was a scrap of paper.

"To The Intrepid Reporter and the Hard-Boiled Gumshoe.

Merry Christmas.

E."

I love that man!

We asked Daddy a thousand times why he and Momma were fired.

He just said "Cutbacks," but he said it like he didn't believe it. Of course, Johnny and I knew why they were fired.

It was because of me.

That was an awful feeling, deep and sharp in me that I was responsible. I couldn't sleep at all well for about a week because of it and the only reason I did not resort to being a sad zombie like Momma was that I was worried that such a mood might tip them off as to my terrible guilt.

Johnny did his best to convince me that I was not to blame, but I knew that I was. I knew that that Winky had put it all together, the girl he saw snooping on him and his son, with the girl who looked daggers at him in Momma's office, both girls being me.

What Winky didn't think about was, now I had nothing to lose. He could only fire my parents once, and that was all he had over our family. As far as I was concerned it was now open season on that old bastard.

ChApTeR 7

It all seemed to quicken at this point, in every sense.

Events began to crash, to push each other out of the way, in a rush to confront us, headlong.

So too, these events began to connect in non-random ways, in knitted patterns that were, for their part, more destabilizing than the events themselves.

Robert Spande
The Born and the Made

The Second Tale of Isobel Whitehead-Patrick
Late September, 1939

It was the final day of their journey. In fact, they were docked at Ellis Island already, moored against the dark, wooded edge of the concrete disembarkation platform. The hold reeked of human tension strained to snapping. It was not the whole of the passengers who would be leaving for the immigrant processing station, only the passengers in steerage like Jake and Sarah, excepting Isobel, who was already a U.S. citizen.

The more well-to-do of the passengers, even those who had never set foot in America, would then head fast for the mainland to be admitted into the country by virtue of less dehumanizing measures.

America in 1939 was becoming suspicious of, and cold to, the disenfranchised Jews of Europe, as the numbers in their fleeing emigrations increased to tipping over some unknown allotment.

"The Jewish People, the people of Zion, are very fond of trees you know, Izzy. We even have a New Year's Day for them," said Jake, returning to the conversation of tree-related matters that had dominated the first day of their trip and had continued intermittently ever since.

Isobel was watching Sarah at his feet chide her few belongings, all of which (including the spool of thread) had attained an anthropomorphic dimension during the course of the voyage.

"I grew up in Zichron, near the sea. It was an agricultural community you know, at first, but by the time I was born, there was a kibbutz. I was among the first kibbutzniks."

Isobel had no conception of what he meant, but nodded just the same.

"The youngest children who knew how to read and write, which is quite young in kibbutz, we were tasked with keeping track of the ages of all the fruiting trees, or – what?"

"Fruit bearing trees," supplied Isobel.

"Of course – fruit bearing trees - thank you Izzy. The youngest had to keep track of the ages of all of the fruit bearing trees in the kibbutz. This New Year's Day, what we call Tu b'Shevat, was what you might say - a mutual birthday for the trees. Tu b'Shavat is an old, old holiday, a mystic one, heavy with Kabbalah. But by my day it had more of an ecological, how would you say... flavor." Jake's face attained the wistful. He said, absently, "Such good plans – if only I had stayed..."

"Then you would not have met Momma and you would not have had me," Sarah protested, quietly.

"Oh, my sweetheart, of course you are right. Forgive me," Jake implored, as if coming to his senses after a mad speech. "If I had stayed in Zion I would only have remained a stupid unloved boy and on the day of your otherwise-birth, the earth would have opened up and swallowed me whole."

Sarah breathed out a nervous giggle that rang in the metal of the bunk. She hugged her father.

Isobel was touched to see how easily the girl was mollified, as if this exchange was a ritual of some kind, as if Jake had unguardedly said these words in Sarah's earshot before. Jake gave his daughter a tight hug. His eyes were rimmed and red, giving Isobel to wonder if he did not indeed regret bringing so lovely a girl into so ugly a world.

Isobel was increasingly sad, almost fraught with gloom, as the time came to say goodbye to Sarah and Jake. The three had become close during the previous weeks. Isobel, Jake and Sarah had coalesced into the approximation of a family, an impromptu arrangement they all fell into effortlessly, if not a little guiltily.

For Jake and Isobel were akin in some indefinable way, a way that lured them, one toward the other. An attraction that brought their shoulders or elbows, or most scandalous of all, their unshod outer wrists into passing physical contact, broken apart in a shock of surprise - surprise at the sudden human warmth amid the cold steel of their circumstances, surprise at how welcome that passing warmth proved to be.

Yet this was never so much as acknowledged nor addressed. Jake and Isobel resolved unspoken to simply bask together throughout the voyage, as a team, bereft of all outward acknowledgement.

"We only have so little time left, Izzy. I mentioned the word Kabbalah just now. Are you familiar with that word?"

Isobel shook her head.

"When I said that Tu b'Shavat was 'heavy with Kabbalah,' I meant that the holiday was once shrouded in Jewish Mysticism, which we refer to as Kabbalah. I want to talk to you about a few aspects of Kabbalah that I think might apply to your theories. I want to do this before we part. I would have brought this up sooner, but I was not so sure I was right in my remembering. I talked to a few of the Rabbis on board and they have set me straight. Do you mind?" asked Jake.

"Do I mind?" asked Isobel with an osmotically acquired terminal uplift, distinctly Yiddish. "I am always beyond delighted to discuss my theories!" she exclaimed with a wink to Sarah, who was befuddled.

"Ok, ok Izzy, calm down now," said Jake patting the air, acting as if she were bouncing off the walls of the hold. Isobel fake-fumed, like in the movies, causing Sarah to giggle behind her hand. They all came to their senses simultaneously, realizing they were having a bit too much fun with each other, and the low guilt returned to settle amongst the trio. As he always did when confronted by these feelings, Jake said a small prayer to his wife, also named Sarah, and to God, and asked them both for forgiveness.

Jake started up again, determined afresh to ignore what padded just outside the glow of their conversational fires.

"Have you ever heard of the Guf?" he asked.

"Did you say the gulf?"

"No, the Guf. G-U-F."

Isobel shook her head. "No, I have never heard of the Guf."

"Ok now listen up. The Guf is a place in the highest heaven, near the Throne of Glory, a treasury of souls, sometimes called the Chamber of Creation, from which are plucked the souls, you know, that inhabit us all. This is Jewish mythology, now. The souls that fill the Guf are blossoms ripened on the Tree of Life in heaven. They grow fat, ripe, and then fall from the Tree of Life into this Guf where they are amassed in numbers that boggle your mind-"

"The mind," corrected Isobel.

"-numbers that boggle the mind. Their brilliance casts the heavenly glow. Yet there is a finite number of soul blossoms. It is said that when the Guf is empty, and people start being born dead, yet alive, like animals, that is when the Messiah will come."

"But, Jake as you know, I conceive of the Tree of Life as a phenomenon that exists on the earth. That is instrumental to my dissertation, my belief."

"Have you seen this tree, Izzy? Is that why you follow this course of study so deliberately?" Jake asked, pointedly.

Isobel looked long at Sarah, who gave no indication that she had been anything but thoroughly asleep when Isobel had bared her soul about the mysterious occurrence when she was 10 in the Heart-Shaped Forest.

"Please Jake, go on with what you were saying." Isobel said, in a tired way.

Jake seemed for a moment to bridle, about to take exception, until it diminished and he shrugged.

"Alright, Izzy, alright. Now this Tree of Life in heaven is a double of the one on earth, so everything is all right, I am not out to explode your precious theory. This is exactly the meaning of 'on earth as it is in heaven,' for heaven's sake. There are two trees, one on earth and one in heaven, and there can be conceived a conduit between them, a column, called the..." and here Jake paused and referred to a slip of paper Isobel only just noticed he held. "...Column of Service and Fear of Heaven."

Jake bashfully looked up at Isobel and gave a little shrug. When Isobel looked again the piece of paper was gone.

"This conduit between the two trees has something to do with the processes of birth and death, the Guf, the Chamber of Creation, the angels and all that. Anyway this myth, this conception of heaven, of which there are innumerable and conflicting alternatives in Jewish mythology, came to my mind when you talked about the bond between humanity and trees beyond death. I talked to a Rabbi, we discussed it for some time, and there is more." Jake considered her face as if searching for permission to continue.

"Please go on, Jake," said Isobel.

"Ok, let's see. We have all kinds of myths about souls. Jewish mythology is somewhat obsessed with them. Some say Adam was created with all the souls there would ever be. Some say there were 600,000 souls exactly, one for every letter of the Torah. Some myths refer to souls of greatness, some, souls that fled from Adam before his fall. Some myths refer to a council of souls, a so called "Divine Assembly," that advised the Creator in the creation of this jewel, the Earth. Some say that male souls come from the Creator, but that female souls come from His Bride!"

Isobel considered this. "I think that's an interesting twist," she said.

This gave Jake a moment's pause, before he continued:

"There was a Rabbi, a devout seeker of knowledge who was called The Ari, the Lion. He lived in Syria in the 16th century and is now considered one of the fathers of all that is Kabbalah. The Ari was seen by his students on more than one occasion talking to the trees, to no person that the students could see.

"The Ari believed that souls not only resided in trees but took refuge, in huge groups, and from what, he never did say, in trees. That, trees were places of souls, where souls resided, where souls hid. He developed rituals that are still observed by some, based on these beliefs. The Ari's thoughts were collected in a book called, coincidentally, The Tree of Life."

"Do you believe all of this?" asked Isobel.

"I believe none of it," said Jake, "Jews are not so literal as you Christians seem to need to be. But there is a knowledge in myth, in poetry, in madness, so I believe that concepts like the Tree of Life, so enduring and pervasive, speak to some ineffable truth.

"The Flood is a good example. There are too many stories, in too many lands, in texts that far precede Judaism or Christianity, that describe a Flood, for me to believe that such an event never happened in the memory of man. As to what all these concepts of the Tree of Life mean? I am too busy fleeing Death, to give it proper consideration, my dear, dear Izzy."

Isobel smiled, sadly. She put out her hand to both of them. First Sarah, then Jake, took her grip and they all squeezed. It seemed the pressure squeezed one tear each from the three of them. They said no words, but communed in silence, for they knew their last minutes together were fast approaching.

"I thought you would like to know these stories, Izzy. It's all I have to give to you," said Jake.

"I thank you more than I can say," said Isobel.

They held on like that for a long while, until the rude stewards (who had been a baneful lot the entire trip) started shoving people out from their section into a moribund line of humanity circuiting steel stairways and crossing further holds, upward into the sunlight.

As the three trudged up, they held on to each other as best they could. When they reached the wooden deck, to the throng pulsing there, contact proved finally impossible. Jake had to lift Sarah into his arms, already laden as he was.

Isobel did her best to stay with them, but when she reached the platform, she was ushered back toward the ship. She was a U.S. citizen.

The group of people from whom she had been plucked, like a fish on a line, continued onward.

The group trudged toward a stately building at the end of a short road that led from the dock. Isobel tried to see Jake and Sarah in that surge, but they were lost.

With a start of horror, Isobel realized that she was weeping aloud. She snapped her mouth shut.

After a mournful trudging through the ships innards, Isobel secured a seat at the bar, where she indulged in copious quantities of Kentucky bourbon, for the remainder of the journey.

~

The next morning found Isobel in a New York hotel room's bathroom, vomiting those quantities into the bidet, instead of the toilet, and realizing it only mid-vomit, which, for some reason, caused her to vomit all the more.

After a quick and necessary wash-down, Isobel fled that place with stunning speed, as the stench from her unflushable exertions emanated into the hallway.

She came out onto 53rd street on a chill morn before the world was awake. Vans and trucks displaying colorfully hand-painted slogans and logos, some even pulled by horses, ambled through the steam rising from the manholes.

She was immediately followed by a pack of boys, who clearly had designs on her one bag. Isobel waited until they were close to making their move, then pointed her Colt Cloverleaf revolver into their midst, which caused them to hoot and scatter. She crossed and hailed a cab.

Isobel spent the next two nights at the Allerton Hotel for Women on 57th.

There, she came into the acquaintance of a girl named Riley, who took her to a seventh-floor apartment to meet the girl's mother, Lori.

Lori had just arrived in New York from Minneapolis, to the promise of employment as a switchboard operator for the New York Telephone Company. Both mother and daughter were thrilled at their adventures in the city.

For Isobel, whose train did not depart until the following morn, and who found New York more confusing than London and Frankfurt combined, it was a comfortable move to fall in with them as they toured New York on their one day before Lori started work.

The three visited the World's Fair, at Flushing Meadows in Queens. The orb of the Perisphere and the spire of the Trylon shone before them, against the grey clouds above. They ambled through the promenades and the pavilions across that massive campus, in a daze of awe.

They spent the most time at the Czech Pavilion.

As Isobel now knew, thanks to Jake's impassioned reportage, the Czechoslovakia that had embarked on this proud, modern building was no longer the Czechoslovakia that existed. Czechoslovakia was now called the Protectorate of Bohemia-Moravia by its new ruler, Adolf Hitler.

Germany had no pavilion at all. Hitler had waffled and procrastinated so long on the decision to join the World's Fair that the New York World's Fair Corporation just went ahead and sold Germany's spots.

Mayor La Guardia said they should go on and make a German Pavilion anyway, as the World's Fair's House of Horrors. That comment may have contributed poorly to the overall situation. He also thought they should leave the Czech Pavilion unfinished, as a memorial to a murdered Republic.

"After the tempest of wrath has passed the rule of thy country will return to thee O Czech People," read the words at the entrance.

On Market street near Rainbow avenue, they stopped at the Star and Crescent for lunch. Isobel had Cold Columbian River Salmon with Mayonnaise, following an appetizer of stuffed grape vine leaves called Yalanji Dolmasi. Lori and Riley shared Half Roast Chicken a la Turque and a Chiffonade salad with Roquefort dressing. They could barely rise from their seats afterwards, they were so full.

~

Isobel could not help but worry about Jake and Sarah.

She knew they were headed to Ashkenazi relatives on a street called Hester in lower east side Manhattan, but beyond that, nothing. All she could do was hope for their safety, since neither Jake nor Isobel had provided the other any future contact information. It was an act of repentance for their unspoken partiality toward one another. At least, that was how Isobel looked at it and now she cursed the decision for a stupidity.

~

Isobel pushed into America, from New York to Chicago on a shiny new steam driven train called the 20th Century Limited Steamliner. The whole train smelled new and gleamed, leather and chrome alike. She slept and gazed out the window of her single coach, and read. She was troubled and perplexed at the state of the world that greeted her in the Times. If she was not mistaken, the clues in today's paper all pointed to yet another World War in the works.

Jake had taught her a lot about the state of things in the few weeks they had spent together. It was a learned and wise, yet terribly uninformed woman who had started that journey. Now that woman had the scales pulled from her eyes by a charming man she would never see again, as long as she lived.

Isobel was now aware of the aggressive competition between communism and nationalism in Europe in the wake of the Great War. She had been advised of the expansionist self-cannibalizing that both Russia and Germany seemed intent on pursuing, to the cost of untold lives, with untold more sure to follow. Both the Stalinists and the Nazis were building up their militaries, even as they protested otherwise. Hitler invaded Poland. Britain and France had already declared War on Germany. It was only a matter of time. Within its own sphere, Imperial Japan was overtaking vast lands and ruinating vast populations, with a horrid disregard. It was all too shocking, too depressing. No wonder she had hid her head in the sand these last years.

From her reading today, she was dismayed to see that America wanted nothing to do with any of it. Like Isobel herself had done until recently, the whole country was hiding itself from the truth. The paper was filled with intellectual arguments against involvement, but all Isobel could think of was the noise of the ship's hold and the dress of little Sarah, that she never changed, not even once. She thought about the surgeon who had to hide as a butler, about the man and the child who had to leave their family in the belly of a very hungry beast if any of them were to have any future at all.

Isobel fumed in silence at the stupidity of the world. Yet, behind all the churning and the crunching of metal over flesh, and the whine of infinitudes of bullets, Isobel suspected that the world was falling to pieces in a way that none of the actors in this idiot's drama even realized.

~

Isobel saw the green line of the Heart-Shaped Forest appear over the darkening grassland.

At the same moment, a wondrous smell suggested itself, a richness scored with subtle rewards increasing to an insistence in the back seat. It was pine and wild grass, petals and earth mixed with something, as-yet unknown, or, at least, up to this moment, unremembered. The heady odor filled Isobel with an upsurge of power and purpose, as if she could smash through the roof of the black Plymouth and soar to her destination on will alone. It was the Heart-Shaped Forest greeting her, specifically her, she was sure.

"Do you smell the forest?" Isobel asked her Mom and Dad, up front.

"You mean that forest?" asked her father incredulously, pointing at the green line. "The one that's at least three miles away? No, I do not smell the distant forest, Isobel," he finished chidingly.

"Didn't think so," said Isobel, with satisfaction.

"Be nice to each other, or I will kill the both of you," her mother said, sweetly.

They stayed silent the rest of the ride, which was fine with Isobel. She knew they were both mad at her for her strange behavior, quitting school and returning home under such conditions as she did.

When Isobel described her trip across the Atlantic in the company of a hold-full of diasporating Jews, her father shook and reddened worryingly, then looked around for a place to spit. When he opened his mouth to emit cutting insight, Isobel stopped him short with a searing look amalgamated of a score of unpleasant emotions that brought the poor man up short of breath. She had adopted far too many liberal European sentiments to listen to homegrown racist junk, the sort of junk for which her father was renowned.

~

They arrived at home around 9p.m. The stars were already out. By their light Isobel could make out colors in the trees that, come morning time, would blaze maddeningly. She made from the car straight for the forest, leaving her parents fretting as to her mental health.

"Isobel!" her father barked.

"Iz-zo-BEL!" her mother bellowed.

In response, Isobel said nothing at all, but scurried out of the glare of the headlamps into the shroud of total darkness just beyond. She was a small animal, no higher than the flurry of her feet, bounding over roots she could barely discern, around mounds of earthen unknowns, ducking the low hanging branches. She came back to herself a good way into the woods. The light from the car made the forest to the west of her glow strangely. Then the light winked out as her parents gave up all hope. The darkness resumed, causing the compensatory machinery of Isobel's eye to dance the black into wild shapes and waves, delighting her even more.

Isobel listened. Other than wind rustle and dab tap of falling things, she could hear nothing at all. Was the Heart-Shaped Forest listening to her, even as she listened to it?

"I'm here," she said softly. "I came back."

She held her breath and listened.

There was nothing. Only the forest, sleeping or listening, or maybe holding its breath too, anticipating what might happen next. She blew out her breath and sucked in another and held it.

Isobel listened.

She caught a weird tune in the air, and then realized it was her mother playing the piano with the window open, probably trying to entice her back on some bizarre level. "I'm Gonna Sit Right Down and Write Myself a Letter" floated to her on the stirring of the trees.

I'm gonna sit right down and write myself a letter, Isobel thought. That is what she had done. She had written herself a letter and a man in a dress walked out of the sea 10 years later and delivered it to her. And she had done what the letter said to do. She came back. She was here!

"Mabel Leone Lighty!" she yelped into the air, immediately regretting the act. The piano stopped.

"Isobel, sweetheart?"

Her elderly father's deeply concerned voice. Coming from between her and the house, somewhere in the forest.

"Dad, stop! You are going to get yourself hurt," Isobel commanded.

"Alright," said the man, with gratitude.

"I'm coming to you."

"Alright," said her dad.

Robert Spande
The Born and the Made

ChApTeR 8

There came a time, some weeks hence, when our parents told us they needed to scope jobs and houses in Hunstable, and other county seats, many miles to the north.

Work at the mill being foreclosed to them, their prospects in Copeland had dwindled to zero. They saw no alternative but to pull up stakes and make a go of it somewhere else.

It came to light, via episodes of espionage on Cot's part, that the Mill had some stake in our house, and was coldly calling in its marks.

All of this lit a fire under Mom and Dad, after their initial weeks of luxuriant joblessness, as our cabinets emptied, with dwindling means to refill them.

Our parents would be gone on this adventure for a period of some days, possibly four.

The situation necessitated that someone look after Cot and me, Lucius being off on his rehabilitation.

I took a choice opportunity, while Dad was fretting at his workbench in our mouse-smelling basement, to put forward the concept of leaving Cot and myself alone while they were gone, with me nominally in charge.

Dad seemed rather grumpy at this prospect.

Yet, I sensed that our parents were reluctant to turn to people they knew in Copeland for help, almost as if they did not want to divulge their intentions to anyone.

This sentiment manifested in an air of uneasiness that settled on our dinners and chores, where our possible futures were furtively discussed, sorted and weighed. We huddled in our insular bundle and made plans in our blind.

To my surprise, Mom and Dad ultimately conceded to my suggestion, probably because it was the method that least called their actions into scrutiny.

It was clear to Cot, from her eavesdropping, that our parents' plan was to disappear with us, some future night, leaving the husk of this house as a depreciated memory (as well as leaving debts and obligations to the very institutions that had brought us so low).

This scurrilous intent required planning and preparation, and necessarily, secrecy.

The word, "Burleymen" was heard by Cot, in her surveillance, on more than one occasion, though never in context, only as a floating word, only apprehended because of its presence on some pre-assembled hot list in Cot's head, as it was in every head in Copeland, and certainly mine.

The morning Mom and Dad left for Hunstable was a Wednesday. Mom tearfully kissed us both and wiped off the damage with her handkerchief. Dad picked Cot bodily up into the sky, causing her to whoop. He caught her just in the nick, settling her to the ground, with a kiss to her forehead.

Dad turned to me.

I will never forget the sense of humility my Dad exuded that day. As if he could not imagine the circumstances that had brought him to this degraded juncture, sneaking away in the pre-dawn hours, leaving his children unprotected, while he and Mom searched for an uncertain future.

Thus it was with a dark solemnity that he transmitted, as though through his grip on my hand, an imperative to PROTECT and to be SAFE.

When he was done imparting, he whispered to me,

"Just lay low."

I nodded.

"And go to school."

"Of course, Dad," I said.

"We will, Dad," said Cot.

We did not.

So began the harrowing final days, each one more amazing and terrible than the last, which conclude this story. Days that found us unsupervised, unfettered by anything but the drive to get to the bottom of the many mysteries that weighed us down in the recent months.

The Mystery of of the Murder of Miss Holly, and that other mystery, which, for loss of inspiration I will simply call The Mystery of Where We Lived, or perhaps more precisely: The Mystery of the Heart-Shaped Forest.

Instrumental to the former was Eli, and to the latter, Molly White.

After our parents left, Cot and I sat down to a strangely adult breakfast of cereal, the jar of sugar left on the shelf as if in signification of the suspension of all things childlike.

There we made our own dark plans.

ChApTeR 9

To suggest that Cot and I played the diligent detectives right off the bat might be an exaggeration.

No, that first morning the luxury of foregoing our school responsibilities wrapped us in a feline indolence too powerful to resist. After our cereal, we repaired to our respective beds until shortly before 9 am, at which time the phone in the living room rang and would not stop.

I was fearful to answer it in case it was Mom or Dad, checking to see if we had skipped class. At the same time, I felt sure it was not them. They were on a mission, one that held all our futures at stake. I doubted they even gave us a second thought.

With no little amount of trepidation, I picked up the phone and croaked my greeting, in case the need to pretend illness became of import. But it was only Eli, asking us to come over.

"How did you know we were home?" I asked, my voice miraculously cured.

"Cuz I waited outside your school all morning long, hoping to catch you two, but you were nowhere to be caught. I just wanted to ask you to come by after school. But since you are both playing hooky, why don't you come over now, and then I will drive you to class."

"Aw Eli!" I protested.

"None of your sauce laddie. By the by, I saw your girlfriend Adria. Quite a looker."

"She ain't my girlfriend, Eli."

"That's not what Cot tells me."

"Here, talk to her then."

I handed Cot the phone before Eli could even reply. Cot started chuckling in a conspiratorial manner the moment she got the phone to her ear.

Damn busybodies, I thought as I fled to my room and fell onto my bed with a bounce.

Of course, I had been thinking of Adria all morning long. The way she had kissed me that day in the forest temple of her departed dog. How she aimed for my cheek but somehow planted that kiss on my neck.

The look of promise we shared afterwards.

Warmth filled my face pleasurably. How comforting, the thought of a living girl my own age, who returned my feelings and shared my world. I was finally willing to admit my enamorment of Miss Holly had become enshrined as something else, an archiving perhaps.

Following that first afternoon in the forest, Adria and I stuck close to each other-- on the playground, choosing each other as partners for activities, our desks even seemed to inch closer together such that we had to occasionally scoot them back into place. I walked her home in the afternoons, holding her mittened hand in my own. One day it was unseasonably warm and all I could think about all day long was that it was warm enough to forego mittens altogether and clasp our bare hands, skin to skin, which we did, in fact, do. It was a mind-blowing experience that I will never forget, in this life of so many other unremembered assignations.

Such reverie was prone to popping like a soap bubble in the mere presence of a nearby Cot.

So, when she burst into my room after her commiserations with Eli, I exploded from my bed, arms flailing, growling like an animal. She was quick to slam the door closed, with herself on the other side of it.

"Eli has something to show us," came her voice, receding. After a short detour to her room, she sat on the front stoop, waiting for me to join her. I could hear her talking out there, to the birds most likely. I pulled on my jacket.

ChApTeR 10

We did not have to walk the whole way. After a short trek between the pines, Eli's car came rumbling toward us in a wake of dusty snow, rolling over the regular sine waves of the gravel road. When he stopped, I quickly got in the back, to give myself whatever distance the interior of his huge car afforded from Eli's strange abilities.

Eli gave me a smile in the rearview mirror, a smile I would come to know later in life as a shit-eating grin.

"What you got for us, Eli?" Cot asked, in her strange adult way, like an Executive Officer asking the Financial Officer for an update. Before he could speak, Cot put up her hand and stopped him dead, adding, "Thanks for the pen and the magnifying glass, those were real nice."

"Yeah, thanks Eli," I quickly added.

Eli didn't say anything for a second. Then he said, "Those were my Daddy's from before the War."

We all looked at each other gratefully, for a split second, before Cot ruined it by saying, "Eli, I hope you don't expect us to go to school if our parents aren't even here to make us go." She clearly found her statement warranted and ironclad, if her stately expression was any indication.

Eli looked exaggeratedly both ways as he turned a corner toward town as he asked, "What in God's Green Earth are your parents doing, leaving you alone like that?"

"I'm taking care of us, Eli," I said casually, as if it were an ongoing situation instead of the unheard-of rarity that it was.

Eli read between my lines and both smirked and snorted.

"You kids cannot be skipping school. That's all I know."

"Eli this is our chance, maybe our last and only chance, to really devote some time to helping you in your investigations," replied Cot.

Eli said nothing as he pulled into the driveway of his house.

As we walked down to the basement, Eli talked distractedly to us about the strangeness and emptiness of the house, so recently occupied by his sister and his mother. Eli told us he had to take all the family pictures down from their perches, just so he could concentrate. I noticed there was a ratty old twin bed in the basement now.

Eli saw me looking and said, "There's no sleeping in their beds."

I nodded.

I did not envy him one bit his status as the only remaining Holly.

I think that, as men, we grow up expecting to be the ones who die first, of bacon-related cardiac pathologies, or by manly misadventures, or perhaps a glorious war-time death, ripped to pieces by a loud bomb. It doesn't seem natural or fit that we should ever live to see our sisters and mothers go before us.

As Eli and I have both discovered, Death takes a different attitude.

"Here's what I wanted to show you," said Eli, as he unveiled the bottle of its velvet shroud.

Cot and I gasped. It was a true miracle. He had completely reconstructed it. The infinitude of cracks described a painstaking attention to detail, that, itself, beggared description. Some of the shards were so small as to be practically invisible. We both started for it, wide eyed, but Eli stopped us bodily.

"Don't touch it for God's sakes!" he practically screeched. We jolted to a halt.

"Did you dust it for finger prints yet?" Cot asked.

"Not just yet," he said, "I wanted to show it to you before I got it all messy."

"I can't believe it," said Cot, awestruck.

Eli was clearly a ball of nerves as Cot and I drew our faces as close as possible to his masterwork of reconstruction.

"I wish you two could have heard the music I heard during all of this. All music from The Private Lives of Elizabeth and Essex. It guided me like never before. I can only think it means that we are really on to something here."

"What are you going to do once you get the fingerprints?" I asked.

"He's gonna check 'em against the fingerprint files, right Eli?" interjected Cot.

I scowled at her.

"He stole the evidence, dumb-butt. He can't take his findings to the police."

"You're right, Johnny, I can't do that," Eli said, clearly uneasy at taking sides. Cot worked her way behind him, ostensibly to get a better look at the bottle, but taking the opportunity to give me the finger.

Eli continued.

"I am going to fast-track my results to a friend in Minneapolis and beg him to sneak what prints I might find into this program they are trying out up there. It uses computers to do in minutes what used to take battalions of fingerprint analysts, days, or even weeks, to accomplish. It might be our only hope to get some resolution on this in a timely manner. Cross your fingers."

Cot immediately crossed her fingers and then looked at me expectantly. I crossed mine and we both looked at Eli. He crossed his fingers too.

ChApTeR 11

Eli made us get into his car for the drive to school.

After Cot got in, Eli held me back by touching my arm and asked, "Your parents are thinking of moving you guys away?"

"That's what they said. And probably not too long after they get back."

Eli shook his head. "That can't happen," he said.

"What do you mean?" I asked.

"You should ask Molly White what I mean."

"Ok, I will," I said.

"Good lad." Eli patted me on the back as I bent down into the car's rear seat.

Cot began screeching into Eli's right ear the second he got in behind the wheel. We drove up County P, toward Rusholme Road where our school was, about a mile down. School kids always made great fun of this intersection. We were ever certain to tell anyone who asked where the school was, to make the appropriate turn at "rush home and pee."

"Eli! School's almost over anyway," Cot wailed!

"We are gonna catch even more trouble if we go at this late hour," she implored!

"Mr. Edwards is gonna smell a fish," she summarized!

Then she started afresh.

Cot kept up like this the whole ride.

I stayed quiet as a grave in the back seat, since I could tell that Cot's shrill voice was getting under Eli's skin. I could see his eyes rolling like a crazy pony's in the rearview.

Suddenly Eli pulled over to the side of the road.

"Jesus Christ and General Jackson! Get out of my car before my damn head explodes and go to school tomorrow or I swear you will know the reason why. I told you not to make a habit of this!"

Eli reached across Cot and threw open her door. She looked as confused as I have ever seen her and hopped out mutely. Eli looked at me in the rearview mirror and jerked his head for my evacuation as well, which I accomplished hastily.

When we were both out, Eli pulled the door closed and turned his car around through a series of backing-up and pulling-forward maneuvers, which I could tell were embarrassing to him, in the wake of his recent exasperation. Finally, he was set in a direction back toward his house and he zoomed off without a backward glance.

"Wow," said Cot.

"He ain't mad," I said, "He's just got stuff to do."

"Well I'm mad!"

"You better not be," I returned. Cot furrowed her brow and set her lips and finally said, "ok," in a little bird voice.

I think Cot had realized that, unbeknownst to her own self, she could be as strident and annoying as anyone.

If I may extemporize, such realizations comprise a hard-won wisdom of disillusionment, the main ingredient of what it is to "grow up." These insights nip at us as we grow, whittling our indomitable spirits down to more acceptable shades of their former selves.

Of course, there are so many people who never attain this sad wisdom, and remain blissfully unaware of the huge pains in the asses they remain, their entire lives.

Would that we could all be epic heroes, like Joan of Arc and Achilles, instead of small, imperfect souls!

ChApTeR 12

With us abandoned so close to the school, my thoughts again lit on Adria and how soon she would be walking this very road toward home.   Cot keenly knew where my mind was turning, mostly due to my fidgeting and sun-glancing and general unease in the direction of the school.

"You are one sickening monkey," she said.

She started walking back the opposite direction and added, "I am going home. See you later."

I made half-hearted monkey-invoking gestures, involving the scratching of my armpits and some shuffling around. But Cot was already walking toward home, away from my funny joke, without a backward glance, just as Eli had done only moments before.

Yet my attitude of enjoyable anticipation was un-derailable by those two. They could piss up a rope for all I cared!

The world had once again begun its funneling toward Adria and her dark, enveloping eyes. I was, literally, a fool for love, unassailable in my thick, dumb armor. I would not have tried to evade a rock, if one were sailing at my head just then.

So, when, from my hilltop crossroads, I saw Adria approaching in the great distance, after a few enjoyment-withered souls had already trudged mournfully past me, repulsed by the energy-of-adoration I was radiating, or so it seemed, I was caught in the belly by a sharp thrill and given to approval of the time honored metaphor of Cupid's Arrow. For it was like catching a quarrel in my belly, of adrenalin and anticipation, radiating intolerable pleasure to my distal parts.

Adria's wavering form resolved into two figures, as her father ran up and locked into step beside her.

My joy was as snuffed as a church candle.

Moreover, a rampant fear welled in me at the sudden prospect of being caught out in my malingering by Mr. Edwards! And on top of everything, my presence there was wholly to intercept his innocent daughter, to trip her up in pretexts of increasing intimacy and, if possible, adventures up to, and including, kissing itself!

I had no choice but to seek refuge.

But there was no place to hide.

I stood in the dead center of a stark country crossroads, Rushholme and P, bereft of accessible buildings or even municipal tchotchkes, such as benches and streetlights. Cyclone fences separated me from the few buildings that dotted the area. One huge Balsam Fir loomed just down the hill, probably kidnapped from its forest home, to live here so that this dreary spot did not propel passersby to suicide.

To that I scurried. I was quick to invade the tree's circumference and start up its branches. I settled in, about 12 feet up, glad to see Adria and her father still deep in conversation.

Yet Adria was nobody's fool.

As she passed me, her father extolling his wisdoms into the air, Adria looked up from writing in her notebook, and winked. It was as if her long lashes were Cupid's bow itself and the arrow of her wink caught me bodily, threatening to fling me from my perch. The thrill was almost too much to bear. I smiled like a madman.

Adria returned her attention to her father's words as if nothing was amiss. She tore out the page she was writing on, and, still appearing to listen to her father's inveigling witticisms, folded the note in half and then half again.

She reached back and put her notebook into her backpack and zipped it smartly. While she accomplished this, she allowed the folded paper to fall to the gravel behind them.

As it fluttered to the ground, I heard her say, "I don't believe that for a second," to which Mr. Edwards threw up his hands in mock defeat. Presumably he was unaware of the note his daughter dropped, but I could put nothing past the man. He was as preternaturally aware as my own father.

I waited for them to crest the next hill before I started down the tree.

ChApTeR 13

But then something caught my eye, causing me to stop my descent. It was a flash of light from a distant hill. The hill was a mound of mottled white and green about a half mile to the south of my location. A gravel road bisected the hill and at its apex there was a car. It was so far away, I had a hard time making out any details.

Then the sun was covered by a cloud and for some reason this helped me make out the specifics of what only moments before had been obscured by glints and shiny surfaces.

There seemed to be a man crouched down behind the car. I could see his silhouette break the smooth line of the car's roof. I don't know how I knew it was a man, but I did. Otherwise the car was too far away to make out anything further. The man behind the car had a good vantage of the whole area around the tree in which I hid.

Then, the sun cleared the clouds and I saw the wink of light again. It seemed to come directly from the head of the man crouched behind the car, as if he was wearing a monocle that glinted in the sun.

I realize now that a part of me must have known what I was seeing.

A fiery brightness occluded the head of the man behind the car.

The bullet arrived to hit the tree directly next to my face before the sound of the shot pierced the day. Splinters of fir tree and hot sap blasted the right side of my head. I lost my hold on the branch above me and fell through the tight-knit branches, to the needle-carpeted ground at the base of the tree.

ChApTeR 14

When I came to my senses, it was at the insistence of Adria's note, which the wind batted against my face, as if urging me to hurry up and read it.

I had no idea why I was on the ground, half under the skirt of a big tree. I sat up and the note remained attached to my face, glued there with some sticky substance. I pulled it off.

"Dear Johnny,

Meet me at the cemetery gates at 6!

Love,

Adria,"

said the note.

I looked around me and up in the sky, dazed and happy. I walked up the road hill, in the opposite direction that Adria and her father had gone, unaware of anything but the note and its author.

A murder of crows blackened the winter sky above me, their raucous laughter piercing the cold air. Perhaps that is what brought me back to the danger of my situation.

Or, perhaps it was the sound of the approaching car, growling toward me on the other side of the hill. The driver was pushing the engine to the brink of its capabilities. The car's ominous scream, as it accelerated toward me, just on the other side of the road's crest, slammed me with the remembrance of what had just transpired.

Someone had shot at me, tried to kill me!

And now I was as good as dead with no time to run. The raging sound of the engine was just over the hill.

My mind lit on Cot, and on Adria, and my Mom and Dad smiling down at me, as I only now realize, in a scene from my infancy.

Then the car screamed its loudest, the scream of a predator pouncing to kill, and came into view of my horrified eyes.

ChApTeR 15

As I said, there was no place for me to go, to escape. There was no time. I turned to run, but was overcome with the futility.

Hopelessness so strong, it bled the animation from my very muscles, suffused me, hobbled me. I dropped to my knees and started muttering the first word of a prayer to a God, who, at that time, I only marginally believed in. I clamped shut my eyes in a resolute acceptance of my death. And I waited for the end.

But the end did not come.

There was a horrible crunching sound and the ground shook before me.

The car was going so fast at the top of the hill that it had shot into the air as if over a ramp. The car sailed clear over my kneeling form and slammed with such force back onto the dirt road that my knees were bruised black and blue for nearly a month afterwards, the result of the tremendous concussion propagated through the road itself. The car's back end slammed into the dirt right in front of me, blowing me back in a shower of small rocks and dust.

I unclenched my eyes to see the rear lights fishtailing in a storm of dust. Whoever was driving got the vehicle under control and the whining scream of its engine caught again, as the car sped onward.

The engine shrieked a different tenor. Now, it seemed like a wail of frightened retreat as the driver, realizing failure, tried to flee the scene under the cloud of dust thrown into the air by the car's landing.

In this, the driver was fairly successful.

I watched the cloud of dust speed up the hill, the only recognizable vehicular features, the two red rear lights, squinting reproachfully at me from within its nebula. It soared over the next hill with another loud crash.

I surged with adrenaline, my thoughts crowded out by disbelief and amazement. I got shakily to my feet and shambled in the direction the car had disappeared. I was alive. I was alive!

I came to the realization that Adria and her father might be in danger, having traversed the very same hill as the marauding car only minutes before. This awareness struck me like a bolt and I sprinted to the top of the hill with all the speed I could muster.

And there they were, two tiny dots on an intersecting road, heading toward the necropolis of Builders Cemetery, and away from the danger of the speeding cloud. Beyond the cemetery lay the skirts of the forest.

From my privileged vantage I could see the Heart-Shaped Forest surrounding the entire town. The sky and the clouds inhabiting it were the closest I had ever experienced. I felt a weird sort of ecstasy, which I can only chalk up to the body-chemicals this reprieve from death left in me. The forest seemed to pulse and exude an undefinable aroma, even in its great distance from me, which caused my head to swim.

I felt strong, stronger than I had ever felt. I yearned to confront my would-be killer, who was surely the killer of my beloved teacher.

I roared after my nemesis.

The car that had tried to kill me was far in the distance, just a mote of movement, ever decreasing. It never turned any direction that might yield a

clue as to its occupant.

More importantly, it sped past the turn-off to my house, where my dear sister waited, unaware of the close call--the TWO close calls--that had nearly taken her brother from her.

Before I headed toward home, there was something I had to check out.

It did not seem possible that the crest of the hill was steep enough to send the killer car sailing over me the way it had. It did not seem possible. I shakily walked the low saddle back to the scene of the crime and examined the hilltop more closely.

I was shocked to find I was correct. The hill on the other side was steep, but not steep enough to make the speeding car fly through the air like Evel Kneivel.

Traversing the dirt road, broken up through its surface, was a tree root as big as a big man's leg. The skin of the root had been ripped away as the car hit it, leaving glaring white wood staring up at me. It was this root that had sent the car aloft.

Yet there was no tree anywhere nearby that the root could have belonged to (save the Balsam Fir some 20 yards away). There was no way the municipal powers would have allowed this ugly obstruction to remain here. I had walked this road every day of my school life and had never noticed a big root sticking up through the road. Indeed I solidly knew that this root was never here before. So why was it here now?

It was as if the huge root had broken the road's surface only moments before the car hit, with the singular purpose of saving me from death, and had appeared, as if from nowhere.

ChApTeR 16

Cot was super pissed that I could not describe more of the killer car.

"It had two headlights," I said.

Cot scoffed disgustedly.

She examined my face and took some turpentine to the sap adhered there.

Through Cot's ministrations, I could sense her fearful imaginings of a world without me. When she was done with her rubbing, she pulled back and looked into my eyes.

Then she gave me a hug of great force, for so little a girl.

ChApTeR 17

It was apparent to us that we could no longer stay at our house. Someone was out to get me, or us. But who? Was it Winky? Ricky Denizen? Or someone else entirely?

These questions dogged me as we made ready to leave.

When we had gathered our essentials, and had winnowed them down to a cartable lot, we slipped out the back door, locked it, and placed the key in the hole of the key tree nearby. We scanned all around us, doing our best to ensure that no one was spying our activities. Paranoia enshrouded.

We made off directly through the forest, past the Donnel shack, and followed the creek down toward town. It was nearly 5 pm and I still intended to meet Adria back at the cemetery, which was in the opposite direction entirely.

"I am gonna drop you off at Eli's. But I have something to do... so I will just drop you off, ok?"

"That is a dumb idea, Johnny. I know you are gonna die if you don't see Adria, but you could get yourself killed, or worse, meeting her tonight," Cot responded between her huffing and puffing.

"What's worse than getting killed?"

"Getting killed twice?" Cot mused, in a quiet way. I could tell her mind was turning, remembering.

We knocked, but Eli did not answer the door, even after we simultaneously attacked the kickplate with abandon.

"He's taking the bottle to his friend, I bet." Cot opined.

I went in back to the rear door of the garage.

I searched under the mat, nearby rocks, and in the garden. I finally found a spare key in the drain spout. We let ourselves into the garage, where an overpowering reek of oil and age assailed us.

There were stacks of stained cardboard boxes, piled in one of the stalls. The top box was scrawled in red, in a child's hand: "Thedas Books."

Around the perimeter, pressboard shelves sagged, overburdened with dark shapes and shadows. The one dirty window admitted a sickly light that made the whole garage seem a sinister place.

I shuddered and motioned for Cot to make through to the house proper. As she did, I turned and grabbed that top box and lugged it into the house behind her. Cot looked back at me inquisitively.

"I want to know about her. I can't help it," I said.

"Are you sure?" asked Cot. "You were just getting back to normal."

I said nothing but kicked closed the door behind me. I put down the box of books and paused, thinking. Then I opened the door I had just closed and went out and locked the back door we had entered by, making sure the crossbar was in place on the garage door itself.

When I went back in the house, I locked the door after me and checked the front and kitchen doors to make sure they were locked too.

I checked all the windows.

I placed the key from the downspout on the kitchen table, next to some salt and pepper shakers in the shape of circus elephants. Salt stood up on its back legs; Pepper did a trunk-assisted head stand.

Miss Holly used to give us stickers when we scored high on certain things, like tests or short stories. One of her favorites stickers was an elephant, pointing to its noggin with its trunk, winking, as if to say, "Good job!"

So I knew those shakers were hers.

As I explored the house (having only spent any time previous in the basement), I saw elephants everywhere.

Crystal elephants of all stripes occupied a vertical display case that stood before the living room window. Light played through their antics and dappled the room in smudges of color.

I brought the drapes closed and all the light winked out.

On the mantel, there was an ad hoc enclosure of #2 pencils bounding a herd of multi-colored pachyderms.

Their pedigree was apparent in the childlike manner of their sculpting, and the half hazard nature of paint applied to them. The thought of children working diligently on these little treasures, for Miss Holly, threatened to get me misty. Why hadn't I ever learned of this secret appreciation of hers? I would have made her a thousand elephants! Ten thousand!

But even as I thought this, another part of me conceded that the gift of ten thousand elephants would probably sour anyone to the idea of elephants ever again.

Such were my feelings for Miss Holly. I was glad at that moment that I had never made them known to her (even if Cot claimed to have spilled the beans to her ghost).

There was little choice at this point, but to look in Miss Holly's room. Eli had told us previously that his Mom had closed her daughter's door and had never gone inside after the murder. Neither did Eli. The police never went in her room, which was surprising, and gave credence to the notion that the police just weren't trying all that hard to solve the murder.

The concept that Miss Holly's room was pristine, untouched, as she had left it on her last morning of life, was powerfully fascinating to me.

I trudged inexorably up the grey carpeted stairs across from the front door. A small stained-glass window cast mottled colors in my path, save where my shadow eclipsed them. Cot watched me go. She made no move to accompany me. My bruised knees ached as I ascended.

I turned the door handle, and swept inside Miss Holly's room with downcast eyes. I closed the door, mindful that Miss Holly had been the last person to grasp the inside handle. My hand seemed to find some inscrutable meaning in this presumption. I worried the door handle with my fingers, screwing up the courage to take the room in with my eyes.

I breathed the faded, female smell of her perfumes, potions and cosmetics. They were strewn on a mirrored vanity next to the laced window. The window admitted a torrent of late sunlight, heating the room in a swath that stirred up currents. Motes danced. Underlying the heat and the scents was the flat presence of a room defeated and unused, unable any longer to perform its lifelong duty to Theda Holly.

I drew close to the vanity. Somehow, the half-hazard positions and orientations of Miss Holly's lipsticks and powders, so reflective of her last moments in this room, demanded a search for meaning where there was none.

I knew there was a particular perfume that Miss Holly used, because she had a special smell, which I coveted and which caused me to stand close to her--closer to her than I should have--on many occasions.

I studied the perfumes, one after another. I held each bottle up to the light and looked through the colored liquid, as if hoping to catch a glimpse of Miss Holly's ghost through the cut-glass facets. I took in the room in this way.

I tested the perfume bottles to my nose as I finished gazing through each. I came to the conclusion that Miss Holly's special smell was the result of a concoction of two different perfumes. One was Jasmine. The other was, of all things, Brut Aftershave For Men! There was a bottle, pink and modern, in which Miss Holly had created this mixture. As strange as the ingredients may sound, it smelled like heaven. In my mind the fantasy played that it was a love-potion I was holding.

I slipped the pink bottle into the pocket of my jacket, turning to the room at large.

It was the room Miss Holly had grown up in, from a little girl. Affectations of her youth, too precious to give up, or leave behind, were everywhere to be seen. For instance, there was a poster of a young man, a supporting character from a decades-old TV show, whose following far outstripped the prominence of his character. The poster hung in an offset way above the head of her single bed.

The bed was covered in a flowered spread and skirted with lace. Atop it, two velveteen elephants, ratty and worn, frolicked motionless among the many pillows.

I found the tenacity of all these juvenilia (there were more that I have not described) both endearing and slightly disturbing. I sat atop the bed, respectfully just at its edge, awash with regret that I could never have known her as a girl, when this bed was new, and when Theda Holly's future stretched limitless.

ChApTeR 18

Cot remained downstairs. After I was finished in Miss Holly's room, I returned to the living room, where Cot sat on the grey carpet, next to the box of books that I had brought in from the garage. She was poring over a green volume, sitting amidst a scattering of other books, like a baby surrounded by a constellation of her favorite toys.

At some significant juncture, Cot deigned to look up at me. We exchanged our usual telepathy and she returned to her book. I grabbed the key from the kitchen and left the house by the front door, locking it behind me.

The ultimate effect of this crazy day was a feeling of elation, of being powerfully alive. The weird strength I had felt on the road was dissipated, replaced by an excited contentedness. The crisp air entered my lungs, uplifting me with happiness, yet mixed, like Miss Holly's love potion, with regret and sadness.

I was all messed up.

It was about ten minutes to six. My knees were starting to kill me. The trees on either side bowed sedately over the avenue, stewards to my destination.

ChApTeR 19

FROM THE JOURNAL OF COT CLEARY

I hate to say it, but I breathed a sigh of relief when Johnny left the house to go see Adria. Even though I was worried for him, I could see his brain was blowing up with Miss Holly thoughts again. It was all the dumb elephants everywhere, reminding him to not forget her.

I was looking at her books when he went out. Johnny had a bizarre expression on his face and was walking like an old man. He was all messed up.

He locked the door that was all I cared and I thought no more about him and his girlfriends.

The books Miss Holly had!

It was a box of books from when she was a kid. Miss Holly read dog and horse books, like one called "Bob, Son of Battle." There were colored-in coloring books and little kid picture books and some paperbacks from later when she was older, cuz they looked kinda racy. Especially the naked book.

It was called "Naked Came the Stranger," and had a woman's naked butt on the cover. On the back it said it was the year's most talked about book. It also said that it made "Portnoy's Complaint and Valley of the Dolls read like Rebecca of Sunnybrook Farm!" I read Rebecca of Sunnybrook Farm. It was good. Those other books were lucky the naked book made them read like it.

I almost read the naked book. But it made me scared and for some reason all I could think about was the life of the girl in the picture. So I put the book on the floor and covered it up with a big picture-book called "The Summer Stallion," which was good, cuz the girl's butt was on both the front cover and the back one.

Finally, like I said, I started reading "Bob, Son of Battle."

Bob, Son of Battle was a dog. An Irish Setter, I guess. The first couple paragraphs of the book had so many words I didn't understand, words like peel-tower, barmkyn and thatching, and weird names, like Tamma, Kenmuir and Sam'l, I almost put the book back down. I couldn't understand what anyone was saying, and it took me a while to realized that Owd Bob meant "old Bob" even though Bob is a puppy at the time.

I must have gotten pretty lost in trying to figure that book out. When I looked up from my reading, it was deep dark outside. That surprised me good. It hadn't been all that long, I guess, but it was weird seeing the sun and then looking up and seeing the sun gone. I got up and checked all the doors and windows on the ground floor and peeked for a long time through the crack in the front curtains.

It was snowing a little and each streetlight lit up its own little bit of falling snow. But it was dark everywhere else. It bothered me how much more dark there was than light. I looked hard into the dark places. I don't know if I imagined it at the time but it seemed like there was something moving behind the houses on the other side of the street. I looked harder but gave up after a while.

I thought I might go up and see Miss Holly's room and so I did.

Her room was beautiful. It was perfect. It smelled real good. The bed was so nice I had to lay on it. I had to get in it. I put my head on Miss Holly's pillow and pulled Miss Holly's covers up to my neck. I fell dead asleep.

I had a dream about Miss Holly and Molly White walking in the woods. They both kept pointing at things on the ground. Both of them, pointing at this and that and this and that. I was afraid to look at what they were pointing at.

Then I looked.

I woke up with a scream almost all the way out of my mouth. I had to bite my hand to stop it.

I couldn't remember then, and I can't remember now, what it was I saw.

That's when I heard the crunching outside. It had been warm during the day, and it must have gotten cold as it got dark. What I was hearing was the ice webs that covered the yard, cracking and crunching as someone made their way around the house.

I noticed it when it was quiet and distant from the back of the house, but by the time the crunching was under Miss Holly's window, there was no mistake. It was a person slowly walking around the whole house. What made me go cold was the way I could hear the person walk right up close to the house, every once in a while. The person was trying to look in the windows.

I was scared, so scared. I was afraid my breath would go again. I didn't want to suffocate and die in Miss Holly's bed. But I kept breathing okay. Then suddenly the crunching got real loud, like there were people running around our house! I heard what sounded like a yell of fright. I was like to collapse in fear myself.

As quiet as I could, I stepped out of Miss Holly's room and crawled like a baby on all fours down the hall. When I got to the stairway that went down to the front door, I peeked around the wall edge and what I saw made fear through all of me.

The golden handle of the front door was slowly turning up and down.

ChApTeR 20

Adria held my hand. Our single mittens were off, which is how we had recently taken to hand holding, even though the night was cold, the wind sharp. We walked along the fence of the graveyard as Adria shared with me her wisdoms.

"You know, when your parents find out about you and me, they are gonna be mad."

"They will not!" I insisted.

"Are they well used to you holding the hands of black girls?"

"No, I've never held hands with any girl. I've never known a black girl, or boy, in my whole life. It's uncharted territory. But my family is good with uncharted territory."

My father, while no saint, not even in this regard, was a pragmatic, realistic fellow. To him, people were, in fact, people. The assertion that everyone had their own merits was one of my father's most vaunted theoretical repetitions, often proffered at the dinner table, usually after one or another of his children had referred to someone as "stupid."

He would say, and I quote, "That person is probably good at something."

While this might not be the most profound sentiment ever uttered, it was uttered a lot, and it left me with the impression of the general morass of humans, as being smart and stupid, venal and moral, able and disabled in similar proportions. Skin color did not seem to enter in.

My Mom was, as I have noted before, a good woman, and a smart woman. She did a lot of thinking, always sitting at the table looking out the window. If she had wanted to give a nefarious importance to the color of skin, she would have brought it up by now.

Really, the fact that I was so smitten with this black girl, was itself the best argument for my parents' liberal outlook on the matter. To my mind, such predilections as racism were the job of the parents to instill, and, as mine hadn't bothered to instill such in me, they were likely free of its burden. I imparted this line of reasoning to Adria, who studied it in the air for a moment before looking at the ground and not replying at all.

"What about your family?" I asked.

"Oh they are gonna flip a tit," she said. I gawped at her.

"No, really, especially my dad, your teacher. You are gonna get F's on everything."

"I don't care," I said.

Adria appraised me gently and I knew I had said the right thing.

"They just don't want to see me hurt. Plus, my grandma does think white people are kinda weird."

"Everybody's good at something," I suggested.

Adria looked at me askance, as if my strange utterance confirmed her grandma's notion.

"It's got a lot to do with the fact that when she was young, she tried to read up on white people and so read this story called, The White People. That story pretty much screwed her up about white people, even though I don't really think the story has anything to do with white people at all."

"What's it about?"

She shrugged. "I don't even know. It's just a weird tale.

"She used to tell me a part of it, about a little girl who goes down this scary hole that no one else will go down.

"Everybody asks her, what's down there? And she just says, colored stones and yellow flowers.

"Then the next day the girl has these beautiful rubies on her ears. Everybody asks, where did you get those? She says, these are just regular old red stones.

"Next day, she's got on this beautiful diamond necklace. They ask again, where'd you get that thing? And she says, these are just regular old white stones.

"Next day, she is wearing a shiny gold crown. Same question from the same people, where did you get a gold crown, for Pete's sakes? She says, this is just a braid of yellow flowers.

"They send her to the king who sees the girl in her rubies, diamonds and gold crown, and thinks she is a princess. The prince falls in love with her, so he asks for her hand. All the people rejoice and agree that she will make a fine princess, since her skin is whiter than the diamonds, and her lips redder than the rubies, and her blond hair more brilliant than the gold crown..."

Adria paused.

"But on their wedding night..."

She paused again.

"On their wedding night, just as the prince is about to enter the bedroom where the princess is waiting, suddenly a tall, black man is standing there, blocking the way. Not black like black people - black like coal, blacker than the dark around him. The black man points at the prince and says,

"'Venture not upon your life,
This is mine own wedded wife.'

"...which sends the prince into some sort of fit. The tall black man goes in the room with the princess and the door slams shut. Till dawn, all that can be heard from inside is screaming and laughing that chills the bones of those outside! They try to break the door down but the wood has turned hard as stone.

"In the morning, the door opens and the room is full of foul smoke. The princess and the black man are both gone, and on the bed..."

Adria paused, one last time.

"On the bed is a pile of red stones and white stones and yellow flowers!"

ChApTeR 21

It is well known, the world over, that the best way to get a couple of humans to close in, to overcome their natural tendency toward awkward solitude, is to put a chill into them. This is why horror movies make such great dates.

Adria's tale chilled us just a little bit more than the winter air and drew us toward each other as inexorably as two frozen birds on a branch.

Our breath mingled in the silence that followed.

Suddenly there came a moment that stopped us, a moment we wanted to see the other side of. Our eyes searched each other's, powerfully curious. Neither of us had any idea of what might occur next, but we shared a desire of it nonetheless.

We stood at the corner of the Cemetery, our hands clasped and drawn up between us, holding us together, yet keeping our distance safe, from what, we did not know.

Before we knew it, and without any conscious impetus from either of us, we kissed, our lips touching to the merest extent. For the first time in my life, I drew in the breath of another human. It was strange, even slightly unpleasant. I didn't quite like it, but I had to have it again. While I drew in toward her, to breathe her breath once more, our lips brushed a second time, with greater force, and a purpose that masqueraded as happenstance.

I was glad our lips knew what to do, because neither of us had any idea at all. A third time our lips pressed and there was no question of intent, or desire, or of anything at all that involved words or description. It was pure Act.

There was more, not much more, but more of a nature too immediate and too special to divulge.

I chose not to tell Adria that night of how I almost died in the tree and on the road. I did not want to ruin what I just then realized was the first kiss of my young life. Our first kiss. I did, however let her know Cot and I were staying at Eli's. Adria looked at me quizzically but did not pursue the questions I saw swirling.

We remained together for a few minutes more. We kissed, in our new-found expertise, like we'd been doing it for years instead of minutes. Assurance and complicity locked our eyes like glue, lending promise to the smiles that forced their way to the surface, even as we did our best to curtail them.

Our parting, a few moments hence, was difficult to accomplish, interrupted as it repeatedly was by further furtive, investigative, communicative kisses.

It was only when I returned to the street where Eli's house stood that Adria's spell was blown all to hell by the sight of a figure running through the side yard of the Holly house toward the dark woods. I yelled at the man and he turned for a moment. His eyes were wide, like those of a horse being relentlessly driven.

Robert Wickley.

ChApTeR 22

"Robert Wickley!" exclaimed Cot when I told her. "That son of a bitch!"

I reared back from Cot's oath.

It was just then that there was a rattle at the front door and it swung open, exposing us in some way, so we shrunk. Eli stood there, wrapped in winter clothes such that his size was increased from giant to gargantuan. In his gloved right hand he held the manila folder in his left, a gun!

"I never knew you were left handed, Eli," said Cot, approaching the huge man.

Eli looked from us to our environs and then scoped to the left and right.

"No one is in the house, right kids?"

"Just us," I said.

"Cuz there is a boatload of footprints out there. There's yours. I could tell those, right off. But then there are two others."

"What the hell?" I muttered, "I saw only one. And that was Robert Wickley. Plain as day. Though it was night. He looked back at me and I saw his bastard face clear as day, Eli!"

"Alright, Johnny, alright," Eli's gun was gone, in his pocket, I guess.

"It's his prints that go to the front door. That's where I saw him."

Cot gushed, "Thank God you came, Eli."

I turned to look at Cot, to remind her that it was I who had run Robert Wickley off, but she burst past me before I could speak. She ran to Eli and gave him a big hug.

After an interval, Eli set Cot off him and went to thoroughly check the whole house, top to bottom. When he was done, he collected us into the living room and had us explain our presence in his house. At the news that someone had tried to shoot me and run me over, Eli's mouth set into a line as grim as gravel. It made me feel good to see it.

"So, what now, Eli?" asked Cot.

"Now, bed," was his reply. He would hear no more from us. Eli ushered us up to his old bedroom and made us get fully clothed into his bed. With nary a word, he snapped off the light and closed the door behind him. His sounds went down the stairs as he took up residence in the living room, from which place his creakings and pacings continued all the night long.

"Big day tomorrow," said Cot, as she drew up the lion's share of the sheets.

"Don't I know it," I said, stealing the best pillow.

ChApTeR 23

The crisped-dough aroma of pancakes twined with bacon smells crept under the door and into our noses.

I doubled over at its insistence and was on my feet before I was even awake. I looked over to the other side of the bed to see Cot standing with a similar attitude of wonderment.

Together we followed the tendrils of scent like cartoon characters, forgoing even the toilet. Eli stood at the table over a mound of meats, a towering stack of amber flapjacks, eggs heaped and potatoes steaming.

He looked around and saw us there, appraising these treasures with the greed of conquistadores.

"Sit down, you two, and set in," Eli said, gesturing.

This we did with no ceremony whatsoever, no words nor even expressions of gratitude in Eli's direction, which seemed to amuse him. Knowing better than to try to engage us, Eli just chomped his food and read of his paper in silence, or in relative silence, since our chewing, grunting and music-less humming were all too audible, perhaps even throughout the whole neighborhood.

When it was accomplished, and nearly all the food had fallen into our stomachs as if from great heights, we pushed our chairs back to accommodate our newly expanded bellies. The grease flowed through our arteries to our brains, making us dumb. After a span, as if sensing our desire to return to our beds without a word, Eli said,

"Since all you can remember about your killer car, is that it had headlights, why don't you tell me a little bit more about them, Johnny?" He took a little notepad and a stub of a pencil out of his right breast pocket, gave it a lick and prepared to notate my response.

I tried to picture the car in my mind, but it had turned into a dusty beast with chrome teeth and glowing eyes. Try as I might, it would not resolve back into a car. But then my eyes lit on the two remaining eggs staring up at me from their platter.

"I think it had double headlights. Two sets of two headlights, I mean."

This provoked a raising of Eli's eyebrows, as if progress were being made, and he was surprised of it.

"Did it have a small ridge going down the middle of the hood?" He quickly drew a small picture in his notebook and showed it to me.

"Might have," I said.

"It did," he said. "How 'bout the back of the car, Johnny. Anything you remember there?"

The memory of the double headlights had done the trick to a certain point. The car in my mind was a car again, and no monster wafting my death through chrome jaws. But nothing more came, other than one small but salient detail. The car was not boxy in back, but sloped downward from the rear window to the rear bumper.

Eli sat there as if contemplating, and his eyebrows did further jumping. He did some more drawing in his notebook and presented me with the result. "You remember any kind of circle on the trunk, like this?" he asked.

"Yes!" I practically yelled in his face. The trunk had a sort of inset circle, like a huge record album pushing up through the metal.

"1960 Valiant 100," he said.

I was about to ask Eli how he had whittled it down so quickly and with such certitude, but then I remembered his music.

"Why can't you just get the music to just tell you who killed your sister, Eli?" I asked. The question had been bothering me, burning in the rear of my mind, ever since Eli told us about his weird ability.

"Oh I have tried, Johnny. I try to get that particular song to play pretty much every chance I get. Nothing, nothing and more nothing. Something I have noticed before. It's as if the music is afraid to weigh in on the matter."

ChApTeR 24

This time there was no getting out of school. We attempted our usual keening and braying, to no good effect. Just short of hobbling us with shackles, Eli kept a stern eye on us as Cot and I trudged from his car and into the school. There was no chance for escape.

I sat near to Adria, as usual. She smelled fresh, like breeze through a blooming tree. The Warm enveloped us together in our secret state of having kissed each other. Our confederacy lay pleasurably on us, as her father's shadow found us throughout the day.

It was one of the longest school-days, ever. All I could think of was the quickening mysteries surrounding Cot and myself, and of the encroachment of danger somehow associated. But the urgency of these thoughts dissipated whenever I glanced at Adria.

I was stricken.

Concentrating on my schoolwork was out of the question.

Cot was studious, however. Instead of doing her math problems, she concentrated with curious intensity on Mr. Edward's delivery of a lesson for the older kids about the history of the Novel. Robinson Caruso was mentioned, which perked up my ears for a moment; I had read all about him, thanks to Classics Illustrated.

But then Mr. Edwards passed us a handout about a Japanese lady and some Genii, or something, and my interest quickly waned. I sneaked the handout to Cot, through intermediaries, to quell her.

As school's end approached, the tickle in my belly increased until it was a ferocious thing. Adria and I had worked out a plan to meet near Buster's forest shrine. We spoke of nothing more, our plans to meet, ending in a figurative ellipsis, under which we agreed, unspoken, to conduct our ongoing experiments in adolescent romance.

After school finally finished, Adria and I met with Cot, who eyed us suspiciously the whole time.

"So, I have to walk to Eli's all by myself, that's what you're saying?" Cot demanded. "There's a killer on the loose, you know."

"Hopefully, for his sake, he won't mess with you. Just lay low and walk with other kids." I motioned toward a rag-tag band of miscreants, just now ambling in the right direction. Cot made a show of rolling her eyes and sighing, but was quick to run and join them.

I watched her go, the guilt of my abandonment just beginning to settle on me. Adria nuzzled up in a dangerous fashion, given our proximity to the school and to witnesses.

She said, "She'll be ok."

Amidst the thrill of Adria's closeness, I continued to watch Cot diminish. She was already making alienating gestures to her walk-mates, of disbelief, or some other irksome stance. They were all yelling at her simultaneously.

I turned my attention to Adria and we started after them, at a distance. When it was safe, we took off our mittens and clutched hands as if we were skirting a precipice, each afraid the other might fall off. In many ways, this was in fact the case.

When we finally arrived at Buster's clearing, we were both dismayed to find that Adria's faithful canine companion no longer occupied it. There was evidence in the snow of some sort of commotion, which we admitted was most likely animals, fighting over Buster's remains.

We walked the area. Buster, whole, or in part, was nowhere to be seen.

As difficult as this proved for Adria, whose furrowed brow gave her away, her troubles seemed to evaporate as I led her a respectful distance away. I drew Adria close and kissed her. She seemed almost astonished, and studied me for a moment.

She kissed me. We descended into a maelstrom of making out.

The world at large fell away from us, like in a cartoon where the main character saws a circle in the floor and instead of falling, the building plummets away around him.

There we perched, on our floating disc of anti-physics, suspended by our juvenile passion, embracing each other's realness. We were finally sure in the knowledge that we were not alone, that there was another in this world who was more than a specular image. Taste, scent, and more than any other thing, the density of each of us made this concept manifest.

No drug compares, and all religions pale.

After many minutes of this notorious behavior, we came to our senses to a small degree.

Ultimately, our transport was snuffed out by the sound of falling clumps of snow from the branches behind us.

I jerked around, my heart a riot in my chest. I could see nothing in the gloom. I held Adria back behind me. Her hot breath on my neck, as she strained to see, threatened to distract me from my sudden terror, by virtue of her living heat's direct communication with my loins.

"An animal?" suggested Adria.

"Definitely. An animal, but how big?" I whispered back.

Bears were known thereabouts. And a sawyer recently saw a mountain lion from his car, he said it screamed at him like a woman, according to my dad. Then there were notions of Bigfoot and the Gollywhopper to contend with.

Snow crunched, wood creaked and more snow fell from the trees to our left, much closer. Adria squeaked and grabbed my arm. I felt like squeaking myself, but I held the squeak in, like a man.

I maintained a protective aura to the best of my ability. After genuinely trying to see what was there, I silently made motion that we should evacuate. As we turned, I caught a shape darker than the forest gloom out of the corner of my eye. But when I turned toward it, I could see only the false night of the forest.

We hurriedly trudged out the way we had come, all the while feeling the steely regard of the real-or-imagined creature stalking us. The shape I glimpsed had been just a little too big for comfort. I breathed regularly only when the twilight of open sky overtook from the canopy of snow-burdened branches.

Adria and I parted ways without a kiss; somehow, we were too spooked to do it.

We squeezed hands and gazed deep before going our separate ways. She whispered my name and let the sound die, suggesting that other words might have followed, if she were braver. I said, "Goodbye, Adria."

I walked backward from her until it became treacherous to do so. Even then, I occasionally stole a glance back, delighted to see her doing the same at me. When she was the size of a gumdrop, she yelled, "I'm gonna call you tomorrow before school!"

I waved and jumped in reply.

ChApTeR 25

Thirty minutes later, the night full dark, found me trudging up to Eli's door. I knocked, but there was no response.

I was just letting myself in the garage door, when I heard running footsteps crashing through the snow on the other side of the garage. I about jumped out of my skin, and so dropped the key into the snow.

I went to my knees with an involuntary cry of dismay, frantically searching the snow for the key with my bared hand. I found it, just as the footsteps neared. They stopped just behind me.

I turned. It was my sister.

"Goddammit Cot, you made me about crap myself!" I barked at her. She said nothing in response, but proffered her hand to assist me up. I ushered her into the garage and into the house. As I locked up, I took in her sorrowful countenance.

"Cot, where in the hell were you?" I demanded, expressing my concern, as I still often do, as panicked yelping. "You promised to come straight here. And where the hell is Eli?"

"I don't know where Eli is! I was up at the diner. Here, look," she said, and produced from her front right pocket what appeared to be an entire Thanksgiving meal, wrapped in a sodden napkin.

I was silent.

I continued to say nothing. I made us some cocoa in silence and delivered Cot's with marshmallows bobbing. Remaining mute, at some cost, I sat down across from her and let Cot tell her story.

ChApTeR 26

FROM THE JOURNAL OF COT CLEARY

As soon as I saw Johnny and Adria going their way to smooch and hug, I split off from the dorks I was walking with and headed straight into town, to see what I could see.

I wasn't looking for trouble.

I know you don't believe me.

What I wanted more than anything was to eat a hot turkey sandwich at the diner. I had been thinking that morning about how to fill my time when my goofy brother went off with his girlfriend (cuz I knew it was a sure thing).

That's when I thought: Hot Turkey Sandwich.

Eli stayed mum about what he was doing today, so it was obvious I was gonna have to fend for myself anyway.

I kept thinking about it all through school, except during Mr. Edward's talk about Robinson Caruso and The Tale of Genji. When I saw Adria and Johnny glomming onto each other, I figured it for a done deal.

Being at Charlie's in the evening-time, without Mom and Dad, was a sad-making experience. I was missing them more than I thought I would. It's weird being without your folks. Even though I hoped a thousand times for them to go away, for one reason or another, with them really gone, I was just worried and scared and missing them.

And now with killers and ghosts all over the place, I sorely wished they were back with me, telling me everything would be okay. Whenever Johnny said everything would be okay, I just never believed him, cuz he was always wrong about it. As a matter of fact, if Johnny said everything was okay, it was a pretty damn sure sign that things were about to go tits up.

But my parents, especially Daddy, had it down.

Maxine, the night girl at Charlie's took my order with the voice that people keep on hand just for babies and dogs. It made me want to slug her, even though I really got nothing against her. I'm no baby. And I'm no dog.

The first bite was heaven on earth. Charlie's put gravy and stuffing and white cheese right on the sandwich with big old slabs of turkey so eating that sandwich was like eating a whole Thanksgiving dinner. There was even a little helping of cranberry slaw on a little dish.

I was already getting sad about it ever ending, when I looked up and saw out the front window this old man shuffling and muttering to himself as he walked past. My heart went out to him, cuz his life was hard. That I could see in one second. Then in the next second it came to me who I was looking at.

Bandana.

I coughed up about a whole bite before I got it under control. Crap! I had half a sandwich left and all the slaw, and Maxie was gonna be coming back with my refill of milk, but I had to see what that old guy was up to!

I wanted to talk to Bandana near about as much as I wanted to talk to Robert Wickley. Why did he finger the twins when he admitted right to them that he knew they were innocent? What did he mean when he told Reg that his life would be in danger if he fessed up what he really saw? Where had he been hiding all this time?

I opened what was left of my sandwich and threw the cranberry slaw right on top and smashed the bread down again. Then I wrapped the whole thing up in a napkin and stuffed it right in the front pocket of my jeans. Right away, I could feel it seeping. I knew Momma would probably kill me for it, but I was on a case!

Just like one of those private dicks in the movies I threw three bucks on the table, like it was nothing (even though it meant leaving way too big a tip for slow-ass Maxie). I was just about to go out onto the sidewalk when I spied something across the way, between the police station and the hardware store, in the alley back there.

It was a black car. Just sitting there in the alley. Shiny and expensive looking, lurking like a black panther. As I watched, it inched forward out of view.

I almost put it out of my mind and went to go follow Bandana, when it popped in my head that the car belonged to Winky his damned self! I stopped and thought about it and came to the idea that maybe Winky was as interested in talking to Bandana as I was.

I stepped out of Charlie's just in time to see Bandana going over the hill out of town on the main road north. The black car passed over the hill a minute later.

When I got to the top of the hill about three minutes later, both the car and Bandana were gone.

I thought about walking some more, following up the road to the exact spot where Bandana must have disappeared. Maybe there was a drop of blood in the snow, from where the Burlymen banged Bandana's head while forcing him into Winky's car.

Or maybe, I might find that poor drunk thrown into the edge of the woods, his head stove full in.

Or maybe, Bandana was just peeing out of sight, in the woods, when I reached the top of the hill.

I had enough. I turned heel and ran all the way to Eli's house, where I found Johnny kneeling in the snow, whimpering like a puppy.

ChApTeR 27

"No they're not!" exclaimed Adria.

"Yes they are, Adria, people are rotten." This was me, in reply to her reply.

"Folks are born rotten and die worse."

I had always felt this, but a story I had heard, earlier in the day, served to confirm the notion.

"All people Johnny? Even us?"

"Even us," I said, and I believed it.

"Johnny. People are born good -- They just sometimes get screwed up by circumstance or happenstance..."

I did not have a response for this. I didn't want to keep disagreeing.

"How come you and me are not bad like that mean old girl from the laundromat?" asked Adria. "That evil Stacy and her even eviler boyfriend?"

"Cuz someone made us good, Adria. Someone took a lot of time and it was a huge pain in their ass, and they brought us up to fight our natural selfish badness."

Adria pulled us to a halt.

"Selfish badness... whoever heard of such a terrible theory of people!" She shook her head at me like I was a foolish, but lovable, dog. Adria kissed me. We continued down the road.

"So you are sayin' that Stacy was made bad, just like we were made good?"

I could tell from her darling tone that Adria was drawing me into some logical trap. I couldn't see it to evade it though. I stared hard down the trail we travelled.

"No. Or maybe no. I don't know! That damn Stacy could have been made bad by someone. Her Momma maybe, or her daddy. But like I said, no one really had to do anything. Maybe she was just kinda let loose, to grow up too much on her own, and her selfish badness just came out naturally."

"And our selfish badness would come out naturally, too, if someone just let us loose like that?" There was a mirth in Adria's voice. I saw no alternative but to continue along the path I had chosen, even though it was about to lead off a cliff, I was certain.

"That's right," I said, in a morally credible tone.

Adria breathed in the breath with which she was surely to deliver her killing blow, but instead, reached into the pocket of her dress and pulled out a thing wrapped in a napkin, as if in defiance of my theories. There were grease spots adorning it and I took off my mitten to accept it as she handed it over. The small white bundle was, amazingly, still warm. I gingerly undid its wrapping.

There revealed, was a golden oatmeal cake, bisected by a purple layer of persimmon pudding. Adria lovingly described the nature of the thing and the ordeal of its creation.

But I never did get to taste it.

For it was then, that the shadow grew ominously across our path and our day changed decidedly for the worse.

ChApTeR 28

I should probably set the stage a bit better.

It was the day following, roughly two thirty in the pm. Adria and I were walking circles in the forest, trails and roads around Adria's house and the cemetery, kissing and talking. The rest of the day preceding our walk had been crap and bullshit, a molasses we had waded through, to achieve this moment.

Earlier that morning I'd awoke to an expected 7 am phone call that lasted all of ten seconds. Adria directed me where to meet at noon.

"Don't be late because I had to pretend I was dying in order to stay home. I'm making you something hot and delicious," she said, before hanging up.

That sounded good to me. I put the phone in its cradle and told Cot that I wasn't going to school. She whooped. I took it to mean that she would be joining me in my delinquency.

Eli, come home at some point in the night, was still in his basement bed at the time. Later, during breakfast, he asked who had called and I just straight out admitted it was Adria. He smirked and shook his head and went back to his eating and reading his newspaper.

Cot acted uninterested in the entire matter, instead focusing her attention on the salt and pepper elephant shakers.

"Why did Miss Holly like elephants so much, Eli?"

"It's a terrible story, I won't tell it," Eli replied.

Cot and I exchanged looks. Curious indeed. I put down my fork.

"Eli... " I said.

"You can 'Eli' me all you want. I am not going to tell it," He said, decisively, from behind his paper.

Cot narrowed her eyes down to sharp blades at that.

"I'll go break a window, or kidnap somebody's cat, or something unless you tell us," she warned.

Eli chuckled. "No, you won't."

But then he didn't say anything for some minutes.

"Oh, fer cry-eye," Eli complained.

"Tell it!" said Cot.

"I will, rapscallion!" rejoined Eli.

He pouted.

"I will tell you just like it was told to me by my own mother," Eli said, with a wistful, faraway look, dripping with drama.

He clearly intended to tell it all along.

"This is a story Momma relayed to us, Theda and me, when we were very young. Theda was maybe six and I was five, or four. My momma told it like she was weaving a spell on us. And she was. Those elephant shakers are the residuum of that spell." Eli motioned at the table.

Eli seemed to summon force from the very air around him, from the table beneath his splayed hands, and most especially, from the expectant faces of the two youths sitting before him. This force, he directed back our way, fixing us with the requisite seat-rooting Eli demanded of his listeners.

"When our momma was a little strip of a thing, perhaps three or four years old, the circus came to town," Eli began.

"The event in question transpired on a fall day, damp and heavy with impending weather.

"This was over in Kingsdock, Tennessee, way back in the teens. Our little Momma was delighted at the circus colors and action. Unfortunately, the sky drew darker, the clouds more pendulous and full. Our Momma could tell right then that the day was amiss somehow. The weather, and the end of the circus fun it heralded, conspired to set little Momma crying, right then. Her grandma had to work to get her settled down. But there was a bright spot, as they discovered on their way back through town.

"Our child-Momma found herself with our great-grandma in a crowd of spectators, watching the circus elephants being brought to water, ostensibly as reward for their fine, though rain-curtailed, performances. The circus folk brought the elephants straight through the center of town, as a form of advertising, I suppose. There were five of them; Mary, Shadrack, Mabel, Ollie, and Topsy. They travelled the way that elephants from the circus are conventionally presumed to, trunk to tail.

"Little Momma was captivated by them, but mostly by the largest of the elephants, Mary. Mary wore an ornate sheet over her back proclaiming her 'The Largest Land Animal in Existence!

"Therefore, little Momma was more than a tad upset when she saw the undertrainer, who was riding Mary's back, give Mary a hard whack on the side of the head, with his wrangling hook, for the crime of leaving formation.

"You see, Mary had become distracted by a gang of pigs that were arguing, as it were, over a watermelon rind in the street. She had wandered that way, when the man whacked her on the head.

"No one was more upset about the blow than Mary herself. With a massive, trumpeting complaint, Mary reached back with her trunk and brought the man down to the ground in front of her, with a crunch that bespoke of broken bones. Mary threw the man into an ad hoc drink stand, set up for the occasion on the side of the road, right near little Momma and her grandma.

"Mary then trundled over, neat as you please, and stepped on that man's head, spilling his brains in all directions."

"Cool!" said Cot.

"That's exactly what my momma thought," said Eli. He drew inward of the breakfast table, as if what he was next to tell was of terrible import.

"Now listen - this is the part that captivated my sister's heart and resulted in the slow onslaught of tiny pachyderms that now invade our home...

"For it was, then, that the town smithy popped five ineffectual bullets into Mary, from his Colt revolver.

"Mary stood there silently through it all.

"The bullets did not seem to affect Mary in the least. It seemed to my momma that the poor beast was somehow stuck inside the limitations of her elephantine species; that, surely, Mary was inside her thick grey skin, protesting her innocence and screaming from the pain of the bullets, but was simply not designed to outwardly express these notions. Whatever the case, the bullets did not kill Mary.

"To the raging crowd, Mary was just a dumb, evil beast, but my momma knew better, and when she told us this part, she cried, and little Theda cried with her.

"And that's how come the elephants are all over the house!"

Eli snapped his mouth closed and brought up the paper and hid behind its broad expanse, continuing to read where he had left off.

Cot was left visibly fuming. When she spoke, it was with a restrained agitation bursting to erupt the newspaper right out of Eli's hand.

"What. The. Hell. Happened. To. The. Elephant. Eli!"

Eli looked innocently over the top of the paper. He cleared his throat, bringing the paper back down. His eyes were in the distance of his thoughts.

He said, "You just ain't gonna believe it."

But Cot was set to explode, so Eli made signs for her to just calm the heck down and continued, with the story of Mary the Elephant.

"Kingsdock, Tennessee was a high-strung town as towns go. Indignation and retribution were constantly in the air, resulting in blood feuds and vigilante justice. Only a few weeks prior, the town crowd had lynched a young black bootlegger as he was being brought to jail.

"The town body protested that Mary the elephant needed to be executed for her crime. They claimed the murder was premeditated and even that, somehow, Mary had conspired with herself to achieve her poor undertrainer's demise.

"An injunction, decrying Mary's lust for First Degree Murder and Conspiracy, was presented by the Magistrate with astonishing speed, prohibiting the circus from packing up and leaving, while the town elders figured out what to do.

"For some reason, it was assumed that the most popular means of execution, bullets, was unequal to the task, most likely due to the fact that the blacksmith's bullets hadn't made much of an impression on Mary. Various outlandish methods were proposed, including field artillery, and even a massive guillotine. Finally, someone proposed simply hanging the beast, although, at first, this seemed a preposterous idea.

"That is, until someone suggested a railroad derrick and crane for the task.

"So, it was, that Mary, a few days later, after a normal day of circus entertaining, was brought to the railyards, to meet her end.

"When Mary spied the derrick, she sat right down on her haunches, like a stubborn ol' dog does."

At this image, Cot's face became a little girl version of the mask of tragedy.

"Only with the use of the other elephants, could Mary be pushed and nudged into approaching it. Some men affixed a heavy chain round her neck and up she was hauled, swinging and spinning. Mary made it about three feet off the ground, when the chain snapped.

"And do you know what the idiots of Kingsdock did then?" Eli asked, significantly.

I spoke for us both, in a croak. "What?"

"They stampeded. Like elephants. The stampede killed an old blind musician. No retribution was ever sought for his death."

"And Mary? Was she dead?" I asked.

"She was not," replied Eli, sadly. "She was all broken inside, and moaning. When the crowd calmed down, and returned to what they had wrought, there was a pervasive regret, and if they could have taken back their civic retribution on the elephant, they would have. But it was too late. They hanged her again, until she was dead, and then dropped her into a big hole and covered it up as quick as possible."

"Did your Mom see the hanging?" asked Cot.

"No," said Eli, glumly, "It is simply a matter of historical record."

Silence reigned at the table, 'til finally Eli said:

"Theda showed me a picture of it."

Eli got up and went over to the living room. He rummaged through a drawer.

Eli showed us that picture, a wrinkled and faded newspaper clipping. There it was, the impossible image of a huge elephant, surely too massive to be in any way hanged, dangling from the end of giant metal arm. It was ridiculous and sad.

Mary the Elephant, like Joan of Arc, was a sacrifice to the brutal history of pride and punishment.

"Our Momma's story left my young sister bereft of joy, impenetrable to solace. For days, Theda was nigh unreachable in her sorrows, until those sorrows, for some inscrutable reason, left Theda, and in place of the sorrow, there started to grow the collection of elephants that parade around the house to this day."

Eli stopped talking about that.

Eli chewed a bit, before finally informing us, as if he had only just remembered it, that the fingerprints from the bottle had produced a name.

We just about exploded out of our seats and through the very roof!

"Who!" was the gist of the plosive and dipthong-ized pleadings Cot and I emitted. But Eli refused to say.

"I wouldn't be so stupid as to tell you kids. You'd be over at the person's lodgings in minutes, and likely murdered yourselves in a few minutes more!"

"So, what you are saying," said Cot, "is that it's someone who lives within a couple minute's walking distance."

"No I am not saying that!" barked Eli, his face darkening. "You kids have to remember that the prints on that bottle might not mean anything at all. Whoever killed Theda might have just picked the bottle up from the ground. It could have rolled over from the garbage area, which was right nearby."

"But it's something," I said.

"Exactly, Johnny," said Eli with favorable wink in my direction. "And it is that something that I intend to look into, this very day."

It was then that both Cot and I saw the manilla envelope under Eli's coffee cup. We exchanged glances. It was the same envelope that we had ransacked while Eli was in the police station stealing the green bottle glass. The name of Miss Holly's killer was very likely in that envelope, added to the other information of her dreadful passing.

"STOP!" roared Eli. He backed up from the table and put the envelope under his arm, holding out the sloshing cup of coffee, as if to ward us off.

"You two stop what you are thinking and desist in your machinations, because you are not getting the best of me! As a matter of fact, I am leaving right now before you can woo and distract me into divulging what I should not."

With that Eli whirled into his coat and stormed out the door before Cot and I could so much as blink. He raced out of the driveway like it was for his dear life. We did not have the presence of mind to see which direction he went at the end of his street.

ChApTeR 29

After eating much of the food Eli had left, we could not help but mosey back upward to our bed. There we sank into the softness and sank again, into sleep. At some point I was aware of Cot getting up and going into Miss Holly's room, shutting the door.

It should be noted that when I left the house to meet Adria, those elephant shakers were gone from the kitchen table. Cot's humming was quiet, but distinct, as I drew the front door closed and locked it.

ChApTeR 30

Which returns us to the road, and to the shadow that crossed it.

You will recall that Adria and I were discussing the problem of human evil, a topic that persisted like a bad taste on my tongue, since the story of Mary the Hanged Elephant. You will recall that Adria employed Stacy Steebler and her boyfriend, Ricky Denizen, as examples of such evil. Then, Adria seemed to wash it all away with the presentation of her persimmon oat cake.

Then, the shadow crossed our path.

That oatmeal cake was smashed out of my hand by the owner of that shadow, with such passion, it fairly exploded against the frozen ground. My hand and wrist rang with pain.

I faced the one who had authored the assault - and a shiver propagated from my knees and up my back, clamping shut the moral outrage about to pour out my mouth.

Of course, it was Stacy Steebler.

Why are our most compromising words invariably conveyed to their most unintended ears? It is as if a supernatural japester listens to our conversations, preferentially collapsing those into reality (from amongst the infinitude) that see our words to their most damaging ends.

There was sound behind us, and we turned to see Ricky Denizen approaching with his weird gait, a silver thermos in one hand, a small black pistol in the other.

"Lookee Cookie! We found ourselves a mook and a spook." Ricky Denizen hissed.

"They were kissin," Stacy said, in a voice, deeper, more cruel, than that of her boyfriend's. "Sounded like pigs in mud."

I was shamed that anyone might be party to our intimacies, much less these two enemies. I looked at Adria's face. She was staring calm and hard at Stacy, but when Ricky's pistol came into her sight, some of her bravado seemed to slip. This outraged me.

I turned to Ricky, but he was entirely occluded by the pistol itself, which he had just brought up to the center of my forehead. Ricky cocked the pistol. The deadly click rose into the trees, with a small sob that escaped from mine, or Adria's, lips. I was not sure.

"You were about to say something Mr. Cleary?"

I audibly snapped my mouth shut.

I hated Ricky, as shame and terror rode up me, for so resoundingly getting the best of us. The fucker!

I wanted to reach for the gun, but the fright of a bullet entering my brains was overpowering; I could barely stand having the gun pointed at me. The anxiety roiled in me, focusing on the point in my forehead at which the small black gun bored.

Yet I spoke. For all the tension snapping like bands inside of me, the imperative descended that I make myself known, before Ricky killed me.

"You were the one. You were the one who shot at me," I said, shiver in my voice.

"Mr. Cleary," he said, with exaggerated consideration, "if I had shot at you, you would be dead."

"Wednesday you shot at me. I was in the tree - you were far off behind a car. Then you tried to run me over."

"Mr. Cleary, shut the fuck up!" Ricky smashed the broadside of his pistol into the broadside of my head. I lost all strength and crumpled.

"If I would have shot at you, I would have continued to shoot at you, until you were dead! Because you, in league with this nigger girl, assaulted my darling Stacy, and deserve to die!"

Stacy pantomimed a garish curtsy. She swept up, and, with a jump, was right before Adria. She grabbed Adria's hair on both sides of her head and screamed a high-pitched banshee scream into her face. Adria squeezed her eyes shut at the onslaught. The sound rang in the air.

Stacy's bizarre excess struck a hollow note in me, and I despaired. She then brought up her open hand in an arc, slapping my girlfriend hard, knocking her down. Stacy's countenance of power-madness and evil delight hit me like a force.

A stillness followed, in which I could hear Adria softly crying. I scrabbled toward her but Ricky grabbed my leg and dragged me back.

"Adria!" I pleaded. Adria looked up at me, her eyes glistening, then hung her head. Ricky slipped a loop around my wrists.

Suddenly, I was all tied up, hands to feet, behind my back. Ricky must have had the truss prepared, it was over me so quick.

I was on my side, facing Adria, the ruts of the road gouging me hard. Adria was up on one arm, crying quietly into her other hand. I could not move an inch.

Ricky Denizen leaned down in front of me and took my jaw roughly in his fingers. He said, "The first time I shoot at you, Mr. Cleary, will be today," and with that, pulled a handkerchief from his pocket, shoving it in my mouth. This was totally unexpected. Again, all I could do was hate him now that even speech was lost to me.

"You're fucking brother! Your fucking brother!" Ricky shrieked, punctuating this repitition by pounding on my ear as if to shove his words in there with his fist. "...got me into no end of trouble when he came clean. He fucked up my whole life! I was going to go to Europe and visit the relatives, but not now! Nope, that was the first thing to go. My beautiful car. I might even have to beg that fucker Winky for a job!" His voice was whiney, genuinely hurt, as if by his self-centered madness, I might sympathize.

I hadn't ever thought of the further ramifications of Lucius' confession to Dad about shooting heroin into his veins. Of course, Dad would have taken it further, gone to Ricky's dad, no matter their social difference.

"And then this little bitch," said Ricky, indicating Adria, "dares to hit my wife, and for why? Cuz she called a nigger a nigger. I just don't understand none of it. I think we should kill you both, fuck your corpses, and maybe skin off your faces and switch 'em around, not exactly in that order."

He moved quickly over to Adria and pulled her by her hair to face him.

"Say 'My Grandma is a nigger,'" he ordered.

"I ain't calling her that, you shit," Adria said.

Ricky whooped and slapped Adria three times in quick succession on the same side of her face. Adria's eyes rolled in her head. I wriggled ineffectually.

"Ok, say 'My grandma is a nigger,'" he whispered, almost lovingly, to her.

"I didn't know you was married," Adria whispered back.

Ricky looked at Stacy, alarmed, like he had let some cat out of some bag. Stacy smiled.

"It was a secret ceremony," Stacy said, "And it will still be a secret tomorrow."

The implications of this hung, like a stench, in the air.

Stacy walked over to Adria and took her head from Ricky's grasp. To my incredulous horror, Stacy kissed Adria hard, on the mouth. Adria spluttered and retreated as best she could, backing hard into Ricky, whose hands squeezed and prodded her. Stacy's voice was breathless and shaken with a terrible passion. Adria shivered in disgust.

"We're gonna kill you both, just like I said we would. We been watching you for a while now. Your secret time together..." Stacy said, practically into Adria's mouth. Her tongue flitted out and then Stacy and Ricky were kissing each other over Adria's shoulder as they compressed her between them.

The depths of their depravity overcame me. Ricky and Stacy had clearly given themselves license to accomplish whatever demented acts their black hearts desired. My state of consciousness stuttered.

"We got another secret for ya'" said Stacy, in her powerful, silken voice. She studied Adria's face as she continued. "Your dog didn't get killed by no car."

Adria and I both froze. Our eyes found each other's.

She erupted, my darling girl, like a volcano.

A shriek of rage, lost and ready for death, ripped from Adria's mouth, even as her hands attacked Stacy's face. But Stacy was ready, stepping out of the way, as Ricky grabbed Adria's wrists, bringing them hard against her own body.

Ricky's face was in my girl's hair. He ground his pelvis into her backside. Adria cried real tears now, since escape, and even protest, were foreclosed to her.

"You evil fuckers," Adria wept.

Stacy and Ricky laughed. Ricky released Adria and she slipped to the ground, sobbing. I continued to weave in and out of reality. It became harder to breathe around the gag.

Ricky and Stacy were close to each other, some feet away. They leaned in to each other. I could see them giggling. The two snorted some drug into their noses from a small bottle that Ricky produced from his pocket. Then they kissed a biting, growling kiss, like werewolves in love.

When Stacy turned back, her face possessed a mask of such immoral delight that my blood ran cold in my veins.

She grabbed a knife from her pocket and pulled it open, breathing raggedly, her eyes strange, as if held open against her will.

"Ricky got your dog to come over with a handful of chopped steak. Such a pretty dog." Stacy carved a symbol into the ground with her knife while she talked. It was an inverse pentacle, just like from the crypt.

"Satan guides me," she whispered and bowed her head in some sort of prayer. Ricky shook his head at her and said,

"Stacy, you sometimes scare even me."

When she was done with her praying (apparently a personal act, not indulged in by Ricky), she looked up into the darkening sky. I admit I had no more hope to lose, but this last act from Stacy laid a weird pall of misery over me that dragged like an undertow.

Ricky spoke: "Last time we were all together, in the crypt, Stacy started praying to Satan, like she does; your fucking brother practically blew the door off its hinges to get out of there! I'm sure that's why he rolled over on us like that. He probably thought we were--"

Here, Ricky was interrupted by Stacy, who breathlessly started pouring out words, in a confessional mode.

"I shot dry-cleaning fluid into your doggy's heart. We have a real long needle for givin' cows shots and shit.

"This needle," Stacy said, and produced an absurdly huge syringe, pointing its business end at my goggling eye. She spoke to Adria, but kept looking at me.

"Your doggy yelped and cried and turned fifty circles in ten seconds before his heart exploded. Then he whined himself to death. Ricky was crying. It was tough for him to watch. But I just pointed in your doggy's face and laughed and laughed while he died. It was funny for me to watch."

Adria sobbed unrestrainedly at this. I heaved against my bonds.

"I want to watch it again."

Darkness impinged on me. I was blacking out, would soon suffocate. Somehow, this was a comforting thought. I was barely able to perceive Stacy opening the silver thermos and sticking the syringe inside. A sharp chemical smell assaulted my nose, pulling me back into reality. She drew a purple liquid into the body of the syringe.

And approached.

ChApTeR 31

FROM THE JOURNAL OF COT CLEARY.

Oh my mind was churning for sure after breakfast. I couldn't sleep a bit. When I heard Johnny snoring good, I got outta bed and went downstairs. The elephant story Eli told us was burning in my head. I held on to those elephant shakers and it seemed to help. People are so terrible.

I took the elephants with me up to Miss Holly's room and read more of Bob Son of Battle. Bob was a good dog, that's for sure. When Johnny finally left the house to go be with the love of his life, I popped out of Miss Holly's bed and set to work.

There was only one place I needed to go. One person I needed to talk to. I'd asked Johnny a million times to do it too, and each time he had some dumb excuse and kept me from it.

Well, now Johnny was playing house and doctor and probably the mailman too with Adria. He'd be busy for hours so I thought it was my perfect opportunity.

Robert Wickley was getting a visit.

I figured if Robert Wickley was the guy whose fingerprints were on the bottle, then Eli's car would be parked out front of his house. If so, then I would probably spy for a bit, just for something to do, then head on to school, feeling good, cuz I would know just how to torture the information out of Eli later. If Eli's car wasn't there, then I would march right up to the front door and knock on it hard, like I was the police.

Eli's car wasn't there, and I thought for sure it was gonna be.

Some of my piss and vinegar disappeared.

Suddenly, marching up and knocking on Robert Wickley's front door like I was the police didn't seem such a good idea.

Robert's house looked real nice, like before, with pretty flowers in the flower boxes and a nice, trimmed yard. From the way he kept his house, he seemed like the sweetest guy ever and not a evil murderer at all.

At the same time, the hotel guy from that movie Psycho looked like a total dingleberry, and he ended up being the scariest murderer ever, so there was no telling just from looks, or from pictures, or even from the way he kept his yard. I was gonna have to talk to Robert Wickley's face, and look in his eyes, while he answered my questions. That was the only way.

The Detective Way.

I knocked on Robert Wickley's door (just normal) after I had a good look around, cuz the last time I was standing there, Winky jumped on me like a vampire and about ripped my arm off.

I almost wanted Winky to be there, again.

I had been thinking a lot about what I should have done when Winky jumped me. Kicking his balls up into his body was high on my list.

My foot just itched to do it, too.

I was practicing kicking Winky's balls up into his body, with the hedge acting as Winky's trousers, when the door opened.

Robert Wickley stood there, behind his screen door. The screen made his face look grey and his blond hair look white. There was music coming from inside- orchestra music.

"Robert Wickley?" I asked.

He didn't say anything, but then I got mad cuz he started smiling at me. Like I was a jerk.

"Yes, I'm Robert Wickley," he said. "You're Cot Cleary. My dad told me to watch out for you."

"Why'd he do that?" I asked. I pretended I had no idea what he was talking about.

Robert Wickley was all of a sudden super quiet. He moved slowly toward the screen of the door and instead of making him easier to see, he was suddenly dark with shadow. His hand came into view and he made a feeble scratch at the screen. He spoke, but his voice wasn't the same. It was a nasal kind of buzzing sound, like the sound of flies around road-kill.

"Because he thinks you know that I killed Theda Holly." he said.

ChApTeR 32

Stacy Steebler wielded the purple syringe in a weird dance around Adria and myself. She repeatedly left and reentered my line of sight, humming to herself some dark tune. Stacy was crazy as the day was long, for certain.

Ricky watched her and chuckled.

"My momma used to show me things," said Stacy. "She told me that if you are gonna make pain on someone, make it good and painful, and the darkness will reward you. She made pain on me plenty. And good."

Suddenly, Stacy was right behind me. Stacy hissed her breath, hot on my neck. She drove the tip of the needle into my scalp, behind my ear. It thudded into the bone there and stopped.

For a moment, there was only the concussion. Then, a searing agony. I was awash with confliction - pain, fear and a betrayal of sexual response from Stacy's hot breath, right before she stuck me.

Stacy depressed the plunger a tiny bit. White hot pain exploded across my head. Fear and revulsion magnified the horror of it. My gorge rose and I vomited explosively around the gag. The ropes bit deeply into the skin of my wrists and ankles. The world turned red and then black.

"Oh my lord, what a baby," said Ricky. I was pulled up to sitting. He roughly tore the gag out of my mouth.

"Adria," I said.

"This is more pathetic than the dog, Stacy. At least the dog didn't puke through its nose. I'm gonna start cryin' again."

Ricky dropped me and I flopped inert. I could see Stacy approaching Adria, who was still crying into her hand. Stacy affected an exaggerated, splayed-hand prowl from one foot to the other, as if Adria were completely unaware of her approach from behind. Stacy dramatically put her finger to her lips, widening her eyes comically,

Quiet, I'm hunting wabbits!

The purple syringe glinted menacingly. As Stacy got closer, Adria started crying even more piteously, bringing her other hand up to help bury her weeping face, as if she could somehow hide there, and find mercy there.

Stacy turned the syringe around in her hand so that it became a stabbing instrument. Even in my stupor, I could see that Stacy was not going to give Adria the light poke she gave me. She was going to drive that syringe into my girl's heart, just like she'd done with Buster.

At my feet, Ricky spun and hid the pistol behind his back, where the sound of its cocking again filled the forest with iron desolation.

These two crazies were building to some deadly climax. Stacy and Ricky's eyes were for each other alone.

They smiled wide.

Ricky shook as if holding back an intolerable energy, threatening to burst from his body. Stacy, clearly thrilled at his performance, brought the syringe up to strike in a savage gesture. Ricky stared right into my eyes and started pulling open the buttons of his jeans with his free hand.

The growling was soft, but it filled the air with a dark, animal profundo.

Coming from neither Ricky nor Stacy, that base growl gave them both immediate pause. The reverberation proved a quick dampening of their sick fantasy, collapsing it, right in front of my eyes.

I was, in my delirium, given to sentiments of gratitude toward the bear, or mountain lion, that emitted the sound. I turned my face toward the noise, suddenly hoping beyond hope that whatever beast was there, it would kill and eat us all, so preferable, that, to what Stacy and Ricky had in store.

The sound was so guttural, so fearsome, I expected to see the most powerful grizzly on record, or the kingliest mountain lion that ever perched to strike.

But that is not what I saw, at all.

ChApTeR 33

FROM THE JOURNAL OF COT CLEARY
Robert Wickley said, in a creepy voice:

"Because he thinks you know that I killed Theda Holly."

I screamed and fell back off the stoop, right onto my butt.

"Oh shit," said Robert Wickley, reassuming his normal shape and voice.

Did he just admit to me that he killed Miss Holly?

Robert Wickley jumped down the steps and knelt right next to me. He put his hand on my arm and I screamed again. He pulled back like I was electricity.

"I'm sorry! That was my best Peter Lorre," said Robert Wickley.

"You, Mr. Wickley, pick a bad time for jokes!" I said in my rudest tone, getting up, ready to run.

"Well, it's not strictly a joke is it, Cot?" Robert Wickley, brushing off dust.

"What do you mean, Mr. Wickley? You just said Winky was worried that we would find out you killed Miss Holly!" I yelled this at him.

"That's just it. My dad thinks I did it!" Robert Wickley sat on the stoop. He motioned for me to sit next to him but I did not.

"Mr. Wickley, look at me and tell me you didn't kill Miss Holly."

He looked right up at me from his shoes, like I had hit him unawares, real mad, for a second. Then he closed his eyes. When he opened them they shone like glass.

"I did not kill Theda!" he scream-whispered.

He took a moment to calm himself.

"Look at it from my perspective, Cot. My beautiful girl gets killed by some monster, and everyone thinks I did it, even my own dad. Not only is Theda gone, but I can't stop worrying about this other crap long enough to even deal with it. And then some kid keeps following us - it's enough to drive you batty!"

"Is that why you visit a head shrinker?" I asked, remembering the yellow appointment slip.

He looked real surprised at that.

"You are a detective," Robert Wickley said.

"Yes, that's exactly why. My dad, for all his shortcomings, has a pretty liberal view of the science of psychoanalysis. He thinks it will help me come to terms with my murder of Theda."

I was warming up to this guy, against my own will. After all, Robert was talking to me like we were old friends. I didn't think that was the way hardened murderers did it.

"You mean, so you'll confess?" I asked.

"Oh hell no. My dad would cover up something like this 'til the day he died. No, he just wants to make sure I NEVER KILL AGAIN!" Robert said this in the same crazy dramatic way as before, and now it was obvious he was just being funny.

I almost laughed

"My headshrinker thinks I did it, too. Heck, I think he prays every night I murdered Theda. Give him some fame if I did, you know?"

I nodded.

Robert Wickley was handsome, that's for sure.

I never really saw them in life together, but what a great couple Miss Holly and Robert must have made. I pictured them together in my mind, but not here in Copeland. I pictured them together in the impossible city where I met Miss Holly and drank hot chocolate.

I pictured them on the busy city street in sunlight, Miss Holly with her wide-brimmed hat, and Robert, in a fine dark suit, his arm casually around her.

But my thoughts were getting off track.

"There's another thing," I said. Our heads were about even, from Robert sitting and me standing. "My brother saw you on Wednesday night, at Eli Holly's house. He said you were running away, into the woods like for dear life!"

"I was there," he said, calmly. "I saw your brother when I looked back."

"So why'd you run off? You act sure suspicious, Mr. Wickley," I said, in my best Raymond-Burr-as-Perry-Mason voice.

"Oh Cot, you are something. I was there to see Eli, for God's sakes. I had heard Eli was in town from my dad, who of course warned me from him. But I used to be friends with Eli. We've got things to talk about, as I am sure you might imagine, Cot!"

Robert fixed me with a hard look.

"I walked on over and was going to knock, when I heard something in the back yard, so I figured Eli was back there. I called to him and walked around the garage, all the while hearing this person, whoever it was, running the opposite way around the house. I got suspicious and called out 'Hey!' and started to run too. I followed that person two whole times around the house before he run off toward the woods and I ran after him. That's when I saw your brother. As a matter of fact, getting distracted by your brother is what made me lose the guy, whoever he was."

"You remember anything about this 'guy'?" I asked, getting out my journal. Robert Wickley looked amused, but I didn't give a whittle.

"I don't mean to laugh, Cot," he said in real tender way. "I should be grateful that someone still cares, since the cops clearly don't."

I huffed. "Don't you think your dad has something to do with that? In fact, our investigations show that it was because of Winky's influence that the police did a horseshit job trying to find the killer. It makes sense, cuz, according to you, he thinks you're the killer! Isn't that right, Mr. Wickley?" I asked.

Of course, the only thing I ever even heard about this theory was from The Cooridy and The Remedy at our kitchen table, and they were just blowing hot gossip.

"Yes, Cot."

I guess I was a mite surprised, him just saying yes like that. I was considering what it meant, when Robert started up again.

"I really don't know what to think anymore. As to the guy at Eli's house. He was a white guy, I think. Smaller. Wiry. Ran real fast. Too fast."

"Too fast?" I repeated. "What does that mean?"

"It means I can run pretty doggone fast, and I could not even hope to catch up with this guy. At the end there, it was almost like he was floating above the snow, instead of running through it. I lost sight of him and I couldn't find his tracks. It scared me. I wanted to go back to Eli's house, to explain what I had seen, but I got afraid. I didn't want to walk back through the woods. So I just continued on to home here."

"Ever heard of a telephone, Mr. Wickley?" I asked.

He chuckled. "Yes, Cot, I have heard of a telephone. I just don't own one." He chuckled again and shook his head. His yellow hair flopped over his eyes and he pushed it back.

He sure was handsome.

"Any idea who the fast guy was?" I asked.

"You know," Robert said, "The person did remind me of someone, a tiny, little guy - seemed somehow familiar, but I can't for the life of me think who it might be."

"Pretty convenient, Mr. Wickley," I said.

Robert got serious then.

"Cot, look..." he said. "I know it's easy to see me as some sort of suspect. One might even say it's 'convenient.'" He looked at me kinda hard again and I felt a pit of shame, and had a difficulty looking him in the eye.

He continued, "What I can tell you is that I loved her, Cot. Do you hear those words? I loved Theda Holly. She was everything to me. When I looked at Theda, my heart was so overfilled with concern and admiration, my chest ached. All I cared about in the whole world was that she was not killed. That she was, always, from now until the end of time, happy and safe. Not murdered! Not taken from me, for no reason, and forever! Because, when you love someone, little girl, you think about such things. Some awful part of your mind knows that it all must end, that such happiness is doomed to failure!"

Robert's voice broke. It was affecting. His look of despair didn't help much. I took another step back. Robert seemed to notice, and when he spoke again, his voice was softer.

"I'm sorry," he whispered. He put his head in his hands and breathed toward the ground. Robert's eyes were in his palms, wetness streamed down his wrists.

"There's just no getting her back," he whispered.

My throat got a little tight. All this time I had been shaking my head at Johnny, so morose over Miss Holly. But Johnny's turmoil was nothing compared to this poor guy. I might be a cold sort of fish, but poor Robert Wickley sitting right in front of me, bawling out his eyes, was getting to me in a way I do not like to be in a public situation for.

Robert looked up at me. His eyes were a mess of tears. I covered my mouth and by God a tear leaked out against my will. I was just fixing to turn around and run, get the hell out of there before I busted out crying.

That's when Robert Wickley put his hand out to me.

What could I do? I was feeling a powerful sadness about poor Miss Holly. All I could think about was that damn picture from Winky's drawer. Them two against the wooden fence, the sprig of flowers, their smiling faces.

I might have been a fool for it, but I took that man's hand. I sat down, practically against my own will, and hugged Robert Wickley. It was all a big surprise to me and I looked at the whole scene like I was an observer, and that observer part of me shook her head like she couldn't believe what she was observing. I might have cried with him some, but never once did I lose my breath.

ChApTeR 34

There was a prominent mound of earth on the south side of the trail, just out of my vision. At the start of the growling, Ricky and Stacy looked there, first with a startled attention, then with a confusion screwing up their brows. To my utter fascination, both of their faces drew, wholly, into masks of dawning horror.

Ricky brought around his pistol, shooting its every bullet at the subject of his panicked gaze, until the thunder of the shots was replaced by the impotent clicks of the pistol's hammer falling on empty metal. The ungodly noise caused me to squeeze shut my eyes and drive my face into the ground (which I did not even note at the time was saturated with my own puke).

As I opened my eyes a sliver, I saw Adria, her face displaying what I can only describe as rapture, draw up to standing, gesturing dramatically with both her arms at the two villains, who were, even then, turning to flee into the forest. I saw that Ricky's wiener had popped out of his open pants, flopping every which way as he ran; he was completely unaware of it.

Adria stood tall, a stone monument to heroism. Through my amazed admiration came the realization of her danger and I croaked at her:

"Adria, run!"

If she heard me she gave no clue to it. Her pointing fingers seemed to damn Ricky and Stacy in their flight. Adria drew in huge breath. The words that roared from her were louder, it seemed, than Ricky's gun had been, her mouth expanding beyond reason, in her massive exhortation.

"EAT THOSE MOTHERFUCKERS!" she screamed.

The trees seemed to shake with the power of her command. Suddenly, dirt exploded into the air from behind me, stinging my exposed neck and darkening the air. Some massive animal erupted into action there, and the ground trembled with the force of it.

There was one whole second of silence as the beast launched itself above me. Its shadow blocked out all light. Dirt peppered my face from that monster as it soared over me, such that I could not keep my eyes open to look at it. All I could perceive was a black, four-legged form, surrounded in the misty blur caused by my half closed lashes.

I could hear Stacy and Ricky crashing through the forest. She was screaming shrilly and Ricky was shouting, "Fuck!" over and over. The black thing flew over me and through the wall of trees delimiting the forest's edge. It landed with a huge crash. Immediately the sound of its charging was joined by panicked screams, as Ricky 's profane repetition morphed into a keening cry, like that of a rain-forest monkey.

Adria was turned that way now. She strained her attention at the forest. When the beast caught up to Ricky and Stacy, and started to audibly mangle and rend them from this life, Adria fell to her knees, bowing her head, in what seemed like an attitude of devout prayer. The growling, like nothing I have ever heard before, purely savage and mad with blood-lust, mixed with the screams and howls of Ricky and Stacy.

There were a couple of instances where the sounds told of either Ricky or Stacy exploiting their spouse's evisceration, by trying to scamper away, only to be dragged back to the locus of carnage by the beast.

They both tried it at least once.

How strange, the tableaux before me, the forest and the black girl in the pretty blue jacket praying before it, while the piteous porcine squeals of the victims echoed off the pines.

Terrible cracking sounds suggested the breaking of sizable boughs. The ripping of fabric tore through the air. I tried to picture what was happening.

It occurred to me that the cracking sound was not of wood, nor the ripping sound, of fabric. At this nightmarish realization, I imagined quite clearly what must have been occurring, no matter how murky my picture of the engine of that destruction.

Through it all, Adria kneeled and prayed.

Suddenly, the sounds were gone, replaced by indeterminate rustlings.

A disturbance at the edge of the forest caused Adria to jerk up from her praying. The beast was there, just out of sight. Two cold eyes floated in the darkness, focused on Adria as she got to her feet.

As in a dream, she slowly walked forward, directly toward the animal presence.

"Adria, no!" I commanded, with as much command as my pitiful, trussed form could muster.

She just turned her head back toward me, and smiled, as the forest enshrouded her in its shadow.

"Adria!"

I strained to hear what happened next. It seemed to me that Adria was under some supernatural spell, being drawn, enrapt, to her doom, like Lucy Westenra in the Classics Illustrated version of Dracula. Adria drew further away, into the dark. The beast bounded after her and I knew it was over.

But when no sounds of violence emerged from the shadows, this eventuality faded into uncertainty, and then, into nothing. I could still hear something, but it gave no picture of what was happening. I struggled at my bonds. I was tied painfully tight, tighter than before, due, in fact, to my struggling at my bonds. When I realized this, I relaxed into a heap of resignation there on the rut-hewn road. Only then did I notice that I was laying in puke, but the realization passed straight through my head as my thinking began to derail.

Time seemed to merge weirdly into my sensorium, such that there was no knowledge of its passing, but instead, that time had frozen into the rustling of the forest trees, the visible swath of the darkening sky. I was there with it, indistinguishable from it, an endless object, ossified into eternity.

Clearly, I was getting loopy. My hands and feet started pounding in protest to the tightness of the ropes. This served to bring me closer to wakeful reality.

Something occurred that snapped me back to myself, straining to grasp what I had just heard.

It was Adria's bright voice, childlike with joy. It broke across an excited rustling from nearby her, floating to my confused ears, like the pealing of a church bell.

Adria said it two times.

"Good boy. Good boy!"

ChApTeR 35

(Note: Since Cot did not see fit to continue writing about her first meeting with Robert Wickley, instead stopping before relating some essential bits, the following is necessarily a reconstruction, from the accounts of those involved.)

Robert's parlor was unexceptional. The one small couch faced a tidy, but well-used, fireplace. A modest chair reposed nearby, presumably to seat some guest of the lovers, who might, in brighter circumstances, nuzzle on the couch. Maybe that's why Robert took the chair.

Robert motioned for Cot to take a seat across from him, but she would have none of it.

She was intent on his small desk, set against the wall, just behind the couch. Cot scrutinized the objects scattered there. Robert conceded to Cot's brazen study of his things, with a bemusement borne of accelerating affection. Cot kept her hands jammed into the pockets of her jeans, occasionally pulling one out to prod this or that object of interest.

Robert continued watching her for a few minutes more.

"What are you looking at?"

"Everything," said Cot, absently.

Cot worked her way around the end of the couch, studying the very wallpaper, it seemed. Her eyes came to rest on the fireplace mantle. Cot inspected it from end to end, and made a huffing sound that, to Robert's ear, held a measure of disapproval.

Robert felt suddenly uneasy. He decided to make for the kitchen and secure refreshments. When he returned, a sweating glass of lemonade in each of his paws, Cot was nowhere to be seen.

Robert was alarmed. He set both glasses on the wooden desk, something he would never have done, had he not been so distracted.

Cot appeared in the doorway to his bedroom, giving him a start. She glanced at Robert and quickly noted the pink incandescence of the lemonade, then turned into the hallway toward the bathroom.

Robert stood, stunned.

"Cot!" he called after her.

"Yes, Mr. Wickley?" she replied from the echoey bathroom. The door was closed.

"Cot... just call me Bob."

The only reply was the flushing of the toilet.

Cot reappeared.

"No way," she said.

Robert was staggeringly uncertain as to how to respond. Turning toward the lemonade, he said, "I got you some lemonade to replenish your liquids."

Robert noticed the water rings soaking into the wood of the desk and was dismayed.

When Cot made no move nor noise nor acknowledgment of any kind, Robert added,

"Because, you know, we were just... um... crying. Not because..."

She approached and held out her hand for the drink.

"Mr. Wickley, you have no pictures of Miss Holly anywhere, not in any room or closet," Cot interrupted, to Robert's great relief.

Robert looked around the sitting area, as if at all the places where Theda's pictures were not in evidence.

"My dad came in here and cleaned me out of them the night Theda died," Robert said, with a stony edge to his voice. "He told me later it was to help me come to terms... to get over her death. But he was really just cleaning the house of things he thought might constitute evidence. Not just the pictures, either. She had some clothes in the dresser and girly things in the bathroom."

Robert looked both angry and sad. Then he seemed to come out of it. He said, "Cot, did you say you searched through my closets?"

Cot had removed her journal from her pocket and prepared to write in it.

"Mr. Wickley, I still want to know where you were the night Miss Holly was murdered."

Cot took a long drink of lemonade immediately after asking this question, staring Robert down with her one visible eye, the whole drink. She then looked for a place to set the half-filled glass. Cot grabbed from a stack of doilies on the arm of the couch, using one to set the glass on the tiny table.

Robert Wickley, approving of Cot's doily usage, readily replied.

"I was building a fire, waiting for Theda right there," he said, indicating the direction of the fireplace. "I laid down on the couch after I got one going. I fell asleep. I woke to the sound of my dad pounding the door down. He came in and looked around, started gathering up stuff before... he told me."

"When was this, what time?"

"In relation to the murder, it was very soon after. One of the men from the Mill called Dad right away. He must have come directly to the conclusion that I did it, cuz Dad came here, even before he went to the Mill, where Theda's body was. It must have been no later than 11pm. Left from here to the scene and he was the one to call the police."

"How did he tell you?" Cot asked, with a little more humanity in her bearing. "What did he say, exactly?"

Robert considered for a moment.

"I was... asking my dad what the hell he was doing in my house, taking my stuff. He looked at me wild eyed and didn't say anything, just went into the bedroom and started in tearing up the closet.

"Then he was in front of me with the box in his arms that had all her stuff in it. He kept asking 'Is there more? Is there more?' I was fixing to basically murder him --"

Robert looked down.

"-- when suddenly he got up in my face, like he does, all outraged and appalled, like he does, preparing to spit a bunch of his venom. Then he stopped, and the expression of outrage suddenly just seemed to fall off his face to the floor.

"Dad's eyes, they filled with... tears. Now, Cot, you must understand, I never before saw anything like that. The only time I ever saw tears in my dad's eyes, they were tears of pure, blinding rage. His tearful eyes stopped me cold, although cold is the wrong word, because my immediate reaction was love for the old bastard. It's like my whole opinion of my dad changed, in an instant."

"I kinda know what you mean," said Cot. When Robert paused, to allow Cot to elaborate, she did not. After one last facial invitation for Cot to explain herself, which was ignored, Robert continued.

"Anyway, right then, he drew up and whispered in my ear, as if what he had to say was too terrible to speak at normal levels, and Dad asked me, 'Did you have to kill her, boy?' Then he studied my face hard.

"I was so taken aback, so confused. I'd just woken up. Everything had been turned into a shambles - I said nothing. When Dad asked me that question, the confusion in my head ramped up to such an insane level of noise, all I could do was stare at him with my mouth hanging open.

"Dad nodded, as if my silence confirmed what he already knew. Then he kissed me, on the cheek. Another lifetime first."

Robert took a long drink, before continuing.

"I was so shocked by these two events, Dad's crying and his kissing me, that I was rooted like a stone to my spot. Dad told me not to leave under any circumstances. Dad posted one of his Burlymen outside my door, so no one could get in or out. One of his Burlymen took my truck. I think Dad must have destroyed it, or buried it, because that truck is nowhere in Copeland.

"It was only as Dad was leaving, that the implications of his question began to sink in. I suddenly realized that Theda had really been killed, for god's sakes, and my dad thought I was the killer! I immediately ran out the door screaming like, well, like a madman. The Burlyman held me back, but all the lights in the neighborhood started coming on at my yelling after my dad. And, of course, Dad, he just drove off.

"So, by the next day, everybody in town thought I killed her. Everyone. I was the last one seen in her presence. I was out of sorts that night and everyone could see it. The next anyone knows I'm screaming about Theda's death like a crazy man, in a peaceful neighborhood on a quiet night and the police hadn't even been called yet!"

"I read the report, Mr. Wickley," said Cot, both to assure him, and to stop his progressively intense rant.

"You read the report?" asked Robert. He was dumbfounded. "The police report?"

"Yes, Mr. Wickley, and it said that you two were at the Rusty Nail and you got drunk and Miss Holly had a coke. You got upset, Miss Holly comforted you and then you both left. It included a lot of interviews with townsfolk who thought you did it. A lot. In your favor, a few people thought it was an orgy situation gone bad and one guy thought it was a mafia assassination sort of deal."

Robert looked at Cot, confusedly. Unsure how to comment, Robert simply returned to what he was talking about previously.

"The town's suspicion of me only strengthened my dad's conviction. His actions continued to affirm everybody's belief that he was keeping the law off me, which he really, actually, was. So, they suspected me even more! And back and forth and back and forth and round and round and soon I got Little Girl Sherlock Holmes banging down my door."

Robert rubbed the back of his neck and rubbed his face some.

It took Cot a moment to cognize that she was the Little Girl Sherlock Holmes being referred to. Upon this realization, she felt an internal twinge of satisfaction. Cot suddenly wished for a deerstalker cap to go with her beautiful magnifying glass.

Cot was Little Girl Sherlock Holmes.

Cot expelled these frivolous thoughts and turned to a consideration of the overall information she had just received. Reading between the lines of Robert's oratory, Cot was better able to see that Robert was a handsome, rich boy-man, of some thirty-odd years, who'd enjoyed a lifetime of privilege and ease. Yet, he had lived without the basic affection and emotional support Cot was fortunate enough to receive in spades from her own parents. Robert also seemed woefully inadequate at dealing with difficulty and hardship. Cot, herself, was far more capable than this man, holed up in his payed-for house, jobless by choice and deliberately blind to the shit-storm of trouble darkening his door.

Cot contrasted and compared the two states, being wealthy and being loved.

After an initial confusion, wrought by mental images of the easy comfort of the wealthy - the mansions, the long pools, the gardeners and the maids, Cot came to the ultimate and inescapable conclusion that, of the two of them, she had gotten the better deal out of life. She wouldn't trade her life and Robert's for all the gold in a mountain of gold.

Yet, something had happened to Robert, something that had promised a reversal of his loveless existence.

A door had opened and, for one luminous moment, Robert had set foot over its threshold. Through that doorway, Robert could see all that was ever denied him, all the affection and support and, most particularly, the warmth of being the most special person in the world to another person, and the intertwined gift of having someone special, all of one's own.

That doorway had been Theda's love, a force sprung up like an unexpected burble of clear, clean water from a rock.

A doorway, now, forever closed.

Cot was wholly, totally certain that Robert did not slam shut his own, only avenue of escape from that lifetime void of affection.

Robert was not the murderer.

The tragic accrual of suspicion to him, and his utter inability to deal with it, even to address the official lines of inquiry, only darkened the picture piecing itself together in Cot's mind.

"How in the heck did you read the police report?" Robert asked. "You are - what? Seven years old?

"I am going on 11, Mr. Wickley!" Cot barked, as if Robert had transgressed the social sphere's most solemn stricture.

Mr. Robert Wickley was maddeningly amused.

He said, "I know, Cot, I was just razzing you," and gave her a dashing half-smile.

The half-smile was discomfiting to Cot, not on the half-smile's own merits, as it was lovely, but because she had a difficult question to ask. The question would probably wipe the half-smile from Robert's face and would likely do so, even if it had been a whole smile.

Robert could see Cot's face change toward troubled. He leaned in to her.

"What is it, Cot?" he asked.

She looked down and seemed to draw some strength into herself, sitting a little taller in her chair and finally meeting his eyes.

Cot asked, "Was Miss Holly pregnant?"

The half-smile vanished.

ChApTeR 36

It took Adria a good 10 minutes to set me free. It seemed much longer to me. Time stretched, so that there was perpetually half an interval to recoup, before catching up to the present.

I was an asymptote on Zeno-Time.

Adria was silent. I could not feel my hands until she worked free the knot, which was fused into a ball of nylon and dirt. It felt like I was holding two burning rocks in my hands, as the blood rushed back into them. I protested into my navel.

Once my hands were free, my legs came loose and I turned to Adria, pulling her to me. We embraced for a long moment.

Adria's mouth moved, but the sounds she issued made no sense to me. I tried to tell her about it, but the sounds I made had no sense either. I shook my head. Shaking my head was a bad idea. I fell backwards.

My head landed on, of all things, Ricky's .38, which he had dropped in his flight to escape.

"Ow!" I cried. My stomach roiled.

"Johnny, there is something wrong with you," said Adria, about a mile away. Her hands were close, but her mouth was at least a mile distant.

Seeing my opportunity, I puked voluminously over Adria's hands.

"Yuck!" Adria protested, definitely, one mile over there.

Then there was nothing. When I woke, Adria was leaned over me, pushing and pulling on my shoulder.

"Johnny?" asked Adria, and I could understand her better than before.

"Adria," I whispered, "there's something wrong with me."

"That's what I said, just before you fell over. I think you had a seizure, Johnny."

"I can't think straight, Adria. It's that shit she stuck in me, in my head."

I tried to get up, but when I did, my skull pounded with such force, it seemed my forehead would pop open like a hatch. Adria helped me back down, careful to avoid the now even more numerous puddles of vomit that riddled my immediate area.

"You sure can puke," said Adria.

I felt a plummeting drop of my reserves, such as those of confidence and hope. Before I could stop myself, I implored,

"Adria, do you still love me?"

It was like the tiny, furry animal part of me muscled up to the surface, bullying the more reserved parts of me out of the way in its rabid search for comfort. The reserved parts protested vehemently, as no one had said such a word as "love" aloud, up to this point.

Of course, Adria no longer loved me, if indeed she ever had.

I was a disgusting purulence, vomiting and God knows what else (I was afraid to take stock). I couldn't even protect her from those two evil figures who wavered in my memory. If Adria had not come back to untie me, I would died like an exposed baby. I could barely even stand.

The world spun and I readied to puke anew.

"Johnny, I love you so much I can barely contain it," said Adria.

Well, that changed everything.

With an immediacy, so immediate, it was truly over before it even began, my stomach settled and the world locked into place. Adria's face flowed before me, inviting, comforting.

"I love you, Adria," I whispered, and passed out.

When I woke the next time, I felt better and the world was even more clear.

Adria was cleaning off my face with a napkin, one she had brought along with the persimmon cake.

"Hi," said Adria.

"Hi," said I.

"Adria," I said.

"Yes?" said she.

"What in the hell just happened to us."

"You were right there."

"I sort of was, and sort of was not," I said.

"Did you see Buster?" Adria asked me.

"I saw a big animal run after those two and it sounded an awful lot like it ate them in the forest."

"Then you saw Buster," said Adria.

Even in my state, the primordially rational part of me balked.

A more recent aspect of me, one that had seen Cot come back from the dead, with a tree in her chest, was more open to the idea that Adria's dog Buster had been revived from death, as well as from being frozen, and from having had his heart pierced with a caustic liquid.

That older part of me was more quick to speak, however.

"He was too big," I said.

Adria smiled. She seemed so calm, so happy. As the murk of my poisoned thoughts cleared by the minute, the remembrance of our mutual brush with murder by sexual torture started reforming. At the very least, we had just been party to the killing of two human beings, no matter how vile, by a dangerous animal.

"It killed those two, it sounded like it ripped them to pieces," I pointed out.

"Buster was always a good dog," was Adria's reply. She helped me up against a rocky mound and looked right into my eyes. I smiled involuntarily and her smile bloomed brighter.

"Don't you see, Johnny? God just saved our lives. Those two assholes were going to kill us and if that was all, we woulda been lucky. They were going to do worse than kill us. They were child raping monsters!

"God saw, and he didn't just save us Johnny, he was ironic about it. He brought Buster back bigger and meaner than ever before and He set my dog on the murderers that did him in. Did you see their faces, Johnny? They knew. They knew they were being punished for their evil, and for Stacy's satanic worship! God just couldn't take it anymore! He had had enough!"

I could not help but argue for my long-held version of reality.

"There has got to be a simpler explanation," I said.

I was thinking pretty clearly now. I sucked in a lungful of air for what I had to add.

"That evil bitch said she had shot chemicals into Buster's heart. Who knows what effect that had? None of us can really say Buster was even dead."

Adria's smile fled her face. She regarded me with nothing short of disappointment.

"Don't you think me and my dad could tell, Johnny? Buster was as dead as a stone by the side of the road. He was frozen into a chunk of ice by the time we found him."

An idea arrived. "That's what I'm saying, Adria. Your Buster froze solid. I have read or heard - a couple of times - about people who were frozen and thought dead, coming back to life like a miracle, haven't you Adria?"

This time Adria nodded resignedly, and her eyes welled up with tears.

Like a stupid jerk, I continued. "I once read a comic called 'The Shape of Things to Come' by H.G. Wells. In that comic, they talk about freezing people for hundreds of years!"

"It was a comic, Johnny," said Adria

"Based on a book!" I leveled back.

"By the guy who wrote 'War of the Worlds' and 'The Invisible Man!' I haven't seen any attacking Martians recently, have you, Johnny? I sure haven't seen any invisible men hanging around!"

Adria was good and angry now. I was putting chinks in the armor of her worldview. But only because she was doing the same to mine!

"Invisible men are kinda hard to see," I said, already sorry I was being such an implacable jerk. Adria gave me a surprised look and turned her face away. But when she turned back there was a hint of a smile there.

She didn't say a thing. Adria rose from before me, the smile still worryingly apparent, even as she wiped the tears from her eyes and cheeks with both her palms.

She stayed standing, still locking my eyes. She backed slowly across the road to the forest there. I felt a chill go through me.

Her eyes were still locked on mine. She said, at a conversational level, "Buster, veni."

At the edge of the road, a veil of a hanging leaves parted, and a creature emerged that took my breath, straight away.

ChApTeR 37

"Was Miss Holly pregnant?" Cot asked.

Robert gawped at Cot like she was a ghost just popped out of an urn.

"How could you possibly know that?" whispered Robert.

Cot, seeing the effect of her question on Robert Wickley, took some liberties at this point.

"I didn't know it, Mr. Wickley. That's why I asked you. The rest is just observation," explained Cot, in her adult way.

The fact was, Cot had, long before, read the account of the Rusty Nail's bartender in the police report, while I fretted over the envelope of police photographs and Eli secured the bag of green glass from the police station. It had been Lucy Semna, the bartender, in her police interview, who originally speculated as to the state of Theda Holly's womb.

As Lucy explained it, Robert had imbibed drink after alcoholic drink, until he was weepy, while Miss Holly drank only Coca-Cola. According to Lucy Semna, "that probably meant something."

Robert seemed almost spooked, as if he were suddenly unsure of the status of his visitor, vis a vis the supernatural. Cot's access to his truths, one after another, left him speechless for a moment.

Cot did nothing to disabuse Robert of his low-grade awe

Cot, it must be noted, never thought to inform her loving brother, your humble author, about Lucy Semna's theory, even though Lucy Semna used to babysit us in our respective younger years, and even though I would have been powerfully interested in the concept of Miss Holly's theoretical pregnancy.

Cot willfully and knowingly withheld this theory from me, for curious reasons of her own.

During the exchange, the part of Robert not totally befuddled by Cot, reflected upon her seemingly forthright decision to believe him - the only person in the happy town of Copeland ever to do so. Given Cot's obvious knack in the arts of detection and pure discovery, this was a comfort not to be ignored. It spoke of a world in which he was no longer enshrouded in suspicion.

Some silence passed, and Robert finally said, "We never told anyone, not even Theda's mom."

"What were you gonna do?" asked Cot.

"Elope. Straight to Vegas. Come back. Live here in my little house. Have the baby. We only found out a few days before her death. It was still just dreams, not even hopes and definitely not yet plans."

Cot said, "That must have been real sweet, Mr. Wickley."

Robert knew that if heaven was a favorite day one could repeat indefinitely, the day Theda told him about the life brewing inside of her was the one he would have chosen. Robert was disarmed by the thought and stepped outside of the house, with a quick apology to his guest.

Cot was left in the tiny parlor, which seemed cavernous with emptiness, heavy with stern remonstrance from the absent pictures of Miss Holly. Cot could feel Miss Holly's disapproval from beyond the grave.

"I'm sorry, Miss Holly. Theda, I mean."

When there was no response from the air, Cot said, "I like him, Theda. I know he's been through a lot. I'm only trying to get to the bottom of this mess."

The silence was being far too judgmental, thought Cot.

"We'll get him. You'll see," said Cot. She finished off what remained of her lemonade and went outside to join Robert Wickley.

Robert was out back, sitting on a bench, looking up at the clouds. Cot sat down next to him.

"You want me to walk you home?" Robert asked.

Cot told Robert that they were not staying at home, but with Eli. She withheld from him that it was because she and Johnny were afraid for their lives.

"And where is Eli?"

Cot was less than forthcoming, until Robert turned to face her with an expectant mien.

"We haven't seen Eli since this morning," Cot admitted.

Robert demanded more information, which Cot was reluctant to release, given that, until recently, Robert himself was a suspect. Robert could sense the nature of Cot's reluctance, and gave her an aggravated look that threatened to wither her where she stood.

Cot only said, "My house ain't safe. I'm scared to go back to Eli's."

"I definitely can't let you stay here, Cot. I hope you understand."

"I do, Mr. Wickley," she replied.

"Do you have somewhere else? Otherwise, I am going to have to take you over to Kamen, which I don't want to do."

"I have somewhere else," stated Cot.

ChApTeR 38

It was Buster, all right.

Buster stood on a berm of the road, his head held way up. His frame, which was of a good size before, now stood at least a third more massive. His black coat was unnaturally sleek, allowing the light to define the oaken muscles rippling underneath.

But it was Buster's eyes, more than his obvious increase in size and musculature, that did away with whatever purchase held me to my former, saner reality. He studied me with a sure intelligence. I felt a moment's desire to hide from it, the way I felt when my father was disappointed in me. Indeed, an uncanny feeling invaded me that I was being regarded through, instead of by, Buster's eyes.

"Good Buster," sang Adria.

Buster looked over at her and released a bark that shook the forest. He wandered up to Adria and licked the hand she offered. Then, to my great apprehension and dismay, the massive beast turned to me and approached. Each of his paws was greater than my own splayed hand. The claws, relaxed though they were, left long dashes in his tracks. As the beast got closer, I could see blood and bits of gore hanging from the flews of his muzzle. I held out my hand for Buster's inspection, if only to give him pause in his approach.

A gag clutched at my throat upon the thought of his tongue rasping against my skin, a tongue over which chunks of our two would-be Satanic child murderers had passed, only minutes before.

At the same time, the comforting reassurance, known to most humans, of a large dog taking you into the folds of his confidence, had a calming effect on my abused, drugged nerves.

I placed my hand on his head and he pushed into it, demanding more.

Buster, whatever else he may have become, was still a good ol' dog in his desire for recognition and affection.

"Good boy, Buster, thank you for saving us," I said, in an obligatory way. He barked his voluminous bark.

I patted Buster and looked up into Adria's eyes as I did so.

"Sorry," I mouthed to her, silently.

I still had reservations regarding Adria's explanation, but there was no doubt Buster stood in front of me. Buster, who was dead and frozen last time we met.

Satisfied, Buster left me and returned to Adria. He met her eyes and there was a moment of silent communion. Then he entered the forest through the same curtain he'd left it.

"I think we are supposed to go with him," Adria said.

"What? Did you just do telepathy?" I asked, incredulous.

"No, he just looked up at me and then moved on, but I still have a feeling we are supposed to go with him," she replied.

I shook my head, no. Adria nodded her head back, yes. We had a short duel, comprised of her nodding against my shaking, until my shoulders slumped as if of their own accord.

I trudged across the road. My head ached from the movement.

We entered the Heart-Shaped Forest, staying to the path of broken foliage left by Buster as he muscled through. Our curious pilgrimage continued for some minutes, when Buster stopped in his tracks. He was looking off to the right. Adria and I followed his gaze.

My eyes settled on a tree-covered area that, at first glance, appeared unremarkable. There wobbled a low, wet, garbled sound from that direction. I noticed a smell of metal shavings, then was alarmed at the undernote of excrement that followed.

Adria drew her breath sharply in. I looked at her and saw the direction of her eyes. I followed.

About twenty yards away, too far to see well, the shifting of highlights and lowlights told me that the ground itself was moving. It looked like a carpet of slimy creatures slipping past, under and over one another. I walked toward this phenomenon and the smell got worse, a base, scraping rasp inhabiting the wet sound I heard.

I stopped dead when I could see what it was.

There was an area, maybe 10 feet square, that glistened and churned. I immediately thought of the horrific debarker my dad had worked on while telling me the history of Copeland. How its toothed surfaces ground away the bark of the logs fed through its maw, with the ease of a child chewing the skin off some Kentucky Fried Chicken.

It was like that, but ironically inverted. I saw a bed of intertwined tree roots, thick and formidable, churning against one another in an incomprehensible wash of movement that glistened red in the brief visits of sunlight.

It was Ricky and Stacy, or what remained of them, being reduced to mush by the slowly gnashing roots. The roots ground together, offering glimpses of white underwood as the rootbark sheared away, only to be painted red in the next moment. More than anything it recalled a nest of slowly writhing crimson snakes.

"Are they being eaten?" I asked, not sure what was doing the eating.

Adria looked over at Buster, who looked over at her. After a moment, she said, "I think they are just being gotten rid of."

It looked like telepathy to me, but I kept quiet.

I looked back at the remains of our enemies, only redness now, seeping through the interstices of the impossible tangle of wood.

I found it silently remarkable, how good it was to watch Ricky and Stacy disappear. I was again brought to mind of the irony of the trees debarking, or rather, de-everything-ing, the pair of humans, in a macabre inversion of the mill workers debarking of the trees.

I did not think too much of how any of it was even possible. The realm of the possible had been forever compromised by the zombie dog that led us on.

Moreover, Buster's reanimation recast all the previous unexplained events, from the tree growing out of Cot's chest, to the fat root that had sent the killer car soaring over my head, in a whole new light. And overarching all, some ironic thinker seemed to be pulling the strings.

It was humbling. One's worldview is, literally, one. My whole self, my likes and dislikes, concerns and approvals, theories and philosophies, seemed suddenly passé, out of fashion and world-weary. I felt like the universe had just passed me by because I was too dumb, or too stubborn, to get on board.

I tried to step out of this former person and enter a new one, one who knew nothing, who was accepting of the unknowable, who resorted to contemplation instead of infernal advocation. It was not very easy to do, and I did not wholly succeed.

However, as I fell into step behind Adria, I decided to try something new. I sent a silent prayer of thankful intentionality to the creature known as God.

Buster led us on for at least a mile. Soon, I had a theory about where we were going. My theory was confirmed when I glimpsed the bright green roof corner of Molly White's log cabin through the chaos of leaves.

Buster stopped at the edge of the clearing. For the first time, he sat down on his huge haunches.

Buster looked up at the girl who was once his master. Adria gazed lovingly down into his dark face.

After a few beats of all our hearts, Adria bent down and hugged the giant black dog to her. A sob slipped out, from deep. Adria caressed Buster's back as she squished him to her, crying softly. Finally, Adria's whispering words, barely louder than her caresses over Buster's coat, floated across the distance.

"Buster, I love you with all my heart," she wept, "I love you forever. Thank you. Thank you."

Her last word was lost in a fit of tears, and Buster nosed at them, trying to nuzzle her sadness away. Adria hugged him even closer. I became concerned as to whether Buster was getting bits of Ricky and Stacy on Adria's pretty blue coat.

Adria got to her feet and came over to me. She grabbed my hand and continued crying, without embarrassment.

We gazed at the majestic animal, and the majestic animal gazed back at the sorrowful, confused humans.

Finally, Buster looked into my eyes, and then into Adria's. Buster turned.

The massive dog moved toward the forest.

Adria said to me, through her sobbing, "I don't think we get to see him again."

Buster slunk with an obvious reluctance toward the trees. He looked back at Adria one last time as the murk overtook him. I watched him disappear and was uncertain - powerfully uncertain – as to whether Buster simply walked into the darkness of the forest, or dissipated, like a dream upon waking.

ChApTeR 39

Eli pulled out of his driveway like Steve McQueen in Bullitt. Having evaded the inquisitions of the children by a hair's breadth, after that damned Elephant Story, Eli made quick for his destination.

The Pink Motel.

Indeed, the single fingerprint Eli had pulled from the shattered bottle of Dell Point Lager had produced a name. But the name made no sense. No sense at all.

Jameson Corr.

Eli remembered that he had briefly told the kids about Jameson Corr when they had stopped in the library parking lot after evacuating the motel that Eli was, at this very moment, driving toward.

Jameson had been a couple years older than Eli. Eli remembered him well, for two compelling reasons.

One, Jameson Corr had been a weirdo who stared at Theda all the time when they were children.

Two, Jameson Corr had been an extremely weird weirdo.

Jameson had been a thin, olive skinned boy whose hair dripped blackly off his head, with two deep forceps scars at his temples from a refusal to vacate the womb in his long-ago matriculation from fetus to newborn. Though he had been a skinny lad, Jameson's clothes were always stretched tight over him, the intervening spaces between the buttons of his shirt agape, exposing of his bleached undergarment.

The memory of Jameson Corr jumping up on his school desk in 1950 was the kicker. That event had given Eli the first creepy sense of the fallibility of the human brain.

"There's one right there!" Eli remembered little Jameson yelling, almost yelping, as if in delighted terror.

Young Jameson Corr had suddenly elevated himself above the kids who were, only moments before, committing their observations of autumn and leaves to Big Chief tablets, but who were now, as one, staring agawp.

Jameson shivered astride his tottering wooden desk, like a statue breaking from its column of marble. He pointed hither and thither, as if in paranoid consideration of unseen events.

"There!" Jameson squeaked, causing the whole class to start.

"Corr, you get down NOW!" roared their teacher, Mr. Divet, a no-nonsense, crew-cut veteran of the Good War. That man's pocket erupted its plastic protector and pens in a shower as he reached up for the boy.

Jameson jerked and jumped from that desk to another, almost taking a blond girl's head clean off. He turned on a toe and faced the man.

"Behind you!" Jameson screamed. Mr. Divet blanched with real horror. He looked back over his shoulder, because he simply had to. Who could resist the certainty with which Jameson Corr asserted the presence of – what?

Of course, there had been nothing behind Mr. Divet. The man fumed and turned to grab Jameson bodily from the desk.

"You little bastard!" Mr. Divet seethed through clenched teeth, but Jameson was already out of reach. He popped from desk to desk, like a sprite in a delirium of excitement.

Jameson stopped atop the corner desk, occupied by Eli's sister, little Theda Holly. She looked calmly up at Jameson, and for a moment, a visage of embarrassment overtook the boy. Jameson bent on knee to her, even as Mr. Divet encircled Jameson roughly in his rocklike arms and pulled him away.

"They're all over you Theda!" Jameson cried, with a depth of concern far too adult for such a young boy. He was mad, as they all could see. Eli shuddered at the memory.

Afterwards, when Mr. Divet had been otherwise occupied securing assistance for this uproar, Jameson had turned to Eli.

"See those shutters?" asked Jameson, in an unsettling whisper. He pointed to the covered window on the nearby south wall of the schoolhouse. Eli said nothing, with as much contempt as he could at that time muster. Jameson turned the little stick and the shutters widened, letting in the light of the afternoon. The light illuminated the dust that rode throughout the beams.

Jameson Corr locked Eli with a Caligari stare.

"My eyes are the windows with the shades open and your eyes are the windows with the shades closed. You see? And the dust is like the monsters. The beams from my eyes light the monsters up. They're all around us, all the time. They want us. They want me. They want you. And your sister."

At that, Eli, large and imposing for his 10 years, emerged from his desk, intent on the simple destruction of Jameson Corr. Fortunately for them both, Mr. Divet was quick to step between, tipped off to the shenanigans by the brightening of the room.

Jameson was taken away in an ambulance. The next day he did not return. He never returned.

Jameson's sister, Rebecca, proud in her new role as Speaker of House Corr, told her schoolmates the miraculous story that Jameson had disappeared from his bed sometime later.

But, that (and Rebecca Corr made this very clear), Jameson's blankets were undisturbed in the way getting out of one's bed in the usual manner disturbs one's blankets. The inescapable conclusion was that Jameson had literally disappeared, vanished into air.

That seemed just the way a bizarrity like Jameson Corr might naturally end, vanished into a smoke, like dry ice. Eli and his friends were all too happy to buy into the tale, because all that mattered was that Jameson was gone.

Some part of them knew Jameson could not have really disappeared, for it was impossible to simply disappear, but that boring and unsuitable part was unfit for playground discourse, and left aside. The official history embraced Jameson's nocturnal sublimation, almost as a comfort.

Eli now knew that Rebecca Corr's story about the evaporation of her brother was just that. A story.

Eli had, some weeks previous, sent the image of the fingerprint down to Minneapolis, where there was an ongoing test of a miraculous new system that could pore through vast quantities of fingerprint images quicker than ever before. The designers of this system included in their release of it, stores of fingerprints from readily available sources, such as federal law enforcement, the military and mental hospitals, all to serve in the fine tuning and enhancement of the fingerprint system as a system, before the system became a tool.

Since the music had seen fit to guide Eli in questions surrounding the bottle, if not the mystery proper, he should not have been surprised when his friend in Minneapolis did a perfunctory, preliminary run of the print against the store of calibration prints, and a match resulted. But Eli was surprised, for the thousandth time, and the sense of being moved by some unseen hand, like a chess piece, rose again in his awareness.

The match had come from a set of calibration stores derived from East Coast mental hospitals.

That was where Jameson had really gone. Not disappeared into smoke, but admitted into the Creedmore Pyschriatric Hospital in Queens New York in 1950, after having clenched into an unmoving thing that no person could reach. His family, being from New York, followed some chain of advice from those parts when looking to commit Jameson. The farther away, the better. They were just glad to see Jameson go.

As were we all, thought Eli.

Some calls out east and the ear of the stately Nurse of Medications of the Creedmore Psychiatric Facility, one Harriet Gorton, was attained, thanks to an entire suite of music from Alex North's Spartacus, again utilizing the love theme to suggest more fruitful investigative pathways, while leaving dead ends to Bernard Hermann's imposing Cape Fear. Eli leaned on the music's guidance during this pursuit in a way he had not before. It was if he were giving up in some way and allowing the music to take a control he had long held at bay. A real dependence on the music was something Eli had long shied from, a door he only cracked, for, to throw it wide open, might ensnare Eli's very personhood in an ever-widening gyre. Today, he let the music take his problem from him and dance it about the room of all possibility.

Eli felt every bit like a tightrope walker, waiting for the wire to snap under him, since the music had, many times, snuffed out when Eli brought it too near the questions swirling around his sister's murder.

Here the musical strains brought him with shocking speed straight to the woman he wanted to speak to the most. Not only was she intimately aware of the history of Jameson Corr, Harriet Gorton was a talky one, an aspect of her suitability only the music could have teased from the field of probability with such uncanny precision.

"That little munchkin of evil, I'll never forget him," Harriet offered the moment Eli mentioned Jameson's name.

"Short guy, was he?" Eli asked.

"Like he never grew, was what it was."

"And what was his diagnosis, exactly?"

"Profoundest Catatonia. You coulda put him on one toe for a year, 'til it broke off. I won't say that we took to posing him somewhat, but if we did, it was within the bounds of decency."

Eli wondered briefly what boundary of decency might include the posing of a catatonic patient. Eli had a feeling that he would never want to be in the institutional clutches of this woman, ever, and that if he told Harriet Gorton of this feeling, she would only chuckle, deep and cigarettey. A sudden burst from another Kubrick film, The Killing (one of Eli's all-time favorites), described Harriet as a hardened tough, but there flew a dispirited motif through the toughness, like a blue thread through sea-salted canvas.

The music told him that to get what he wanted, he had to say it right now, so that it came out of the sun like a blade and split Harriet Gorton open.

"It is my opinion, as a federal investigator, and as a brother, that Jameson Corr is the man who murdered my sister, Theda. He cut her throat and left her to die near some garbage cans in the back of a building." Eli told this with unfeigned gravity, even though he was certain of only some of these things.

There was no sound on the line. The music in Eli's head described Harriet Gorton's thoughts and body sensations, a spooky action-at-a-distance of over a thousand miles.

At Eli's words, adrenaline slammed down into Harriet Gorton's guts and her face flushed, hot tears over-coursing the brims of her lids. This was all silent, of course, presumably undetectable to her interlocutor.

The weight of her association with the institution that allowed Jameson Corr to escape and murder this good man's sister threatened to suffocate Harriet Gorton as she sat deep in her plastic-covered La-Z-Boy rocker, on the second floor apartment of a blocky brownstone.

Harriet's Siamese cat, Mongkut, sensing that an emotional storm that had just blown in, jumped off her lap for more restful climes.

This transpired, without a sound, over the space of three seconds.

"I am so sorry to hear that, Mr. Holly," said Harriet Gorton with a clear, professional voice. "You just ask me anything."

Eli found himself touched, even as he was shamed at exploiting this woman's particular sadness, that blue thread of a long-ago loss. A child, perhaps. He was a marred man on a mission, that was for a surety.

"Thank you, Mz. Gorton."

"You call me Harriet. You say you grew up with Corr?"

"I went to school with him in the years preceding his commitment," said Eli.

"So you talked to him?" asked Harriet Gorton.

"Only once and he told me that his eyes cast beams that illuminated monsters the rest of us could not see."

"Monsters, huh? That sounds right."

"I would like to talk a bit about the night Jameson Corr escaped," said Eli.

Harriet Gorton inhaled for a long time, the kind of gargantuan breath that Eli knew was sure to be followed by a shitload of information. He set pen to paper.

"All right, here it is," said Harriet Gorton, "some of it is a little hard to swallow but it is all true. I was not in the direct care vector for Corr, but I gave him meds every day and was in the loop, as much as I would have cared for it to be otherwise. I gave him medications for 14 years and he never moved once. Not a tic, not a hiccup, nothing. Plus, he stayed the same size the whole time. He never got bigger than the 12 year old boy he came in as, although his face did get older, eventually."

Eli was intrigued by that last word, but did not say anything, letting Harriet continue.

"I never liked going in that man's room, much less putting drops in his mouth, or patches on his back, or, perish the memory, administering a suppository. Now, I said he never moved, but he did move in one, particular way. Whenever we would close his eyes they would pop open sometime later. It became part of my job to close his eyes every morning and every night, after administering eye drops. To help with the dryness, you know.

"It wasn't giving him the meds that was so bad. It was just being close to the man, intimate-close, all those years. I looked into those grey eyes too many times."

Eli stepped in. "Grey eyes? Could you give me a quick description?"

"Yes, Eli, grey eyes with flecks of yellow. Obviously, a small fellow, little over five feet. He used to have black hair, but last I saw him it was mostly grey. It was long, at, or past, his shoulders. The temple scars of course. Not much in the way of flesh on his bones, but what muscle he had was hard, which was odd, given his lack of exercise. That was one of the things that made me worry."

"What do you mean?"

"About two years before he left us, I began to get the impression that Corr had woken up, and was only pretending."

"Pretending to still be in a state of catatonia?"

"That's right, Eli, pretending."

"What gave you that impression?"

"Well he stopped opening his eyes. Some two years before he escaped, every time I would come in, his eyes would be closed. Unless someone was messing with me and closing them right before I got there, he was doing it himself."

"As if Corr didn't know he had been opening his eyes all those years. Corr thought he needed to keep them closed in order to perpetuate the charade – is that what I'm hearing?"

"Exactly what I was thinking at the time. Then there was his muscle tone, which increased significantly in those two years. And he aged."

"Aged?"

"In those last two years he aged. His face got lines and his hair greyed. Before that he was always the waxy same. Just like, I thought a million times, just like a figure at Madam Tussaud's."

"Was there a camera in his room?"

"No, I'm sad to say."

"Okay Harriet, let's turn our discussion to Corr's escape."

"Lord, what a night that was."

"Tell me."

"Oh, Eli," sighed Harriet Gorton as if she and Eli were old friends, "I work the night shift, a 12-hour shift, so I give the clients their bedtime and their morning meds. Don't do much between the two times except read and sneak z's whenever possible, and give the occasional nighttime med.

"That night, it was a Saturday, the alarm went up and there was a lockdown, so everyone was running around like shoppers on Christmas Eve. We all have special duties during a lockdown. Mine are to secure the med cabinets and lock the two doors leading to the med room, but I am not allowed to be in there during this time. I have to go to the front office. I was sitting right there when security came in and told everybody there was a dead body outside the loading dock in a terrible state."

"Tell me what you mean by 'terrible state.'"

"I mean the head was bashed in and the face was missing, brains all over, the stomach was ripped open, two small ribs were broken off and were embedded in the eyes of the victim, sticking straight up. The intestines, large and small, were removed and placed around the corpse like murder tape. The victim's genitals were missing and there was extreme trauma to the upper thoracic area. The heart was pierced numerous times. The police said it must have taken hours."

"My God, Harriet, did you see this?"

"No I did not, but I saw the people who saw it, and that was harrowing enough, thank you."

"Who was it?"

"The dead one? It was him."

"Him who? Jameson Corr?"

"Yes, Jameson Corr, Eli."

"How…?"

"The corpse's head, under all that mess, had two forceps scars at the temples. It was a tiny little guy. Longish hair. That pretty much decided it."

"I'm confused," admitted Eli.

"We thought it was Corr for about a day, but then the M.E. discovered it was a woman. Turned out it was an orderly, the one who used to bathe Corr. Her name was Rey-Rey, or that's what we called her. We think Corr mighta talked to this girl. Somehow charmed her into helping him. Made her feel special by telling her some bullshit, like that she was the only one he could trust to confide in that he was awake, some shit like that. There is no denying that by the time of his escape they looked very much alike. She was in charge of his bathing and his hair cuts; we think she brought their looks into alignment at Corr's behest. She was a smidge retarded. High functioning but easy to trick. I miss her, even now, especially now, I am not ashamed to tell you."

"It seems that I am not the only survivor of Corr's mayhem. I am sorry, Harriet."

"Thank you, Eli."

"So then, I can imagine how a person might confuse a body to make a woman look like a small man, but how do you explain the temple scars?"

"The M.E. determined that they had been pounded and cut into the victim's temples with a knife and a hammer. No one could tell that those scars were new trauma verses old trauma. They just saw the shapes of the depressions in the skull. The skin was mostly gone, Corr just cut the hell out of everything."

"The upshot being that no one was looking for Corr for about a day."

"Correct."

"Which is, presumably, why he did it, to buy some time."

"That's the theory."

Eli felt a little selfish, but he breathed a real sigh of relief that Theda had not suffered such destruction.

ChApTeR 40

Eli pulled around the back of the Pink Motel. He rode past a long wood-paneled station wagon parked behind the motel office. Sweeping the lot with his practiced eye, Eli caught the shapes of a few covered automobiles up against the back fence. Eli slowed. The one on the left could be a 1960 Valiant.

Sure could be, he thought.

Eli pulled around to the front of the office and parked. With nary a pause, he flung open his car door and started for the office.

Eli's hope was that an imposing presence might loosen whatever tongue he found in that office, since the music was suddenly no longer in evidence.

The music's recent absence, which Eli guessed must have occurred sometime during his drive to the Pink Motel, proved both comforting and worrisome. It made Eli feel like he was on the right track, but that he was all on his own. After recently relying on the judgment of the music so heavily, it was a desolate feeling.

Eli pushed open the office door. A bell jingled somewhere in the back. There was no one at the desk.

Eli cleared his throat loudly and slammed his massive hand down on the desk chime, an act that simultaneously triggered and muffled the little bell. Eli decided that one finger would suffice. He set that finger into position and let it loose with vigor. Thirty or so seconds later, a door opened in the back, shaking the shoddy little office.

"You sonovabitch! Unless you wanna draw back a stump you best stop that dinging!" came the buzzing complaint of a tall man who suddenly loomed in the doorway.

Unfortunately for the tall man, who was clearly under the impression that he was tall enough to say this rude thing to a person he had not so much as seen, Eli was a good 4 inches taller and untold pounds more massive.

"Oh," said the man when he saw Eli.

"Oh, indeed," growled Eli. "You just called my dear, departed mother a bitch."

The tall man realized that this was technically true, and just the sort of technicality oft used in the justification of a good nose-punching.

"I am terribly sorry sir, I spoke out of turn, I just woke up," said the tall man.

"I am inclined by your rude comment to put you back to sleep," said Eli.

The man was mute.

"However, in the interests of time, and since you will no doubt use better judgement into the future of our conversation, I will hold off on that. For the moment.

"My name is Elijah Holly. I work for the United States Government. Department of Defense." Eli let the man drink in his official I.D. even though its imprimatur gave Eli no warrant whatsoever for his present behavior. However, the I.D. did look terribly official and important, replete with watermarks and repetitive filigree, so the tall man was impressed, if the absent nodding of his head was any indication.

"You Theda's brother?" asked the man.

"I am. And you are?"

"Denny Freemantle. I own this joint."

"Ah, yes Mr. Freemantle, I recognize you now."

"Real sorry about your sister, and about your dear..." Denny Freemantle was about to say "your dear mother" but came to halt before giving name to the person he was about to punched in the nose over.

"You're too kind. But, as I said, time is of the essence. I stayed in this establishment some weeks ago."

"I remember."

"You may remember that I pulled up stakes and left here in something of a hurry."

"I do."

Eli set his face into an attitude that suggested that no nonsense would be borne in answer to the question he was about to pose.

"I would like to get back into my room. It was room 14, I believe. I think I might have left something in there. Can you help me with that?"

"We go over 'em pretty good, Eli."

That answer constituted nonsense and made Eli scowl most impressively. He made a show of laboriously returning his I.D. to his wallet and pocketing it, as if to free his hands for ensuing activity.

"Of course, we can get you back in there, Eli. Just one sec," Denny said, hurriedly. He picked up the phone earpiece and leaned back to look out the window. Eli saw that the man was trying to ascertain which room the cleaning lady was servicing. Denny dialed a number, presumably the number of the room she was in.

"Gladys? We need you to open up room 14 real quick. Got someone needs in there. Yep. Right now. Thank you, Gladys. No, Gladys. Gladys, I cannot talk about your paycheck right now. Gotta go. Gladys! Open the goddamned room 14! I will talk to you about your paycheck right after. Thank you, Gladys. No, Gladys. Thank you."

Denny Freemantle motioned Eli to the door with the mien of obsequious submission. Eli nodded affirmation and approval. He walked back out into sunlight so strong, Eli had to put his hand up in a fruitless attempt to shield his eyes. Across the dust of the parking lot, Eli could see Gladys trying to open the door to room 14.

Eli stepped it up to help, but just as he got to her, the door popped inward, taking Gladys with it. So intent was she on the lock, she forgot to let go of the key. Eli stepped in after her.

The room looked just as it had the day he had arrived in Copeland. He hadn't really left anything in the room, of course. He simply wanted to lift some fingerprints, to see if he could match the one from the bottle. It would tell Eli a lot if he knew absolutely whether it was his sister's killer who had broken into this room those many weeks ago. He did not want Gladys around as witness to this procedure.

He reached into his pocket and secured a few coins. "Thank you, Gladys, you've been a great help."

Eli held out the change for the woman. Gladys looked up into Eli's face from her own negligible height. What lovely eyes, thought Eli, as she reached up for the money. Grey, with flecks of yellow.

"So good to see you after all this time, Eli," said Jameson Corr.

ChApTeR 41

The man who opened Theda Holly's throat like a sacrificial lamb, and the man who later rifled through the motel room of her surviving brother, Eli, were the same man. Together, they were the same man as he who Robert Wickley pursued through the side yard of the Holly house, losing the small man in the darkness of the Heart-Shaped Forest. And also, it was he, who nearly blew my brains out the side of my head as I hung in the tree at Rusholme and County P.

They were all Jameson Corr.

Yet he no longer used the name Jameson Corr. Jameson Corr was his old self, his lost and wandering self. Jameson Corr had been gone so long, in that shifted place known as the Askance. Twenty-five or more years he was there, and those years had changed him. Now, he was back in the world, a new man.

He used a different name, because he was so different a man.

Shortly after he found himself free of the Askance, but before he returned to Copeland, Jameson befriended a musical traveler, thumbing rides over the skin of America. They became close friends over time, hitching and riding the rails south and west, until, one night, Jameson opened the stunned traveler's throat with the same knife he would use to do in Miss Holly.

Jameson bemusedly watched the musical traveler deflate like a balloon. This transpired behind a great yellow barn, turned white by the night.

Jameson had chosen the traveler because of their similar builds and hair color. Now, when he was asked his name, Jameson Corr proudly gave the name of the musical traveler as his own.

Gladys Turnbuckle.

347

So proclaimed the driver's license for which poor Gladys had given up her soul. That document now resided in the compression of Jameson Corr's homemade leather wallet, and was presented from his purse many times to weave his new identity across the sleepy town of Copeland.

That Gladys Turnbuckle had given up her soul, and not merely her life, was an absolute certainty to Jameson Corr.

Jameson had watched her soul do its best to ascend, until it was snatched asunder by the Swimmers of the Air. He fearfully regarded the snakelike creatures fight over, and gulp into their foul gullets, that soul, as it rose defenseless from Gladys' slumped form. The soul tried to fly away at the last minute, across the land, but the imperative to rise had proved far too powerful, giving the Swimmers their foul reach.

(A soul, Jameson explained, looked like a diaphanous projection, see-through and wavering. Was it a churning confusion of internal organs? roots? it was hard to tell. If you took a heart and a liver and some tree roots and leaves and put them in a meat grinder and were somehow able to film their grinding from inside the grinder, and then projected the image from a projector with a weak, flickering bulb onto a dirty screen. That's what a soul looked like. A soul shot from the topmost surface of a person like a flare from a castaway's gun, a semi-opaque thing of roiling meat and vegetable matter. It was just then, when the soul first left the body, that it was vulnerable to the needle teeth of the Swimmers of the Air, Jameson said.)

Jameson watched the Swimmers feed on Gladys Turnbuckle's soul. He shivered, because he knew how slight the froth between the real world and the Askance had become - thin enough to allow the Swimmers farther through than ever before, far enough to hijack the shocked soul from its upward journey.

Jameson's relief at being freed from the Askance knew no bounds. It was a terrible place, so close, yet so immeasurably far from the real world. Return to the real world had always seemed an empty hope, at best.

Jameson spent his twenty-five years in the Askance walking the streets of Copeland, and later, all of America, but shifted just to the right of common reality, passing through others who passed, unknowing, through him.

And all the while, the tormenting Swimmers nibbled at his coherence, his consistency.

His first fifteen years in the Askance were aimless, except in one respect.

Theda Holly.

Jameson Corr watched Theda for every one of those years, and loved her.

Jameson had watched Theda in the years before the Askance, too, when they were school children together in Copeland, the horrors to come not even eventualities, yet.

The 1940's, it was, with the War coming to a close. Theda was two years younger than he.

Jameson watched Theda on the playground every day, from his desk by the south window. One day, he caught her eye and smiled. Theda looked right back at him, calmly, pleasantly, and he loved her.

Theda was always respectful to Jameson, but distant. Yet Jameson took it as a sign of their mutuality, on some obscure level, that Theda did not treat him like shit, as did every other kid in that school.

As the school years progressed, Jameson kept Theda always in his vision if she was nearby - in his thoughts, if she was not.

However, Jameson knew that Theda's large brother, Elijah Holly, would rip Jameson's head from his shoulders should he ever be made aware of Jameson's strange, abiding interest in his sister. In any event, Jameson was mortified at the prospect of doing anything to dim the glow he accrued to little Theda. Something like actually getting to know her might do that very thing.

So Jameson kept away. He admired Theda from a safe distance. It was a normal case of perpetually unrequited juvenile favor. A crush, never declared.

They grew together, yet apart, and even when the Askance began to impinge upon the pubescent Jameson Corr, and he started acting bizarrely, Theda remained kind to him, because she forgave him, as she would one day forgive me, for loving her.

In 1950, when Jameson had gotten atop his school desk to warn his classmates of the nightmares trying to push their way through the shimmering skin of the Askance, his eyes were wild, his lips flecked with saliva. Yet the child Theda had gazed solemnly and patiently up at him.

The beams from Jameson's eyes were so powerful in his puberty years; he could no longer shut down their illumination of the awful Swimmers or the shambling Horrors darting and jerking just to the right of his unwitting classmates, every moment of every day.

If only they knew of the frightful creatures that regarded them all from mere spaces to the right of their reality, his peers would gibber and drool with madness!

And behind and above it all, the Agents of the Askance schemed, eternal.

He'd had no choice but to warn everyone!

He was abducted into the Askance before he could make his classmates fully aware of the horrors to come. The Agents of the Askance had snatched him from his bed in the night, for shouting Their secrets to the world, or so Jameson had initially believed.

But as the years beyond the veil of the Askance progressed, Jameson had to amend this theory. He ultimately discovered that his captivity had nothing to do with his rant in the classroom.

It was his interest in her.

It was Jameson's enduring fascination with Theda Holly that invited the Agents' horrid scrutiny upon him.

Theda Holly.

The Agents of the Askance were as unnaturally interested in Theda Holly as Jameson Corr ever had been. In the years before Jameson's abduction, They watched him watching her, and They thought,

(this boy might be of some use!)

So, They slipped open the Askance, and through that opening, Jameson's sleeping, still-pajama-ed form had plummeted.

Once mired in the Askance, confusion and loss pummeled Jameson. The boy's dawning knowledge of the dreary realm to which he had been banished brought a savory glee to The Agents who had captured him.

The Agents indeed seemed to delight in all manifestations of human misery.

For a while, They played with the boy.

Their favorite desolations were horror and shame. These miseries the Agents provoked unceasingly, for two whole years, driving Jameson quite insane.

But the Agents had bigger plans for Jameson, and when the game became finally tiresome, the Agents directed Jameson toward his ultimate solace.

Theda Holly.

When finally allowed, Jameson was attracted to Theda like a castaway to a beacon.

Theda glowed from the other side of the veil, luring him, yet repelling him, like a camp fire does a forest wolf.

At first, Jameson's approach was tentative, as he could hardly believe she could not see nor sense him in any way. To Jameson, Theda was right there, shimmering, warped by the half-mirrored curtain that separated them.

When he became comfortable with this state of things, Jameson hovered endlessly, just to the right of all of Theda's doings, with the slavish, addicted quality of a co-dependent pet.

Year after ghostly year, Jameson followed Theda through the most intimate avenues of her life. He watched her sleep every night for thirteen of those twenty-five years. Jameson watched Theda's every shower, every use of the toilet. He hovered over her homework like a jealous cat.

Jameson watched Theda's first fumbles at sexual intimacy. He hung just to the right of Theda Holly as she wept over the corpse of her dear, dead father.

His thirteen years watching Theda only strengthened the intensity of Jameson's gaze. His obsession made Jameson into a haunt, and it was Theda he haunted.

One day, as Jameson watched a twenty year old Theda, newly a teacher, newly Miss Holly, mixing perfumes at her mirrored vanity, the truth came to him.

Theda performed the delicate task in front of her eyes, waving the tiny glass bottles under her nostrils, which twitched or flared, according to their tastes. The truth seeped into Jameson as he watched this lovely act, like the unfurling of a poison in his veins.

The Agents of the Askance wanted Jameson Corr to kill Theda Holly.

The Agents allowed Jameson to see this much: Theda Holly was a danger, or somehow contributed to a situation that worried the Agents of the Askance a great deal. Jameson saw the image of a small tree, a narrow stalk topped with the green profusion of a leafy ball. The tree was part of what the Agents feared, a landmark maybe, or, merely a metaphor. How it related to Theda, Jameson had no clue.

Once it became clear that he was aware of their designs, the Agents themselves came forward with a Deal for Jameson Corr. They towered before him, a crowd of ill-defined leviathans warping the Askance at the limits of their forms. Jameson was held in a field that compressed him, like a fly in amber. The Agents studied him from every angle, turning him over, passing Jameson between them. When their interest was satisfied, the Agents offered him the Deal.

Freedom from the Askance, for the death of Theda Holly.

Right off the bat, Jameson Corr reared like a spooked mule at the prospect of killing Theda. He backed away from the Agents, far away. He left Copeland entirely and was the shade of a hobo, travelling the night of America for a whole decade, skirting the snapping jaws of the Swimmers of the Air.

Indeed, the onslaught of these eel-like creatures, that coursed in unruly sine waves and breached the skin of the Askance like hooked marlin, seemed only to increase. It was as if the Agents themselves had tasked the Swimmers to torment Jameson's every moment, and nibble him down to nothing. Jameson's form was whittled inexorably away, forcing him to flee never-ending, whipping through rural lanes and city streets to evade the swimming forms with their circle mouths of sucking teeth.

Over time, Jameson Corr discovered a curious paradox that finally secured him some relief from his tormenters. He observed that the numbers of the Swimmers were greatest in proximity to human violence, where they waited in rabid hunger at scenes of murder and fearful death, for the victim's soul to ascend into their toothed maws.

However, and here was the paradox, it was in such proximity that the Swimmers showed the least interest in the dwindling thing that was Jameson Corr.

The shade of Jameson Corr realized that he could always hide in plain sight, if there was human gruesomeness afoot.

Jameson became a watcher of a different stripe.

Jameson watched men erupt and kill one another in alleys and parking lots. Jameson watched in the air just to the right of many a once-earnest suitor, as he choked the life out of his beloved.

Jameson ultimately theorized that it was the shock of murder itself that gave the Swimmers just the advantage they required, to seize a soul from its skyward flight. For it is (and has always been) the fate of murdered folk to disbelieve their impending end with an ungovernable force. When murder comes, your average person is quite taken by surprise, from the suddenly expired to the long condemned. The not-murdered, those other dying, shoot their souls up as if from a cannon, with purpose and intent.

The murdered soul doesn't quite know how to act for a short, fatal span.

Jameson came to the conclusion that the despair of the victim lent the fleeing soul a tang the Swimmers just could not get enough of.

In Gainesville, Jameson came upon a killer of girls and women. The killer studied the movements of his prey for days before falling on his victims, in moments of solitude and weakness. That man loved to torment the girls and the women to death, and avail himself of whatever charms he had not sliced or burned away as, and after, they passed. The Swimmers of the Air ripped and churned over the innocent victims like sharks a-frenzy, as if the souls were the very juiciest to be found.

In Lafayette, the shade of Jameson Corr watched a family of four, heartlessly murdered by a pair of thugs. The two villains drank beer from a cooler they had brought along, chuckling with anecdotes of truthless bravado over the corpses of the man and the wife, the son and the daughter. The men set the bodies on fire, unaware of the grotesque feeding of the Swimmers of the Air.

Jameson watched, fascinated, as one of the souls of the victims fled this carnage, indecisive in its flight.

That soul fled away instead of up. The soul got away clean, and hid in a nearby tree. The Swimmers could not overcome the tractor pull of the Askance to retrieve it into their mouths.

Yet, Jameson knew the soul was doomed to a fate not unlike his own, shifted away from its kin, as insubstantial in the real world as he was, in the Askance.

A ghost.

The two men were arrested as they walked out a side door.

In a Georgetown University cornfield, just outside of Maryland, Jameson Corr watched over the right shoulder of a man forced to dig his own grave. The two mobsters watched the man's efforts with hollow eyes of absence until it came time to kill him, which they achieved with a hammer.

Then, their eyes became bright, like stones.

Jameson Corr became a student of these acts.

His wisdom of violence and corruption at the end of that decade surpassed any ripper or stalker ever to darken a victim's path. Jameson's observations of the limits of the human soul to endure purposeless pain and abject humiliation outpaced any doctor of medicine or philosophy, any torturer for war, or pleasure.

In essence (for essence was all that Jameson was), Jameson Corr became a villain who knew only villainy, in its hideous forms and filthy methodologies. All the rest of him had been nibbled away. And when Jameson was nothing more than a mote of this villainous density, They returned to him.

The Agents of the Askance were quick to remind him that, despite the camouflage lent by the violence of men, Jameson could never wholly escape the hideous mouths of the Swimmers of the Air. He was inexorably dwindling, a mere wisp, destined to break apart into a webby nothing like a patch of scum on a busy sea. The Agents reminded Jameson of the Deal that they had offered ten years before, the Deal that had sent him running.

Kill Theda Holly.

Of course, Jameson had no choice but to agree.

In his very last moments, Jameson reached out.

The Agents plucked him from his circumstance, before the Swimmers of the Air rent him to nothing. Jameson found himself back in the real world once again. The vitality of reality jolted him and he breathed for the first time in 25 years.

But it was an entirely different Jameson Corr who drew in those virgin breaths. The confused, sensitive lad who had fallen into the Askance all those years ago, was now wholly comprised of the dismal remnant the Agents had saved. The more refined elements of Jameson Corr, such as sanity, and the milk of human kindness, had long ago become food for the lamprey-mouthed Swimmers of the Air.

The new Jameson Corr wanted nothing more than to visit his special knowledge on the object of his lifelong obsession. He wanted to finally caress Theda Holly, but with the edge of a just-sharpened blade. He wanted to slide his hand into Miss Holly's slippery innards and confuse her beating heart with his bare fingers, until it burst in her chest.

So, Jameson went out into the world, and returned to Copeland in Gladys Turnbuckle's guise. He got a job and worked hard. He found Theda, and found her in love. With William Wickley The Third's son, Robert.

Jameson watched Miss Holly for weeks, as he had learned to do from the killer of women and girls.

He studied Miss Holly's routine with the absent eyes of the mobsters who'd made the man dig his own grave.

Jameson Corr killed Miss Holly, however, with the hands of the men who murdered the wives and daughters who loved them.

He left the scene of the crime, and returned to his false life in Copeland, with the shallow disregard of the thugs who burned the family of four.

Jameson Corr's only regret was, he was not allowed ample time with Theda Holly's corpse, to enact all the depredations of his bottomless, limitless fantasy. For this, thanks can be given to the indigent itinerant, Bandana, who shuffled on scene far too soon.

This history, as fantastic and depraved as it was, came pouring from Jameson Corr's own lips as he frenetically paced the room. He still wore the outfit of a cleaning woman, the nametag proclaiming "Gladys," his long grey hair tumbling past the scars at his temples.

The pressure to finally tell the whole tale, in one sitting, to a captive audience, was too precious to pass up.

"You are one crazy shit-bird," said the one member of his audience.

Jameson's eyes darted hither and thither, as if in a paranoid consideration of unseen events.

At his pacing feet, lay the man who spoke. The man was chained, foot and hand, to eyebolts in the floor, such that escape was impossible. He was a singularly large man, with a spot of grey in his beard at the chin, and tiny glasses falling off his face.

"You weren't in no Ass-Cans, you crazy son of a bitch," said Eli Holly. "I know all about you, James Albert Corr born right here in Copeland. You were a nutter when we were kids, and you are still a raging nut-ball, if ever I saw the like!"

Tiny Jameson Corr smiled down at the wriggling giant. He seemed to wait for what Eli had to say next. Eli took the opportunity.

"Do you think I just waltzed right over here? Hell no! I made some calls and studied you up right good, you degenerate."

"You didn't just remember me?" asked Jameson, hurt.

"I remembered you from when we were kids - when you got up on that desk and showed us all the workings of your addled brain. Blabbering about things in the air. You look like shit warmed over now. And a woman, I guess. Very effective disguise."

Eli continued,

"When we were kids, your sister swore up and down that you just disappeared from your bed soon after that ridiculous spectacle. And we believed her, because that was a weird and fitting end for your bizarre ass. But that ain't the truth is it, Jameson? That's not what happened at all."

Eli squirmed to make sure his eyes were good and locked on those of Jameson Corr. Eli's next words were colored with barely concealed disgust.

"For the past 25 years you have been a honored guest of the Creedmore Psychiatric Hospital in Queens, New York. And you didn't move a muscle the whole time. I talked to Harriet Gorton about you. Harriet Gorton spilled about what you did, how you escaped. Is any of this ringing a bell, you deranged loony fucking fruitcake?"

Jameson Corr's smile never wavered a bit.

"Of course, it rings a bell, Eli," said Jameson, calmly. "For that is precisely what did happen. But so did happen... what I told you. It all happened. It's all still happening.

"It all happens together, on both sides of the Askance."

Jameson beamed down at Eli. Jameson's long grey hair framed those uncanny grey eyes with murk, even as his strange, glossy pink lipstick glinted in the gloom.

The music in Eli's head suddenly returned, for all the good it could do him now. It broke through amid a repetitive string motif that Eli immediately recognized as a variation on Bernard Herrmann's Psycho theme.

However, the music arrived in a telling way. Eli now realized that when the music had left him, generally when he thought of his sister's murder, it was being turned down. Some third party with influence over the music interceded and sequestered it from Eli's knowing, and Eli did not think it was Jameson.

Again, Eli envisioned some overarching intelligence guiding his actions, and now he knew beyond doubt that this intelligence had a nemesis. It was the nemesis who had been shutting out his music.

Now that Eli was in chains, his music could do Eli no good, so the nemesis gave it free reign once again, almost as a taunt. Eli knew he would have to try to somehow use this to his advantage and he had a curious idea as to how to do just that.

Eli was enmeshed in a larger battle, like an ant caught up in fistful of sand thrown into a man's eyes. More true, thought Eli, I am the sand.

The Psycho shrieks continued, with subtle variations that told Eli that Jameson Corr believed every single word he said about the Agents and the Swimmers, the Askance, and the thinning veil that separated that place from common reality.

But only one thing was certain.

This was the foul man who had murdered his sister, Theda.

And Eli was in no good way to enact justice, or revenge.

Part 3

The Tree of Life

"I want to tell you some important things before we start our journey. I lived through it all. That's one problem about relating events in the first person. The reader knows the narrator didn't get killed."

-Robert McCammon, Boy's Life

ChApTeR 1

Adria and I were quaffing steaming cups of hot chocolate when Cot and Robert Wickley walked in the front door of Molly White's cabin. I would like to say I was surprised, or somehow adversely affected, but I took it in stride. Robert's status as my once unwitting adversary did not so much as nudge in my consciousness. I was becalmed close to a stupor by hot chocolate and by the intensity of the events I had just survived.

My hand still smelled of Buster's gory chompers. My head still buzzed with a chemical burn.

Adria sat beside me. When the two burst through the door, she set her cup down quickly, splashing its contents, in preparation for some defensive move. I set my hand on Adria's thigh, to settle her, and Cot's eyes locked on the action. Impropriety nearly loomed, but could not win out.

"Gar, wot a frantic pair ye present," said Molly to Cot and Robert, filling her tea pot from an imposing iron pump lurking in the corner. Molly heaved up the heavy iron handle with a groan and pushed it back down, almost lifting the rest of her from the planked floor. A strong stream of water splashed down the kettle's tin hole.

Robert waved his arms as if we were a crowd of agitators instead of a room of three. "Hello everybody, my name is Robert Wickley. Cot asked me to bring her here. Her parents are out of town, is that right? I hope I did the right thing, bringing her here."

Robert stuck his hand out for someone to shake.

When no one approached to take it, Adria rolled her eyes at yet again being the only polite one of us in the presence of a Wickley, and pushed herself out of her chair.

"Nice to meet you, Mr. Wickley." Adria said, and shook his hand.

"What about you two?" Cot asked of Adria and myself, with a suspicious tone. "You go and get married and have a kid or something? You look like a couple of tired old adults."

I fixed Cot with a steely glare for this grievous critique.

"Cot, if you –" I only just began, when Molly White cleared her throat quite menacingly. I clamped shut my mouth.

"We got some bit o' talk to talk I'm thinkin'," said Molly, motioning for Cot and Robert to sit, which they hastily did. She brought over some cups of cocoa and Robert looked about for something to rest the very hot objects upon. Molly noted his dilemma and grabbed a small stool. We all set our cups on it.

Molly pulled up another small stool and set it down. Then she left the room.

"Been havin' adventures?" came Molly's voice from beyond the door. "Learnin' and listenin'. Questioning."

Cot looked a little spooked.

"Young trout John almost broken with 'mazement and confusion. His love, not nearly so. Cot like to burst with new knowledge. Robert Wickley, unburdened of so much, he's finally left his house!" Sounds of rummaging came through the door with Molly's words. Her summation of my own and Adria's situation, rendered in the sparse, weird way I was finally able to unravel, was spot on. This probably meant that Molly's words about Cot and Robert were true as well. But how? And what did she mean by Cot's "new knowledge" and Robert being "unburdened?"

Robert seemed aghast.

"You do know this woman, right Cot? She seems a bit…" Robert searched for the words.

"Like a crazy forest lady?" offered Cot.

"That's it. Yes, exactly."

"Here we be, me garland!" Molly shouted, in the other room.

Cot nodded. "That's just what she is. But I love her. She saved my life."

Robert was struck speechless by this response, and said nothing further.

Adria reached over to me and grasped my hand. I looked up at her and we smiled because we could not help but to. The Warm filled my face and my chest, just like I used to feel, sitting across from Miss Holly, all those eons ago.

Molly White emerged from the other room, carrying a green book. She was clad in strange garments - a striking leather jacket with broad lapels, and a long leather skirt. I can tell you from my present vantage that Molly looked more than anything like the Katherine Hepburn of A Lion in Winter had donned the attire she wore in The African Queen, a stately, elderly female adventurer, such as might be glimpsed as mother or aunt to the hero, in the nearest Mummy movie.

Molly twirled in a girlish way, causing the hem of the long leather skirt to ascend to the slightest degree.

I fretted as to Molly's mental stability. I turned my attention to the book in Molly's hands, to banish the cognitive discomfort provided by her behavior.

The book was thin, and had the dimensions of a magazine, like LIFE magazine, which is to say taller and wider, yet thinner than your usual book. It looked old in her old hands. As she brought the book closer, one of those old hands splayed across the cover in a brushing motion that was more akin to presentation than to dusting.

Molly brought the volume close to her chest as she glared disapprovingly down at the cups of cocoa.

Without a moment's hesitation, the four of us collected our respective cups from that surface. Molly replaced them with the green book. The title, once gilded, now little more than depressions in the green weave of the cover, was many words long. Over that tiny landscape was scrawled a different, shorter title in white wax pencil.

Molly reached into the pocket of her dress and drew out some small thing. I was sure that it was the same small thing that claimed her attention when first we met, under the Old Cross bridge, the little thing that she'd kept removing from her pocket and looking down at.

She set it atop the book.

I knew what the small object was. I had seen such a thing in an old comic, not a Classics Illustrated, but some reprint of horror comics from the 40's. The story was about an old Rabbi in a place called Prague, who made a man out of clay whom he called the Golem.

The object in question appeared in that comic. A small child played with the thing in the looming shadow of the Golem, just before the Golem ripped the poor urchin to shreds. The object was like a small wooden top, hewn in a geometrical way with strange glyphs cut into each face. I thought hard and came up with its name.

It was called a dreidel. I looked below the dreidel to the scrawled white title of the green book.

The Tree of Life.

Molly suddenly brought herself up to a different height than I was used to with her; she stooped no more.

She drew her arms back and clasped her hands behind her.

Molly studied all our faces one after the other.

She paced a bit, as if summoning fortitude, finally turning back to us with a swoosh of her long leather skirt. Molly planted herself in the other stool and set her hands majestically on her knees, like a king looking down from a throne.

"I suppose the first thing to do is drop that silly way of speaking. I cannot tell you all the times I have regretted taking it on. My god, this is nice! I haven't spoken in a genuine way to another soul in 30 long years," said Molly White, in a lilting voice, in perfect, Bridgeford English.

We were all cast into stone-stunned silence. Molly White fixed us with a beaming smile.

"I am ever so pleased to finally, truly meet you all, and especially you, Robert." Molly's eyes lingered on him. It seemed she had something of a crush on the man, even at this early moment in their association. Molly pored over his features with her eyes. I began to feel some embarrassment for Molly and glanced to Cot and Adria to see they were wrestling similar notions.

Molly broke her regard of Robert with some difficulty, it seemed, and turned her attention to all of us.

"You have known me as Molly White, because the times demanded it. Well now times have changed, and drastically. It is time you knew me by the name I was born by.

"You may call me Isobel. Isobel Whitehead-Patrick."

We were all simultaneously saddened at Molly's sudden downturn in psychological functioning. We exchanged furtive looks with each other and with various objects in the room, but not at Molly, whose smile, I could see out of the corner of my eye, diminished away.

"Of course," Molly said. "This is why I have brought out these objects, and dressed in these clothes of my youth, which I barely fit any longer, to lend some physical proof to the tale I am about to tell you. Right now you think me quite mad, and that is more than understandable. I can only hope you can find it in your hearts to forgive my long deception, and to listen to my tale."

Adria, Robert and I were like wooden statues of ourselves. Cot, however, was nodding her head sympathetically.

"We will, Molly. I mean - Isobel," said Cot, tenderly.

Molly's eyes got shiny and she slowly nodded her head.

"Thank you, Cot. Thank you all. When my tale is done, I will ask favors of you. After you hear what I have to say, I think you will see the importance of my deception, and of what I will ask you to do. Please open your hearts to me, and work to suspend all that has you invested in the ways of the world as you know it. For the world is not as you know it.

"The world is not as you know it, at all."

Robert Spande
The Born and the Made

The Third and Final Tale of Isobel Whitehead-Patrick
1939-1941

For one entire year Isobel waited.

The first month was an excruciation of expectation. The second and third months were anxious confusion. The fourth month through the eighth, Isobel shifted through a depression that sapped her hollow.

The year closed with a steadfast decision to resume the project of her life.

High on the resultant list was a job. Nowhere on the list was a boyfriend. Yet fate saw fit to saddle her with the latter before fitting her with the former, through a bizarre series of non-encounters.

The young man she would love became known to her by his non-appearance at a string of events where his absence was vocally noted by childhood friends Isobel was attempting to ingratiate, as she clawed her way back into the Copeland social scene.

"Where is Billy?" complained the presumptive head of their small company, Roger Mahn.

"Who is this Billy who never shows up?" Isobel asked.

"Just a fop!" someone offered.

An explosion of derisive laughter.

A girl Isobel knew to be otherwise bright and resourceful, called Sadie Brown, who would one day drop dead at her own daughter's funeral, under the name Saide Holly, snorted and brayed to Isobel, alcoholically, "Don't you remember?"

The small group guffawed as one, save Isobel.

"C'mon Isobel! You remember," screeched the girl. "The water hole? When we were kids?"

Isobel did remember. When she was eight or nine, swimming with the girls.

A group of boys arrived. In that group was a lad who seemed out of place, thoughtful, or otherwise preoccupied. Unlike the others in the group, he was not raucous, nor did he guffaw. It was to this somber lad that the shame of that afternoon accrued, the embarrassing display that named him forever after.

The lad had no conception that his swimsuit was split down the back; no realization, that, whenever he bent over to pick something up, or prepared to dive, he displayed quite garishly that part of himself that he would have otherwise shielded from every eye in the universe, to include his own, until the day he died.

That part, sadly, being his anus.

To the others gathered on that idyllic summer afternoon, this opportunity proved grist for their schemes, and the boy consented unwittingly to accomplish many seemingly innocent tasks at their behest, causing him to re-display that staggeringly intimate part of himself for their unquenchable amusement, all afternoon. When he finally realized what game was afoot his embarrassment was tantamount to true horror, while his supposed friends, including Isobel (to her subsequent shame), laughed at his misfortune. Isobel rarely saw the lad again.

"Do you mean Winky?" Isobel asked, using the name the young William Wickley The Third acquired that day. "Whatever happened to him?"

"He is a richy rich you know. Dad owns the damned sawmill. Winky studied abroad after the 'Afternoon of the Asshole.'"

"Isn't that Debussy?" asked Thomas Egan.

This proved a comment side splittingly funny for all but Isobel, who remembered William Wickley The Third's shame, how he ran into the forest verging tears, to leave their lives from that point forward.

"He came back about a year ago. All is forgiven! He is a true chap. He doesn't like it if you call him Winky, though. Therefore, we do, whenever possible," said Chip Williams, a 26 year old epicurean, well on his way to morbid obesity.

"However, I call him Sir Winky to acknowledge his pedigree."

"He doesn't show up much," added Tom Tietze.

"I wonder why?" asked Isobel disapprovingly.

"I recall you nearly doubled over with laughter, Belly," returned Tom, using the name this very same group had bestowed, to her great dissatisfaction, all those years ago. That was when Isobel realized she did not like her childhood friends much anymore.

They had not grown up sufficiently, she noted.

In later days, William Wickley the Third was much on Isobel's mind. Isobel fantasized about him a bit.

William was surely tall, and likely handsome, if her ability to gauge the morphology of faces over time was any good. He was also educated abroad and wealthy, being the son of William Wickley the Second, the owner of the sawmill. Unless he was a complete foppish boor, Isobel believed she and William were destined to click on some level that eluded her friends from childhood.

Isobel set William Wickley The Third, otherwise known these long years as Sir Winky, of the Afternoon of the Asshole, in her sights.

Which is not to say she saw William with her actual eyes. Via deliberate investigation, Isobel discovered William Wickley's favored haunts, but whenever she haunted these places herself, Isobel invariably arrived some minutes too late, or hours to soon, to catch him.

Yet her investigations did produce one thing.

Some of the residents to whom Isobel turned to for information, noted, remembered and conveyed her interest into the cloud of gossip that hung, like a miasma, around Copeland.

It was only a matter of time before someone whispered Isobel's name into William Wickley's own ear.

That Sunday, after Isobel and her parents returned from church, while Isobel hacked into a watermelon for Sunday Lunch, somebody knocked, with seeming purpose, on their front door.

Isobel answered the door, opening it wide enough so that her mother, at the table painting glaze on a hot ham, saw a besuited William Wickley The Third darkly looming against the bright of the outsides, with a grim and cranky aspect, which caused the woman to inadvertently, yet unmistakably, shout "Yipes!"

Isobel's father, instinctually activated by his wife's favorite exclamation of surprise, popped to his feet from his rocker, where he had been fiddling with the radio console. The only person among them who remained coldly composed was Isobel herself, from whose face flowed no telling emotions, nor any hints of intent, nor any suggestions of purpose.

Her eyes settled on William's.

Their effect on the relatively savage beast that existed behind those eyes, caused William to forget all that he was poised to say.

William had intended to upbraid the woman who was tracking him through town. When he found out that it was this Whitehead-Patrick person, one of the group who had shamed him for their tawdry amusement at the water hole all those years ago (the whole of whom he had been conspicuously avoiding), his anger ramped to a level unprecedented.

But when Isobel's eyes fixed William's, these impulses fairly flowed out of him.

"I heard you were looking for me," said William, finally, more tenderly than he intended.

"Indeed, I am," said Isobel, who then walked out onto the front step with William, closing the door behind her.

This left her parents fretting yet again, an activity that had dominated their sensibilities ever since Isobel had returned from Europe. To their dismay, they watched through the stained-glass window of the door, as the two smudges representing their daughter and the Son of the Most Malevolently Powerful Man in Town, stepped down, out of the frame.

They both rushed to the window over the kitchen sink, causing a tin colander to clatter into the living room. Their daughter and William Wickley were now talking near the front of his white Daimler. Isobel and William sported little smiles on their faces. Little flirtatious smiles such as those Isobel's parents employed to ensnare one another in their own youths.

Isobel's parents both arrived at similar endgames from the initial condition of those flirty smiles. For Isobel's mother, this evolution of events gave her great hope and great solace. Indeed, if one could have entered her mind at that point, one would have marveled at the tapestry and pageant of the fantasies derived from this merest prospect of joining with the Wickley clan.

Isobel's father, however, fled his own similar thoughts on the matter, at high speed, slamming mental doors behind him and throwing down psychic obstacles, until the thought of his lovely daughter marrying into that den of capitalists grew tired of the chase.

William Wickley glanced toward the house. Isobel's parents were quick to duck his notice.

They resumed their surveillance.

Isobel looked at William with expectant hopefulness. William gazed at his own feet. Finally, William nodded and Isobel gave him a hug, for god's sakes!

Isobel's mother and father grasped the available parts of the other, and squeezed.

Isobel turned back to the house with a big smile on her face, a smile that William could not see. He watched her until she closed the front door. William looked down at his shoes again, shaking his head bemusedly, smiling to the merest extent. Then he got into his car and drove off.

Only then did Isobel's parents relax their perch and notice that Isobel was standing right behind them.

~

Isobel and William saw each other every day, shortly after that Sunday encounter. He took her far and wide in his white Daimler. He refused, however, to give her a tour of the sawmill.

"That place is disgusting, I'm ashamed of it," whispered William.

This was shocking to Isobel, who was quick to ask him why.

"It is going to eat the entire Heart-Shaped Forest from the inside out!" he spat. "This beautiful place is not going to be so beautiful in a hundred years. My dad doesn't know how, or care even, to slow down to a respectable level of cutting. He does no replanting. He does not give a care as to the safety of the sawyers, who die like flies in an oven, from accidents and disease. He's horrible."

This took Isobel quite by surprise, for she thought that, as next in line to steward the sawmill into the future, William would have an entirely different outlook.

"I will die before I take over that mill," he said, with finality.

And that was the moment Isobel fell, to her own reasoning, finally and completely in love with William Wickley the Third (or Winky, to his enemies).

Their relationship, from that point, followed a trajectory to which they were not active participants, but instead, subjects under the power of something simultaneously external, and intimately internal, to them both. Their hearts were at the wheel, driving them inexorably onward, farther into each another's embrace, than they ever thought possible.

Their so-called peers were offended, for reasons no one cared to articulate, and treated Isobel and William as embarrassing pariahs, which only brought the two closer together.

Isobel, who had had only the one, glancing experience of love (barely achieved, while crossing the Atlantic) was, even so, the tutor for William, who had no experience whatsoever in these realms. He looked to her for guidance and permission in all things romantic.

While such a tendency in a man is often bothersome to the women of this world, for Isobel, it was a comfort. She was happy to take William's hand and lead him tenderly through the potential pitfalls that successful relationships must circumvent, at least in her theories.

Isobel was therefore especially careful, as she led a both reluctant and expectant William, to her bed.

Not her bed at home, of course, but a bed of leaves and pine needles deep in the Heart-Shaped forest, which Isobel and William had recently taken to exploring, and over this particular patch of which they frantically cast a tartan blanket.

The event represented the first real sex for both of them. As such, it was a painful and embarrassing mess, but also an earth-shaking discovery, making them not just lovers, but co-conspirators in love, the discoverers of a strange and beautiful artifact that no one on earth had ever found before, discoverers who, instead of sharing their discovery with museums and the rest of the world, decide to selfishly secret the artifact between themselves, and clandestinely visit it, whenever possible.

One of the places they would visit the amazing artifact was in the back of William's Daimler.

As William's forehead dripped sweat onto Isobel's back, he was mesmerized by the transitions and shimmerings of her gloriously white backside. He slid his hands wonderingly over that slick expanse and did his best to understand the notions he derived from this unprecedented behavior.

William was brought to mind of the film he and Isobel had seen together some weeks ago, The Wizard of Oz. William was totally flummoxed as to how they, the filmmakers, near the start of the film, had accomplished the menacing tornado that seemingly whipped in the distance, kicking up enormous clouds of debris at its foot.

The twister was, he later learned after some digging, a special effect, a completely non-magical yet utterly compelling illusion, which physically inhabited the set with the actress who played Dorothy.

So it was with sex and Isobel.

Somehow, amid the drudgery and pain of life (for the drudgery and pain of life were paramount in William's worldview), there existed an amazing illusion of contentment and oneness, derived from the basest physical act that William had ever performed.

It did not matter where the act occurred, thought William, as his neck began to ache at the way the Daimler's roof made his head bounce unnaturally against his own shoulder. Sex, William was sure, was the one special effect that life offered.

William marveled that he was allowed to experience it with the most alluring woman who ever existed, a woman who, when not engaged with him in the act of sex, was his better in the realms of language, logic, philosophy and physical science. A woman, to whom he could turn with any question or problem that had ever vexed him.

When they weren't talking to one another, the aesthetic pleasure William derived, from simply drinking in Isobel's image, made his lungs stop working correctly.

To William, it was beyond any serious doubt that Isobel Whitehead-Patrick was the woman he would marry.

~

Isobel was not so sure. She took some convincing.

The Grand Convincer was her own mother, of course, whose first act was to shock-muzzle Isobel's father from any of his own opinionated offerings on the matter (threatening pains only a wife can inflict on a husband, and, of which, every husband is genetically aware, and afeared).

When this was thoroughly accomplished, the Convincer sidled up to the Convincee.

There began an onslaught, such as that the Colorado River performed on the Earth those many years ago, gouging it into the Grand Canyon with amazing speed, geologically speaking. The Grand Convincing started as a primordial trickle, cutting new grooves into Isobel's thoughts on the theoretical matter of her own marriage, widening and deepening those widenings, via logical and unassailable argument, into the much vaunted sure thing that was, in the mind of Grand Convincer, the inescapable certitude of her daughter's future union with William Wickley the Third.

Her mother used her Womb Voice, bypassing Isobel's meager, socially acquired firewalls. The Convincer caressed Isobel's hair from her temples as she spoke, the nails tickling her scalp, an act long producing of a certain somnambulance in Isobel, from a kid.

William had to do none of the Convincing at all, and the Convincer made well and sure he never heard of the Convincing that took place, essential so that William did not get cold feet himself, which would have taxed the Convincer's powers of Convincing beyond all measure.

In fact, William was surprised and pleased at how quickly Isobel returned to affirm their assignation of marriage.

~

You will remember Isobel and William's first sexual encounter in the Heart-Shaped Forest. We must go back there, I'm afraid, though not for reasons of prurience. We will only look out through Isobel's own eyes, and Isobel never even once glanced down to see what was going on. The visual displacements singular to their activity may simply be assumed to have taken place, and need not be described in tired mode of "… the scene bounced chaotically in her vision as his…" etc. etc.

There may prove, however, some need to become sexually expository to the tiniest degree, and for this, the author is blameless.

For, during their ruttage, Isobel was gazing hard at a nearby hillside, a hillside denuded of trees and studded with stumps. There was a road that wound up its slope from the roughly east to the roughly west, crossing the hill's crest exactly at the middle. In the center of this road, at the very apex of the hill, was the small tree Isobel knew from the mysterious occurrence of her youth. It grew right up out of the road, as it would, some 30 years later, grow right up out of Cot Cleary's chest. The tree was as she remembered it, a tiny stalk topped by a ball of green sprinkled with little flowers, perpetually shivering.

The sound came to her ears then, the choir of lament, as Isobel had come to know it in the examining of her own recall. The lament assailed her ears even as the chemical surge of the forest's heady odor invaded her nostrils.

Her eyes were locked on the tree throughout William's exertions and then, after one particularly savage thrust, the tree was gone, producing a hitch in Isobel's awareness that unfurled into an orgasm the likes of which, any girl in the world would be grateful to experience during her own devirginization.

This development pulled from William his own mind-splitting and reasonably simultaneous orgasm, due mostly to Isobel's lurid writhings amid her otherwise classically beautiful charms, charms that William associated with the public sphere, and this association (between her writhings and the public sphere) did his erotic center well-in.

The semen fairly exploded from him, inundating her womb and impregnating Isobel Whitehead-Patrick with all spermatazoan haste. And sperm do not dawdle.

Isobel and William's status as being "made for each other" and being "two halves of the same whole" was by this orgasmic moment cemented. Considered mathematically, the turgid moment was at least 64% responsible for Isobel and William's engagement, even though the mutual orgasms' biological end-product would make their marriage a foregone conclusion, only a few months hence, when Isobel's pregnancy became undeniable to any who cared to look.

But far before such obstetric morphing took center stage, or even made itself noticeable to its host, Isobel set out on her own, secret mission.

She returned to the place where she and William had lain that day and gazed across at the razed hill at the road that cut its center. The tree was no longer there, of course, but Isobel made her slow way to where it had stood, then continued down the dirt road for some miles, as the devastation of the logging finally gave way to real forest again.

As she strongly felt she would, Isobel caught the irregular horizontality of a roof line some yards off the road, just as her feet were becoming strident in their protestations.

It was a small wooden cabin, but as Isobel drew close, she saw that it was overrun on every surface with the tendrils of boughs from the trees surrounding it, and by strange overgrowths of the grasses and flowers around it. Roots broke from the ground in ungraspable profusions, carpeting the porch and siding the house, even overgrowing the roof. Mycelium ghosted the base and crawled up the corners. Through the separations in this rhizomatic web of impossible growth, Isobel could see that a regular old log cabin existed underneath it all.

Isobel entered the one room through the portal at the front, the door overgrown, stuck open into the room at an eternal angle. Inside were sharp shafts of light falling like a shower on the figure that lay in-state there, reminding Isobel of the painting of the deceased King Arthur, from her children's book of the Knights of the Round Table.

How the very forces of nature seemed to draw near, to honor the dead king: the light falling, the petals in the air, the somber visitation of the animals themselves in the borders.

It was Mabel Leone Lighty who lay there, long dead, wearing a shift of dirty white, her silver hair tumbling off her head to wind down into the roots of the floor itself.

Mabel Leone Lighty's hands, such as they were, lay drawn to her chest, clutching some thing between them, some green, living thing.

As Isobel withdrew the thing from the deceased dame's grasp, she saw that it was a large, folded-up leaf, still attached, at its base, to a green and winding connection that joined the woody tendrils covering the wall.

Reluctantly, Isobel detached it, with a tug. She unfolded the green leaf before her eyes. An acorn rolled lazily out of the leaf, along a fold, bouncing on the root-hewn floor, coming to a rest under the couch upon which the dead woman reposed. Isobel barely noticed, until she read the ragged slip of paper that lay in the cradle of the opened leaf.

"ISBEL SWALO TE ACORN," said the note, written in a jagged scrawl, in what appeared to be dried blood.

After Isobel fished it out, she studied the acorn some, gauging its swallowability. She was fortunate in that it was a tiny breed, but nonetheless sporting of the conventionally rough cap, which caused some apprehension in its appraiser's mind.

Oh, she was going to swallow it all right. She just needed to know what she was getting into. Indeed, that rough cap scored Isobel's throat good, but she got it down.

When it was down, Isobel did not wait around, to shoot up through the roof, or turn into a tree, or for any magical thing to transpire.

She just walked out the doorway, even as the house started to creak and crack at what Isobel knew would be, some minutes after she left, a clenching demolition of the shrine-like abode housing Mabel Leone Lighty's corpse, by the infinitude of tentacular branches and ropes of green.

~

While it was known, for a surety, by the acorn that Isobel had swallowed, that it was the author of the madness that soon consumed her, Isobel herself was not so sure.

The cause was ultimately unimportant, since it was not a wholly unpleasant madness, to its subject, but to the rest of the world, and especially to William, the madness rent reality asunder.

The madness began immediately, that very night, in Isobel's dreams.

"It must be protected," said Mabel Leone Lighty to her, to some her that walked with Mabel Leone Lighty in a thick wood. Isobel noticed that Mabel's speech had changed. Now she talked, well, just like Isobel did.

Mabel Leone Lighty stopped.

There was the tree before them, small, yet somehow majestic, like the tallest, sturdiest oak.

The tree reached out to her, in just the way a tree would communicate to a person, in Isobel's long-held fantasies. It was a complexity, slow and tentative, that washed over her, under and into her senses, a meaning that expanded and settled into her awareness.

Isobel realized that she was at class.

Mabel Leone Lighty was the teacher, and the class was how to talk to this tree.

In the real world, Isobel was beset by noisome physical symptoms. She began to bat unconsciously at her right ear, at a buzzing pain that tortured her there, like a fly in a never ending cochlear seizure.

An insistent itch settled on her, everywhere, but especially at her outer arms, and one other place too, one other, impossible place.

Her brain in her skull set to itching like crazy, which was crazy, since Isobel Whitehead-Patrick had never felt her brain before, nor had any person she had ever heard of. There was a cat in her brain, perhaps, along with the fly, thought Isobel, too many times.

"You are going to have a baby," said Mabel Leone Lighty, with a lovely smile that filled Isobel with hope.

"You are going to have a baby," said Dr. Mowlem, with a paternal look of disapproval, which leeched away any of the natural enjoyment that might normally come with such an announcement. Isobel's mother rested her face into her lime green gloved hand and sobbed.

Isobel was furious at them both. She batted at her ear.

"You huge jerks," was all she said and would say no more.

Isobel made her mother drop her off at the library, where she met William. Isobel told him the news in his Daimler. He whooped with joy and did a little jig outside the car. This gave Isobel great pleasure, which overcame the buzzing and the itching for a short, sweet while. They drove some miles and made love against the car with whole and total abandon.

But William was already noticing a shifting in her.

Isobel was irritated now, much of the time. He saw her bicker at her parents and them take it admirably, with great patience.

Whenever William presented Isobel a question, no matter the kind, she was cross. He often had to question her, because much of the time she was hard to comprehend. Every question was, to her, an interrogation filled with subterfuge and motive.

William told himself it was just a normal aspect of pregnancy, even as a wiser part of him knew better.

Isobel's room became a chaotic mess that she would collapse anywhere into, in a sleep so deep, it caused her parents much dismay (and many placings of a pocket mirror under her nose, to ensure she was breathing).

Isobel was simultaneously livened, and deadened. Indeed, this contradiction was the madness that flowed over Isobel.

To that which is commonly considered the matter and stuff of the universe, she was reborn, delighting in the smallest feature of whatever aspect of that matter and stuff rode before her consuming vision.

Isobel was aware of the non-human biomass that dominated the planet, in a way never she never before imagined. She filled her days with study of the Heart-Shaped Forest, reading its stanzas and drinking of its vintage.

But with regard to the world of people, Isobel was losing her footing. People seemed sort of ridiculous and laughable, when they weren't being noisome and full of bother.

This sad impression even accrued to William, who could feel its cold bite in the spaces between every word Isobel deigned to speak nowadays, which were far too few, and far too far between.

But Isobel still loved him.

Oh, how she loved William.

Sadly, the part of her that loved him, was fighting hard to keep from being subsumed under the new part, the part of her that thrilled at the living world so intensely, there was no time for human love.

Even thoughts of the baby inside her, whom Isobel loved with a force that paled the other loves, filled her with a desire to be done with it, to be on the other side of it, so she could get on with her new role.

Isobel was a mass of contradictory impulses and thoughts. A walking, distracted thing, pulled hither and thither, as the part of her still named Isobel fought, desperately, to keep hold of her new family.

"You may not love," said Mabel Leone Lighty, with tender firmness. Mabel held Isobel's hand and Isobel was an old lady in a shapeless shift, just like Mabel herself had lain in.

"You may only dream one dream at a time, you know. This dream."

Isobel's heart was broken in a sadness, so epic, she was undone, and crumpled to the forest floor.

They found her sleeping on the roof. Isobel had apparently grabbed the overhanging branches of a nearby tree, to wind them somehow around herself. She clutched in dreams that would not let go of her, even as the firemen slapped at her cheeks and yelled into her face.

Only when they chopped the winding branch, did Isobel pop awake and allow with them to send her down the ladder.

After this event, Isobel noticed that her thoughts had changed. It might be better said that the way Isobel thought skidded into a wholly novel arrangement.

Isobel knew damned well, by this time, that it was no cat nor fly that deranged her. She knew it was that fucking acorn.

Isobel knew this so resolutely, because she was now in constant communication with that acorn, as it resided there in her belly, awash with acids that strangely had no effect whatsoever upon it.

The little acorn advised her ongoing, using the new language the rearrangement of her mind demanded.

The language of the Tree of Life.

Isobel heard her parents that night. They were planning to send her to a madhouse in Hunstable.

"You must run!" Mabel Leone Lighty screamed.

Isobel shot awake. There was no light under her door.

She grabbed her shoes and pulled out the box with the leather Amelia Earhart outfit, her dissertation, and the tiny wooden dreidel that Sarah had given her, held desperately out to Isobel, dropped into her outstretched hand, even as Jake, unnoticing of any of this, stepped onto Ellis Island and away from Isobel, forever.

Isobel thought of that man, and the other one, the one who put the baby in her, the one who was diminishing somberly away, such that the two men resided together, only in her head, and not at all in the real world.

She ran straight from her bed into the Heart-Shaped Forest, and not her parents, nor William, nor anyone else, ever saw Isobel Whitehead-Patrick again.

~

Seven months and twenty three days after Isobel Whitehead-Patrick was last seen, there was a booming at the front door of the Wickley mansion.

The wind was howling in deepest midwinter.

The booming was so awesome and fearful, William Wickley the Second could not help but think it a terrible night for his millworkers to choose to finally attack his door with a battering ram.

The corpulent old man got up to see whatever it was all about, only to have his son shoot past him and bolt in an unseemly hastiness down the center stairs.

William Wickley the Third, or Winky, to his enemies, ran right up to the front door in his pajamas, and began to work at the locks.

"William, wait," said the father, with even more than his usual torpor.

But William paid the old man no heed at all.

He whipped open the door. His father was quick to notice that William's expectant eyes were fixed on a level of height that would have otherwise corresponded to the eyes of Isobel Whitehead-Patrick, who was, the father noted, sadly, not there.

William's shoulders slumped.

This act naturally brought his gaze downward, where his eyes settled on a strange object. It looked like an oblong wooden bowl, so finely wrought, it appeared almost as if the wooden bowl had been grown into its shape. There was something in the bowl. The whole thing steamed white in the night, as snow streamed down against it.

"I thought I was going to be murdered," muttered the father to himself, contentedly patting at his girth as if to confirm it was still there. The old man returned to his room without a second glance.

William bent down. After investigative touchings, he grabbed the object and brought it inside. The wooden bowl was warm, like wood left out in direct sunlight, though it was darkest night in a terrible December storm. In the bowl was a bedding of the greenest grass William had ever beheld. This extreme vision may have been contextually affected by the weather.

Atop the green grass lay a mossen bundle, roughly the size and shape of a human baby.

In fact, William knew it was a human baby there, under the strange blanket of warm moss. He knew it was his baby. For one horrifying moment, William dreamed a fever dream, wherein Isobel had, in her madness, birthed their baby and cooked it, and here it was, cooled by the storm but still warm, for William to eat.

This nightmare was quickly overturned by stirrings under the blanket, and a small sigh.

William did not uncover the baby just yet, for William was no longer that man who had danced a jig upon hearing of this creature's eventuality.

That man's propensity for love had been abandoned as unsafe nonsense.

William had, of late, taken up more with his father's way of thinking. Only in the young man's dreams did he allow for, hunger for, the world of Isobel Whitehead-Patrick and their once-future together.

Their happy possibilities were not allowed back into cold reality with the waking William, who became armored with a thick air of malevolence as he entered the world he had chosen instead.

The world of his father.

The world of the sawmill.

William did not think he wanted this baby. But even more than that he did not want to want this baby.

That sort of sentiment, William determined, must be kept well at bay.

War was, after all, just on the horizon.

A dark beast.

Hungry for wood.

But his duty was clear. William pulled up the baby from the wooden bowl. He would name the thing Robert, he decided. It was the name of a man who'd been hurt at the mill that day, the first name that came to mind.

Robert did his level best to make some kind of eye contact, but William would have none of it, and summoned the maids.

Robert Spande
The Born and the Made

ChApTeR 2

As Isobel Whitehead-Patrick, or Molly White to her friends, finished her tale, there was a knock at the cabin door.

Isobel's head jerked that way. She looked back at us and said, "Oh dear."

Adria and Cot were immediately alarmed. They rose to their feet. Robert Wickley sat still, his questioning eyes locked on Isobel Whitehead-Patrick. I slowly got up and looked to Isobel/Molly for instruction.

"I am certainly not expecting anyone, John," she said to me. It was lovely to hear my name without a "trout" in front of it. So lovely, in fact, that I decided to think of her as Isobel from that point forward. I put my hand on Isobel's shoulder and slid past her to go to the door.

"Absolutely not, dear John. You get behind me. I may be old, but I have a few tricks left." Isobel looked vibrant, young and defiant of all that might cross her. I nodded and slowed behind her.

"Absolutely not!" exclaimed Robert Wickley who was, evidently, Isobel's son.

The man shot to his feet.

"I may have only just learned of you... you... person who is apparently my own mother... but I'm not about to let you face something that clearly has you alarmed. You just get behind me and we will sort out who is who to whom when things calm down. You get behind me."

Isobel covered her face with her hands. She threw her arms around Robert and wept. Robert hugged her back confusedly, his face a-bother.

"The door?" said Cot, rudely, fed up with the emotion people were evidencing at every turn.

"I have so much more to tell you! So much more to say!" cried Isobel into Robert's shoulder.

My knowledge rang with the story that Isobel Whitehead-Patrick had just relayed to us.

The way Isobel had almost died as a child, just like Cot. How she had been visited by a woman who resembled the Molly White I thought I knew, even more than Molly White did (given that Isobel was not a person named Molly White at all). How the tiny tree had saved Isobel, healed her, just the way it had done with my dear, bullheaded sister.

Isobel's youthful romance with, of all people, a young and less terrible Winky! That part was way more unbelievable than any other part of her story.

"I made William into what he is, dear Robert," Isobel had whispered, with a shaky voice, after explaining the truth of his tortured lineage.

"It was all my fault," she had sighed.

There were so many questions. Isobel's story opened up more mysteries than it solved. As I had gotten so used to doing, I resigned Isobel's fantastic story to the shelves in my mind where I housed all the unbelievable circumstances that had preceded.

There was an aspect of Isobel's story that left me worried, however. Something that I could not forestall thinking about.

If Isobel's life was saved by this Mabel Leone Lighty person, who then pressed her, by virtue of this debt, into throwing away her own happiness, in order to protect this tree, this Tree of Life – did Isobel Whitehead-Patrick expect to do the same with Cot?

Isobel let loose of her son with reluctance.

Robert strode past his newfound mother to the door and opened it wide.

ChApTeR 3

Kimberly Lewis left out the front of Kimberly's Liquors, in state akin to frenzy.

What caused her frantic exit? Why was she on Main Street deep in the night, in a hard snow?

She had no idea. Something had pulled her from the residence at the back of the liquor store, tugged her out to this spot by unknown and worrisome means.

She sped down the avenue, whipping her head left and right, in search of the cause of her undefined dilemma.

Was it music she heard stuttering through the snowflakes?

Not just any music. It was familiar, yet not the kind of music one hears on the radio or on a record album. It spoke a raw phrase that repeated over and over, scratching, gnawing at Kimberly's awareness with a terrible grating.

It was dramatic, annoying, repetitive. Definitely movie music. And, after a moment of internal reflection, she knew what movie music it was.

It was the all too memorable murder music from that crazy flick about the motel guy who knifes the woman in the shower. The music from that very scene whipped in the wind of the night, sounding like no music Kimberly Lewis had ever heard, and everywhere, as if emitted from the very snowflakes themselves.

Now she remembered the name of the movie. It was called Psycho - that nightmarish Hitchcock movie they went to some years back. They had seen it at the drive-in over on 104. Psycho had given poor Kim at least a week of anxious showers.

Kimberly stopped. She studied the big flakes of snow as they chaotically descended about her. Kimberly drew close to one, particular flake as it fell, lowering her face along its journey.

The music came again, that siren-like scream of repetitive shrieks.

The snowflake vibrated, as if in sympathy. Kimberly looked from one snowflake to another with dawning amazement to see them all vibrating just like that first one.

Kimberly passed a parked car and caught in the side mirror an oscillation that caused the scene in its frame to jigger. She brought her face close and could see the whole car vibrating in sympathy with the music, just like the snowflakes were. She went to a streetlight, quickly perceiving that it pulsed to the music like everything else.

Kimberly realized that all these objects were, not synced to the weird, bleating music that brought her out into the night, but were somehow producing it.

All the cars, buildings, trees, snowflakes and every single thing around Kimberly was oscillating, vibrating like a harp string. Though each thrumming object created no more than a wisp of disturbance in the air, the whole of the disturbances added together, producing a suffusion of musical sound across the whole night.

Kimberly saw some lights go on, far off.

She was amidst the so-called business district of Copeland -- there were no residences on this street. But it was clear to Kimberly that the music was, while weirdly localized, invading the surrounding neighborhood.

Indeed, there was a directionality to the music. There was an epicenter somewhere. Kimberly was drawn that way, whichever way it was, as the piercing music struck at her again and again.

Suddenly, to her left, in the small lawn that graced the front of the Pink Motel, a huge oak tree dumped all the snow from its branches with a whump!

As Kimberly watched agog, all the other trees surrounding the motel did likewise, one after another.

A few moments later, snow began to dribble off the roof at the far end of the structure. At the next repetition of the musical phrase, which Kimberly now realized was only a small snippet, like a car-sized cicada's song, all the snow slid away from the weakly pitched, roof, revealing the motel's ridiculous pink shingles.

The music was louder. Not louder, really, but more strong, more... something. Whatever the quality was, it was most pronounced at the far end of the motel.

As Kimberly approached, a sharpening anxiety roiled in her. This tension did not come from within, but from without, from wherever the music was originating.

Kimberly followed waves of sound and unease toward this source, which ultimately proved to be in the vicinity of room 14. There was no room 13.

Kimberly entered room 14. It was empty, yet thrumming like a bumblebee. She looked in the bathroom, where the paper cups were bouncing on the counter, and behind the shivering shower curtain. Peering under the vibrating bed, the legs of which drummed on the floor in time to the repetitive motif, Kimberly saw a door in the floor, located unobtrusively between the bed and the wall to the bathroom. It was a conventional access door, carpeted like the rest of the floor, with a pull ring for grabbing it up. Kimberly figured the door opened onto a set of downward stairs, to a storage area for cleaning supplies, bedding and the like.

As she descended, Kimberly saw this was in fact the case. However, all such thoughts winked out of existence the moment she saw what else occupied the small space under room 14.

There on the floor, trussed up like a roast and chained to bolts in the ground was Elijah Holly. Standing over Eli, a tiny old woman with long grey hair frantically gesticulated. She was dressed in the garb of a motel cleaning lady in a striped, skirted dress with a green apron. The old woman was faced away from Kimberly and toward Eli's bound form.

The old woman screamed at poor Eli, who beamed up her with a big, shit-eating grin.

"Stop it! Stop it, Eli!" the Cleaning Lady shrieked. Eli just kept smiling like crazy.

The voice told Kimberly that the Cleaning Lady was really a man. It was a man dressed as a woman, in a motel. Just like in the movie, Psycho.

Kimberly suddenly realized that the music was coming from Eli himself. Eli was the generator of the unbelievable phenomenon overtaking Main Street. The little Cleaning Lady Man was becoming unhinged, screaming at Eli to stop making the music.

Suddenly, the music snuffed out entirely. Silence reigned in the room. Kimberly took the opportunity to examine the space, and her eyes alighted on a nightmare.

Above the Cleaning Lady Man, snaking around the ceiling, were creatures that made Kimberly start with horror. They squirmed into the air above Eli, who seemed not to notice them at all, a writhing mass of creatures with thick looping snake-like bodies. The faces of these creatures were disturbingly like those of human babies, but with circular mouths rimmed with needle teeth.

The snake-like creatures churned in the air as they took their place above Eli. They seemed to expect something, like a pack of hyenas at the zoo, waiting for the meat to be thrown through the bars.

At Kimberly's startled reaction to these monsters, the Cleaning Lady Man turned around and looked right at her, the first living human person ever to do so (save her own living sister, of course, who was, even now, sleeping in her bed at the residence at the back of the liquor store).

"Hello there," said the Cleaning Lady Man, with an inviting grin.

Kimberly was far and away more frightened of this living man who could see her, than even the disgusting creatures swarming the ceiling. Yet the tiny man simply stood his ground, waiting for Kimberly to reply.

The swimming snake creatures were not so sedate. They poured over and around the Cleaning Lady Man, towards Kimberly's shaking form, and Kimberly figured it was high time to get the hell out of there.

But not before Eli, whose head was whipping about after the Cleaning Lady Man had spoken, bleated, "Kimberly! Is that you? Go get your sister! Tell her to get Molly White!"

Kimberly rose, out, away from the repulsive swimmers, who did not seem able to follow, through the floor and walls of the Pink Motel's room 14. Kimberly arrived in her sister's bedroom, at the rear of the liquor store, a split second later.

Kim's snoring shook the room the way Eli's music had the Pink Motel. Kimberly whispered softly into her sister's sleeping ear, for she knew that if she yelled, Kim would shoot awake in a storm of anger, and might take too long to calm.

And they needed to leave right now!

ChApTeR 4

Robert swung open the door.

Standing in the doorway, her olive drab parka dusted with snow, a pink bathrobe poking out from under, was Kim Lewis, owner/proprietor of Copeland's only liquor store, looking discomfited in the extreme.

Kim took in the room.

"Dear God," she said, "A more unlikely assemblage I never did see. This night just gets weirder and weirder."

Kim said this last part to the air beside her, and I was reminded that she was given to such odd behavior.

The circumstances of Kim's appearance had, for a moment, banished my memory of her lifelong behavior of speaking, as if to her twin sister, who had died in the womb, all those years ago.

I realized Kim had said it to her sister and not to us.

Isobel, obviously relieved that it was someone she knew, approached Kim.

"Please do come in," she said.

"What the hell, Molly? When did you start talking like Mary Poppins?" Kim demanded.

"Since well before you were born. The Crazy Old Lady thing, the speech patterns, it was all an act. Whatever the case, I can't imagine you want to discuss my way of speaking. Cot, get the woman some cocoa. Ms. Lewis, do let me take your coat."

"No Molly, I only got a robe and boots on."

"Please, call me Isobel. Isobel Whitehead-Patrick. I'm very pleased to finally meet you like this," said Isobel, putting out her hand.

Kim ignored the hand and walked into the room.

"Jesus Christ in a sidecar," she said. "You're still Johnny and Cot Cleary, I hope. And you're Winky's kid, Robert." Isobel eyed the man with undisguised suspicion. "And you, you're the teacher's kid, right?"

"That's right. My name is Adria."

Adria put out her hand and Kim ignored that hand too. Cot gave the woman a cup and Kim set to warming her mitts and face with its radiations.

"What brings you all the way out to see me?" asked Isobel.

"Bad news, of course," said Kim, who was distracted in her warming. "It's Theda Holly's brother, Eli."

Here, Kim glanced sharply again at Robert.

"He is in some trouble."

"I knew it!" exclaimed Cot.

Kim looked at Cot like she was wailing baby at a wedding ceremony, and Cot was cowed.

"You know about me and my sister, right Molly?" asked Kim.

"Isobel. Isobel Whitehead-Patrick. Of course, Ms. Lewis. I am well aware. More aware of such things than most, you might say. Your lovely sister Kimberly is standing to your left, presently, attired in white dress with lace filigree on the skirt and a choker collar. She is sporting a matching parasol and holding a wide-brimmed, matching hat. In fact, she seems to be dressed just like Audrey Hepburn, in the film, My Fair Lady."

Kim Lewis, who was exceedingly difficult to impress, was impressed.

"That's her," said Kim, who was, herself, the farthest from Eliza Doolittle imaginable.

"We go see movies at the drive-in. She's been taking on airs since we saw that one."

"How delightful," responded Isobel, "I must rely on trades with the covers ripped off, rummaged from the dumpster behind Bill's."

Isobel continued.

"Kimberly, you look utterly charming."

Isobel regarded the invisible subject of her utterance with a respectful dip of her head. It seemed an invisible curtsy was returned, because Kim rolled her eyes in an exasperated fashion.

"So, Kimberly here was called to by Eli," snapped Kim, still looking into the cup. "She says Eli sent her a song or something. It was a song in the night and it pulled her out of the house. She went and followed the music, like a dumbass, over to the Pink Motel, where she found Eli all tied up, or some such?"

Here, Kim looked to her invisible companion for confirmation.

"Kimberly ain't makin' a lot of sense. I can't say I ever saw her like this before, either. Kimberly says Eli is bein' held in room 14 of the Pink Motel, in a room underneath, that you got to get to by a door in the floor, on the far side of the bed.

"There, I said it," finished Kim, who talked daily to a ghost, "This is way too weird for me. I need to leave."

Kimberly's reply was apparently in the negative, as Kim's eyes goggled and her lips pressed and she breathed sharp from her nostrils, like a bull.

Adria grabbed my hand again. I wondered how she was taking all of this. Our teacher, her father, was probably over at the police station right now, it being so late. It had to be around 9 pm. Isobel's story had mesmerized us all, all for different and personal reasons. Time had snuck past us.

How could anyone presented with such world shaking information, after having undergone such a nightmare of evil and saved by such extraordinary means, give a cold crap about getting home on time for dinner, no matter the consequences?

But I felt bad that her dad and whole family were likely beside themselves.

Isobel spoke up.

"Kimberly, could I see you in the next room? It won't take but a moment, and then Kim, I assure you, you may leave."

Kim Lewis raised her eyebrows at that. We all watched Kim, watching her sister follow Isobel into the bedroom. Isobel drew the bedroom door closed behind her.

Then Kim was in huff of solitude, peering down into her cup.

"Dumb," she muttered. "Stupid."

"We gotta go to Eli right now, I don't know why we're standing around talking!" Cot said, sharply. She almost looked like she was about to start crying.

Then the door to the bedroom opened and Isobel emerged. Kim set down her cup and was already walking out the door, bitching up a storm.

After a moment, I heard Kim, outside, yell, "What! There is no chance in no Hell that we..." The rest was lost to distance and the wind.

"Isobel, we must notify the police," said Robert.

"This is not a police matter, my dear boy. This is a matter for us, of utmost importance. For us. Going to the police would only worsen matters, and surely get Eli killed.

"No one understands the nature of these events but me, I assure you," whispered Isobel, almost to herself. She gave us all a faltering smile, seemingly of apology, and resumed,

"The events before us comprise more than a simple murder myst   --"

Isobel put her hand to her mouth.

"Forgive me, that was a poor way of stating it. It's just that if we fail tonight, human life as we know it, will begin to wither. I know that sounds impossibly dramatic."

Isobel appeared as if she were about to lose her composure. She could tell her words made no sense, and even worse, seemed like raving.

"I will say this quickly and once.

"We, humanity, are an experiment. The Experimenter feels that if he interferes in any way with the experiment, he will taint the data. Others want the experiment to fail, and are trying to sabotage it, though not through direct involvement with the subjects of the experiment, which is to say, us, but by subverting the experimental equipment. These others want to pierce the tubes, wet the burners and crack the flasks!"

"The Tree is that piece of equipment, without which, the whole experiment fails. The culture turns grey with death and the Experimenter hangs his head in defeat, leaving the experimenting to others, less good, less noble.

"They have been at this for a long time, our Experimenter's enemies, all of modern history in fact, slowly pressing mankind into an ever-increasing violence and territoriality.

"This century we have reached the endgame, for, now, the Tree has only one place to hide from the inferno of War and Industrialization that has overtaken the world in the last 100 years.

"Here. The Heart-Shaped Forest. Smack dab in the middle of the only temperate landmass not beset by such horrors. The Tree's service to the experiment has already been undercut. It no longer travels where it is needed, where the bodies are piling, clogging the pathways of the experiment.

"The Tree is compromised and overworked. Cracks are appearing. It must be looked after. There must be one of us, one person, always nearby, always vigilantly watching. Those of us who take this mantle, are not only protectors, but mediators, interpreters, friends, to the tree. There is always one, at every destination. A network of us, and that network too, is broken.

"And let me tell you, the effects of all this brokenness are evident, if you only look. World events are cascading ever downward, even now, just now in fact, as a direct result of the Tree's compromised state.

"New wars. The country torn asunder in civil strife. Criminality and murder stalking the highest offices. The earth screams from misuse. The money changers decide the course of history now. The disparity widens between the rich few and the many poor.

"The enemy forges ever ahead to prepare the death blow, and it need only strike us. Just us. Me and anyone who might succeed me. Us. Five people, and human life begins its slide... toward what, I honestly do not know. All I know is that the tree is life, and the Tree of Life is dying!"

Isobel stopped and took Robert's hand.

"Your love was not killed by lustmord, my son. Your dear Theda was my student. She was going to take over when I passed.

"That is why she was killed."

Robert studied Isobel's face. He visibly milled her words into unknown thoughts that played into unreadable expressions. His eyes narrowed, but did not go cold. He grimaced.

Adria advanced toward the mother and the son, to step in the way should son decide to take a swing at the mother.

"Was Theda compelled, as you were?" Robert asked.

"No, my son. No acorns for that one," said Isobel, with the merest smile of remembrance. "And I would not say I was compelled, in the conventional sense. I wanted it, more than anything else in the world. More than you, my dear boy. I was... insane." Molly looked into her son's eyes with a profound regret.

Robert said nothing, so Isobel continued, "I approached Theda as a child. Through her mother, who was known to me and I to her. Her mother and I grew up together, you see, and she was on to me, which is to say, aware of my journey, who I really was, and had a certain knowledge of my... transformation.

"I wanted the one who was to follow me to be taught, over time, and while I was still alive to teach her."

Robert nodded slowly.

Isobel looked at me. "I was gauging your mother for the task, John. But I do not think she wanted it. Not like Theda."

"And now you want Cot, right? You want Cot to give up everything and take care of your goddamned tree!" I barked.

"What makes you think that, dear John?" asked Isobel, taken aback. She studied my face, which was trembling, surging, but which must have transmitted something to her, for a look of dawning comprehension suddenly overtook.

"Because Cot was saved by the tree, just as I was. Is that it, John?" she asked.

I never got the opportunity to reply, or find the answer to my frantic question. I looked to Adria and Cot for their opinions of events, to see Adria's eyes worriedly scanning the room.

Cot was not there.

"Where is Cot?" I asked, to all.

ChApTeR 5

FROM THE JOURNAL OF COT CLEARY
I left those dipshits theorizing. I went out the bathroom window. They were so caught up in their talk, they didn't even notice.

I watched Kim and Kimberly's car lights shoot through the trees and over the Old Cross Bridge. The lights went out of my view but I knew they must be passing my house, and the thought of my house made my breath hitch a little.

More like a crying hitch, not a dying hitch. I made it go away and ran after the lights.

When I passed my house, I stopped and gazed at it, knowing I had not long to live there, where I was almost nearly born, but where I was surely named my strange name.

It took me about 20 minutes of good running before I was back in town. I looked for Kim's car by the liquor store, but all was dark, and her car was nowhere to be seen.

The Pink Motel glowed. The dumb pink roof blazed in the moonlight. I wondered what Denny Freemantle was trying to say. He was always a little nuts, according to my Daddy. One day, the motel was just pink, as Daddy remembered.

There was a real bad feel in the air. I figured it had to be my fear, but it seemed so much to come from outside of me. I think that if the pink of the motel had a name, like my momma's lipstick did, then "Menacing Carnation" might sum it up real nice. The dreadful bad feeling in all that pink painted onto the snow and into the very light of the night.

On the way over, I was trying to figure out what I would do. How could I possibly save Eli from his predicament?

That's when I remembered that comic Johnny had let me read, The Iliad.

Those guys, the Spartans, had made a big wooden horse, the size of a double decker bus, and rolled it up to the gates of Troy. The guys inside Troy, the Trojans, brought the horse inside, thinking it was some kind of gift. But the Spartans had filled the horse with soldiers. The soldiers came out of the big horse and took over Troy and won.

That sneaky idea was just the sort of thing I needed to do. But I couldn't think of anything that fit.

That was ok, because somehow thinking about the Trojan Horse made me light upon the idea of stealing a car, driving it through the wall of room 14, and when the bad guy came up to see what was going on, running over his head and spilling out his brains, the way Mary the Elephant did.

That was a perfect idea.

Even more than perfect, because I knew Denny Freemantle kept his station wagon in back. It was more than like that his keys were right in the ignition.

I creeped that way along the wall of the motel office, approaching the long, wood-panelled car in a crouch. When I got to the rear driver's taillight, I got on all fours and crawled toward the driver's door like a baby.

I looked behind me to make sure no lights were coming on from the back of the Office, where Denny slept most nights. He wasn't married. I don't think his life was too fun. But there were no lights.

I reached up to handle of the driver's door.

There was some kind of sound or vibration in the air that stopped me short. Was it breathing? It was just, exactly like breathing, and close.

I looked under the car to see if there were legs standing on the other side. Like if someone had been standing on the other side of the car the whole time, and I just couldn't see them in my crouching. That would be just the luck. But there were no legs.

I listened. The sound had stopped. I listened good and hard, but it didn't come back. I reached up for the handle and tested it. I felt firm resistance and feared it was locked. But I continued to pry it open with a screech, followed by a super loud thunk.

The door popped open a bit, but I held it so as not to let it screech more, if it was so inclined. I looked back to the office and was relieved to see no lights come on.

I slowly pulled open the car door. It screeched like a hundred-year-old ferris wheel. It screeched through the night, so bad, my eyes watered and my guts sang a tune.

When the car door was open sufficient, I snaked my body inside, which popped the door open some inches more, and the metal screeched another good one.

But it did not matter much, since when I finally set myself in the driver's seat, I was sitting in the lap of Denny Freemantle himself, because that son of a bitch had been sitting there the whole time. It was his breathing I heard!

I felt a whole new kind of scared when Denny put his big hand over my whole face, so it was hard to breath. Denny held me against himself with the one hand. With the other, he picked up a little silver flask he had been drinking from, and some mail, and nudged the already-open door, all the way open.

I get a little panicky when my breath is impeded for any reason, as you know, so all I could think about was trying to get his hand off my face, but I couldn't do it. He was too strong.

He lifted me up tighter with both arms now and saw that I couldn't breathe, so Denny adjusted his hand a bit.

I started lung-ing it through my nose.

We didn't say nothing and I was way past putting up a fight. My eyes were moons and I just stared into Denny's sad eyes, while the air whooshed in and out over the side of his palm, as if from a creature separate from me.

That thing that wanted to live saw death peeking again, and was doing all the work, leaving me to stare terrified at the tall man's face, as he carried me right to the office, in a matter of seconds.

I wished I had something to drop on the doorstep, to leave as a clue to my fate. All I could do was grab at the doorway. To Denny it seemed I was trying to keep him from pulling me inside, but I knew that was a fool move. I was just trying to leave a mark for Johnny and Isobel to see. I felt some snow, but I don't know if I left a sign.

The scenery behind Denny's big head was bouncing and sweeping, making me dizzy. I started shivering in his grasp.

I suddenly remembered that I was not a detective. Not even little girl Sherlock Holmes. There was no Sherlock Holmes about it. I was just a little girl.

When Denny Freemantle closed and locked that outside door, I realized that I might never see the other side of it, ever again. It was dark in the room and he turned on no lights. I started crying real bad. Denny just clamped his hand over my mouth harder.

He lifted a door in the floor and stepped down into even blacker dark. I thought for a moment I would start screaming, because of the closeness of the dark. I couldn't even tell if my eyes were open or closed. Denny found some switch.

We left the small room that was lit, through a rickety door, and started down a long, narrow hall, toward another door.

It took us at least a minute to get to that far door, all the way at the other end of the Pink Motel. By the time we reached it, the light had reduced to plunging us again into an awful murk. I listened to our breathing as the light gave way to black.

Then, Denny was through that second door, into a bright-lit room that was too much for me.

I squeezed my eyes shut tight.

But the moment before my eyes shut, my brain took a quick, bleeding-bright snapshot of the room.

That horizontal smudge on the floor, that had to be Eli. And the vertical smudge to the right, that had to be the person who killed Miss Holly.

I knew that when I opened my eyes, I would be looking at the person who killed Theda Holly.

ChApTeR 6

Eli felt a bolt of shock when Denny Freemantle carried Cot through the door.

Cot's weird compliance created a host of possible scenarios in Eli's fevered thoughts as to why, and none of them good. Eli felt an emotional volcano threatening to erupt through a long-frozen caldera. Eli's perception stuttered a moment, so enraged was he at the sight of Cot's situation.

Eli wrenched at the chains that bound his feet and felt, more than heard, a weakness in the arrangement down there. Eli pulled and pushed toward whatever situation of his body strained those chains the most.

Denny set Cot down on the floor, where she lay still for a moment, before springing into a crablike shuffle, away from him, toward the far wall, damning the man with her eyes. Denny looked at Cot sadly while she retreated from him. Denny turned to face Jameson Corr, as if waiting for instruction.

"Scaring little girls is your game?" growled Eli. "You best kill me now, Denny!"

Eli realized that it must have been Denny who'd snuck up in room 14, the very moment it dawned on Eli that Jameson Corr, himself, stood before him, dressed as a motel cleaning lady named Gladys. Denny brained him with some dense, metal object. Eli had awoken, after God only knew how long, to his current predicament.

"Eli, restrain your silliness for a moment. I want to introduce you to someone," said Jameson Corr, with disturbing gentility. Jameson turned away from Eli and faced the wall by the stairs, the wall adorned with shelves and motel items.

"The brilliance of your scheme is manifest!" Jameson yelped into the air, his voice embarrassingly high-pitched and wretched.

It was good-old, garden-variety insanity, all right, thought Eli. The type best brewed by decades of institutionalization.

Eli only hoped that Kimberly really had been here, had followed the music he had somehow, in his extreme state, sent outward, and was, even now, getting help.

Jameson continued his pleading speech.

"Soon the crone will be here, along with any other possible replacement, just as you foretold!

"Come! Come and witness!" Jameson shrieked.

Eli looked back at Denny and was disgusted to see the tall man weeping like a baby. These crazy bastards, thought Eli. How did I let us fall into their clutches?

He wrenched himself around to face Cot. "Don't you worry about a thing, baby! I'm not going to let these loony idiots do nothing bad to either of us!"

"I ain't worried, Eli. Not any longer," said Cot.

Eli smiled as bravely as he could, all tied up.

But then his bravado faltered, as Eli realized that Cot was only humoring him, and was resigned to something else entirely.

This realization was just the nudge required. The volcano inside of Eli exploded.

Eli curled, wrenching up his tree-trunk legs. He did it once, twice, three times, each time becoming a shuddering, reddening machine at the business end of the action.

With a groan, Eli ripped the very boards to which his feet were moored, out of the floor. The violence of their loosening sent Eli's legs wriggling into the air, shaking off the chains sufficiently so that he could stand. However, Eli was still attached to the floor at his arms and wrists. He got to his feet and pulled at those chains with all his might.

Eli realized there was an ugly sound in the room, a bothersome noise that made him sneer in disgust, like a barely heard fart in a roomful of people. The unmusical sound grew, even as Eli tried to drown it out with his epic effort.

Eli turned, in his Samson-like struggle, toward Jameson and the noisome sound, to see reality itself peeling inward from the center of the wall. It was as if the shelves and motel items were simply hyper-realistic paintings, rendered on slowly opening curtain.

Eli stopped his pulling for a moment, but only a moment, as this magic widened before him.

A scene was revealed by the separating curtain of reality. It reminded Eli of being at the movies, when everything is lit just so, and timed just right. When the movie starts its playing against the non-reflective red velvet of the curtain, so that when the curtain parts, the light of the projected movie hits the reflective screen and pierces the darkening room, with the certainty of another world.

Just so, another world was here revealed. This curtain opened on a gloomy plain, against a dreadful sky. Far away, there were dots, scattered against the moody land, enlarging. The dots grew to a group of man shapes, walking toward the mind-bending window in reality, toward the widening aperture in what was, moments before, merely wall, and shelves, and motel items.

Toward Eli and his friends.

The Nemesis! thought Eli.

Jameson Corr was not to be distracted.

Denny, however, came out of his overwrought state, and started determinately toward Eli, who was wrenching again at the chains that bound him, even as his gaze remained affixed on the broadening tableaux before him.

Denny picked up a mop on the way to Eli and raised it to strike.

"Leave him alone!" screamed Cot, like a wild animal.

Denny did no such thing, but brought the mop handle down with great force against Eli's right knee. Eli turned to Denny, seemingly unaffected, said, "You are gonna smoke a turd in hell for that one, my man," and lunged for Denny, who was quick to scurry back, out of range.

There was a trundling sound that added to the confusion of weird noise in the room.

Jameson whipped around at the sound, which came from behind the door through which Cot and Denny had just arrived.

"They're already here!" Jameson whispered. He was no longer possessed of his previously enlightened composure.

No, now Jameson's voice was a bit frantic, as if things weren't going precisely to plan, as if the possibility that he might be embarrassed in front of some very important people had begun to creep up on him.

Jameson looked back at the scene that overtook the wall, as if to gauge how far away the dark men yet were.

Denny was back by the door.

He swung it open, stupidly, and was immediately bowled back into the room by an unknown person, which caused Denny to projectile-vomit a loathsome spray into the air, as if in welcome.

ChApTeR 7

When I saw that Cot was nowhere in any room of Isobel Whitehead-Patrick's cabin, it was all I could do to keep from balling. The wretched realization made me dizzy. Isobel pulled up right in front of me.

"Not to worry John. We are leaving now and we know just where Cot is going. I'm sure we will catch up to her on the road."

Isobel turned to Robert's fraught face. Their eyes exchanged an amended version of this statement, which, I have no doubt replaced "I'm sure," with "I hope."

I pulled from Isobel's grip and stood at the front door, in a moment.

"Well, c'mon!" I shouted angrily, winding my arm in a come-hither-and-thru pattern. Adria went right by, tugging on her mittens. Robert followed on her heels, with a respectful nod to me. Then, it was Isobel herself who briskly shooed me on through the impossibly packed front porch, into the night, as she closed her front door behind her.

Isobel paused outside the porch-door. She looked about her feet, here and there, here and there.

Suddenly, Isobel sighed, "Ah." She bent over, pulled some thing out of the snow, brushed it off and put it gingerly into her outer pocket.

She came up to me and whispered, "We walk into a trap, Trout-John."

"I don't care!" I whispered back.

Isobel smiled at me, sadly.

We did not see Cot, but we saw her running footprints. When we walked past my house, Robert asked if there was a car there we could use.

There was not.

Adria and I ran ahead, against the protestations of Isobel and Robert. We said nothing, but sped, until the library passed, and then the liquor store. Kim's car was not there and it was dark. The lurid Pink Motel lay waiting beyond. I hoped that Eli was ok, but did not give him much more of a thought.

He was a big fellow who could take care of himself, even if the worst came to the worst.

But poor Cot. I worried about her breathing.

I worried.

Adria walked carefully to the back of the motel, skirting the brighter spots in the night. I was right behind her. There was something there that made me go cold.

Denny Freemantle's gargantuan station wagon was parked in its usual spot, it's driver's side door opened wide. Snow had accumulated somewhat on its inner surfaces. I gauged it had been doing so for only a short while, for the wispy structures flew away at the slightest disturbance.

In itself, the open car door was odd, but contextually, it did make my guts scream like a banshee. I looked at Adria. She was similarly spooked.

We studied the scene some more. Sure enough, back toward the motel, there were Cot's small footprints, bearing the distinctive wavy lines of her blue rubber boots. But they disappeared at the edge of the lot, and by the car, only Denny's long feet and long strides could be seen, walking over to the back door of the Motel Office.

I studied that door like I had never studied a thing before. The handle betrayed nothing, but on the jamb, there were three tiny half-moons in the dust of snow, that could have been from the tips of Cot's fingers.

Those marks, if they were from her, spoke to my bones. I pulled Adria close to look.

By this time, Isobel and Robert came up. We ran back to tell them of what we had found.

Robert was quick to try the door. It was locked tight. He backed up and appraised the whole building, looking down the entirety of the motel.

Adria yelped, "Johnny come here!"

She was over at the window by the door, doing a chin up on its sill. I looked in over her shoulder. The room inside was dark except for one odd feature.

A trap door in the floor was yawned open. Weak light seeped from its maw. I pulled Robert over to see it, and when he did, he wasted not a moment.

Robert ran over to the station wagon and swung open its back door. After rummaging around, he hustled back with a tire iron that he used to slowly force open the back-office door. It was clear he was trying to be as quiet as possible, but the wood crunched as he forced it, causing dismay among us.

We spread out into the dark room, and gazed apprehensively at the trap door. There was no sound coming from the hole in the floor, but instead, a swirl of luminescent dust. That could mean there was someone moving silently around down there, gazing fixedly from below, like we were all doing from above, wondering what would happen next. Wondering if, in the next moment, they might be beset by forces that would undo whatever awful plan they were enacting.

Whoever it might be, they surely were not picturing two kids, an old lady and a forty-year-old shut in. That was an advantage we should press. I walked heavily to Robert, who was shocked by the noise I made.

"Can I make a suggestion?" I quietly asked.

"Please," whispered Robert.

"Please do or please don't?"

"Please do!" Robert practically whistled.

"All right, first off, you stop whispering. You have a pretty deep voice. If there is someone down there, they have no idea how... weak we are. Let them think we are a group of adult men."

Robert nodded his ascent and we all therewith abandoned our sneaking and took to generous heavy footing around the room. Robert started up a conversation with himself using a deep voice and a deeper voice. It was, in retrospect, comical.

"Hand me that gun," said Robert, in a deep voice.

"Here ya go, Joe," Robert replied in a deeper voice.

I impatiently motioned to Robert, who was getting a bit carried away, to peek his head over the edge of the hole to see what he could see. He did so with reluctance.

Robert got bolder in his looking, finally poking his whole upper body through the trap.

"There is no one down here," he informed us, again adopting his sharp whisper. Robert stayed like that a long time; I guess he was listening.

Robert pulled out of the hole.

"There is a real strange sound coming from an open door down there. Like, a rumbly, squishy sound. I never heard anything like it."

I took Adria's hand this time, for comfort. She petted my hand, attempting to give me some ease, but the furious way she accomplished the act gave her away.

Robert jabbed his finger at us and looked terribly angry.

"You three stay here!" Robert whispered, with force. I could see he was just trying to be mean and scary so that we would comply.

"I ain't staying here," I told him, calmly.

"You may be wholly assured that I will be accompanying you down that hole, Robert," assured Isobel, wholly.

Robert turned to Adria.

He said, "Look Adria, I know I probably cannot stop Johnny, or Isobel, because they are too hard headed, but there is no reason for you to continue to endanger yourself. I insist you walk out that door and head straight home."

"No fucking way," Adria returned. We all ducked as if a bird were attacking, so surprising her epithet.

Robert was shocked into an immediate sort of submission, and shook his head slowly as he began to descend into the light.

I regarded Adria with an accustomed admiration, as she walked determinedly to follow. Isobel and I were right behind her. I steadied the old woman's arm as she tentatively negotiated the steps downward.

Once below, we all stood as still as anticipation itself. We listened, and the sound Robert had described became known to each of us.

It was a nasty sound, somehow offensive. The delicate, wet grinding, was an undulation of chewing softness, such as the way eating a juicy chocolate sounds to one's self.

There was a roaring sound, like the roaring of a lion.

"That is Eli!" I announced.

There followed a crunching destruction of wood, and a girl's voice screamed words that took me a moment to quicken into sense:

"Leave him alone!"

The voice was Cot's.

Utterly unbeknownst to my own self, and leaving my companions agape, I was halfway down the darkening hallway, toward the far door, before any realization of my actions caught up.

"Johnny!" Isobel, Robert and Adria shouted in unison.

I kept running. Before I got to the door, it opened wide, blinding me.

I thought to stop, but knew it would only weaken my position, so I stepped it up and bowled directly into the tall figure that stood in the light of the portal.

I put my shoulder right into his gut, and he "Whoof!"ed, shooting out a spew of whiskey vomit into the air, much of which landed right in my hair and on my back. We tumbled together for one disgusting second. I heard my companions tearing down the hall toward us.

Somewhere in the room, Cot yelled, "Johnny!" There was terror and delight in her voice, both.

I tried to get to my feet, but suddenly there was a person attacking me from behind, someone different from the bowled-over puker, wrenching at my hair and scratching at my face.

The attacker was hidden, but the nails adorning those torturing hands belonged to a female. They raked my face some good ones. I bit down on a finger and a pitched squeal resounded, like that of a wriggling pig.

I turned my whole body in this woman's grasp. I can tell you now, the desolation of horror that struck me when I did so, has never been repeated in my long life. I doubt it ever could be.

For there was, behind the old woman who rode astride my bucking form, spraying me with hot spittle as she snarled and tore at my face, a separation in reality.

The walls of the room beyond the raging woman ended somehow, warping into the gap that appeared there.

The strange, chewy sound came from the hole, but I could not tell if it were being emitted from the place on the other side, or was, instead, some epiphenomenon of the amazing occurrence itself.

A dark, dismal vista lay through that portal, and towering in that realm were a group of huge, wavering figures. They approached the opening, a procession of massive, dark men, like the blacker-than-black man of Adria's "White People" story. Their darkness was not the absence of light, but the absence of all things.

All hope, all future.

The shadowy giants were the witherers of human life, to whom Isobel had referred in the warmth of her log cabin. Gazing in horror through the impossible opening, I suddenly and for the first time, came to believe every word she had uttered

The small woman began to choke me, her soft hands pressing my neck down into the floorboards, impossibly strong. The pressure in my head grew till I felt my temples would blow out.

Then Adria was behind the old woman. My girlfriend snarled as she reached over the woman's head and hooked two of her fingers into the old woman's nostrils, pushing them way in. Adria fell back, using her own weight to rip the old woman off me.

The old woman emitted a nasal shriek of anguish that told me that it was no woman at all, but a man dressed as a woman. This creepy apparition fell back on my love, who was quick to wrap her arms around his neck and her legs around his thoracic.

Then Robert was there. He arrived at a run and booted that villain right up into his dress, one epic kick that would have sent a football all the way downtown.

When Robert's foot met the man's testicles, I do believe at least one of them popped like a watermelon thrown to the pavement from a great height, or so it sounded.

The lady man doubled up sitting, his eyes like overfilled balloons. He emitted a piercing hoot-owl hoot that warped into a throaty gurgle, like a death rattle.

Adria disentangled herself and was away from the little man with great speed. The creature I would soon know to be Jameson Corr, the murderer of Theda Holly, curled into a fetal position, wheezing an airy whistle.

I took in the room. Eli was some yards away, on his feet, though encumbered in chains and broken floorboards. He pulled in an epic way on a chain that still fastened his massive arms to an eyebolt in the floor, snarling like raging animal. He was so fearful and awesome, my admiration for the man quadrupled, even in his bondage.

Then there was the wavering hole in the world itself.

It took up almost the entire wall and a large portion of the ceiling.

The vantage had strangely changed, as if the hole, to the dark giants, was represented in some object they could change the position of. Now, they regarded us, as if from above.

The huge, dark men made no attempt to breach the opening, but were gathered like a collection of farmers looking down a well, calmly observing.

One of the dark giants indicated toward the fallen lady man. Another was looking steadily at Eli. Another was looking at me. One of the giants was looking behind me and I turned to see Denny Freemantle, tall and gaunt, pressing a small black pistol to the head of my sister.

ChApTeR 8

Denny cocked the small black pistol he held to Cot's head. "You all step away from Mr. Corr. Now."

Adria and Robert joined me. Jameson Corr was still heaving in pain, his baleful eyes burning at our company through the tangle of his long grey hair.

Denny Freemantle loosened his grip on Cot.

Cot rushed over, to me, encircling me with her arms, burying her head in my neck. She cried silently.

Denny kept the gun pointed in the general direction of our heads, non-verbally directing our group to a corner of the room.

Jameson Corr stirred up from his position in nothing short of agony. That, at least, was delightful to see.

I watched Eli pulling at his chains. The big man was tiring, the bonds not giving. Our eyes met, but Eli looked quickly away, so that I would not see his hope abandoning him, but I did.

Jameson Corr hobbled over to Denny Freemantle, and looked high up into his minion's face. Jameson whimpered something up to Denny.

"What was that, Mr. Corr?" asked Denny fretfully, leaning his ear down to listen.

"I said shoot them. Shoot them all. Then reload your weapon and shoot them again, in the base of their skulls," whispered Jameson Corr, weakly.

From the corner of my eye I discerned our dark observers draw close to their window, with interest. Jameson Corr noticed this too, and it caused him to shrink a little, as if the dark men's heightened scrutiny upon him was more than he could bear.

Denny screwed up his face. It was clear that killing us was distasteful to him. But then, the tall man literally shrugged the problem out of his mind and pointed the gun at Robert's head.

Behind Denny Freemantle, a tiny thing floated out of the blackness of the open doorway, the doorway I had burst through. I could not make out what it was, only that it flitted lazily, a smudge against the coal dark entryway, dancing in the air, about head height.

Glancing around me, I suddenly noticed that Isobel Whitehead-Patrick was nowhere in our company. I came to quickly realize that Isobel had never even entered the room with Robert and Adria, but must have hung back in the dark of the hall.

The floating thing bobbed past Denny Freemantle and Jameson Corr, as if suspended on a jerking string, circling unhurriedly along a sinewave course toward the hole in reality, through which the dark men regarded us.

It was a leaf. The autumn-browned leaf that Isobel had picked up out of the snow as we left her cabin, spinning in the air toward the dark men, who suddenly apprehended its journey toward them.

When they noticed the leaf ambling through the air, these giant apparitions, whose aims and abilities included, without doubt, the snuffing out of all human life, startled, as if in alarm, and backed away from their well hole, leaving only the dismal sky of their realm to waver in view.

This drew Jameson Corr's attention, which pulled the notice of Denny Freemantle, who was eager to be distracted, in any event.

Eli never noticed the leaf at all, but continued to violently pull at his chains, as the dead leaf wafted right past his head.

The rest of us followed the delicate, forward pitching of that leaf, hypnotized by its lazy journey.

The leaf mosied through the window to that drear landscape, as if it were an open window, which I do not believe it was, and suddenly the whole impossible image winked out of existence with a squishy pop of displaced air, that tickled the whole room. The wall and shelves and motel items reclaimed their previous positions.

"NO!" screamed Corr. The little man's face weirdly parralaxed between the genders as he broke into sobbing that shook his tiny frame.

"Kill them, Denny. Do it NOW!"

"Yes sir, Mr. Corr," said Denny as he once again raised the gun to shoot Robert.

"Shoot the little girl," insisted Corr.

Denny was troubled, but adjusted his aim to Cot's head, which was still buried in my neck. I spun us around so that my back was to the man and waited for the shooting.

Some person pulled up the trap door at the top of the stairs and let it bang fully open.

Denny Freemantle let out an exasperated huff at this further interruption (for which he was, again, actually, quite grateful) and moved his aim to cover the top of the stairs.

I shot bolts of reproach and hatred at Denny, which he diligently ignored, as I watched him over my shoulder, keeping myself between his weapon and my sister.

Denny Freemantle's long face became even longer with dumb awe, as he saw who it was, coming unconcernedly down the steps.

The new arrival had to stoop low to negotiate the opening and was not able to re-achieve his considerable height until he was well down the stairs.

William Wickley the Third, the most cadaverous man since Solomon Grundy, gazed placidly at our scene. He glanced briefly at Eli, as he smoothed his tie and then shot his cuffs. He took in the information of our situation with transparent distaste.

"Denny Freemantle!" Winky suddenly boomed, when his eyes alighted on the fellow.

Denny jumped in his shoes.

Denny suddenly realized he had his gun pointed at William Wickley the Third, a man whom Denny Freemantle had feared, preternaturally, his whole life long. Denny lowered the gun and hid it behind his back.

"Mr. Wickley! Ah God! I am... I... uh," stuttered Denny.

Behind Winky, more legs appeared and Burleymen started coming down the wooden stairs, all of them sporting firearms – pistols, rifles and shotguns. Their peppermint striped shirts and red suspenders were vibrant in the gloom of the underground room, refreshingly so.

Jameson Corr hugged Denny's legs in terror, his tearful eyes peeking over his shaking shoulder at the men descending into the room.

"Is that the person who killed Theda Holly, Denny?" asked Winky, indicating the shaking form at Denny's feet.

Denny quickly disentangled his legs from Jameson Corr's grasp. He put some distance between himself and the desolate mound of Jameson Corr, pointing his finger accusingly.

"That is correct, Mr. Wickley. That is the man! Jameson Corr! Right there!"

William Wickley's eyes left Denny entirely, proceeding sorrowfully to those of his son, Robert. Winky and Robert regarded one another in silence for some time, before Winky broke the spell.

"Denny," said William Wickley, "were you involved in the death of Theda Holly?"

Denny exploded his answer all over the room.

"Not one bit! That evil little bastard did not take over my mind until some weeks after. I thought he was my goddamned cleaning lady, Mr. Wickley!" Denny set to weeping himself, in a repulsive display. He covered the side of his mouth and confided through his mournful crying, with an exaggerated whisper: "But, it turned out he was Satan, Mr. Wickley! Satan, his damned self!"

Winky's face was grim. He walked to Denny and put out his long hand, with domineering expectation. Denny slowly brought the gun around and set it in Winky's palm.

"And the key to Mr. Holly's shackles," said Winky. Denny fished the key from his pocket and shakily gave it to the man I once derided as reminiscent of a dead baby bird. The comparison was lost on me now. For here before my eyes was a man of true power.

What power, you ask?

The power to make a younger, stronger and armed man shake in his boots, a power Denny was responding to, like a submissive pet.

"You may go, Denny," stated Winky calmly.

Denny nodded with a frenzy of gratitude and skirted the old man, without a moment to lose. Denny hurried through the parting Burleymen to the stairs.

"Denny?"

Denny stopped still.

"Yes, Mr. Wickley?" Denny gasped.

"Denny, you must go far away and you may never return."

"Yes, Mr. Wickley. Thank you," which was greeted with silence. After waiting a sufficiently respectful moment, in case Winky had anything else to say, Denny rushed up the stairs and was gone.

Winky tossed the key to Eli, who grabbed it out of the air with a nod of approval and, possibly, thanks. Eli twisted the key into the iron that held his wrists and arms. Within a moment, Eli was free. The big man threw the chains to the floor, disgusted at how simple becoming free finally proved to be.

"Elijah Holly, would you care to tell me what is going on here?" Winky asked, his manner reaching back millennia to the landed lords and their peasantry. "I was hauled out of bed by a very insistent Kim Lewis, who explained under some very intense... questioning, that I would find the real killer of Theda Holly in this place, which I apparently have."

Here, Winky turned his attention to Jameson Corr, who was in a heap against the wall, sniveling incomprehensibly. Jameson pressed his face against that wall, muttering to it, his pink lips brushing the wood as he seemed to beg something of it. His manicured hand absently caressed the texture as he urgently whispered, at just below the volume of apprehension.

He was, almost silently, pleading some case to that wall. I moved close to the man, so I could hear him. Though Jameson Corr tried numerous rhetorical inroads to that wall's apparent opposition, the entreaty Jameson repeated boiled down to just one, hope-challenged sentiment.

Take me back!

Eli said, "I really got nothing to add. That's the man who did it, for crazy reasons of his own. Your son, Robert, had nothing to do with any of it."

When he was done talking, Eli set to examining his wrists, which were covered with wounds from his escape attempting.

"It was them!" shrieked Jameson.

If Jameson Corr's pointing accusation had been a javelin, it would have buried deep in the wall that had been, only minutes before, the window to an uncanny, unsettling land, but was now, just wall, and shelves, and motel items.

"Get him, boys," was all Winky said at this juncture.

The Burlymen leisurely swept past Winky, six powerful, irritable, small-town sociopaths, eager to claim their reward of violence for coming out on this cold night.

The biggest one, the Alpha Burlyman, grabbed Jameson up by his long grey hair and shook him in the air like a bag of bones.

"For Theda!" he roared, and shook Jameson some more. The group returned that cry with a savage sound, a resounding, unhinged male chorus, and Robert and I were in that group, two irrefutable madmen.

Jameson clutched wildly at the Burlyman's arm, trying to find some purchase, to free his scrawny neck from stretching along gravity's sudden incline.

The Burlyman put Jameson Corr down hard.

The group converged on the fallen man wearing the cleaning lady dress. Robert and I were not among that group.

Jameson Corr started keening almost immediately, his cries barely escaping the press of Burlymen around him.

The Burlymen did not put Jameson Corr on a figurative rail, or otherwise raise his wriggling form into the air, but dragged Jameson Corr amidst them, along the ground and roughly up the stairs. When they pulled him through the trap door, he cried a repulsive, high pitched "Nooooo!" and managed to hook his foot on the edge.

Only for a second though, after which, Jameson Corr was pulled violently upward, out of sight, with no ceremony, or significance, whatsoever.

The man who had murdered my dear Theda was gone, never to be seen again.

William Wickley looked about the room. He took our sorry lot in, including his son. He nodded briefly at the confederacy comprising Adria, Cot and I. There was no malice in his face. What there was, I could not say, but no malice.

Winky also gave a brief nod to Eli, and it finally came to me that a brief nod was Winky's way of offering a heartfelt apology for being an epic asshole. Winky turned to his son.

"Robert, I will see you at your house, later."

Winky gauged his son, waiting for a response.

Robert betrayed no signs of emotion, or intent, but seemed satisfied at receiving more than a brief nod.

Robert said,

"Yes, Dad."

Winky smiled sadly and dusted off his hands, as if of unpleasantness.

Winky turned his lanky old frame toward the stairs and made up them.

As Winky bent his head through the trap door, Isobel Whitehead-Patrick suddenly appeared from the hallway behind us.

"William," she said.

Winky froze. Slowly, those long, spider legs backpedaled down the steps until he could see into the room again.

William Wickley looked at Isobel Whitehead-Patrick, and immediately knew her. His jaw dropped and his mouth started smiling, when, suddenly, Winky seemed to realize that he had reason to be bothered with this woman, given her long abandonment of him and Robert, as well as her seemingly genuine transformation into a crazy forest lady.

Winky became quite cold.

"If it isn't the fabled 'Molly White!'" he sneered, the quotes audible. "I haven't had the pleasure yet to meet you. I remember someone, but she was not you.

"Indeed!" Winky continued, "Indeed, I know all about you, Molly White. I know who you really are. I know you have utterly given up on a normal life. I know you talk like a crazy woman, and haunt the woods hereabout, and that you have a cabin in the Heart-Shaped Forest.

"In fact, I have stood outside it, many a time, " Winky finished, as if in confession.

"I know, William, I watched you, many a time," responded Isobel Whitehead-Patrick.

William stood confused.

He clearly intended to say some more nasty things, but it seemed that seeing Isobel across the room upset the workings of his tired brain. Isobel had always possessed the facility to disarm William's weaponed mouth, if her tale was to be believed.

It was like the moment they first met, her eyes defused him now, as then.

I could see that Winky's confusion exceeded the intellectual, piercing the emotional. If the wrinkling and unwrinkling of his brow were any indication, Winky's whole head was soon to explode in a shower of gore from all the confusion.

As if taken in hand by uncertainty itself, Winky started toward the mother of his child, with uncertain steps and an uncertain bearing.

Isobel watched him approaching, and when the man she had so nearly married in her youth was close, she grasped his hand in hers, and slowly turned into the dark hallway she had just emerged from, Winky only a step behind.

He closed the door behind him, but popped it back open a couple inches, a few seconds later, most likely to admit some light.

We could not hear Isobel and William at all, so what was spoken behind that cracked door, I cannot say, for it was never divulged to me by either of them. There are many things in this tale that I did not witness, but were told to me later. However, this transpirance is not among them.

Cot, who was still entangled in me, smiled up bravely, but then her face broke and she started bawling again. She stuffed her face back into my shirt and cried like never to end it. Adria tried to smile at me bravely, kind of like Cot had tried to do, but then she started to break up crying, too! Adria grabbed my face and kissed me on the lips and set to weeping on my other shoulder.

I looked at Robert, who was alarmed by this behavior, but I took it all in stride.

Women just deal with world-ending near-misses different from the way men do.

I resigned myself to my own methods of dealing with all that I just experienced, which I knew would include yelling at others, and falling host to pathological behaviors, later in life.

Then the door opened and a shaken William Wickley walked out. His alarmed expression betrayed a knowledge, a knowledge Winky did not possess prior to his ensconsement with Isobel in that dark hall.

He rushed, as far as he was able, to the stairs. Before he went up them, Winky turned back toward his old love.

Isobel Whitehead-Patrick.

There she was.

Finally.

Winky and Isobel locked their eyes a last time. She mouthed some words to him, to which he nodded, somewhat enthusiastically, for such a wizened old bastard.

It took me some days to work out the words Isobel mouthed. I just couldn't figure it out, no matter how hard I thought, or how many fitting permutations I applied. Then I saw the Classics Illustrated version of The Iliad lying on its hallowed stack, that epic telling, even in comic form, of such great men as Achilles and Hector, characters so mighty in thought and deed, their shadows still fall upon us, even to this day.

"Go, my hero," Isobel's lips had shaped.

Winky started up through the trap door.

"Mr. Wickley!"

It was Cot. She had raised her head and was looking in a pleading way at the lanky old man.

"Yes, Cot?"

"Can my parents have their jobs back? Please!"

Cot delivered that last word with such an uncharacteristic look of supplication, she did not, for a moment, appear to be Cot at all, but another person entirely.

Winky came back down the stairs and gazed into the tensely expectant face of my sister, who had unraveled herself from my ministrations as if they were never needed at all.

It was strangely as if Winky respected Cot too much to yell what he had to say from across the room. He placed his hand on her shoulder.

"No, Cot. Actually, your parents can not have their jobs back. I am so sorry."

Winky bent down and wrapped Cot in a hug which I have never seen the like of.

One of the huggers, Winky, had his eyes solemnly closed, intent on imparting a goodwill message totally at odds with the words he had just spoken.

The other hugger, Cot, was in a sort of paroxysm of ill will and bad intention, emitting repulsion and looking more than anything like she would, any second, vomit all over Winky's back the way Denny Freedmantle had done over mine.

Then the hug was over. Winky turned and was up the hole as fast as his ancient appendages could convey him. We all heard him slam the door to room 14, and then the engines of many cars came to roaring life just outside. The sounds diminished toward the mill.

I looked around. There were no bad guys left. Only good guys.

Cot said, "Did you hear that son of a bitch? I swear to God, what a jerk that guy is!"

Eli approached and seemed about to speak, when a sudden realization spread across his face. He turned to climb the stairs.

"Where on earth are you going in such a hurry, Eli?" asked Isobel.

"I am going to see if Denny Freemantle is still around, and if he is, I am going to kick his ass. If he isn't in the area anymore, I'll come right back," Eli responded, and then he was gone, up through the hole.

ChApTeR 9

We went up soon after, to find a long black car and a Burlyman waiting for us. He walked to the back of Winky's own personal conveyance, and opened the door. Winky wasn't there, but had left it for the Burlyman to see us all to our homes.

Right when I was about to get inside, Eli yelled, "Hold up!" from down the street.

He huffed and puffed to the front passenger door, which he pulled open and entered without a word.

I gave a glance back to the pink of the motel, and the rest of the snowy night.

I was just about to get in the car when a low siren started in the far distance. Not a siren really, but an increasing machine whine that produced a siren-like tension, from the locality of the sawmill. Unlike a siren, this sound never retreated, only increased in pitch, reaching a plateau, which, even at this great distance, set my teeth on edge.

I knew that sound. I had heard it before. It came from that toothed engine of fearsome machinery, which, as I have admitted to you, haunted my dreams.

The Debarker.

ChApTeR 10

Cot and I slept the next day entirely away, in our own beds.

We were awoken by none other than our long-lost parents, finally returned from their unsuccessful job-hunting excursion.

I grasped my Mom in a desperate hug she had to wrestle from, in order to escape.

"My gosh, kids!" she exclaimed, "I've never been hugged so hard in my life! My ribs hurt now."

My dad came in my room and seemed in a generally good mood.

"What the hell? Why you two sleeping?"

"Cuz we're tired," I said.

Dad looked around the room. "Everything around here looks pretty good," he said. "Non-destroyed, I mean."

Dad smiled and I got out of bed and hugged him a good one.

"What smells?" I asked my parents. I parted my curtains, expecting to see a waning day, given the time, but seeing only dark night, the stars occluded, as if by heavy cloud.

"The mill," said my Dad. "It's burning up."

Cot and I watched the glow over the tops of the trees. My dad left and came back and told us that the mill had started on fire early, maybe 2 or 3 a.m.

The firefighters were in a defensive mode, he said, suggesting that the sawmill was a loss. Dad said people in town were acting mighty strange, few giving up any real information.

Just when the mill fire was threatening to jump the Meritimus River herself, a violent rainstorm, the like of which the town of Copeland had never experienced, exploded out of the sky. That sky was a procession of dark leviathans out of the east. One could barely look up at them, so heavy the downpour that day.

Cars were carried away in mere hours and the Meritmus exceeded her banks in a few hours more, flooding the whole of the mill yard. The mill fire raged a few hours further, above a lake of floodwater and below a torrent of beating rain, but it could not retain the modicum of violence required to remain aflame.

The returns diminished, or were sodden, until finally the fire gave up the ghost.

The fire and the rain finished, miraculously, at just about the same time.

But that wasn't the weirdest part.

The weirdest part was that Winky was nowhere to be found.

The official story was as follows:

Winky, driven mad by his son's culpability in Theda Holly's murder (and haunted by the ghost of Theda Holly's mother, Sadie Holly, who may have, according to some, tormented the old man into madness out of unadulterated revenge-from-beyond-the-grave-type-dissatisfaction), arrived in the mill during the night shift, and told all his workers to vacate immediately (which part was actually true - Winky did at some point that night burst onto the work floor and make all the workers leave the mill grounds), after which, Winky poured about accelerant, making sure to saturate the walls, and, flinging a final match, fed his insane feet into the maw of the churning Debarker, as the world of the mill exploded into heat and light and William Wickley The Third, or Winky, to his enemies, churned himself into red gravy .

But the official story was written by people who had no idea of the real events of that night. Also, they were idiots.

I pictured it the truth of it all very specifically:

Winky ordered his Burlymen to bind, and maybe even bag, Jameson Corr. Winky then went into the mill and made all his workers leave. After the last car was out of sight, Winky dismissed the Burlymen.

After the last of them was out of sight, Winky dragged Jameson Corr from whichever trunk he was put in, all the way to the Debarker.

Winky turned the machine on.

He may have talked to Jameson, but I think not.

I think Winky did it all real silent, as Jameson pleaded and begged for release. Or maybe Jameson was pleading to the Gods who had abandoned him.

I picture Jameson pleading.

Then, William Wickley set Jameson Corr to grinding.

I imagine there are some among you who are disturbed by the gory fates our enemies met.

Bad men meet bad ends, is all I have to say about that, as Ricky and Stacy and Jameson all discovered.

Then I got to thinking, what if Winky or his Burlymen killed Jameson Corr, but someone *else* burned the mill?

Any one of us, Robert, Eli or Cot (but not likely Adria) had motive, for days. I knew I didn't do it. But the others, and particularly Cot, were more than up to the task, especially if the Heart-Shaped Forest and its magic tree were somehow essential to all human life!

Any of them could have done it late that night, when everyone was asleep. I watched Cot close after such thinking, and, while she looked guilty the whole time, I couldn't say one way or another.

And what about my own parents? They had an ax the size of a quarter moon to grind with Winky. Coincidentally, my parents showed up back in town, shortly after the fire started.

Finally, I decided on the answer.

Winky did it, that's for certain.

When Winky and Isobel went into that hallway, Winky was received of knowledge that transformed him from the sedate overlord, just done restoring order to his hamlet, to someone else entirely.

Winky was changed into someone who still had stuff to do, whose mission was yet before him.

Whether Isobel's hold on William survived his natural response to her abandonment, or if Isobel had pulled out some crazy magic and hit him in the face with it, is unclear.

What is clear is how Winky seemed charged with purpose and strangely happy. It was clear as day on his face, right before Cot ruined it by asking him about our parents' jobs.

Maybe, Isobel showed Winky the Tree of Life.

Whatever the case, Isobel called on William to save the day.

I think Isobel reminded William of his younger self, his younger ideals. Isobel made him into her knight right then and Winky gladly donned the armor.

Go, my hero, she had sent to him, like a wish before battle.

ChApTeR 11

All concerns became moot, some year and a half after the mill burned to the ground.

The Heart-Shaped Forest was suddenly declared a National Forest, and renamed "Henry James National Forest," after the famous author.

No one seemed to know exactly how it happened, but one thing is for sure.

The President who signed his name to the amazing declaration, was the selfsame, big nosed politician who shook a young William Wickley's hand in the photo on Winky's office wall. Cot and I had appraised it during our ransacking.

"What a couple of maroons," was Cot's estimation, at the time.

ChApTeR 12

Robert refused to discuss his father, or elaborate on his legal commiserations, or speculate as to the future of the mill, the forest, or any of us, though he was uniquely positioned to do so.

The impression I got was that he was sworn to secrecy by Winky himself. Robert was damn well going to accomplish that secrecy.

Robert moved in with his mom, so we saw them all the time. Robert sold his pretty house to the government for next to nothing.

Robert made it known to his mother, and Isobel made it known to us, that her cabin and its inhabitants were legally inviolable within the cloth of the Heart-Shaped Forest's new, protected status. No one from the Forest Service would ever molest them -- one last, gallant gesture from the "ghost" of William Wickley.

When I last saw Robert, I made sure to give him the bottle of Miss Holly's love potion. He just stared at it in his hand and that's my last living image of him.

When the Heart-Shaped Forest was finally nationalized, whatever fund Winky had set up to accomplish it, was fallow and dry.

But it was accomplished. Winky had, as if from beyond the grave, deployed a field of young and hungry lawyers to his bidding, and, with the help of his son, slain the dragon for his princess.

ChApTeR 13

My family stayed in our own house, since no one seemed to own it anymore, until some months after the Heart-Shaped Forest turned into the Henry James National Forest.

Dad was made to feel rather low by a congenial sheriff who visited us one day, about that time, for squatting there, but Dad told the sheriff his side of the story and together they appraised its virtues on the porch, over beers and cigarettes, long into the night.

We moved out a few days hence, and up north with Ben and Lucius, who had chosen to remain upon the end of his rehabilitation. Lucius was hale and strong like I had never seen him, in mind and body, both.

He was kinder, which is to say, less abusive.

Cot was forced to forgive Winky for denying our parents their jobs back, given that he knew, at the time he said it, that he was going to burn down the mill, and no one who worked there would have a job come morning.

His hug afterword was read in whole new light by Cot, who always had struggled with an admiration for the lanky old man.

ChApTeR 14

Eli was never quite able to scourge the pain in his eyes whenever we saw him. He was clearly embarrassed in front of us, feeling low at not having escaped those chains.

Cot found this bothersome. "There were gods of evil gazing at us from the wall, and on top of that, a wily psychopath and a moron with gun. So, Eli ain't stronger than that chain! Who cares? Get over it! Join the club, right Johnny?"

I nodded a reluctant admission I probably could not have broken the chain either.

Eli's sadness was also the weight of his family dying around him. Without the thrill of the hunt to dissuade his thoughts, Eli was struggling with morosity and downright depression.

"I know we did right by her, Johnny," Cot said, gazing up into the ceiling.

On Eli's last day with us, Cot camped outside the man's door. She remained there about an hour, never even knocking, when the door suddenly opened, and the man emerged.

Cot stood in his way.

Eli had his red suitcases in hand, and it appeared to the girl as if he might be trying to skip town without saying goodbye to her.

"What is going on, Eli?" Cot demanded.

"I am packing to go," Eli responded with unfeigned irritation.

"Kinda looks like you are doing more going than packing."

"Nonsense," Eli huffed, "I do not leave until tomorrow."

It was Cot's impression that Eli amended his leave date, from the present moment, to "tomorrow," right then. She was pretty certain Eli had been about to scurry away and out of Copeland without a word of farewell.

"Why would you do that?" Cot asked. Her eyes brimmed with tears and she started breathing heavy.

"Momma Donna," said Eli, under his breath, not so much at Cot's crying, but at its accompaniment, in his head, by music from the film Bambi, the mournful chorus that swaddles the realization that Bambi's mother will never return.

The music told him the depth of Cot's emotion, emotion the brimming tears underreported, by a long mile.

"Cot... I don't... " Eli stuttered.

"Oh, shut up Eli," said Cot, wiping at her eyes.

"Cot, I swear to you I would have dropped by and said goodbye to you, but I do admit... it would have a been a quick farewell."

Eli disclosed this with no little shame.

"It's not enough," cried Cot.

"It never is, little one," said Eli, admitting of the sentiment informing his ill-advised attempt to leave.

"I know you're sad, Eli. Part of it is that you couldn't get out of that chain, isn't it?"

Eli said nothing.

"Join the goddamned club!" Cot barked. "I can't even get out of my shoe unless it's untied. Do you think I am disappointed in you? Is that it? I knew you couldn't get out of that chain before you even tried. But you tried. Oh boy, did you try."

Cot indicated toward the white gauze circling both of Eli's wrists.

Cot said, tenderly, "That's all I care."

Eli looked down at his wrists and felt a warmth of pride for the very first time about the situation. Then, Eli felt ire and embarrassment at being psychoanalyzed by a child.

He huffed, starting toward his car with his suitcases.

Cot had to back away for him to pass.

Eli placed his suitcases, shuffling them into the largely empty trunk, repeatedly adjusting them, as if their precise position in the wealth of space was of importance. His big face was still down in the trunk as he pushed his suitcases to the farthest location, when Cot softly said,

"I am so, so sorry about your sweet Momma and dear sister."

Eli hung his head in the trunk.

He felt no end of shame at surviving his mother and sister. He deeply regretting his years-long distance from them. Eli would never have the opportunity to repair that distance. The coda to this adventure was going to be their silence, forever more.

Eli felt Cot hug what small portion of his massive haunch she was able to, still all bent over as he was. He pulled himself out of the trunk and sat down right in the snow. Eli opened his arms in silent invitation. Cot stepped into them and practically disappeared into Eli's hugeness for many warm, comfortable moments.

Eli dropped off Cot at our house. I went out and said goodbye to him, no big deal. I was sad to see Eli go, but I was happy to be done with the creepy feeling that someone was reading my mind.

Eli was a good man. He did not deserve his fate, as neither his mother nor sister deserved theirs.

We watched Eli's car slide away, over the rolling hills, smaller each time it returned to view. Cot was quiet. I let her precede me back to the house, so I would not see her eyes filling, if indeed they were.

Cot went into her room, and I went into mine.

ChApTeR 15

I received, some years later, a strange package. The package had no address, nor postal markings of any kind.

When I opened it, I was horrified to see it contained a mason jar, with a red spider inside, and a roll of dark leather.

There was a lovely white card that told me what to do, in Isobel Whitehead-Patrick's own hand.

I spread out the roll of leather, rough side up, and poured the red spider out onto it, whereupon the little fellow set to furious activity.

The red spider started spinning a web over the square, employing a method that finds nothing to which to liken it, until recently, with the arrival of 3-D printing.

Over and back, following a blueprint far too complex to be housed in its miniscule head, the spider worked, dizzyingly.

I watched this play out for hours, until I got bored.

When I woke up, the spider was waiting at the edge of the leather mat, and I swear to you, this is true, the spider was tapping a single foreleg, as if in impatience for me to see its work. The tapping was faintly audible.

The square patch of leather had been turned into something akin to a photograph, by the exact spinning of spider web over the leather, the dark of the leather acting as the shadows, and opaque layers of web, acting as the highlights. At appropriate places, where the webbing was less than opaque, there were midtones.

Like I said, the arrangement of webbing described an image, an image much like a sepia tone photo.

There were four figures in the image. Isobel Whitehead-Patrick stood sedately in the middle of the figures. On her right, were two people, a man, and a woman holding a baby. On her left, an old man stood, looking sour.

The man on Isobel's right was clearly her son, Robert. I had worried so that Isobel would take Cot to be her successor. I worried for nothing. She had always intended to induct her son, after poor Miss Holly was taken away.

Which brings us to the woman with the baby. Neither had much for detail, but were, in both their dark and their light, murky. They were the only persons in the picture the spider did not render with exactitude, which follows, since they were both ghosts.

It was Miss Holly and her baby.

Robert might have had to give up his future as a normal person, to steward the Tree of Life, but there were, apparently, some benefits to the situation.

On Isobel's left, the old man scowled most fearsomely, but not nearly as fearsomely as he used to do, just walking down the street.

It was that old bastard, that shining knight, otherwise known as Sir Winky of the Afternoon of the Asshole, William Wickley The Third.

Winky stood, hunched and unwilling, as if he knew he was posing for a photo.

This sort of thing was old hat to me now.

Nothing -- not the spider, its work, nor what that work depicted, amazed me.

It was like I was looking at a normal, everyday sort of photograph that showed some married friends, who everybody agreed were made for one another, with their new baby and a set of in laws, thrown in for good measure.

It did not amaze me.

But it sure did make me smile. I went and got my wife and brought her over. It didn't amaze her either. She smiled wider than I did.

You may know of her. Her name is Adria.

Adria and I shared some hot chocolate following that.

After, we returned to find the spider was eating its web off that leather.

When the web was all ate up, the red spider hurried down the table leg and straight for the back door.

I opened the door for the spider, for which it seemed grateful. It scurried across the back porch, disappearing over the edge, and that was the last supernatural thing ever to happen to me.

Until the next time.

THE END

Special Thanks go to
Carri Sampson-Spande, most of all, muse and polisher.
Next, Kim Lewis, Susan Whitehead, Lori Patrick,
Jordann Hoff (If there is a beautiful tree alone on the
cover of this book, she was the artist) and Jenna Lynn
Isabel Spande and Sam Leslie, my stalwart apprentices,
Dave Gysbers,
Sam Levine,
Katie Ploetz-Sanchez (beefreehonee.com),
Brian and Lucie Freedman,
Zach Peterson(zpproductions.com),
Lucy Peterson,
Marlene J Spande,
Greg Ketter (dreamhavenbooks.com),
Ryan Paramore – printer extraordinaire
(www.bloomington.minutemanpress.com),
Jennifer Arnold (jenniferarnold.com),
Rex Carter,
Katherine Young (katherineyoungcreative.com),
Linda Rock and Marianne Teresa Wipson,
Ebba SN...

A note from the author.

If you find something about The Born and the Made that you would like to discuss or critique, drop me a note at bobspande@gmail.com.

I look forward to making the book better, and if I take your suggestion, your name will be added to the ever-growing acknowledgments section in future copies.

With Sincere Thanks,
Robert Spande
Minneapolis, MN
March, 2016

Made in the USA
Columbia, SC
15 July 2021